THE
KEPT

THE KEPT

A Novel

JAMES SCOTT

HarperCollins*Publishers*Ltd

HarperCollins books may be purchased for educational,
business, or sales promotional use through our Special Markets Department.

HarperCollins Publishers Ltd
2 Bloor Street East, 20th Floor
Toronto, Ontario, Canada
M4W 1A8

www.harpercollins.ca

Library and Archives Canada Cataloguing in Publication
information is available upon request

ISBN 978-1-44341-838-6

Designed by Renato Stanisic

Printed and bound in the United States
RRD 9 8 7 6 5 4 3 2 1

FOR TAYLOR

BOOK I

Elspeth Howell was a sinner. The thought passed over her like a shadow as she washed her face or caught her reflection in a window or disembarked from a train after months away from home. Whenever she saw a church or her husband quoted verse or she touched the simple cross around her neck while she fetched her bags, her transgressions lay in the hollow of her chest, hard and heavy as stone. The multitude of her sins—anger, covetousness, thievery—created a tension in her body, and all that could ease the pressure was movement, finding something to occupy her wicked hands and her tempted mind, and so she churned her legs against snow that piled in drifts to her waist.

While the miles passed, the sky over Elspeth became nothing but a gray smudge and weighty clouds released their burden. She loosened the scarf from her face and the cold invaded her lungs. As soon as a drop of sweat slid out from under a glove or down a curl of hair, it turned to ice that flickered in the last of the light.

In her pocket, she kept a list of the children's names and ages, the years crossed out two and three times, so that when she bought gifts, she forgot no one. She carried a fish scaler for Amos, fourteen, a goose caller for Caleb, twelve, a hunting knife for Jesse, ten, a fifty-inch broadcloth for Mary, fifteen, a length of purple ribbon for Emma, six, and a small vial of perfume for both girls to share. Wrapped with care against the elements, hidden at the bottom of the bag, were strawberry hard candies, gumdrops, and chewing gum. For her husband, she brought two boxes of ammunition and a new pair of sheep shears. Collectively these goods had cost her only a fraction of her four months' midwife salary. The rest resided in the toes of her boots.

The valley stretched out behind her; the tracks she'd left were already erased. When she'd stepped off the train in Deerstand mid-morning, the snow had been a lazy flurry, but the closer she got to home, the deeper the snow became, and the more furiously it fell. It was as if, she thought, God wanted to keep outsiders away as much as the Howells did. "We are an Ark unto ourselves, waiting for the floodwaters to rise," her husband, Jorah, liked to say. She heard his calming voice in her ears, over the sighing wind and the whisper of wet snowflakes, and she missed him. She longed for his silken hair against her cheek at night, his soft footsteps as he left in the morning to milk, and his smell—of leaves, of smoke, of outdoor air.

She'd meant to come home in October. The baby had been born before the snow covered the earth, and she went by every day to check on its well-being, to touch each of its little fingers and their pearly nails. The child grew as October gave way to November and the calendar flirted with December. The city—any city—always had need for a midwife. Even that morning, looking out the window, warm by the fire, she couldn't bring herself to leave, and failed to get on the train before dawn had broken, revealing a clear, bright day.

Still a ways from home, something nagged at the back of her head, threatening to push forward and topple her. She hurried, but the rush made for careless steps. The path shrank, and she passed between naked oaks and shivering pines. The light emanating from the snow turned the color of a new bruise as the day died, glowing just enough to mark her way. The terrain leveled again and she broke through the woods. Elspeth knew by the rolling of the ground that she crossed the cornfields; the dead stalks cracked beneath the ice and snow. She tromped alongside the creek that brought them their water, frozen at the surface but trickling below. It was then that the fear that had been tugging at her identified itself: It was nothing. No smell of a winter fire; no whoops from the boys rounding up the sheep or herding the cows; no welcoming light.

She crested the last rise. The house nestled in the bosom of the hill. The small plateau seemed made for them, chiseled by God for their security, to hold them like a perfect secret. She held her breath, hoping for some hint of life, and heard nothing but the far-off snap of a branch. Everything stood still. She could not make out the smoke from the chimney, and despite the late hour, no lamps shone in the windows. Elspeth began to run. She tripped, and her pack shoved her into the snow. Clawing with her hands, digging with her feet, she pushed herself upright and rushed toward home.

Closer, she noticed a hollow in the snow, next to the front door. A bear, she thought, a wolf, but nausea welled in her belly and said different. A glimpse of color spurred her on. The hole drew her toward it, and she feared that it would swallow her, as she'd once seen—from this very hilltop—a tornado envelop a hundred-foot oak and leave nothing but a ragged gap where the roots had been. The color flickered again, a small swatch of red reaching out from the darkness like the Devil's forked tongue. The screen door clapped against the house as Elspeth pitched herself forward and fell to her knees. There, dressed in her nightgown, lay Emma, the youngest, her blond curls matted with blood. The red ribbon holding her hair waved in the wind, almost free. The snow had melted and then refrozen in an obsidian mass beneath her. A fine layer of powder had settled on her gown and face, and Elspeth removed her gloves to brush it away. Emma had been shot. The cold had puckered the skin around the clean bullet wound on her forehead, the blood there a thin red ring. Elspeth whimpered a small, ferocious noise, and rubbed her hands together before she dared to pull a few loose strands of hair from the wound and tuck them back behind the girl's ear. If these images didn't cause Elspeth instant revulsion, Emma might merely be sleeping. The snow gone, her hair in place, Emma looked more like herself, and that made Elspeth's pain burn brighter. She wished to call out, to scream for someone to help, but their Ark had been chosen for its isolation; Deerstand was the nearest town, a six-hour walk that Elspeth had barely made in daylight. She looked to the barn, where Caleb slept, and saw no signs of life there, either. The cold that they warded off with their structures and their fires had won: No warmth lingered on the hill. Nothing could be done. No help could be summoned.

The screen creaked behind her as Elspeth pushed open the front door. The house, usually heated to bursting on an early winter's night, offered no respite from the cold. The kerosene lamp stood unlit in the middle of the kitchen table, the matches beside it. She removed her pack, and shook the snow from her hat and shoulders, stalling. She didn't want to see what the light would offer.

In the darkness she grasped the coatrack Jesse had built. Jackets hung on every hook. They were cold. She bent down and touched the neat alignment of shoes and boots beneath the windowsill next to the door and found no puddle of melted snow beneath them. She left her own buttons fastened and her laces tied tight.

She struck a match and touched it to the soaked wick of the lamp, the brightness causing her to turn away. She adjusted the flame and let her vision acclimate. Not three feet from her, Mary sprawled across the stovetop. Elspeth recognized the pattern of the dress Mary wore, a gift from an earlier trip. She, too, had been shot, but from behind. The stitching of her dress—tidy and taut from the girl's own hand—kept her off the floor, the fabric tangling in the hardware of the stove front. As Elspeth backed away from the body, lowering the lamp, she made out Amos on the ground, four steps from his older sister. He must have been helping with the meal. He'd cut his hair since she'd last seen him, when it had hung down like a girl's, almost to his shoulders, and he'd developed a tic to keep it from his face, a sudden flick of the neck. Elspeth squatted to touch the bristly hair and wondered if the tic had remained after the hair was gone, the same way her father had sometimes fallen in the morning getting out of bed, forgetting he'd lost his leg to the millstones. She thought that Amos's eyes had been stolen, or shot out, but when the lamplight struck his face, she saw that two large brass buttons, the type found on overalls, obscured his blank gaze. She fell back onto her hands. She couldn't tell if her heartbeat had slowed to normal or stopped altogether. Like an insect, she crept backward, away from the bodies, until she hit the wall. They'd been babies once, swaddled and cradled in her arms. The crowns of their heads had smelled so sweet. How she'd held them. How she'd nuzzled and kissed them.

In the silence, she heard a low whistle and froze. It continued. Then she felt it, on her bare hand, the outside forcing its way through the bullet holes that dotted the house. They announced themselves to her, ten, twenty, countless large bullet holes, then dozens, maybe hundreds more from the pellets of a shotgun. The room contracted and she bent over and clasped her hands to her knees. When she recovered, she moved to the living area, a rectangular space that ran the length of the building, and discovered Jesse facedown in front of his parents' door, both arms extended above his head, as if he'd been shot diving into a stream. Elspeth had to step around him, her foot leaving a patch of snow in the crook between his arm and his body.

She opened the door, but shut her eyes before the lamp confirmed her fears. She inhaled. The bedroom smelled how she remembered it, of Jorah sleeping, his breath filling the air. She lifted her eyelids, their weight palpable. Upon seeing her husband, she moaned and pressed her fists to her temples like she could hold her thoughts together with pure force. Jorah lay in bed, his face frozen in a grimace of anger, his eyebrows knotted and teeth clenched. His bare torso bore his wounds. One soil-stained foot touched the floor and she allowed herself to think of his soft padding steps trying not to wake her in the morning. The wind insisted, drowning out her reverie, rasping a ghostly noise through their bedroom. The bed itself was stained black. She kicked dozens of shotgun shells and rifle casings that littered the floor and they chimed against one another. She could not bring herself to touch her husband's gray skin. Usually, when she'd returned from one of her trips, Jorah would be sleeping on the same sheets that had been on the bed when she'd left. She could place a fresh set on the dresser, and in her absence it would do nothing but gather dust. Weeks later, when she came back, the sheets Jorah had been content to lie upon would be stiff with dirt: from the barn, from the fields, and from his own sweat. The springs squeaked beneath her when she knelt on the bed to pull the linens from under his weight. Jorah's joints had locked; she hefted his legs onto the mattress and fought to straighten them, but still would not touch his skin. She stripped the thickened sheets as she'd learned with bedridden pregnant women, gently rolling him onto his side when she needed. Once she freed them, she pressed the bunched linen to her face, and breathed in the odor of her husband. The blood didn't bother her; it was, after all, his. There, on the dresser, sat the clean sheets she'd left for him. She snapped them open, the only sound in a house normally so filled with noise that Elspeth used to retreat into the fields to think or to pray or to worry over the growing thrum of temptation in her body. The new sheets glowed like snow, reflecting the lamplight. She drew them taut under Jorah, pulling as gently as possible, because every time his body moved with the motion of the sheets, it was just that—a body. Not a man, not her husband. When she'd finished, she lifted Jorah's head, replaced the pillowcase, fluffed the down again, raised his head once more, feeling the back of his neck, formerly soft and warm, now cold and firm. She shook her hand as if the sensation would slide from her fingers like drops of water. He'd never looked so small, her protector. To her, he'd loomed over everyone and everything, blanketing them with all the safety and the comfort he could muster.

She extinguished the lamp and lay beside him as the wind erupted and swept through the house. Outside it pushed the clouds south, and the moon rose, casting silver light onto the floorboards, the boots Jorah set beside the bed each night, and the empty shotgun shells.

ELSPETH THOUGHT AGAIN of Caleb. She pictured him at first small and bundled in a yellow blanket, his skin against it a harsh red, mouth toothless and wailing. But twelve years had passed—he walked and talked, he had hair the color of fertile soil that flopped down to his eyebrows, and he'd lost his last baby tooth the previous autumn. He was a solitary boy, and spent most of his time in the barn, sleeping among the animals, talking to them when he got lonely. One spring morning, she'd gone to see why he had yet to bring the milk and she came upon him leaning against the fence surrounding the pen with his chin rested on his folded hands, telling the sheep that the cows were not being cooperative. When Elspeth brought it up to her husband, he said he'd seen it as well, that the boy talked more to the animals than to his own family. Jorah reserved a special tone for Caleb, a sensitive timbre, as if the boy would frighten easily, like a skittish horse.

Caleb's body wasn't in the house. She hadn't been able to think—her head pulsed and thudded with her heartbeat—but gaining some clarity in the familiar itch to move, to do something, she rushed to find him, skidding on the shells, catching herself on the doorframe. In the moonlight, the bodies of her children existed only as shadows. She picked her way across the living room and the kitchen and out into the cold again. Through the howling of a wind that burned her face and a falling blanket of snow she called Caleb's name. The barn crouched in the dark, somewhere under the pines. Without the full glow of a lively home to guide her, she wasn't sure of finding her way there, much less back. The moon had been lost to the storm. She walked as far as she dared, one foot in front of the other, until her legs finally gave out and she slipped and called his name again. Had Caleb survived, she thought, the barn would be lit; the bodies wouldn't be in such a state.

She shut herself inside, out of habit hanging her jacket with the others, and stopped to listen, as if the house itself might tell her what had happened. With the multiple weapons used, the sheer volume of shells and cases, and the fact that Jorah hadn't even risen from their bed, it was apparent more than one murderer had stolen into their home. She imagined an army of them, crawling over the house like spiders. No one had ever followed her on the long journey from Deerstand; she would have seen them, heard them, sensed them behind her. A man would have to travel far out of his way to stumble upon the Howell farm, set as it was on what most would consider the wrong side of the hill for farming in an expanse of northern New York so vast and empty that even those looking for the house would have had difficulty finding it. No one lived close enough to know them, as they'd wanted, as had been necessary. Of course, Elspeth had her enemies, and her sins were tied with the Devil's strings to those she'd wronged.

Sickened, she cracked the ice that covered the surface of the drinking bowl and sipped some water from the ladle. In the main room, three logs stood on end against the wall, next to the large woodstove, and she opened the grille and saw that Jorah had left the fire ready for the morning. Perhaps that explained his presence in the bedroom—Jorah often went back for a short nap between his morning chores and the first blush in the sky, and she would pretend to be asleep as his weight reshaped the bed beside her and she, too, drifted off, listening to the sounds of his breathing.

She retrieved the matches, stepping over Jesse's body once again. Seeing her children sprawled in the kitchen affected her more now that the shock had worn off, and her whole body began to quiver. She stood there, shaking, sweating, not certain where to start. Her numb fingers went to work trying to untangle Mary's dress from the range, and she stopped to breathe into her cupped hands to warm them. Mary shook like a doll with her efforts, but it was no use. Elspeth would have to cut her loose tomorrow. How Mary would have cried at that thought, after the many hours she'd spent in the yard clutching her dress in her arms to keep it from the dust. Even the chickens seemed to understand her concern, and did not nip at her toes or flutter at her feet as they did the rest of the Howells. But everything would have to wait for tomorrow and the light of day. She would place the bodies out in the barn with their brother

Caleb. Once the house heated, the smell would be too much to take. Burial was out of the question this time of year. Even Jorah would not have been able to dig deep enough to safely keep the bodies.

As she straightened Mary's dress, she heard a scratching in the pantry, and it relieved Elspeth to have company, if only a mouse. Her voice almost leapt from her throat to call the boys, who loved to catch the mice and keep them in homes they built from scrap wood. She approached the door gingerly, afraid of frightening the animal. The floor creaked. A bright flash and she was thrown into the air. She landed on the kitchen table, nostrils and throat full of a burning smell, her body rent. It felt as though she had fallen apart.

THE PANTRY SMELLED of gunpowder. The acrid smoke swirled and then disappeared, sucked through the hole in the wall created by the elbow of Caleb Howell and the kick of his gun—his prized possession—a twelve-gauge Ithaca shotgun. The thirty-inch barrel ran most of the width of the pantry, leaving no room for recoil. Six more paper shot shells sat in the mass of blankets between his legs. He cleared the spent rounds, still smoking, and awkwardly loaded two more before pressing his face to the pantry door and looking through the hole created by the shot. It was warm on his cheek. He'd heard the grunt as the pellets hit and the scraping of the table legs as the murderer's body dragged it across the kitchen floor.

Through the smoldering gap in the wood, he saw one hand draped over the side of the table, blood dripping from the index and middle fingers. The steady tap helped him keep time. He waited for twenty, then another set of twenty. Caleb couldn't count higher than that.

Moments before, it had been comforting in his delirium to hear sounds again other than the fabrications of his terror and the incessant moan of the wind through the bullet holes and the scratching of the elm against the roof.

He had been asleep when the men had come last. The first shot had sent him scrambling to the edge of the hayloft door. The sun threatened to rise. His sister, who'd been coming to fetch him for breakfast as she did most mornings, lay in the snow. When the men stepped into the doorway and over the threshold, Caleb caught only a few details: the long beard of the first; the gangly, unsteady legs of the second—like a newborn calf; and the way the third moved like water. Each carried a gun. Each wore a red scarf: the bearded one dangled loose about his shoulders, the gangly one wrapped around his neck and the third tied his long hair back with his. Caleb heard another shot and moved into the darkness of the loft. The crack of gunfire kept coming and he willed himself to press his eye to a knot in the rough wood. They emerged from the house, the three of them, and the gangly one glanced toward the barn. Caleb's pants grew wet and he backed up, wriggling down into the hay, covering himself, his hands clenching at the straw.

Sometime later, maybe minutes, maybe hours, he thought he heard voices, and then nothing.

When he finally rose and picked the hay from his clothing, the house was dark. Emma's body was only a small shadow. He climbed down from the loft and fetched his gun from the rack at the rear of the barn. Ithaca in hand, he sprinted across the yard, head swiveling, certain he saw red scarves behind every tree. He paused, and—with a careful touch—brushed the snow from Emma's face. Once inside, he passed through each room as quickly as he could, running past the horror so he could not fully take it in, shoving open his parents' door, the smell of gunpowder strong, his father's rifle untouched in the corner. On his way back through the house, searching for any remnant of life—a groan, a twitch—he was met with stillness beyond his imagination. It made so little sense to him that he pressed his hand to his mouth until his jaw hurt, for he feared he would laugh, his throat and stomach dancing with the possibility. When that subsided, he grabbed his wrist with his hand and hugged himself hard. He couldn't leave the bodies, didn't want to be so alone, and he hid in the pantry, where he felt safe, confined. The moaning of the wind accompanied his sobbing while he awaited the return of three men. In the depths of night, he emerged to stretch, check for signs of intruders, and wipe Emma's face and body clean from the snow that never seemed to stop falling, then crept back into the pantry, where he waited with the loaded gun.

He'd been asleep, again. But this time he woke and did not wait, did not let his hand prove unsteady or his legs grow wet. This time he had been brave. This time he had done what his father had been unable to: He'd protected them.

Once he felt certain no one else lurked in the shadows, he emerged from the pantry, his knees cracking, his legs cramping at being bent so long. He shifted his Ithaca to the crook of his shoulder. From the doorway, he saw the boots. He knew them. He let loose a scream from his rusted vocal chords. The lamp glow—diffused by the cracked chimney—lit the face of his mother. Her slate gray eyes were shut. He removed her hat, and her black hair unfurled onto the table. The scarf around her neck staunched some of the bleeding, so he left it. To see her not moving seemed impossible; in his twelve years he'd never so much as seen her sleep.

He prayed—not for himself, because he'd long ago lost the place in his heart for God—but for his mother, who believed. His prayers were half answered by the rise and fall of Elspeth's chest, infrequent and unsteady as it was. Most of the shot had missed her, peppering the wall and the cupboard containing their dishes and cups. One or two had cracked the chimney of the lamp. The rest, however, had lodged in her chest, her shoulder, and her neck. Caleb opened his father's whiskey—Jorah wasn't much of a drinker, only a sip for Christ's days: Easter and Christmas, the day before Ash Wednesday and Epiphany—and he poured the brown liquid over his mother's clothes, soaking the wounds like he'd seen his father do when he'd nicked his own leg with the ax or when Amos had stepped on a nail. Unlike Amos, who'd screamed so ferociously that Caleb had felt it move up his feet and into his core, rattling his rib cage, his mother made no noise. He was certain she would die and that he'd killed her. The thought made him numb.

All he could do was busy himself. To keep warm he pulled his nest of blankets from the bottom of the pantry and wrapped two around his shoulders. As he did every night, he traded the wide berth of his Ithaca shotgun for the distance and precision of his father's rifle. He laid two blankets over his mother's feet, and one under her head. The rest he draped across the kitchen chairs to air out. He lit the small stove at the foot of his mother and father's bed, and resolved again to move Jesse. When he stepped over him he tried to concentrate on the reflection of the lamp in his mother's wet footprint rather than his brother's tousled hair and the curve of his ear. He would move Amos, too, and Mary and Emma, and bring them all to rest. The fire would soon make the bodies rot— the cold had been their preservation—and Caleb had lit nothing more than twigs since the three men had killed his family. Nothing would make him careful now. He didn't care who saw the smoke or smelled the burning wood; everyone he knew in this world had moved on to the next. The lengths he'd gone to over the past five days—or was it six?—would no longer be necessary. With his mother's presence came a strange sense of freedom: They were all home, and he had nothing left to wait for, nothing to fear, but his mother's last breath.

His feet wrapped in old pillowcases to keep them warm and silent, he shuffled into the living room and stared out into the snow. He saw his mother's tracks extending out toward the barn. Once more he heard the solid thud of her body hitting the kitchen table and the screeching of the legs gouging jagged lines across the floor. He thought there must be some elemental knowledge stuck deep in his blood that should have prevented him from pulling the trigger. Shouldn't he have been able to tell, even in the darkness of the pantry, even through the wood and the roar of the wind, that the person on the other side was his mother? He checked on her again—sat beside her, crying—and once he'd seen her chest rise and fall twenty times, he composed himself, wiped his tears until his face turned raw, and dragged a chair to the window in the living room to wait out the night.

The exposure of sitting in plain view unnerved him. To soothe himself, he shouldered Jorah's rifle and took shaky aim at the landmarks he could pick out in the dark: the dead pine that held their swing in its scraggly grasp; the boulder that marked the start of the stream; the farthest fence post of the sheep pen; and the stump where he, Jesse, and Amos played Chief. If anyone had followed his mother, if anyone waited for them, if anyone smelled the fire or saw the lights, he hoped he would be ready.

It wasn't difficult to keep from sleeping. Everything was painted in the shades of the killers—a face in profile, an outline of a body, the long legs and the beard and the greasy hair. Before hiding, he'd taken in the weapons slung over their shoulders, their vivid scarves. He remembered their gaits, how they hunched against the cold and walked gingerly over the thin coat of ice that covered the snow, careful not to slip. In the kitchen his mother coughed and he double-checked the rifle to be sure it remained loaded and patted his pockets, where the bullets clicked reassuringly.

THE NEXT MORNING, Caleb found his mother's sweat cold, her breathing shallow. He didn't know what to do. He wished to crawl back into the pantry, where the days had been lost to him, a collection of hours spent listening intently and shivering and sleeping until time bled together. He knew he had to ignore this impulse and left her, set the Ithaca and the rifle against the dresser in his parents' room, and lay down on the floor in front of the stove, the warmth and give in the boards amending his pantry-bent posture and relaxing his muscles. Perhaps an hour later, he went to the kitchen, taking a path he'd memorized to keep from seeing the faces of his brothers and sisters, first looking at the window, then the mantel, the scratch on the doorframe, the crocheted quote Mary had made—AND IF IT SEEM EVIL UNTO YOU TO SERVE THE LORD, CHOOSE YOU THIS DAY WHOM YE WILL SERVE; WHETHER THE GODS WHICH YOUR FATHERS SERVED THAT WERE ON THE OTHER SIDE OF THE FLOOD, OR THE GODS OF THE AMORITES, IN WHOSE LAND YE DWELL: BUT AS FOR ME AND MY HOUSE, WE WILL SERVE THE LORD. This way he stepped around Amos, Jesse, and Mary. He tried to pretend the bodies were no longer his siblings, but pieces of furniture.

Caleb sat on the chair by the door, the tidy row of boots beside him. He'd been wearing Amos's old pair, which were worn thin and much too large; his father had stuffed the toes with scoured wool, but this made his feet itch and didn't stop his heels from chafing on the leather. Jesse's boots were snug but comforting. He laced them tight and prepared himself to visit the barn. The animals had not been fed in almost a week, and he wondered how many of them would be dead or dying, or missing, or eaten by another. The cold air made him cough. The sun stung his eyes. To block it out he held up hands stained with his mother's blood, and slowly, through his fingers, he could see more than the blazing white of the landscape. Emma lay at his feet and he stooped to clean the snow from her face for the first time in daylight.

It took great effort to reach the barn. When he did, his body had turned to a confusion of sweat and chill, pain and numbness. He'd grown weak from eating nothing but the preserves and pickled beets left in the pantry. The bread had run out on the first day. Mary would have baked more once breakfast was finished, and he recalled the sound of her pounding the dough. The snow had blown against the grand doors, and, his small store of energy sapped, Caleb could not fight them open. He tried to climb the woodpile to reach the window, but his hands refused to grip the sill. He stood a log on end and tried to pull the doors from the top, but they wouldn't yield. Beaten, he finally allowed himself to break open, weeping and kicking at the snow.

When he was empty and calm again, he tapped on the wall of the barn and pressed his ear to a small gap in the boards. He heard rustling inside, but not the usual collection of snorts and huffs that met any intrusion. He gave the side of the barn one last pat and steeled himself for the trip to the house.

WITHOUT THE FEAR of killing his mother or injuring her any worse—he was certain she was going to die no matter what he did—he heated his father's butchering knife over the kerosene lamp. He rolled Elspeth onto one side and spread a blanket underneath her, then rolled her onto her other side and pulled the wool taut. She made no sound. The hand that had been hanging, bleeding onto the floor, had swollen fat and purple when Caleb placed it in her lap. He plucked the necklace from the blood on her chest and wiped it clean with his thumb. A pellet had dented one of the arms of the cross, imprinting a small half-sphere in the silver. Worried about damaging it further, he turned it to lie next to her head. When he slid off her boots, something fell to the heel, and he reached inside and found a wad of damp papers. He thought of the wool scratching his feet and he pressed the papers back into the toe. He slit her dress up the middle and it dropped away, baring her flesh. Caleb averted his gaze, each glance bringing him more of her. His mother kept her body private. She never washed in front of them or swam in the stream in summer, rarely exposing even her arms. Caleb knew that there was no time for modesty. Over each small puncture wound he poured a few drops of whiskey. He pressed the tip of the knife in until he felt scraping or heard the small clink of metal. If the pliers did not fit in the opening, he wiggled the knife around so they would. Blood drained into the new space, spilling over and trickling down her hot skin. Most of the shot concentrated in her right breast, and Caleb took less and less care of where he placed his hands. The thick and unwieldy pliers took two or three tries to fish each ball of lead from her, especially where they'd lodged in her muscles, which were taut and difficult for him to maneuver. He dropped the pellets in a tin coffee cup; each landed with a satisfying clink. As he dug the stray shot out of her neck, she stirred. Caleb yanked the pliers out and stepped back from his makeshift operating table. A trickle of blood seeped out of her neck and then stopped. Her eyes fluttered open. She moaned loudly.

"God," she said.

"It's me, Mama, it's just me," he said. "Caleb. Your boy."

With that, she turned and coughed up a small gob of blood, her body racked with the effort, and she went limp with a loud sigh. Caleb waited, hugging himself in defense, until she took one long breath, and then another—shorter—and another.

CHAPTER 2

The fever boiled away the excess, burned off the fuzzy edges of her memory. Elspeth felt she'd risen from great depths to bring her head above water, and everything that had been obscured by guilt and sin was once again made clear.

She remembered her father's moustache, how he would wax and comb it last thing before heading out the door to work for the van Tessels, tending their gardens. Mr. van Tessel would give the last of his tin to her father, who would dutifully scrape out the remnants. She remembered the stomp of his wooden leg and the small sigh that escaped him whenever he bent down. She remembered the scar on her mother's cheek where she'd been bitten by a sheepdog as a child, and how in summertime it turned silver when the sun tanned her skin. She remembered running in bare feet, the heat of the dirt on her toes, and the grass sharp on her soles in August when God starved the land.

The burning in her chest—for certain the first flames of her eternal damnation—brought about thoughts of Mary. She saw her face as it had been in infancy, the cherubic cheeks, her mouth without teeth but always smiling, and the hairless head that bounced and bobbed with each of her uncoordinated movements.

Mary had been her first. It was September, but an Indian summer had flared across the Northeast, bringing death by heat and humidity. Aboard the train in Rochester, as the compartments filled with harried men and women, everyone sweating in the oppressiveness of the motionless cars, she panicked at the thought of the child perishing before ever reaching its new home, before she and Jorah could even present it with a name and baptize it in the creek that seemed so perfect when they'd stumbled upon the clearing that would hold their house. When she'd left, the building was new enough that the walls smelled strongly of cedar, the pine furniture sweated sap, and the floorboards creaked in the afternoons from the drop in temperature.

Elspeth hurried down the train's thin corridor, people not even giving way to a woman carrying a child, everyone rushing, the temperature unbearable. The passageway emptied; people had settled in their compartments and at each Elspeth was met with the snap of a shade drawn in her face or the angry cries of a full car. Toward the back of the train, she saw through the dusty window one empty, plush red bench. She opened the door slowly, afraid of what it might reveal. A woman lay on her stomach, her face hanging off the edge of the embroidered cushions. Elspeth thought the old woman might be dead but was too exhausted to care. She dropped her bags on the floor as quietly as possible, and crumpled into the seat opposite her. Elspeth exhaled and looked out the window. Rochester had been her home for eight months, yet she knew she could never return. As if powered by this thought, the train began to move.

"Hello," the woman said and sat up with tremendous difficulty, her eyes shining with tears as she propped both of the pillows high up on her back. The face had been lost to Elspeth over time, but in her fever it appeared before her with clarity: The stitching of the cushions left red impressions on the woman's sallow cheeks, and her green eyes sank into her skull until it seemed they peered out from caves. Her gaunt face stood in sharp contrast to the thickness of her ankles, so swollen they dwarfed her calves.

"The compartment wasn't full," Elspeth said, "but we can move."

"No, please," she said, and smiled through a wince of pain. "I'll enjoy the company." Elspeth nodded, unsure of what to say. "My brother lives in Syracuse," the old woman continued, "and I've been sent to stay with him there. Sent." She sniffed and ran her hand along the latch of the window. "Like a parcel, shipped off."

The baby was hot on Elspeth's shoulder and she moved her to the other. Thinking of the word of the Lord, but unable to contain herself, she asked, "What's the matter? It's best to know, for my child." The mere phrase "my child" made Elspeth tingle.

"Oh, no need to worry," the woman said. "But you're right to, of course, for the child's sake. Bright's disease." She explained to Elspeth the swelling of her kidneys, and how the blood that used to course safely through her veins was escaping, leaking into her flesh and threatening to kill her. Would kill her. Each heartbeat, in fact, brought her closer to death. The train's wheels clacked with exacting rhythm, and the woman cocked her head to the side. "Listen," she said, "that's the sound of my heart."

The woman smiled at the baby. She reached out a shaking hand and slid her fingers over its near-bald head. Elspeth, too, had come to know the delight of the warm skin and the hints of downy hair. The woman withdrew quickly. "I'm sorry, I shouldn't have." Elspeth told her she understood.

A vague whiteness at the corners of her lips showed when she opened her mouth to speak. She swallowed. Then she began again. "If I may," she said, and then—despite the great pain that made her teeth gnash together and her breath hiss between them—she stood on her bulbous ankles and adjusted the infant, placing it across Elspeth's arm, with its head at her left biceps and its torso supported by her right. The tension that Elspeth hadn't realized she'd carried in her shoulders disappeared. The baby stirred, then eased back into sleep, the pink skin of her eyelids adorned with purple veins.

The woman stroked the child's tiny ear with the back of her finger, and Elspeth would have sworn to her Savior that the old woman's cheeks filled and flushed, and the crevices and shadows on her forehead dissolved, everything about her beaming. After a time, she collapsed back onto her seat. The cushions were thrown into disarray behind her. "She's young to travel," she said, and glanced out the window, her skin sagging.

Elspeth rocked back and forth in time with the swaying of the train as it barreled down the tracks, the trees and hillsides merely a blur. "We've no choice."

IN THE KITCHEN, Caleb crouched beneath the coatrack. The sleeves of his father's jacket tickled his head, and he shoved them aside. From his vantage point, all he could see of his mother was a few strands of black hair that spilled into space, and—when she took one of her rare breaths—her chest. But he could hear the noise, an unholy groan that she produced deep within her, and he plugged his ears against it, the sound deadening into a bass hum. He waited for her chest to rise, and held his breath until he saw it again. Soon he felt light-headed.

As he drew close to her, he removed one finger from his ear but replaced it immediately. She sounded like death: as if her life was being pulled from her body forcibly. He imagined her spirit like a wisp of smoke, but one with talons and teeth that it dug into her insides and the groan was those nails and teeth being dragged across her ribs, her throat, and her lungs as it fought to keep its place. He cried and cursed himself and uncovered his ears and let the noise tunnel through.

She frightened him, always had, even before he'd moved to the barn, but never as much as she did with her blood seeping from her body and that noise clawing its way out. Soon, he thought, she would be empty. His surgery seemed to be speeding the process: His sloppy digging and cutting had made the wounds worse. Her hair, flecked with rogue strands of gray, had become matted and tangled. He patted her bare arm. The heat had been replaced by a cold clamminess. He wasn't sure he'd ever touched her before he'd shot her. During her long absences he remembered her immense strength— greater than that of any of the boys. Her shoulders were sloped with muscle, and her knotted arms were thicker than Amos's. He pushed up one of her eyelids and saw nothing but white streaked with blood. She would not survive, he thought again. He picked the pillow up off the floor, where he'd dropped it the last time, before he went scooting like a mouse beneath the coatrack. Some of the goose feathers scattered on the floor and stuck in the wide puddle of blood that had accumulated beneath the table. He raised the pillow over her head, and plumped it between his hands. He clutched the fabric. Every time the courage built within him to crush the material down on her face, stopping forever the spasms and the terrible sound, she would cough or murmur and turn back into his mother. He held his position until his arms shook. A droplet of sweat formed at her widow's peak. As it traced the curve above her eyebrow, she squeezed her eyes tightly, and he recalled her making the same expression when he and Jesse had come tromping into the kitchen one night. She'd held her eyes shut for long enough that the boys knew to retreat back the way they'd come. This had stayed with him, because the next morning, she'd left and they wouldn't see her again for six months. He threw the pillow across the kitchen, where it collided with an empty jug that used to hold their sugar. The pillow landed on the floor, while the sugar container spun on the shelf, rattling around on its base before it got too close to the edge and tumbled. It landed, however, directly in the center of the goose down. This small piece of fortune made Caleb smile, and he brushed his mother's hair from her face and the sound ceased. The calm was worse to him, and when she recommenced, he pulled a chair to the table and laid his head on it, next to his mother's hip, where he felt every raw breath reverberate through the wood.

WITH DARKNESS, THE fits ceased. The fever dulled. But her memories continued to unfurl before her, and uncovered events she had worked hard to forget—arguments, trespasses, lies—and she relived the aftermath of the first time she'd spoken to Jorah, who was known then as Lothute.

"A savage," her father said in a whisper—all of their conversations whispered so as not to disturb the van Tessels. Their nook of the building had always been the servants' quarters, and as such, did not hold noise as well as the house proper, the boards not as tight, the corners not as square, the walls and floors unadorned. Worried even about his steps, her father removed his shoes, placed the tired leather next to her mother's boots, and straightened the two thick, woolen socks that muffled the thump of his wooden leg. "You've embarrassed the family over a savage. We must assume Mr. van Tessel has been told."

"All I did was say hello," Elspeth said and her father's hand snapped her head back. Her lip throbbed but did not split. She'd only heard Lothute speak that morning, never before, and his voice had surprised her, light and airy where she expected gravel crunched underfoot. She'd pretended to shake a rock from her shoe in the cool of the barn while he mended a horse's saddle. Elspeth had been warned to keep away from him, but she saw them as paired in their silence—neither was spoken to, neither was expected to speak. Besides his darker complexion, he looked the same as they did, wore the same clothes, ate the same food. He did not run around with a tomahawk and a belt full of scalps like the Indians in her books. His eyes were kind.

"The van Tessels deserve to see better of us," her father said with crimson cheeks and straining neck muscles, his anger loosed but his volume contained. As if summoned by the mention of his name, or by the harshness of their whispers, the shadows of Mr. van Tessel's fine shoes appeared at the crack beneath their door.

Her mother wept, and Elspeth knew better than to look to her for support and instead glanced around the room, her home—the bed her parents shared, the straw mattress at their feet where she slept, her small trove of books that the van Tessel girls had grown out of, her mirror, another van Tessel castoff because it had been warped somehow and stretched one's appearance at the edges of the gilded frame—and she knew, even before she heard the slither of her father's belt being drawn from his pants, that she would not see any of it again.

She squirmed to get away, but her father grasped both of her wrists in one strong hand and brought the leather down upon her back and her head. He struck her again and again, and she cried out. Her blood dotted the floor as it flew from the buckle. She screamed for him to stop, and the two shadows shifted beneath the door and then disappeared. The beating ended. Her father wrapped the belt around his hand like a bandage. He even seemed to whisper his ragged breathing. When Elspeth pushed herself onto her feet, he leaned against the dresser on his fists.

"It's time you go, child," her mother said. "Here." She opened a drawer and presented Elspeth with a neatly folded pillowcase, pressed between her two palms. "For your things." When Elspeth reached for the linen, her mother retracted her hands, as if she'd be scalded by her touch.

Less than a mile from the van Tessel estate, Lothute caught up to her and matched the rhythm of her careless steps. He handed her a cloth, and she held it to her head. "Is this my fault?" he asked her.

She stood there, shocked and crying, her few possessions in the pillowcase—yet another van Tessel hand-me-down, already torn—wondering what this man would do to her mother and father if she told him the truth.

"I don't know where I'll go," she said, the echoes of the lashes racking her body.

"I'll protect you," he said. She looked out at him from between eyelashes caked with blood. He took the cloth from her and dabbed at her injuries, swabbed the clots from her face, then examined the wounds, his face inches from hers. "All shall heal in time. I promise." He smiled. She smelled his sweat. He nodded to her belongings. "I'll return with my things."

He walked through the woods, and she followed his white shirt flitting among the trees until she could find no trace of him. Only after he'd left did she consider the beating—or worse—that awaited him at the van Tessels, and she prayed for his survival and tried to reassemble the day through the miasma of her shock. She'd only wanted to say hello. But after this, they had no choice. After this, he was hers, and she was his. And so she sat down to wait.

CALEB SPENT TWO days listening at his mother's hip, thinking each wretched breath might not be followed by another. From the shelf in the living area he'd fetched one of their Bibles, and though he could not read it, not well, he set it next to her limp hand, thinking it might comfort her, wherever she was. The pillow he'd tucked beneath her head. He couldn't bring himself to end her pain and leave himself alone in the world.

Once he grabbed her hand but it was so feverish and wet that it felt like no hand at all. She hadn't improved, nor had she gotten worse. Caleb opened the house to the outdoors and let the cold and the light flood the kitchen. The wind dried his tears. He hoped the fresh air would dispel the odor of his brothers' and sisters' deterioration, but by dusk he had to tie a handkerchief around his face to fight the smell. Yet the snow gave way to ice and the ice to frozen ground and the frozen ground to a land strewn with slate and limestone, and in an hour with the pick he hadn't made a grave fit for a chicken.

ELSPETH HAD BORNE Mary up the hill, the path at that time unfamiliar and unworn. Several times she had to turn around to try to find an easier route. Small trickles of water made footholds treacherous, and she would brace herself to stay on her feet. Her clothes became soaked in mud and torn by small branches. The baby, strapped to her chest, gurgled with each bounce.

In the yard, freshly shorn sheep chased one another around their makeshift enclosure. Jorah stood on the porch, as if he expected her, his black hair blown across his face, while Elspeth forged through the mud, the smell of animals and urine thick in her nostrils. He squinted at the bundle in her arms. As she drew closer, his expression broke into one of pure joy, something she'd never before witnessed, and he leapt from the porch and ran to her, his unshod feet sliding in the mud and the turned earth of the field. She said, "It's a girl. Our girl."

"Our girl," Jorah repeated and lifted Elspeth into the air and spun them around until they tumbled to the damp soil, dizzy, clutching at each other, and when they were through laughing, Elspeth's cheek touched the vulnerable spot on top of the child's skull where—in their excitement—the hat had fallen from it. She ran her fingers across the crease where Mary's impossibly tiny head met her even more unlikely neck, where the tufts of infant hair grew long and softer than anything in her imagination.

CALEB WENT BACK outside and placed Jesse on top of Emma and Mary and Amos, who lay in a pile atop the chairs from the living room, which he'd broken with Jesse's boots and the butt of his Ithaca. Splinters of wood and useless nails surrounded them, all of it startling against the previously uninterrupted snow and ice. Amos's bulk had been enough to force Caleb to reconsider where he'd lain Emma, and he brought her to her older brother and placed her on top of him, twenty steps from the house—he counted them as he brought the others. His father he could not budge from the bed. Caleb would wait for his mother to pass, and then let them lie together.

As a child, Caleb hadn't known of death. He saw cows, sheep, and pigs butchered, but he and his family—people—were different. When his father read the stories of the Bible, Caleb assumed those men and women were still walking the earth somewhere. But two years prior—his tenth birthday less than a month past—he had gone late at night to check on the sheep, guided by the moonlight and his perfect memory of each stone and root in the path. He'd watched as a man crossed the fields below, the grass waist high. The man stepped with great deliberation, and Caleb knew enough not to move. He carried a gun; Caleb saw the moon reflect off the steel. A shot rang out, and Caleb ducked and waited for the sting of the bullet. It was the man, however, who jerked backward and disappeared from view. Caleb's father—he recognized his upright walk—emerged from a stand of trees at the foot of the hill, waded through the grass to where the man had dropped, stood over the depression in the grass, and leveled his gun. A second report chased the man's small cry out into the world. At that time, Caleb had lived in the house and slept in the same bed as his brother, and for months after that, when they were both woken by his nightmares, Jesse would cover Caleb's mouth with his hand and hug him, muffling his screams, squeezing Caleb back into himself.

Water plinked all around him, falling from the branches and the roof. He stopped and listened. He stood beneath the elm tree that hung over their house, and found himself in the path of one of the steady drips, each as cold and finite as a bullet. This would be the last time he would ever see them; he'd been careful to hide their injuries. Mary—her dress in tatters, cut away to untangle her from the stove—stared out from beneath Emma. Mary looked whole, and he thought of her standing in the barn, waiting for him to show himself. She would fold her arms and stand there sternly, until his giggling would turn to laughing and the chaff would sift down through the gaps in the floorboards, falling like dun snow, and he would lean his face over the edge of the loft. "Father needs you," she'd say. "Father needs you for something." He heard these words with such clarity that he became angry with her for not speaking or getting up, for lying there like an old cow on a rainy day.

The easiest to move, weighing no more than a lamb, had been Emma, the one who understood him least, who asked him questions the others didn't. *Why did he live in the barn? Why didn't he like to talk or sing? Why did he sit at dinner only after their father had already said the prayer?* Caleb would lean down, look her in the eye, and muss her hair. Somehow that placated her.

Underneath her, facedown, was Amos, the eldest boy, who could silence them all with the same look their father gave, who one morning after milking had gotten his hair caught in the latch to the barn door and no amount of tugging or twisting could free him. Caleb had been forced to cut him loose, leaving thick, sandy locks of hair waving at them. Their father had made Amos wait two weeks before he'd let Mary even it out, a large gap in the bangs that he flicked and pushed from his eyes. "*Oh, ye sons of men,*" their father quoted, "*how long shall my glory be turned into dishonor? How long will ye love vanity, and seek after falsehood?*" Caleb thought they were praying, and paused on the steps, hat in hand, the scent of stew readying his stomach. No one dared smile at Amos's crooked haircut. Even in death, he held sway with that expression, and Caleb had cut the brass buttons from a pair of overalls his father would never wear again and had placed them over Amos's eyes.

And Jesse. Jesse had been the only one to know him at all. They would sit on hot summer days in the tall grass, far enough away not to be able to see each other through the shifting stalks, close enough to hear the occasional sigh or hiccup, together but apart, waiting for the fog to roll over them and the moisture to collect on the blades before they'd lie down, their bare arms and shoulders cooled by the dew. He had used the remnants of Mary's dress to cover Jesse fully, but somehow when his brothers and sisters settled into one another, things had shifted and now his dirty fingernails pointed at Caleb. He took his brother's hand, pretended it felt capable and human, and tucked it beneath Mary's back.

He avoided his mother when he took the lamp from the hook above the stove; he couldn't stand for her to know what was happening. He no longer bothered to close the door to the house. When he ventured back outside, a rabbit scampered across his path, leaving its prints in those of Jesse's boots, the sight of which gave a brief leap to Caleb's heart, but then he realized the boots held his own feet. He removed the chimney, the collar, the burner, and the heavy wick from the kerosene lamp and dumped the contents across the four bodies. On top of that, he emptied what was left of the oil in the small barrel they kept in the kitchen. He clutched the tinder in his hands. The kerosene soaked down to the snow and began to melt it in small rivulets, like the view from the hillside when the streams swelled in spring. The rivers radiated out from the mass of bodies, and as he contemplated them, his brothers and sisters came alive. He heard their voices; he saw them move.

He couldn't do it. It would have to wait for nightfall, when he could no longer see their faces or their familiar features, and re-member them speaking and playing and singing and praying and crying and laughing. Sometimes, on the quietest of nights, when the moon hung heavy in the sky and the light could guide him as well as the sun, he would tiptoe to the front door of the house, sit on the step, remove his boots, lift the latch, and in stocking feet walk silently from room to room, watching his siblings sleep.

The house offered no solace. His mother's irregular rasp chased him from the kitchen. He avoided the stained shapes on the floor as if his brothers and sisters were still there, and entered his parents' room. The book Jorah had been reading to the children lay on his bedside table, a red ribbon marking their place. Beneath that sat his frayed Bible. The only thought in Caleb's head when he'd heard the shooting was that his father would stop it. He'd done it before. With each shot, Caleb had wondered whether it had come from his father's gun and he'd hoped his father would wave to him from the front step, telling him all was well, but then the three men had slunk out into the yard. He shuddered, and caught himself with a hand to the frame of his parents' bed. His father looked shrunken, his clothes tattered by the shot and bullets. In life, he'd been in constant motion, only sitting to eat or read the Bible. When he put his shoes on, in fact, he did not sit on the chair next to the coatrack as everyone else did—he remained standing. Jorah's manners and movement had given him size and weight, but in death it seemed as though he'd been wearing a coat much too large and had shrugged it off.

The wind had ceased, and with it, the whistling and moaning of the house. Sometimes he caught himself humming along with it at the base of his throat, and he'd wonder how long he'd been keeping himself company.

Caleb turned his back on his father's body, his horrible grimace, and almost tripped over a pile of sheets on the floor. Not sure in their bloodied state what they contained, he nudged them with his foot, then noticed the clean linens on the bed. Even though he thought it had shattered altogether, his heart broke once more, for his mother, for his father, for his brothers and sisters.

He gathered the sheets and added them to the pile of bodies and broken furniture, and sat on the fence that he and Jesse had constructed to pen the pigs. It had been crooked the first time and they'd rebuilt it until they got it right, their father never saying anything but, "*And he built fenced cities in Judah: for the land had rest.*" On his knee Caleb rolled a cigarette from the tobacco he'd uncovered beneath Amos's pillow. Jesse had showed him how to pinch the leaves and wind the papers tight and occasionally allowed him a puff here and there for his services.

The valley unfolded before him, undulating lands with small patches of forest, everything covered in cottony snowfall. When the wind came, the whole world would quake with movement—every tree, leaf, and blade of grass—moving in waves like liquid. But the snow and wind had subsided and everything was at rest. The world, too, waited.

The short day grew dim. Caleb vowed to wait until sunset, but the clouds rolled in again, thick and gray like the mounds of sheared lamb's wool that cluttered the barn at first thaw, and the sun disappeared. Once he'd finished smoking, he would say goodbye. Caleb lit another cigarette. He didn't like the taste but enjoyed the warm sensation in his throat and his lungs. Before long, the papers burned his fingers and he spat on them, rubbing them back and forth to ease the pain.

Their first night together, baby Mary slept between them, and Elspeth worried that Jorah kept the child awake with his constant touching: cupping the heel of her foot in his palm and looking over the miniature toes with delight, placing a finger in the dimples of her elbows, giving her his pinkie and laughing when she suckled on it. Over her husband's protests, Elspeth took the infant into the main room to feed. She could hear Jorah shifting on the bed to see through the open door, but she held her back to him, silently urging the child to drink. She had been practicing, but the baby at times refused her, or latched on painfully, or, most often, the milk refused to come and Elspeth would look away so Mary could not see her crying.

Jorah built a crib, and some nights Elspeth would find him sitting cross-legged on the floor, watching Mary sleep. When he returned to bed, he would recite his observations, speculate on the baby's dreams, remark on her beauty. He would drop into slumber, his brow clean and smooth, his lips bent into a slight smile while Elspeth examined the shifting shadows on the ceiling until the dawn chased them away.

On a clear July day, the heat filtering through the trees, Elspeth stood on the bank of the creek, holding Mary in her arms. She'd made a tiny dress from her nicest white scarf and the pillowcase in which she'd carried her belongings away from the van Tessels'.

Jorah positioned himself on two steady rocks, his legs staggered for balance. He wore a white shirt and his finest trousers, which he'd rolled up past his knees, but the rushing water soaked the fabric anyway. He sang in a register lower than his speaking voice, "*O Father, bless the children, Brought hither to thy gate.*" He gestured for the child. Elspeth edged closer to the water and reached out and Jorah took Mary in his sure arms and continued the hymn. When he finished, he handed the child's bonnet to Elspeth. Mary's large eyes worked against the sunlight. Jorah said something quiet that Elspeth couldn't hear, and dipped the baby's head in the rushing creek.

Elspeth watched the sky. Cottony clouds lazed on the horizon. She didn't know what she'd expected. Certainly she didn't think the child would burst into flame or the earth would crack open and swallow her whole, but she didn't expect Jorah to hand Mary back to her and for the child to act perfectly happy and for Jorah to smile as well, unrolling his pants and saying the Lord's Prayer. With Mary's breath on her cheek, she heard herself reciting the passage she'd memorized the night before, "*And Mary said, 'My soul doth magnify the Lord, And my spirit hath rejoiced in his God my Savior.'*" Jorah looked upon her as if she'd come straight from heaven. This only made her face flush and her legs waver as she retreated back to the house.

CALEB MONITORED HIS mother through the glass. Nothing made this an interesting pursuit—at such a distance, her breathing was imperceptible—but he could attend her and at the same time measure the strength of the sun as it tumbled down the sky in the gleaming of the window. He focused on his mother and then the sun and back and forth so many times his eyes were adjusting slower and slower and his head throbbed.

From this spot, he could imagine the path of the killers as they walked around Emma's body, her life already leaking away, into the kitchen where Amos froze midstride and Mary didn't have time to turn from the stove, and then through the great room, where they shot Jesse as he ran to Jorah. Even if he hadn't witnessed the man falling in the waving grass and didn't know of his father's capabilities, Caleb would have fled to him, too, and he pressed into the wall of the house, thinking of his brother's shoulder against his as they scrambled toward safety. There they would lie forever, side by side. Jorah had failed them, hadn't even gotten up, and Caleb burned every time he thought of his father's body in bed, and the unused gun in the corner.

When he was nine and exploring their land for the first time on his own, Caleb had discovered a magic, silent place on the other side of the hill: four humped mounds in a small clearing covered by curving moosewood, the striped trunks gnarled and growing over rocks as if pinning them to the earth. The trees and the grass were well maintained, and Caleb felt at home there, safe. Two days after seeing the man die, Caleb ventured to his private spot to try to arrest the hammering in his chest and stop the nightmares that had plagued him once he finally managed to sleep. The peace had been shattered, though, by a new mound where the turf sat in clumps amid freshly exposed earth.

ELSPETH HAD GIVEN Jorah the money she'd earned in town, and he'd wrapped it in a kerchief and left for a period. During those quiet nights, she held the baby in the rocking chair, sometimes not getting into bed before a pink flush crept over the sky. She stared out the windows, walking from one to the other, awaiting his return, restless. He came back with a cow and two wicker baskets full of chickens. In his hat, he ferried half a dozen chicks. By then, Mary had begun to walk and burbled the beginnings of words. He placed the hat in the grass—the chicks chirped and squawked and tried in vain to mount the edge of the hat and escape—and he knelt down, holding his arms wide for his daughter, whose lurching steps filled him with laughter.

Her brown hair grew long and fine and curled at the tips. More and more Elspeth left the care of the child to Jorah, who relished it all, every soiled diaper, every burping. Mary tottered on her feet and chased the chickens around the yard, but they'd turn on her, and—with useless wings flapping—knock her to the dirt. Jorah would drop his shovel or his pitchfork and scoop his tearful Mary up in his arms and place her on his shoulders. She would press her cheek against the top of his head until she cried no more. Elspeth observed this with worry and envy. When the days grew shorter, she left again.

PAST NIGHTFALL, CALEB sparked the tinder and lit a handful of hay. It reflected off the ice and made everything sparkle. He let it burn. Then, as it illuminated Emma's face looking up at him, he dropped it onto his brothers and sisters. He shut his eyes and ran.

The sound came first, a whooshing like a bat flying close to his ears, but all around him. Next came the sudden rush of heat, and he fell. Before he could pull himself from the snow and ice, the smell hit him, the noxious odor of burning hair and flesh. He scrambled to his feet and—vomiting on his way—fled from the pyre. He followed the path he'd made to the barn, back to safety, and from two hundred yards away, in its shadow, the fire looked like any other. With a ball of snow, he wiped the bile from his chin. He picked up another tight fistful and sucked the water from it.

With no warning, the wind tugged his hair so hard it hurt his scalp and brought with it particles of ice that stung his face and neck. It drove the flames along the ground, following the tributaries of oil and kerosene, low and slinking like fog. The fire covered his twenty paces in an instant as if following his trail. The house withstood only a couple teasing licks before the roof ignited, the wooden shingles and gutters clogged with pine needles. The attic window, shuttered for the winter, popped behind the wood. He was already running toward his mother. The roof had proved to be little but tinder, and—weakened—it dropped down onto the rafters in less than a minute. The gap between the barn and the house had never seemed so vast. The ice cut his ankles above his boots. He held his scarf to his face against the smell.

Once through the door, the house roared around him. The heat was astonishing. A section of ceiling closest to the pyre caved in on the living room, and he saw the rocking horse they kept in the corner—though they were all too old for it—crushed by a beam. His mother did not move, despite the stifling smoke and the thunderous noise of the house falling down around her. Caleb screamed, urging her up, his mouth an inch from her ear. He slapped her cheeks. Sweat beaded and rolled down her forehead. He took her under the arms, and dragged her from the kitchen table. She yelped as her feet slammed on the floor. His vision blurred, and when he coughed it felt like he spit flames. He clutched his mother, fighting to pull her along with him, the heat so intense, so close, that he thought they wouldn't make it.

The air from outside slipped in the open front door, bracing and new, and it brought life to his lungs. He leaned back and dug his heels into the floorboards, and soon enough he lay gasping in the snow, his mother half on top of him. When the tears cleared from his eyes, he was surprised to find the fire more docile. It was sure to swallow the house, but now seemed like the milk snake he'd seen eat a mouse in the barn: content to finish its job, but in no great hurry.

Caleb thought of the Ithaca and his father's rifle sitting in the kitchen next to the door, and his mother's bag beside the coatrack. They would need them. He allowed himself a prayer—he thought of his mother, said her name, so that maybe God would listen— asking that the wind wouldn't pick up in the short time he would be inside. He pulled his scarf back over his mouth and nose. The doorframe held. The heat leeched all the moisture from his skin and lungs, leaving behind an aching dryness. He wrapped his hands in his sleeves so he could touch the hot metal and threw the weapons out into the snow, along with an old coat of Jorah's, his mother's bag and jacket, a pot, a pan, a bag of oats and one of cornmeal, and a few blankets.

The wind resumed and the fire screamed with approval. His prayer hadn't been answered. He threw himself out the door. As he turned over, shimmying away from the inferno, he heard a frenzied hooting. An owl emerged from the small triangular gap above the door, and swooped through the smoke. Then another. The windows cracked like gunshots.

His mother lay where he'd left her. He wadded his shirt and tucked it beneath her head, and sat in the snow, shivering. He placed the back of his hand on her forehead. The snow seemed to have brought her fever down, but he knew he couldn't leave her exposed for long.

Half of the house collapsed. The living room bent outward, then flattened altogether, sparks exploding into the sky like fire-flies. Sheets of ash, borne by the wind, their edges glowing orange, floated away like demonic leaves. The flames found the kitchen, and he watched the table withstand the onslaught through the darkening windows and the open door. His head filled with the impossible wish for the table to survive. At that moment, another owl burst forth. As it took flight, its wings beat frantically against the flames blooming from its feathers. He stood and watched it careen through the smoke-filled air, flying erratically in uneven spurts, the light consuming its body, until it dropped and landed in the snow with a hiss.

CHAPTER 4

The morning sun, as if recalling the fire, scalded the sky with bright oranges and reds. His mother lay inert next to him, bundled tightly in the few blankets he'd saved. The chill, however, seemed to have done her good; her face appeared less pallid and translucent, more solid. Caleb dripped some water onto her lips and she drank until she coughed and he turned her head so she didn't choke.

He threw aside the canvas he'd hoisted to protect them from the elements to find that a few inches of crisp, granulated snow had fallen in his brief sleep. He put on Jorah's coat, which came to his knees, and he had to roll the sleeves in order to see his hands. The smell of smoke clung to everything and thickened his tongue. He hacked and spat an evil black stain onto the new powder. The house smoldered and popped. Caleb refused to look in the direction of his siblings, not yet ready to see what the flames had left.

The barn door still wouldn't budge. They didn't keep any shovels in the house; they were all in the barn as Caleb would be first to wake in the morning and, if the snow was deep enough—he would leap from the opening to the loft, first tossing a shovel out before him, where it would penetrate the unblemished white like an explorer's flag laying claim to a new land.

He shifted some logs in the woodpile so that he stood high enough to push open a window. His fingers held on long enough to pitch himself up and onto the sill but, his boots and jacket slippery with snow, he lost his grip and crashed onto the hard-packed earth below. Above him the rafters lurked dim but brighter than the coal black of the ceiling. The odd stillness of the space made him uneasy—usually his presence would be met with swallows dropping from the darkness and swooping in wide circles and the animals rousing themselves, even though Caleb, as close to one of their own as existed, seldom made noise. The animals were worse off than he'd feared.

The pump had frozen, and he kicked at it with the heel of his boot—Jesse's boot—to break the ice that encased it. Caleb filled pails and took them around, dumping them into the bone-dry troughs behind the enclosures that separated the animals from one another. It was as if their bodies had been hollowed out, their stomachs bloated with hunger, their legs stripped bare. He, too, felt as if his necessary parts had wasted away, his empty shell held down by nothing but his brother's boots. He couldn't bear to light the lamps. The stench was stunning. He took fistfuls of oats and hopped the fence and tried hand-feeding the horses, who were alive, but barely, their ribs pronounced beneath skin dotted with sores. He poured trickles of water directly into their mouths from the pail. Their parched tongues worked at the water, and even this slight movement cheered him. Two of the pigs had died, and the others had taken nibbles from the carcasses. The sheep were mostly gone—but only the infirm or pregnant were housed in the main barn, the rest were high up on the hill in a small outbuilding. The cows appeared to be the hardiest, but even they were sick, their skin thick and

hard, their breathing slow, their reactions muted. Caleb moved between them, absorbing their warmth. The milky edges of the cows'
eyes were exposed as they searched for him, questioned him. He responded by patting their flanks and humming softly. For two years,
this place had been his sanctuary. He stood in the middle of the
barn, his eyes welled with tears, his chest tightened with anger, and
he dropped the bucket with an apocalyptic clatter.

THE COLD AIR seeping in under the canvas reestablished order to
Elspeth's thoughts. They'd become jumbled in the fire, losing their
thread and pitching her into hellish dreams of rotting corpses with
their long fingernails pointing, and their skinless jaws opening and
snapping shut.

The sun reminded her unconscious body not of the teasing fires
of hell, but of a happy warmth. She was rocking back and forth, the
boards making a pleasing creak with each roll of the runners, baby
Amos in her arms, the floors slick with the sawdust Jorah carried in
on his clothes and in his hair that would turn their feet pure white
by the end of the day. The child slept, warm on her skin, his tiny
forehead lined with purple veins like a subtle map of some fantastic
land. She would trace those lines, the longitudes and latitudes of
their new son—Mary nearly forgotten—as through the window
she watched Jorah frame the barn. Soon she would have to rise and
put Amos back in his crib, make sure Mary was occupied, and help
Jorah and the horses heft the timbers. He would say nothing but
she could sense the questions building. Outside, he exchanged his
saw for a hammer and she watched him pull a red cloth from his
pocket and draw it across his face, and when his eyes emerged, they
fixed upon her, dark and hooded.

Amos grew, and as he did, so did the clouds across her thoughts.

She would rock the boy furiously, trying in vain to recapture that feeling, the heat of the baby against her chest, the peace of watching out the window. He hated to be idle, would not give her the rest of sleep, did not depend upon her wholly. When she relented and put him down, he pulled himself up by the rungs of the chairs and stayed standing on his own. His gurgles sounded more and more like words with each passing day, and he possessed a soft mat of hair. In the sun it was like gold, and Elspeth hated it. She caught herself wanting to cut it off, to take Jorah's straight razor and restore the baby to what she thought of as its natural state. Mary played quietly in the corner, stacking blocks Jorah had fashioned from scraps of wood. She knocked them down and Elspeth bit her lip, wishing the child to stop. But whenever these thoughts struck her, Elspeth would cradle Amos and read her Bible to herself, surprised it didn't ignite in her hands. She clutched him to her, hard, and once she left a series of finger-shaped bruises on his arm as he wriggled to be free, to be placed on the floor to run through the open door and out into the fields where she would never get him back. The bruises went from black to blue to yellow, but sometimes, even when Amos grew tall and muscled, she would see them on his upper arm, black as pitch, and she would look away.

CALEB BUILT A fire in the makeshift stove, a pile of bricks arranged in the shape of a box, topped with a flat stone, with a hammered and bolted chimney capped with chicken wire that carried the smoke through a hole in the side of the barn. Before he'd installed the wire, a family of raccoons had crept down the metal shaft, drawn by the scent of food, and when he lit the fire the next morning, they came screeching and snarling from the bricks. Caleb had been forced to stab one with a pitchfork when it got cornered in the horses' stall, the horses stamping wildly, the raccoon screeching and clicking and baring its teeth.

In the loft, his bed, his lantern, his bedpan, and his small pile of clothes were exactly as he'd left them. A biscuit—the last thing Mary had cooked—sat fuzzy with mold on the crate where he kept his things: a few books of animal pictures his mother had brought back with baby Emma, a collection of arrowheads, and another of feathers he could not identify. They seemed silly to him now, a child's playthings, and he was embarrassed by how he would sit in the weak light of his lamp and rub the feathers against his face, thinking of the strange birds that had left behind these clues, species he'd never seen that flew only at night.

The door to the loft looked down on the smoldering rectangle where the house once stood and the rustling canvas under which his mother slept. He threw the shovel as hard as he could, and almost reached the first fence around the barn, which separated the pigpen from the pasture. The snow was not deep, but he jumped anyway, enjoying the brief moment of nothingness, his body no longer his own, the wind screaming past. He landed with a thud and rolled forward, coming to rest on his back. The sky was gentle blue, unaffected by what had happened beneath it.

WITH THE HORSES, the mule, and their greatest efforts, the barn had been built. Jorah leaned the new walls against trees as they did so. He sat in the branches to hammer everything into place, and once he'd finished he cut them down to make room. Her husband went about his work with a clouded countenance, which she first took for concentration, but then understood to be something far deeper. She lifted a protesting Amos into her arms. Mary played with pinecones a few strides away.

"We should baptize that boy soon," Jorah said. He pressed his hand flat against one of the corner posts of the barn and then aligned his foot with the base, checking its orientation. Satisfied, he slapped his palms together.

"Of course," she said. "Today?" The afternoon threatened to slip away, and the wind had picked up, signaling a storm or—at the very least—rain.

"Now," he said. "Mary's dress is on the top shelf of the closet."

Elspeth started to say that she knew exactly where the dress was, and there was no way it would fit the heavier, taller Amos, but she remained mute.

By the time she'd cut the back of the dress open and affixed some ties to keep it shut, evening had descended on them. Amos fought her as she tried to put his arms into the sleeves. The door slammed and she heard Jorah's footsteps coming toward her. Instinctively, she held the child closer.

"Now," he said. They carried no lamp, and Jorah pulled Mary along by the hand, more than once lifting her by it when she stumbled, unable to keep up with his pace or to know the dips and holes in the earth as he did. Amos cried on Elspeth's shoulder. As they approached, the creek grew louder, the spring melt lending power that made the water roar.

Elspeth could see little but the white collar of Mary's dress, and the black shape of her husband stepping down into the creek. She heard the water splash against his thighs and his sharp intake of breath as the icy water enveloped him to the waist.

"Give him to me," he said. He sang the same song, but not in the lilting, patient way as before, this time more of a chant. "*O Father, bless the children,*" he began. Amos wailed. His white dress glowed in the dark. Jorah sang louder. "*Lift up their fallen nature, Restore their lost estate.*" Mary, too, started to cry, and she grasped at Elspeth's skirts. The wind grew in strength, and the trees rocked toward them and then away. "*Receive them, cleanse them, own them, And keep them ever thine.*"

Elspeth saw the dress dip and Amos stopped crying for an instant, but then recommenced louder than before, and Elspeth pictured his tiny mouth opened wide, his face turning purple. Jorah did not hand the child out, but stepped onto the shore with the boy in his arms, and Elspeth felt the cold radiating from her husband, and heard the chattering of his teeth.

THE RHYTHM OF the shovel consoled Caleb as he dug out the barn door. The task gave him something to concentrate on and he wrapped his hands in rags that grew wet with perspiration. Soon blisters opened on his palms. When the sun lowered behind their hill and the chill sharpened, he stopped, jammed the shovel into the pile of snow and, setting his feet, pulled on the door. It swung open, scratching a half-moon of dirt, the rich brown earth shocking against the snow.

Inside, he piled straw on the floor as close to the fire as he dared. One funeral pyre had been enough. He covered this in his thin set of sheets, and though the straw poked through the cotton in places, it would have to do. His footsteps crunched as he followed the path of his own prints back to the tent. He removed the canvas from over his mother and laid it on the snow. While the chill had eased her fever, he understood another night might kill her. Bent at the knees, he imagined lifting her like a swaddled child and placing her on the canvas as gently as he could, but all he could do was roll her. She grunted. "Sorry, Mother," he said, and at the sound of his own voice, he looked to the hills behind them, as if even that brief speech would bring the murderers out from the trees, screaming and waving their guns before they leveled their steel and the shots cracked again. Caleb dragged his mother toward the barn. He contorted his neck to avoid the black mark where it all had originated.

With the back of his hand he felt his mother's forehead, leaving a small smear of blood at her temple as he did so. Her fever had fallen. The grip of her muscles had loosened, her brow had relaxed, her jaw no longer flexed until small striped shadows developed on her cheeks, and her eyes no longer squeezed tight as if against a bright sun. He gave her some water and spoke to her as he did the animals, nonsense, a collection of soothing tones and syllables, near-words. Caleb thought it did his heart more good than hers. He placed his head by her hip, the straw poking his face, but he didn't mind. He listened to the crackle of the fire and the small rustle of the animals in their pens.

After a short sleep, he rose. The day didn't have the bite of the last and yet he wrapped his arms about himself. He focused on a tree so he could avoid an accidental sighting before he was ready. When he sensed he'd drawn close, he looked down upon what he'd done. Their home lay in ashes that the wind had smeared across the snow, as though the house were slowly escaping. The four thick posts that had formed the perimeter of the house remained, charred and shrunken. In what had once been his parents' bedroom, in a far corner, the bones of his father had been scattered into disarray. Stark white, in a smaller circle of ash no more than a yard from where he stood, rested the skeletons of his brothers and sisters. They had fallen in on one another, arms wrapped in arms, legs hooked around legs, rib cages intertwining like hands in prayer.

IN THEIR BED that night, Elspeth had pulled the quilt close to her chin. Jorah knew. He entered the room without a lamp. His weight settled on the edge of the mattress, but he didn't lie down.

He cleared his throat. "I'm sorry," he said. Elspeth's body became confused, her heart trembling an uneven beat and her mind racing and then slowing. "I don't know," he continued, "whether this is because of some wrong I have committed." She could feel him undoing the buttons of his shirt and peeling it off. Marring his uncovered back, she knew, were the crisscrossed, ropelike scars from his beating at the hands of her father and Mr. van Tessel. When she doubted how he could love her, she remembered these scars and the torn fists that had held his meager belongings when he had found her in the woods, his knuckles split nearly to the bone, the cuts so deep they hardly bled. He'd read the Bible to her at night as they searched for a land to house their new life together, and had renamed himself for her and for God, to show his new dedication. He'd liked how it had sounded, *Jorah,* so smooth and unlike the ugliness of Lothute. Those memories held small comfort for her in their bedroom, his broad back to her.

"I don't know if perhaps I made you feel some necessity or urge," he said. Elspeth tensed, fearful that he might strike her, thinking of the flash of his eyes as he demanded she hand him Amos while he fought against the raging creek, the water piling up and around his torso, the white foam spectral in the dark.

One of the children cried in the other room and they both held their breath. Elspeth pictured herself making the journey down the hillside, her effects secure on her back, her customary letter of reference folded among her things. She only hoped that he would allow her to spend the night before leaving.

When it seemed enough time had passed and the children had resumed their sleep, Jorah spoke again, his voice even softer. "I also know that I made a promise to you, to keep you safe and protected. Haven't I done that?" Elspeth's feet tingled. She'd gripped the quilt tight enough to cut off her circulation and yet her fingers clenched ever harder, the material gathering in her hands, where it quickly grew damp. Jorah sighed, his shoulders rising and falling. A milky stream of moonlight washed over the bedroom. "I've protected you. And I will continue to do so." He reached back and took one of her hands, cupping her fist much as he had Mary's heels. Elspeth relaxed, and he turned to her—everything about him soft—and tugged on her arm. She heard the tender pat of his feet hitting the floor. The quilt slid from her and she felt levitated, like her own feet never met the ground, and hand in hand they walked into the next room, where Amos slept in his crib, his belly protruding, his tiny hands clenched beside his head, and Mary slept also, her brown hair splashed against her pillow in the bed Jorah had made and inscribed with a letter *M* on the headboard. They each breathed deep and even.

"They look nothing like us," Jorah said, and Elspeth's body jerked and she made to run away, but he latched his arms around her and held her as tight as she'd ever held Amos, and he said, "Whose children are these?"

The clarity of the memory startled Elspeth. She coughed, and tried to sit up, but the pain was too intense. At first, she thought she was in a high-ceilinged hotel room in another strange town but soon realized she was in the barn on her back in tremendous pain, and she couldn't recall how she'd gotten there or how she'd been injured. A crow called to her from off in the darkness. She remembered walking up the hill and the fever-soaked nightmare of the bodies strewn about the house and then the flaming hot pain and understood she'd been shot and her children were gone. She cried out again, and Caleb appeared before her. *It couldn't be*, she thought and tried to move, but she was too weak.

"Mama, it's okay," he said. He truly was alive—the knowledge sent a spasm of happiness through her, and the surge proved enough to roll her eyes back once more.

The night of Amos's baptism, when the children had been put to bed, Jorah had told her that he'd seen the bodies of mothers before, and he knew Elspeth had not had a child. He sighed, letting the bookmark from his Bible slide between his middle and index fingers, and said, "For a while I convinced myself that it was possible.

That the child could be"—he chuckled, an angry sound—"I thought it could be a child of God." He ran his hand along the leather binding, but said nothing else and asked her no questions. Implicit in his silence was an understanding, she thought, that Amos and Mary would be enough for them. She left to work and trudged up the hill again with more money stuffed in her shoes and everything flowed well for a while. After two years, though, the urges returned. She spent entire nights cradling her arms and rocking on the balls of her feet in front of the windows.

When she'd come back with Caleb, Jorah hadn't spoken to her for days. One evening, however, after she'd fed the baby and held him on her shoulder to burp him, she sensed Jorah in the doorway, watching them, and knew that something in him had thawed.

CALEB DRAGGED THE dead animals through the woods— the smallest first to create a track that became tamped down and smooth—and to the edge of the cliff where he and Jesse had taught themselves to chew Amos's tobacco, spitting thick streams of juice onto the rocks below. He threw the dead chickens, rolled the dead sheep, dragged the smallest of the dead pigs. The others he could not manage, though he tried. All this took the better part of the day.

He looked in on his mother every hour or so, wiped her forehead with a cloth despite the fact that the fever had abated, and fed her from the bowl of eggs he kept warm by the fire. The color had returned to her skin. He thought that she might live, not merely for another sunrise, but to stand and walk again. But with standing and walking came the prospect of speaking, and he would have to explain himself. He didn't know how he could tell her about his fear, how it had clenched him into a ball and forced him down into the hay. He didn't know how he could tell her that he'd heard Emma's short scream, like the bleating of a lamb. How he'd hidden. How he'd seen them—had been within a hundred yards of his Ithaca and another few to the open loft door, from which he could have sighted at least one, aiming for the red scarf. How he'd shot her.

They would need a plan, and for the first time he began to think of a future. All he could tell his mother was that he planned on killing them. He assumed she would want the same. He sat in the open door to the hayloft with these thoughts. Snow fell, only scattered flakes at first, but then in thick sheets, erasing the stars. His feet hung free. He chewed on an old boot string. His father's rifle sat across his thighs.

He imagined himself leaping down from the loft as the birds scattered at the first shot. Perhaps before that. He would have heard them coming, or detected some change in the air, like the mornings when Emma would come to get him for breakfast and he'd be at the edge of the loft even before the creaking of the door. This would be the opposite, a call like the one that had brought his father to the other side of the hill late one night, a low, rumbling thunder like a storm miles off, so faint it might be nothing more than the creaking of the trees, except somehow his bones would know different, and he would have jumped down from the ladder and grabbed his Ithaca. He loaded it as he crept along, the shells clicking into place. Emma saw him and he motioned her inside. Her eyes betrayed no fear, so strong was her faith in her brother. Or maybe he picked her up under one arm and placed her safely in the house, telling her to latch the door. He edged along the periphery of the pen bent over, under the cover of the fence. One hand planted on the post and he vaulted over it. He circled back around them, down a path in the hill between birches and elms and evergreens that only he knew, and as he came up behind them he would say, "Put those weapons down. There'll be no killing today."

But of course he would kill them, because they would not drop their weapons, and he would feel no remorse. Afterward, his father would find the perfect Bible passage to make everyone feel that what he'd done was right with God. Even Caleb would listen. And he would believe it—and the man who was saying it—deep in his core.

They would bury them in the plot on the other side of the hill, where Caleb had first discovered death, a simple marker their only connection to the living world. He could also penetrate the frozen ground and dig a perfectly rectangular grave. That was what the Caleb who could kill would do.

The Caleb who could not fire his father's outsized rifle into the night sky, imagining the bullet losing speed and falling harmlessly into one of the rolling fields below, perhaps sending up a small cloud of snow, probably not. His shoulder throbbed from the kick of the gun and he knew he'd have a bruise for a week. The sound was lost in the descending blanket of snow. It was a call to the killers, a sign from Caleb that he would find them, that he would be different when he did. Or so he hoped.

Elspeth murmured. When he got to her, everything appeared to be the same; he wondered if he'd imagined the noise. He checked the bandages, cleaned the wounds with whiskey, and dabbed at her forehead with the rag. When he withdrew it, her unsteady pupils tried to follow him. "Caleb," she said. She forced a smile and small dots of blood burgeoned on her cracked lips.

Caleb feared she saw his guilt, but hoped she saw how he'd changed: He would defend them, he would find those men, and he would kill them for what they'd done to his family.

ELSPETH HAD BEEN living in dreams so long the pale dawn confused her. The bandages made no sense, either, and then she remembered the shot, and her last seconds of consciousness. The wraps were clean but loose and tied with poor knots. In spite of the pain, she tried to stand, and surprised herself by getting to her feet. She shuffled to the barn doors and leaned her weakened body against them until they opened. The air struck her and nearly knocked her over, and she searched for her balance, the task made more difficult by the dizzying effect of the snow swirling lazily outside. Nausea rippled within her.

The house was gone. In its place, a blank hole. The elm that had overhung their home had shriveled into something black, no longer quite a tree. In the clutch of her fever, she'd thought it strange that they slept in the barn and now she realized why—the men who had shot her and her family had razed their home. The closest trees had their branches shortened and twisted by the heat of the fire. The ice clinging to the bark had saved the forest, preserved the rest of the yard so that it appeared as though God himself had plucked the house from this world, as one would a blueberry from its bush. Elspeth noted the four posts that had been the entirety of the house she'd left on her first trip. The fire had made them its grave marker.

The cold mud pulled her down, down into the embrace of the Devil. Her hand went to her chest, where her cross always resided, but all that met her fingers was a naked chain. She gave in, the faces of her children turning away from her, and when they turned back, they were as she'd found them some days ago, waxen and unmoving, fear and accusation stuck forever in their skin. She struck her knee on a stone in the mud as she yielded. Something rustled above her—the wings of a demon beating, flying down from the rafters, close to her. The heat burned her face and the only relief she could find lay in the mud and she surrendered, allowing the cooling powers to provide for her, knowing all the while that they were a gift of the Devil.

C ALEB SHOOK HIS mother lightly. She groaned. He pulled the blanket over her bare shoulder. Even in the icy mud, her skin was hot. She'd bled through her bandages. Her eyes, glassy and unfocused, pointed in the direction of the house. His image of her rising, yawning, and stretching away the shotgun pellets he'd inflicted upon her, ready to take off after the men who'd murdered their family, was completely gone.

She hadn't done serious damage, merely opened a few wounds with exertion. Rivulets of sweat wiped the dirt away in thin stripes. He melted snow over the fire and used one of the clean rags to set about washing her. She'd lost weight, and it laid bare her veins and muscles. He started at her feet and worked his way up until he reached her thighs, then he worked inward from her arms. He removed what was left of her dress. As he did so, she called for his father in a feeble voice that cracked and turned to breath toward the end. The sound of his father's name made him shake. His eyes averted, he even removed her muslin drawers, which were badly stained. He could smell them at arm's length and added them to the fire. He blindly dabbed at her, and dunked the rag in the bucket, the scalding water forcing tears to his eyes, his skin prickling and he withdrew his clenched fist quickly, sending a wave of steaming water across the floor of the barn. The hay needed refreshing and the bedding needed cleaning, so he spread a blanket on the ground for her. To keep her warm while he worked, he dressed her in some of Jorah's old work clothes that had hung on a peg near the horses, the buttons on a flannel shirt giving him greater access to her bandages than a dress could afford. He draped the wet sheets and quilt from the rafters over the fire, and the drops of water sizzled on the stone. Of all of this, he felt proud.

He stared at the space where their home used to be. He heard them, his father's high voice reading to them, the boys laughing, the girls arguing. There was nothing to mark where they'd been. He considered the other side of the hill, the four lumps that would remain there even though his father would no longer pull the weeds surrounding them or tend to the tidy field of grass.

He crossed the yard. When the snow melted each spring, rocks would appear in the fields where before there had been none, like the earth had given birth to stone eggs. The large pile of cleared rocks formed a sizable hill, bigger under its wintery cover. During the summer, the loose rocks would provide housing for snakes and rodents alike, and Amos would sit in the tree with his hand-carved slingshot and hunt. He would send Caleb to collect his prizes.

Caleb climbed the small hill, tricky with its uneven footing, and hacked at the ice with the shovel, his grunts deadened by the snow covering the ground and the trees and the bodies of his brothers and sisters, mercifully obscuring their intertwined skeletons. The blows—hard, thudding strikes—soon relented as the ice gave way to powdery snow. Each shovelful hit the earth like a whisper. He rested, the sun beginning to fade from the sky behind the hill, the warmth ebbing from the afternoon. His shoulders tightened up toward his neck. His hands bled. The work occupied his mind.

He kept on in the dark, his hands ringing with the cold, operating on muscle memory alone, digging because he didn't know what else to do. The shovel finally clinked against a rock. Caleb widened the hole, and worked his raw fingers around the stone. This first marker—small and smooth to the touch—would be for Emma. He placed it beneath the elm, gnarled by the fire, but in its former life the girls had sprawled under it, looking up into its branches and whispering. He retrieved a large, rough rock for Amos, and placed it next to Emma's. Hours passed, and he persisted. Four rocks, one for each of them, arranged in a square around the tree.

IN THE BARN, the fire glowed as it had been for the past few days, and one of the lamps had been lit. Its light fell on Elspeth, seated on the edge of her pallet, facing the bags and supplies Caleb had piled in preparation to find the killers. "Mama," he said.

"My necklace," she said, her voice harsh and dry. Caleb found the cross had twisted around to her back, and he apologized for moving it out of the way. "Did you see them?"

"There were three men," he said. He told her about the red scarves but he stumbled over their descriptions, not able to put them into words.

"It's okay," she said. She patted his hand. "You pulled me from the fire?" she asked and Caleb said that he had. "Where were they hiding? I didn't see them," she said. Caleb drew a breath to confess everything but she slumped and he helped shift her feet onto the bed as her head collapsed into her pillow. "My necklace," she said again. He laid her hand over the cross and she tightened her fist around it. "Where were you?"

"Making gravestones," he said.

She nodded, "Good." She said it several times, and then faded away once more.

He leaned against the wall of the barn, his hat in his hands, boots on, and slept for two or three hours—heavy, black sleep. When he awoke, the brightness of the world startled him, and he reached for the Ithaca, as if this light was one of the marauders for whom he'd been waiting.

CHAPTER 6

They went on like that—Elspeth and Caleb—for nearly a week. Each day Elspeth could sit up for longer and stomach a bit more food. Each morning, noon, and evening, Caleb changed her bandages, and the wounds no longer seeped liquid, and the scabs started to meet in the center like ice over a puddle. The snow continued, too, and the black shadow that used to be their home became lost in the sweeping, slow-moving drifts. The four broken posts turned half-white with driving flakes that stuck to the sides like moss.

Inside the barn, the revived animals heated the air enough for Caleb to walk around without two shirts and two pairs of socks. His mother's growing strength made him look upon the meager provisions he'd collected with new eyes. He packed and repacked, preparing for the journey ahead. Into an old rucksack that must have belonged to his father, Caleb placed what dried meats they'd stored in the barn for the winter. He rolled a thick wool blanket around clean shirts, extra rags for bandages, empty jars for water, a length of twine to hang their shelter, some matches, and—buried deep at the bottom—one of his favorite feathers, curled and so deeply black that when the sun shone against it, the edges appeared purple. He cleaned and oiled the guns. He took boxes of ammunition and stacked them in his arms, impressed by their heft.

For lunch he made cornmeal cakes, picking out the grubworms with quick hands, trying not to burn his fingers on the stone. The animals perked up at the scent, and Caleb knew their interest signaled the restoration of their health. He sometimes thought of staying but pushed the wish aside by shutting his eyes tight and thinking of the gunshots and the emptiness in the faces of his brothers and sisters. For the first time he lit the lamps that lined the middle of the barn, and he saw the animals, thin but alive, their bones cast in sharp relief beneath their taut skin, their shining eyes watching him. At the last stall, he discovered the horses had died in the night. He slammed the bucket to the ground and the water sloshed out and puddled at his feet. The horses—hardly recognizable as such, they'd grown so thin and frail—had fallen together, curling into each other. Caleb got down in the muck and folded himself into their embrace as well. The mud was cold and stiff. The horses had materialized one day, grazing in the valley below. Jorah had owned some workhorses once, but they'd died before Caleb knew them. Sometimes Amos pretended to remember them, but Mary would dismiss this as nothing but dreams, pictures culled from the words of their father. Caleb and Jesse had spotted these horses at the same time, but it had been Jesse who went to tell Jorah. Their father's look had not been one of delight, as theirs had been; he shielded his eyes from the sun with a flattened hand and scanned the horizon. The horses—he would explain later— had been broken and wore the marks of being saddled. He ushered everyone inside and sat on the rock at the edge of the cornfields and watched the animals for most of the afternoon before he whistled for Amos and the two of them disappeared down the hill. When they'd returned, Caleb had been awed by the horses' size, their knotted muscles, their veins thick as one of his fingers.

As he curled against the belly of the horse, he thought of his move to the barn, which had begun after he'd watched the man in the valley spasm and fall, the sound reaching Caleb's hiding place long after the flash of the powder. Day by day, he spent more time with the animals—who were simpler and easier to understand—waking earlier and staying later, Emma or Mary bringing him his lunch. After one fitful night in which gunshots sprung him awake again and again, and Jesse clamped his hand to his mouth each time, the two boys paced the inky darkness of the yard, then spent a while on the fence—not talking, Jesse keeping Caleb company—before Caleb wandered into the barn. He'd slept in the loft with no nightmares. The next night in the house, he woke screaming. In the barn, tranquil slumber. He grew used to the outdoors, but inside he would flush and burn with heat. Part of him thought perhaps Jorah radiated evil, and at night it seeped into his head and poisoned his dreams, and he yearned to ask Jesse about it, but he could never manage to find the words.

ELSPETH PRACTICED WALKING. She creaked her way to her feet and took tentative, choppy strides, reminded of the children's first steps—their first betrayals—how when Amos had begun to walk, she'd rushed to the lip of the hill and stood atop a stump, contemplating whether to throw herself off.

Down the aisle of the barn she limped, and considered how it must affect Caleb to see the animals in such a state. She didn't know the boy well—she barely knew any of the children—but she understood, of course, that he loved the barn and the animals it contained. The walk quickly drew the breath from her, and she rested against the railing of the final stall, where the two horses' bodies shrank each day, their teeth baring themselves and their rib cages poking through their tightened skin.

On the second day, she made it to the end of the barn and back. She felt more herself, and though her body wasn't ready, she couldn't bear being locked up with death any longer. Every time she glimpsed the wreckage of the house, her skin itched with her damnation. This limbo could hold her no longer. "Tomorrow," she said, walking back to her bed, knowing he listened from the hayloft, "we leave at first light."

Though from the state of her injuries and the fact that she'd woken in Jorah's clothes she presumed that Caleb had seen her body, Elspeth retreated into the back of the barn out of modesty and wrapped bandages around her chest, drawing them tight with her teeth until it hurt to breathe, the fabric groaning each time she did.

Caleb paused at the top of the ladder, wiping sleep from his eyes. His mother fastened her bandages with a series of pins that made her look as though she'd been stitched together with metal. "It's time," she said.

"What about the animals?"

Elspeth put one arm and then the other into the sleeves of Jorah's shirt, trying to ignore the pain, knowing that worse—much worse—would come. To leave the animals must be hard for the boy, she thought, and their eyes followed her with rapt attention, awaiting their fate. Their snorts and shuffling steps amplified in her head. "Perhaps we set them free?"

"They'll die," Caleb said. While he stood within a yard of his bed and his feeble belongings, his heart begged for a few more moments of childhood. He forgave himself his whining. He pictured his animals roaming the hillside sickly and weak. He hoped he'd meant much to them. "They won't know what to do."

"You could stay," she said. He came down the ladder, his twelve-year-old form so small in that giant space. The animals didn't care, she thought, that he'd buttoned his shirt incorrectly and it hung crookedly over his tiny frame, or that his hair stood on end in the morning and then flopped into his face by midday. He'd found his place. Her head and stomach eased at the thought of walking off by herself like she had a dozen times since she and Jorah had settled in their small nook on the shaded side of the hill.

Staying had of course occurred to Caleb. His mother had said it aloud and so it pushed its way to the front of his thoughts and hung in the air in front of him, easy enough to grab. He could live like this forever, among the animals. But his mind had been made up and his family depended on him, and he walked down the rows of pens, unlatching them as he went, unable to look at the expectant faces. While the chickens milled about under his feet, he slid the pack over his shoulders and took the Ithaca and Jorah's rifle in hand.

They swung the doors open. The cold air gripped their skin and turned their lips dry, and they tugged their scarves up to cover their mouths. The snow crunched underfoot. Caleb fought the urge to look back. The faint sounds of the animals called to him, begged him to reconsider. But then he passed the small lump of snow where his brothers and sisters lay entangled in each other's arms and his resolve hardened. He hitched his bags higher onto his shoulders.

Legs heavy and head dull, Elspeth stared at the empty space where her home had once stood. She saw the four stone markers, and the line Caleb's footprints had drawn to them. She prayed silently, asking for a safe journey for both herself and Caleb on their mission and also for her children and her husband as they sought their way to heaven. Abraham had been willing to kill his son for God, and so He spared them both. On the altar of sacrifice that receded with each step, she had given not one, but four children and a husband. She wondered whether God had become so much crueler with the passage of time. Instead of giving thanks for what she'd been spared, she grew angrier at what had been taken from her, and a hunger grew deep in the pit of her—in the imaginary womb where she carried and bore the children she'd taken as her own—to find the men responsible and snatch everything from them with equal cruelty.

Elspeth, usually as sure-footed as a mountain goat, stumbled and slipped along the icy rocks and steep descents. Caleb didn't offer his help before she slid down an embankment and crashed onto the thick ice atop the stream. Her scream penetrated the thick air of the morning. Caleb tucked the Ithaca—safety on—down the back of his shirt, where it formed a second spine and helped him feel upright. The cold metal stuck to his skin. The rifle he used as a walking stick. He took Elspeth by the crook of her arm, and they made their way awkwardly, the path not wide enough to accompany the two of them side by side. Elspeth lost herself in pain—let herself be buried by it—her only focus to keep her feet moving.

Caleb remained quiet, concerned that any conversation would lead to the logical questions. They'd never spoken much; Caleb didn't speak unless spoken to—sometimes not even then. He had one strong memory of his mother, and he'd stored it away, much the same as his books or his feathers.

One autumn morning, he'd risen early to fish in the eddies of the stream. He stepped out of the woods on a long, flat rock that jutted out over the water. The surface looked placid, but he and Jesse swam in it in the summertime, and the current spun them around like tops. The cool radiated up from the water onto his face and hands as he sat down to fish. His cork swayed in the stream, his feet kicked at the air, and a cigarette dangled from his lips when he heard his mother coming up from the lower path, a basket of laundry in her arms. She hummed to herself, a hymn he could hear them singing to Emma as he tended to the animals, *"There's a home for little children, Above the bright blue sky."* Elspeth, preoccupied and harried—having recently returned from months away—set the basket down and removed one of her husband's shirts, which she held up to the sun to look upon with a bewildered expression, as if she'd never seen such a thing before. Caleb stared at the shirt as well, at the way the sun shone through the thin fabric.

Elspeth saw Caleb and flinched, skidding on the muddy embankment, and would have tumbled into the water if the shirt hadn't caught on a rock. When she lifted it to the sun again, it had been clouded by mud and torn down the middle. She got to her feet, brushed herself off, and tilted her head at him. It was his turn to start, and he tossed the cigarette into the water, where it made a small hiss—enough for both of them to hear—and looped around in a spiral before it disappeared over the edge of the rocks. Elspeth smiled, dangled the shirt over the stream, and let it drop from her hands. It waved underwater, pushed and pulled by the indecisive current, and then it, too, went over the falls, like the ghost of a drowned man. Neither made a sound, though when Caleb caught a trout and brought it wriggling from the water, she smiled at him again. He strung the fish and tied the twine around a root that protruded from the ground in a wooden loop. He'd only needed one fish, but he liked sitting there in the weakening autumn sun with his mother so close by, doing her work. When she finished, she nodded to him once and walked off, the laundry basket in front of her like a belly full with child. Only then did Caleb gather his things.

That golden fall day had been the longest the two of them had ever been in one place by themselves. It was their only shared secret. The gap between them had widened again after their brief connection and he felt it yawning even as he clutched her arm and helped her down the jagged path that split the hillside like a bolt of lightning. He worried that if he told her what he'd done she would leave him, and he would spend the rest of his days alone.

Elspeth was distracted by the map she had stored away in her mind. As her trips had become more and more frequent, she prayed constantly that the next child would bring her peace. The town of Caleb's birth, Watersbridge, had wide, dusty streets and when the wind howled down their corridors the air filled with sand so thick one had to close the windows even in the height of summer. The church's imposing steeple punctured the sky. Caleb had looked like a lumpy, disheveled angel, and Elspeth had tried to help herself, had sworn she would be happy with what she had, but this promise did not last his first day on earth. The train ride home had been short, and Elspeth marveled at her forked tongue, which could lie with no effort to other passengers about her reasons for forcing a newborn to endure such a journey. When she was met with Jorah's wordless anger, her breasts would not produce for the child, and so she dipped her finger in milk and sugar and the infant Caleb would hang on with tenacity. She'd been gone for eleven months. Once Jorah had connected with Caleb—when the child peered over her shoulder at him—the boy had been like the rest. But not quite. Caleb and Jorah had never settled into a comfortable rhythm, not like the others. She'd waited another two years before Jesse, whose mother had turned to alcohol and laudanum, and she'd presented this as evidence to Jorah, and he'd accepted another child without question.

She tried to stop. For four years she swaddled, nursed, and delivered, not immune to temptation, but not succumbing to it, either. Emma had proved too difficult. She brought the baby home with no explanation, and Jorah had been sullen and taciturn. She heard him praying morning and night by their bedside for her salvation. Nothing could have made him break his word to her. Though she often tried its strength, she knew it to be true.

"WHICH DIRECTION WERE they headed?" Elspeth asked. She leaned down until their foreheads almost touched. They'd come a fair distance, and Caleb risked a glance back toward home but couldn't see the barn or the tops of the trees he knew by heart. This section of the hill wouldn't be visible from his fence post and the realization chilled him. Caleb had seen the footprints, their trail in the snow like a long snake of guilt, winding its evil way into and out of their house. He raised a snow-covered arm and pointed.

Elspeth pulled at her bandages, and thrust a finger into one of the wounds. The pain cleared her mind and brought her breath rattling back to her, gave life to her legs. The boy had pointed her back the way she'd come. She flipped through images of the towns and cities she'd visited, as if turning the pages of a book, examining them, looking for sidearms on the men, listening for the pop of shots as the taverns spilled their contents out onto the streets. "Hapsburg," she said, remembering stepping around a broad puddle of dried blood outside her hotel one morning, and hearing the constant hammering of the overworked coffin maker. "It's a good place to start." The journey would be slow, she thought, and they would not come back this way again.

THEY COULDN'T FIND the energy to talk, nor did they have much to speak about. Elspeth recalled the long miles to Hapsburg and understood her crawling pace meant days of travel, days spent inside her own head, attempting to piece together where the men had come from and how they'd discovered the Howell farm in the middle of so much nothing. Rocks rose up out of the ice to snag her boots or appeared under her heels, sending shock waves of pain through her. Caleb's thoughts zipped from his siblings to the fire to the great expanse of the world he found himself walking across.

As morning turned to afternoon, a low fog rolled in, thick as smoke, creeping its way up the mountain like a living thing. It wrapped around their ankles and then their waists and within minutes it became difficult for them to see their hands in front of their faces. Caleb held on to his mother, as she knew the way by heart.

She shook violently. He leaned in and saw her face wet with tears, her mouth contorted in a grimace of sorrow. "Would you like your Bible?" he asked, attempting to console her.

"They're all gone," she said.

"Yes, Mother."

"The house, too. The house your father built."

"Yes, Mother."

The wind picked up for an instant and the fog unwound itself from their bodies, and the snow began again, landing with wet thuds on their hats. "He spared us," Elspeth said. This was the cruelest punishment. "Why would He do that?"

THE MIST PRESSED in on them again, heavy and smelling of rot. Rain fell. Elspeth's calves cramped, but her thoughts moved in an endless circle. And then, the bottom dropped out from under her. She stepped forward, and expected the pain of her stiff leg, but no ground met her foot. She slid through Caleb's arms. She let herself go limp, moving with shocking speed. The sound of the ice rushing past produced a steady growl. One of the scarves around her neck caught on a broken limb, and she thought it would hang her. She hoped that the earth would disappear beneath her again and she would feel nothing.

But the scarf unraveled with a brief heat on her neck and the hill leveled off. The roar in her ears subsided. She remained on her back, listening to the ticking of the rain. She'd gone under the fog, the land covered in a low ceiling, all white and flat and impossible to tell one direction from another.

The fog hung so close that Caleb had to kneel to see that rain had washed out the edge of the path, and two slick lines in the snow marked where Elspeth's boots had gone over the edge. He called to her. The air looked like dirty dishwater. He stood at the lip of the washout, and told himself to jump several times, but his body wouldn't allow it. He thought of his brothers, how even Jesse would laugh at him, and he wished for Amos's hands to come out of the mist and shove him. He longed for their taunts and their goading. Below him, somewhere in the murk, he saw something move. He slid. His pants rose on his ankles, and the ice started to burn his skin, so he lifted his feet, moving even faster. The object that had caught his eye became visible again as he crested a bump. He leaned left as he slid, stretching, trying to steer himself. The damp fog had made the surface of the snow so slick and he moved so fast he didn't think he could get there. He reached. His fingers closed on the wet wool of his mother's scarf, and he freed it, though the brief resistance sent him spinning and he continued down the hill backward. At any moment he expected to hit a rock or a tree and he braced himself for impact.

When he'd come to a stop, Caleb rolled over onto his stomach and checked the back of his pants. The ice had nearly rubbed right through the material. His ankles were hot and raw, and as he watched, dots of blood sprouted and pooled on his skin.

About twenty yards away, his mother made a strange noise from her stomach. His bleeding ankles forgotten, Caleb rushed to her. As he approached, he could hear with clarity the sound he'd confused for coughing or choking: Elspeth was laughing. Gales of it rolled from her broken body, throaty and gruff. Caleb laughed just hearing her.

For the first time in a long time, God had handed her a gift. She'd been lying there, trying to figure out how to locate Caleb in the murk, and as she'd decided to stand, she'd heard a noise, growing louder and louder, and then Caleb, his legs stuck up in the air, had blasted through the fog, spinning like a top. When she thought she'd controlled herself she heard Caleb's helpless giggling—something she'd heard only a handful of times in her life, few enough to count on one hand—and she started all over again.

"The rifle," the boy said, his laughter stopping abruptly. "Father's rifle. I dropped it." He flexed his hand like it might reappear.

"It probably got hung up on a root," Elspeth said. He held back tears and she could see that losing the rifle had further damaged his mangled heart. She would do her best to fix what she could, and traced the outline of the items lumped in the bottom of her bag. Inside it smelled of cedar and smoke from the fireplace of the hotel where she'd stayed while working as a nursemaid due to a thankful overabundance of midwives. After going unwashed for so long, her packed clothes had solidified into a filthy, mildewed ball that she left in the snow; they could not be saved. Besides, she enjoyed being surrounded by the scent of Jorah's hard-earned sweat. Underneath her clothes were the gifts, and they made her breathe harder, each gasp causing more pain. Elspeth pulled the stopper from the small vial of perfume she'd purchased for the girls, and the tart scent stung her eyes. She placed it on the ground at her side, and the angular glass refracted the dim light, casting slight rainbows on the clean snow. She unspooled the ribbon meant for Emma. The three yards of purple fabric spilled across the snow, and when the wind tugged at it, Elspeth gave it up, letting it slide away like a colorful snake. From the very bottom of the bag, she brought forth the smallest packages, wrapped in brown paper and tied with twine. She undid one to reveal several chunks of pink gum. "Don't swallow it," Elspeth said, handing a piece to Caleb. "It's gum. Just chew."

The pinkish blobs looked to him like newborn squirrels. Once he got over the association, however, and the gum softened, he smiled.

"Let's forget the rifle," she said. "It was too heavy, anyway."

Clouds rolled and undulated, moving fast across the sky. She put her arm in his, and led the way toward Hapsburg. The rain resumed. Caleb learned to trust the lean of her body when she steered him in an unexpected direction, but it was always sound and level. In minutes their backs and heads shone with the same glaze that had settled over the landscape. She forgot the bottle of perfume in the snow, but it would soon be buried.

When they came to a group of evergreens that provided some cover from the weather, they made camp in the remaining light. The pines stood close enough to one another that Caleb could string up the canvas, and shortly they were beneath it, rain and fits of hail loud overhead. There wasn't much to eat: a few nuts, three strips of salted pork. Caleb checked his tobacco rations and saw that he only had enough for one small cigarette. He rerolled the bag and replaced it in the breast pocket of his shirt. It smelled like Amos. He managed to start a fire, though the pine made for poor, smoky fuel. He located a dead birch at the edge of the firelight, and stomped on it with Jesse's boot to break it into pieces. Rotted, it burned too quickly. They shared a jar of water and then Caleb filled it with snow and placed it close to the fire to melt.

"Did you see the house burn?" Elspeth asked, her hold on the events slippery. He said he had. "Where were they?"

"I don't know," he said. He took a pine branch—the sap hissing as it boiled and dripped from the makeshift torch—and wandered away looking for more wood, hoping his mother hadn't seen the expression on his face. He hadn't lied, he thought, but before long he'd have to tell the story, and he still worried she'd wander off and leave him there and he'd spend endless days trying to find their home again.

Elspeth watched Caleb's torch rise and fall with his steps in the middle of the darkness, her feet throbbing and her body alive with pain. She got her Bible from her bag, shifted it closer to her chest, and fell asleep.

Not far from where he'd found the first, Caleb fetched another dead birch branch and dragged it back to their camp, the papery bark sliding off and shredding in his hands. As he approached, he made out a black form creeping along the ground, near the edge of the halo of firelight. At first he thought he'd imagined it, but then it moved again, sideways, close to the ice. Caleb moved to the side as well, in an attempt to keep the fire between himself and the animal. Its eyes glittered orange. The fire popped. The rain intensified.

Caleb drew near the canvas. The animal flirted with the light, allowing a paw—claws sparkling like jewels—to enter here, a muscled shoulder there. As Caleb leapt the last few feet to his pack, the animal growled, a low, guttural noise that stirred his bowels. But in the seconds he ducked under cover to pull the Ithaca from his pack, the animal disappeared. Emboldened with the gun, he walked out of the light, toward where the beast had stalked them. He made out a few footprints, claws digging into the ice, before he backed his way to the canvas, and sat under it, his head out of the rain, his Ithaca across his knees. Here he was, his mother shivering with fever, farther than he'd ever been from home, and he couldn't help but feel that the world had turned against them.

EARLY THE NEXT morning, Caleb caught a snowshoe hare by following it back to its den. He checked for leverets; he wouldn't take a mother. As he lifted it by its ears, the animal's huge back feet kicked at the air and it produced a hoarse bark. Caleb let its weight stretch out its body then grabbed the feet and pulled. The spine snapped. It convulsed twice. He cleaned the animal, the meat purple and quivering in the cold, steam rising from the blood, the insides warm on his bare hands. He inspected the organs for spots, and threw them into the creek bed along with the feet and head, where a scavenger wouldn't let them sit long.

As a boy, he'd once sliced right into the lower intestines, ruining the rabbit, the fetid stench staying on his hands all day, even as he crawled into bed with Jesse, who had made him sleep on the floor. Caleb woke early, the light blue. Jesse must have told their father, because Jorah grabbed Caleb by the hand and led him to the small pen the girls had made, where he grasped a rabbit by its hind legs, and it glanced around, confused but not panicked; the girls did all sorts of strange things with the animals, and they'd become inured to such rough treatment. Caleb's eyes stung with tears that he didn't allow to fall.

"Go ahead," Jorah said. He held the animal out to him. This was before Caleb knew what Jorah was capable of, one of those brief days when he thought the square plot of grass on the other side of the hill was his secret, a magic land left for him alone.

Caleb put his hands behind his back. "It's Emma's."

"It's our Father's," Jorah said and grabbed the rabbit by the head and flicked his wrist. Caleb heard the crack and looked back at the house, sure the girls were watching from inside, sobbing. "This is a lesson you will learn."

Caleb tried to run away, afraid he would make a mistake in front of his father, who—at that time—he loved so much that he watched him in secret, trying to copy his walk, his mannerisms, even his voice. Jorah caught him with a strong hand. *"He is in the way of life that keepeth instruction,"* Jorah said, *"but he that refuseth reproof erreth."* Caleb dropped the knife with a clanging and buried his face in his hands, then tried to lean into Jorah, but Jorah kept him upright and wouldn't permit his son to find solace in him. "The girls will forgive you," Jorah said. *"Receive the Holy Spirit. If you forgive the sins of anyone, they are forgiven."* Caleb didn't know what his sin had been.

"Mama," Caleb said, "did you always understand what Father was saying when he quoted the Bible?"

It was the first time either of them had mentioned home, and Elspeth had to gather herself before answering. "Your father understood things I never will." She left it at that and leaned on her elbows and let her head relax back against her shoulders. The fact that Jorah had seemingly memorized the entire Bible and could call up passages at will for any problem or occasion had frustrated Elspeth, but it was impossible to criticize. She'd only wished he would use his own words. She rested while Caleb built the fire up and speared the rabbit with a sharpened stick. Smoke rose into the murky sky, and the sizzling could be heard above the pops and cracks of the forest.

During their early years together, Jorah would tell her tales of his time away—small jobs on farms, minor carpentry—and the cruelty of the larger world. Often his skin color would cause him trouble in the form of thieves or employers who refused to pay his wages. He told her of how he fought, and how he held back, and sometimes he ran, knowing his young wife slept alone in an unfinished house without enough food or money. Despite their violence, the stories made Elspeth itch: her feet, her legs, her hips spasming with the desire to move. As time passed, and he became more immersed in the Bible, he sometimes didn't even come to bed, the faint rustle from the next room of the thin pages turning the only sign of his presence. The pages spoke through his mouth, whole chapters, psalms and hymns in their entirety. It was as if he had turned piety into a contest and Elspeth lagged far behind. Of course, he knew her secrets. Her feet twitched in bed at night, and Jorah told her it was as if she ran from him in her dreams.

ELSPETH HAD NEVER needed a compass and she led them with confidence even blinded by pain and fever. They walked on what had once been a grand thoroughfare. Great elms stood in lines on each side of the road, and their branches met overhead, so that beneath them the snow was only a pale dusting on the frozen dirt.

Caleb had never experienced such silence. The snow on all sides muffled everything. He stopped to let it wash over him.

"What is it?" she said.

"It's so quiet."

"It's a road," she replied. "But they never built the house to go at the end of it." The last time she'd passed this way, the elms had been smaller, and others had been cleared and chopped to produce the tidy lines. She placed her hand on one. Her fingers were dwarfed by the size of the trunk. "Do you mind if we rest? Only for a bit."

Caleb hesitated. They'd only walked a few miles—four

perhaps—since they'd set out that morning. Then his mother stripped off her jacket, and he saw the blood had soaked through again. "We'll rest until you're ready," he said.

When Elspeth had traveled down the new road alone, the horses that had planed and leveled the way whinnied and clomped their hooves. A man in tweed suit pants and a matching vest emerged from a large tent, wiping a pair of glasses on a handkerchief. When he placed his glasses upon his nose he smiled, his cheeks rising into small apples, his teeth pure white.

"Hello," he called out. Elspeth returned the greeting and kept moving. "Would you like some water?" Elspeth agreed—the summer heat leeched her strength, even in the shade—and the man winked, as if she'd confirmed a previous order. "My men have gone scouting for a higher location from which to survey the property." He ladled a cup full of water and Elspeth accepted it with both hands like a child. "Our employer plans on building a farm on this land." He took the empty cup from her and refilled it. "Good soil here." He kicked at the new road with the toe of his boot, as if to expose the dirt's quality. She watched him over the brim of the cup and wondered how different her life might have been if she hadn't been cast out with Jorah. If only she'd met a man like the van Tessel girls had surely married, she told herself, a man like this, things would be simpler.

"Looking for work, by chance?" he asked. "We have plenty."

She wanted to say yes. She stuttered some guttural consonants. Before she could block the images, she envisioned Jorah waiting for her, the children gathered around him in the doorway, the children she'd brought home against his wishes, that he had taken on as his own. She handed the cup back to the man, said she had to be on her way, and practically ran down the new street that arrived at nothing.

WHILE ELSPETH SLEPT, the quiet began to exert a kind of force on Caleb, the trees seemed to bow closer, and he imagined himself stuffed inside the pantry again, his legs folded over one another, the smell of his blankets, the oil from the guns, the stench of his own body overwhelming the usual pine. "Did you ever know about the rabbits? How I learned to clean them?" Caleb said. He asked his question again; this time his mother heard him.

She said she hadn't, and he told her the story, uncomfortable at first, his voice wavering. His mouth went dry and he took a sip of cold water from one of the jars. It hurt his teeth. He continued. It helped him not to look at her. Instead he gazed up at the white canopy above them, the branches like veins, and it seemed that the pictures he described drew themselves on the snow like etchings in a book, with straight lines and dark shadows. He said that the girls had not said a word to him about it, though surely they noticed the missing rabbit, and had eaten the stew that evening; they must have known. As his story drew to a close, Caleb knew he was ignoring the center of it: that his father wasn't the man he said he was.

She knew that he awaited her response. He'd maintained a far-off look while he talked, but now that he was finished she suspected he hoped for an answer to some question he'd posed in the telling. "It sounds like your father," she said, trying not to make the word sound strange. "Though I suppose he easily could have waited for you boys to trap another rabbit. I can't say I understand his lesson, either."

Caleb smiled at this unexpected union; he'd guessed his mother would admonish him for disagreeing with his father, perhaps even tell a parable of her own. Instead, they were paired in their confusion. The branches above seemed to him to exhale, relaxing.

"He did the best he knew. He didn't have a father of his own."

"Did you have a father?" Caleb asked.

"For a while," Elspeth said after a time.

"Did you have brothers and sisters?"

"No," she said. "Not like you. It was just us."

"You and your father and—your mother?"

"Yes."

Caleb had never heard about the parents of his parents. It had never crossed his mind, and—as when they'd left the borders of the earth he'd seen from the top of his fence post—the world opened up at their acknowledgment, strange people suddenly born into his imagination. He felt closer to his mother than he ever had and helped her to stand. They left clean footprints in the thin veil of snow that penetrated the canopy, and when they cleared the line of elms, the sun made them squint, the wind caused them to shiver, and in step with his mother, Caleb didn't notice that the snow was much deeper than when they'd entered the shelter of the trees.

CHAPTER 8

Caleb daydreamed of cities, houses like theirs but as tall as the tallest trees, swaying back and forth in the wind. From the topmost room, they would scan the horizon, searching for the killers, their bodies growing used to the steady rocking.

He waited for his mother to say something, to continue their conversation from earlier, to somehow acknowledge their closeness. Each step took all of her concentration, however, and silence reclaimed her.

They slept in a hole created by a fallen tree, and rose the next morning with the sun high in the sky, hidden from them by the mass of roots and clods of dirt. The cold had sapped what little strength Elspeth possessed—had stolen into her joints and locked them in place. Every time she stood, it surprised her to be on her feet. As they resumed their task once again, they broke through a line worn clean in the snow; animal tracks paced a clear circle around their camp.

The straps were giving way on Caleb's pack, but when he wondered whether his mother would be well enough to make the stitches strong again, he saw that she, too, had weakened. Her face, which had been regaining some of its old complexion, in the sunlight appeared ashen and drawn. He dug through her bag, and found a package fastened by loose string. Rather than chewing gum, the parcel held small, sugared gumdrops. After all the white and brown of the dead of winter, the blazing yellows and oranges brought a smile to Caleb's face. He gave a red gumdrop to his mother, who tucked it into her cheek and tried to match his happiness.

ELSPETH'S BODY WORKED on its own while her mind slept in fire. Sometimes she jerked away from the burning and became dimly aware of Caleb's hand at her elbow, and she would try to thank him, but her voice had left and her lips had become so racked with fever blisters they were more water than skin. Other times she heard the calling of birds or the squawking of crows and she would be certain that Caleb had been forced to leave her and she was facedown in the snow, waiting for her last breath so the birds could take their portion of carrion back to their young. Somehow this last image improved her mood, and when Caleb's arm wrapped around her waist and she understood they'd never stopped, she felt cheated.

They had no food. Their clothes were beginning to wear out, beaten by the wind and the snow. Elspeth's breath came heavily, sporadically, with a strange wheezing like a baby's rattle. They walked over long, rolling hills. On all sides, trees cracked from the weight of the snow as it melted in the sun. Sometimes a branch would fall with a massive whoosh and a dead thud. Caleb would jump with fear but his mother wouldn't react at all.

Together they crested another in the unending line of hills, the land like waves on the oceans and lakes his father read about in his stilted tongue as the children huddled in his bed at night and Caleb sat outside, crouched underneath the windowsill.

Elspeth identified something that had been dragging along in her mind. "Were you in the barn?"

He stumbled. She had given all of her weight over to him. Her feet barely made contact with the ground. He knew that to stop was to die. "I hid," he said. All the reasons, the excuses he'd readied sounded hollow. "I did nothing."

A large hill loomed in front of them, and he knew it would be their last. His words seemed to have wrenched the final bit of strength from his mother, and she could no longer lift her feet high enough to clear the snow. He imagined what it would be like to die but it simply sounded like rest. They would rest. And they would not wake again.

His body climbed. He wished it to stop, and tried to communicate this to his limbs, but his head had drifted away and was no longer connected to the rest of him. Atop the hill, Caleb crashed to the ground, his mother falling with him. She made no noise. He squinted in the harsh white blur. The endless land surrounded them, naked, no trees, nothing but smooth snow. An indentation—as if God had taken a scoop out of the earth as one would a cup of flour—sat half in shadow, half in sunlight. Tall and alone at the edge of the dent stood a building.

"A house. Mama, there's a house," Caleb said to Elspeth, his voice cracking. She didn't move. He placed her on their tarp, along with his pack, the Ithaca, and her bags, and tied it as well as he could. With the rest of the twine, he attached the cocoon to his pack, though with each tug the straps dug into his shoulders and threatened to tear entirely.

From the hill, the house had appeared to be less than a mile away, but from the bottom of the bowl it seemed at least twice that. Caleb stopped. He ate some more gumdrops that his stomach immediately rejected in a bright sunburst on the snow. A hawk circled overhead, its call like the earth being torn apart. Caleb stood on unsteady feet and returned his pack to his shoulders, where the skin burned, rubbed raw. Jesse's boots dug into the snow for traction. "One more."

A strap went. "Hold on, Mama." He kicked his toes into the powdery snow and strained to keep the tarp from sliding backward. "Hold on." Caleb took the last few steps at a run, and collapsed at the top of the hill. The other strap gave way with a small sigh and a pop and he spun and caught the twine as it tried to slither away. The coarse fibers peeled his skin until he wrapped it around his wrists, stopping the cocoon's descent and bringing it next to him. He lurched onto his stomach. His dwindling heat melted the snow, and sleep started to hug him. Even in his exhaustion, Caleb knew if he closed his eyes whoever lived in the house would find him lying there next to a small, clean spot of yellowed grass where his breath had left him and—next to him—his dead mother swathed in a tarred canvas tarp. He pushed himself onto one knee, then one foot. He grasped the Ithaca and dragged it out of the cocoon by its barrel. The gun had never felt so heavy. He worried he wouldn't be able to lift it to fire. The house rose ahead, and as he advanced into its cold shadow he saw how massive it was: at least three stories, with a long porch that extended the entire length of the first floor. Chains for swings rattled from the ceiling. The windows were as tall as a man and had each pane intact, but none glowed with lamps. No smoke billowed from the chimney. Caleb took a look back at his mother. Her parched lips didn't move; no breath clouded in the crisp air.

A shot cracked the sky and Caleb dropped to the ground, pointing the Ithaca at the house as he did. Stinging life rushed back into his limbs. Silence as the report echoed down through the valley.

"Who's there?" a man's voice called.

Caleb didn't dare move.

"I think I got him," the man said.

Caleb heard the creaking of a door and aimed the Ithaca at the front porch. An old man, cradling a shotgun half as big as his body, let the screen slam behind him. Caleb had never seen someone elderly, nothing more than drawings in books that depicted the ravages of age as soft and giving. This man shuffled at an angle, as if he ducked under a low branch, and most of his scalp shone through thin strands of white hair. Every movement brought a new sound—a sigh or a sniff. On his feet he wore bundles of rags. His clothes were layers of burlap, some torn and filled with holes so that the ones beneath poked through. Caleb didn't know how the recoil hadn't knocked him clean off his feet.

"Are you dead?" the old man called.

Caleb had him in his sights. "No," he replied, his voice louder and stronger than he could have hoped.

"Did I hit you?"

"No."

"You alone?"

Caleb relaxed and the gun barrel dipped into the snow. "My mother's with me."

"Where is she?"

"Did he say 'Mother'?" said a woman's voice from inside the darkness of the house.

The old man turned slightly. "Hush, Margaret," he said. "I said, where is she?"

"She's here," Caleb said. He didn't think the old man had seen him yet but could track him by the sound of his voice. The snow was deep enough to conceal most of him, and the afternoon shadows did the rest. Caleb thought the man was going to step out farther into the snow. Instead, he set his rifle against the railing of the porch and sat down on the top step. He placed his chin in his hands. "I'm an old man," he said after a while. "I can wait."

"Wait for what?" Caleb asked.

"Yes, wait for what?" the voice from inside said, more clearly this time, as if it had moved closer to the door. He'd called her Margaret. This made Caleb feel safe.

"For you to show yourself, and show you mean us no harm." He pointed to the rifle at his side. "I showed you I mean none."

"You shot at me," Caleb said.

"Ah," the old man replied, "that was before you had a voice. Now you've got one and you sound like a boy. Are you a boy, son?" The old man brushed something from his sleeve. He certainly didn't seem threatening.

"Tell that boy," Margaret said, "that we have pie."

Caleb's stomach throbbed with hunger.

"I will do no such thing," the old man said. "I aim to wait for this boy to show himself and then I'll know what to do."

Caleb left the Ithaca in the snow, but memorized its exact location should the man fire again. He got up and the blood drained from his upper extremities. He wanted to sit right back down, so heavy was the wooziness inside his head. He swayed, as if he stood in one of his city buildings.

"What are you doing here?" the man asked.

Caleb, his heart brimming with the answer, could only say: "We've been walking."

"And where's your mother?" the old man said.

"She's behind me. She's real sick."

"Dammit, why didn't you say so?" the old man said.

Caleb heard the woman talking quickly inside, but couldn't make out the words.

"Son, why don't you and your mother come on in the house?" the old man said.

"Okay."

The man picked up his gun and as he reached for the door, he paused. "You've got to tell me one more thing: Do you mean us any harm?"

"I mean no one harm." He raised his hands, as if that's where malice hid, and realized that he'd told a lie. "I mean you no harm."

The fact that they had arrived somewhere brought energy surging back to him. His mother, however, looked even worse than when he'd packed her up, forehead dull with sweat and her mouth pinched shut. It was the color of her skin, however, that nauseated Caleb—a bilious green so thick she looked less like a person and more like the slugs he and Jesse had found under logs, stomping through the woods in search of things with which to scare the girls. Caleb dragged the tarp to the house.

The door creaked again and the man's boots thumped toward him. "Your momma, what's she got?"

"Shotgun pellets," Caleb said and put his head between his knees. He thought the man might take his gun up again and force them away.

"Guess it's not contagious," he said and sniffed. "Let's get you two inside. Soup's almost ready."

"There's pie," Margaret said from somewhere inside the house.

The old man snorted. "Wipe your feet."

Out of the constant howl of the wind, Caleb's ears were emptied of everything but his own heartbeat. As his eyes adjusted to the lack of light, he saw a house unlike anything he could have dreamed. Lamps sat on every available surface. Walls were covered in decoration. Tables had glass tops. Chairs were adorned with elaborate carvings. Floors were hidden by thick carpets, their strands woven together to form beautiful flowers and branches, all in exploding colors. To Caleb, used to the dull wash of snow, the occasional tree, and the rare gumdrops, it was like staring straight into the sun. His head ached.

The old man stood at the other end of the room, his arm around his wife, a woman of similar stature, her clothes the same worn fabrics, her skin as weathered and rutted as his. "Where's your mother?" she asked.

Caleb waved his hand toward the door.

"Well, don't stand there like a statue, boy, bring her in," the man said.

The air outside felt better to Caleb, and he realized he'd been sweating in the house, streams running down his back and the middle of his chest. He'd forgotten how he overheated indoors. The sweat dried and froze on his skin. He managed to carry Elspeth up the steps to the porch, but then his strength failed him. He had to drag her into the house on the tarp, taking care not to bump her head as he pulled her over the doorsill.

"My goodness, get her out of that coffin," the man said, and rushed forward. He fumbled open a folding knife and cut the twine that fastened the cocoon together. Caleb saw his mother as they must have—filthy, sweating, fevered, with a wound bleeding through her shirt, and he believed himself a failure. They tried to calm him with comforting noises while they looked over his mother. "My name is William H. Wood," the man said, "and this is my wife, Margaret." Caleb introduced himself.

"Where are you coming from, Caleb?" Margaret asked, patting his hand.

"Far away," Caleb said, knowing that but little else. "Very far."

Before Caleb could realize what was happening, he had placed his head on Margaret and began—for the first time in front of anyone but Jesse—to cry. She patted his back vigorously, as he would a sick sheep. This made him cry harder. Through the haze of tears, he noticed that William had unbuttoned his mother's shirt, and her bandage lay half open on her chest. Caleb rushed forward and wrenched the old man's arm behind his back. William dropped the knife, but Caleb maintained the pressure. The old man squealed and asked him to stop. Margaret yelled and tried to pull at Caleb, and when that failed, she simply put her arm around him and rubbed his head, as if what he truly needed was reassurance. When Caleb glimpsed William's pained expression, their words made it through the haze of anger and he released him. Caleb's world went fuzzy. "Sorry," he said, and backed against a couch.

"Just trying to help, son. But I understand. My mistake. Here,"

William said, and handed Caleb a clean, damp cloth. He knelt at his mother's side, wiped the last of his tears, and used his body to block their view as he pulled the final bandages aside. The blood had caked onto her skin, small pebbles of clots and scabs, which he dabbed away. William presented him with some clean bandages and Margaret took away the dirty ones.

"Let's put her in a bed upstairs," William said.

"Oh, no," Caleb said, his words sounding as if they came from the end of a long tunnel. "We couldn't take your bed."

They laughed. "We wouldn't want that, either," William said, "but we have plenty of empty rooms and empty beds."

"Nothing but empty rooms and empty beds," his wife said.

Caleb stumbled. He was aware of William's arms behind his neck and at the small of his back, and as the world faded around him, he heard William say, "Perhaps we need to take care of you first."

SHE'D STOPPED WALKING. She wanted to call out for water, but her throat could not carry out even this simplest of instructions. The constant chill that had assailed her bones no longer wrapped its cold fingers around her. She could sense nothing but the soreness of fever and the invasive confusion of dreams. She prayed she still clutched her Bible. In her more lucid moments she hoped for a parable that would give her strength, but her knowledge failed her. Jorah would reach onto the vast shelves of his memory and find the exact passage, the exact lines to suit her situation. Her own mind, however, seemed frozen. No words of God, no images struck her to bring light to the dark place in which she lay.

Out of that darkness came a pair of sullen brown eyes, and a small, pointed nose. Gusta van Tessel had been a year younger than Elspeth, and as Elspeth went about her chores—helping with the cooking, sweeping the floors, and tidying the shelves she could reach—Gusta followed, silent and watchful. As Gusta aged, she hardened and turned mean, her black hair long and shimmering and often curled into an elaborate bun that Elspeth's mother would worry over for too long, until they'd have to rush the lunch preparation and the van Tessels would raise their eyebrows at the undercooked vegetables and the uneven slices of bread.

As a teen, Gusta fell ill, and the family fetched the doctor from town. Their usual physician had been an ancient man with a bulbous, broken-vesseled nose, but this doctor was handsome, with thick blond hair, his carriage well appointed, his medicine bag oiled, the leather new and buckles gleaming. Gusta's sickness ran its course, and the doctor, who even the boys fawned over, departed. No more than a month later, Elspeth came upon Gusta on the south lawn, stretched out on a bench, arms extended, stark naked. Gusta didn't notice her, and Elspeth retreated back to the house. The sunburn brought fever and the young doctor. Not long after, it was announced at the dinner table that Gusta and the doctor would marry. Elspeth sank into herself, doing her chores day after day, trying not to think, letting time pass. She hated to see the empty place at the table where Gusta had once sat.

The following spring the well-appointed carriage returned, and the doctor—now with a small beard that aged him somewhat—took Gusta's hand as she stepped down, pale and painfully thin. Her brown eyes had shrunk since childhood, but in her skeletal state they stood out again, like coffee-soaked saucers. Elspeth's father unloaded enough luggage for a lengthy stay.

On the first night, long after dinner, Elspeth lay awake at her parents' feet, fanciful images of the doctor's house in her head while the moonlight played through the curtains. She imagined Gusta's life often—the fabrics of their chairs, the patterns on their carpets, the softness of their sheets. The rapping of harried footsteps upstairs made Elspeth and her parents sit upright, so finely, tightly attuned to the needs of the household that they must have looked like the three prongs of a hinge, opening in unison.

Upstairs in the hall, the doctor stood with his hands at his sides, shoulders slumped and head down. An overturned candle had sprayed the floor with wax, and Elspeth considered how to remove it without scratching the wood. Her parents, however, did not look at the stain and stood side by side, hands loosely entwined. Expectant, Elspeth stationed herself a foot behind them at the threshold of the bathroom. In the wobbly light of Mr. van Tessel's lamp, Elspeth saw past Mrs. van Tessel's crouched form to the body of Gusta. She drifted in the overfilled tub, her hair swaying back and forth, her eyes and mouth open. Her pallor had fallen to what appeared to be no color at all, an absence of shade so profound it took Elspeth's breath away. Occasional drips of water from the edges of the tub and the doctor's hands were the only sounds in the large room. Everything shone with wet reflections, casting glimmering shapes on the walls, the ceiling, and their stunned faces. Gusta's nightgown had been made translucent by the water, and even in the wavering, weak light, Elspeth could see the dark spots of her areolas and the black mound of her pubis.

Gusta's husband never left; he sold his marriage house and—in spite of the van Tessels' offers to the contrary—stayed in the same room he'd been in the night he awoke to an empty bed beside him and grabbed the candle from its holder and sprinted down the hall, too late. Sometimes Elspeth would end up alone in a room with the doctor and not notice him for several minutes, as if he could not muster the force required to be present. When one of the van Tessels became ill, the doctor would get out his medical bag, which year by year grew shabbier, the leather cracked, the clasps broken and then missing. He'd wandered out of the sitting room one summer afternoon, having immobilized Ginny's turned ankle, and Elspeth waited to let him pass, both of her hands grasping the handle of a bucket that steamed with hot water to scrub the hall floors. Alexis's voice came muffled from the room, but then Elspeth heard Ginny stating something that had been whispered for years: Gusta had been unable to bear children. The doctor's halted expression and rushed steps confirmed it. Elspeth looked down at the bucket, her watery reflection staring back at her.

Outside of those infrequent events, Elspeth seldom thought of Gusta after her death. After all, there were more van Tessels, four girls and five boys, and they all needed as much—if not more—care than Gusta. But years later Gusta would come to her in her dreams, peeking around corners, mouth twitching, hoping to be noticed.

CALEB AWOKE IN a bed cloaked in white sheets in a white room. He had been stripped to his underwear. Someone had washed him; he could smell the soap. They'd also cut his hair, and he touched the jagged edges. Once his eyes had adjusted to the light, he saw that his room stood at the front of the house, looking out onto the bowl he had dragged his mother across. Though he would have guessed only a few hours had passed, their tracks had been covered over and blown away so thoroughly that he must have slept for at least a day. He surveyed the room: his clothes folded in a tidy pile on a chair next to the bed; a shelf crowded with books, their spines brilliant red leather with gold lettering; and a framed painting showing three children. Caleb pushed the covers aside and stepped onto the cold wood, his toes curling from the shock. He wiped the dust from the frame. The children all possessed the same brown hair.

"Those are our babies," William said from behind Caleb. He

wobbled across the floor in his surrogate boots. "Sorry to startle you. Wondered if it was you I heard moving around." He handed Caleb his pants and shirt, stiff and unfamiliar and smelling of flowers, and Caleb dressed while staring at the portrait. "Did you sleep well?"

"They all look the same," Caleb said.

"I've apologized to them for that," William said and laughed. "They have my big nose and flat face, though their mother's lovely chin and hair. Some of God's grace in that, I suppose."

Caleb shifted his gaze from William to the young faces and back again. He pictured the children as separate parts stitched together and shivered. "They all died?"

"Certainly not. They've all moved away, married, had children of their own."

"Children of their own?" The idea was not completely foreign to him; he'd seen the animals give birth, he'd learned of the parents of his parents, he knew of the families from the Bible, but he didn't understand how one could simply decide to have children. He wondered if he, too, could have children of his own.

"Do you have brothers and sisters?" Caleb ignored the question and continued to stare at the picture. William spoke of the farm that they'd helped run before moving on to their own lives. He pointed out the window and told Caleb about the sinkhole that had once been a cornfield, verdant and lush. "Then one day, once they'd all left us," he said, "the earth started to fall in on itself, as if someone had pulled a plug on a drain." The wind blew across the field, and by instinct Caleb covered his face. The snow drifted up from the hills like smoke. "You must be hungry," William said.

Caleb followed William down a long hallway, something he'd never seen or experienced, and the tight space made him duck his head. "Where's my mother?"

"She's doing much better," William said. "I think it was more hunger and fever that got her than the pellets—you did a fine job, son." William opened the door to the next room. It was larger, almost the size of Caleb's entire house. The walls were painted yellow, the ceiling white. The floors were sparkling wood, but spotted with small rugs. In the center of an enormous bed—the head and foot decorated by intricate, wrought-iron curves, the breadth of it enough, he thought, for two horses—his mother slept in blankets that piled high around her like she was floating on colorful clouds. She appeared better, healthier, than at any time since her hand had dangled over the edge of the kitchen table, her blood counting seconds on the floor. "She's a strong one," William said. "A lesser woman—shoot, most men—wouldn't have made it as far as she did."

"She'll be okay?"

"I truly think she will."

Caleb placed his head next to his mother's hip. The rattling wheeze had left her lungs.

"Let's get you some food," William said. He placed a light hand on Caleb's back and brought him down to the kitchen, where Margaret stood at the counter, a mixing bowl in her arms. A hulking stove took up much of the room, a fire crackling and filling the air with the smell of burning wood. Everything, even the sounds of spoons scraping bowls and cupboards being opened and shut reminded him of home. He listened to Mary and Emma bicker over who had to sift the flour and heard Jesse tromp in and plop down onto the seat next to him.

The old man looked at him with concern. "What have we got for the boy here?" William asked and rubbed his hands together. Caleb ate everything set in front of him: ham, bacon and eggs, toast, apple cider, corn cakes, fried potatoes, and, at the end, a thick slab of blueberry pie. Margaret apologized that the blueberries had come from a jar and said the pie would be better in summer—William said that her worst blueberry pie was still the best in the world—but Caleb hardly heard either of them over the deep, rumbling satisfaction in his stomach. He sat back in the chair, happily bloated, and drank the last of another glass of milk.

William and Margaret showed him out to the parlor—William had been right about the meal, his steps were sure, his head clear—where he noticed for the first time the fireplace had been covered up with boards, nailed across the hearth, descending from the mantel, in such a thick latticework that no opening could be seen. The cold overwhelmed him.

"What happened to the fireplace?" he asked. He'd loved his small fires, sometimes sitting in front of them for hours, mesmerized, listening to the pinging of the tin chimney as the metal expanded with the heat.

"Oh," William said, his expression changing. Margaret looked away, clicking her fingernails against one another.

"You're alive," he said, "with blood pumping through your veins and a soul stitched onto your body like a well-fitted suit, correct?" Caleb nodded, though he was unsure. "Well, we have some in this house who are not alive, who do not have blood pumping through their veins, but who, more importantly, are nothing but the thin suit of the soul."

For Caleb, the world had opened up again like the sinkhole out front, and he was liable to fall into it and never be seen again. The things he caught out of the corners of his vision, the glimpses of movement from his brothers and sisters, had a cause and an explanation.

"Don't worry," William said. "We know how to deal with these souls." He motioned toward the fireplace. "Most of them were coming in through the chimneys, attracted to the smoke and the embers." Like the raccoons, Caleb thought. "We never saw them, of course, they wouldn't allow us to, but we heard them talking to us, calling out."

Once it had been said, Caleb heard the voices himself—hollow sounding, alternating high and deep, speaking too slow or too fast to understand.

"We stay in bed most of the time," Margaret said. "We push the dresser against the door. Our fireplace is more carefully barricaded than this one." She reached out and touched the bricks, ran her fingers along the mortar. "Stoves are okay; they're too small and too hot."

"At night, we leave the back door open—no matter the cold—only a touch, a mere inch."

"Why?" Caleb asked, even though the idea made more and more sense to him, because in this world, where people slept in the beds of kings and everything had been coated in beautiful colors, where children bore children in a never-ending circle, loose souls wandering the cramped hallways and vast rooms did not seem so far-fetched.

"If any of them squeeze in through a crack in the night," he said, "we need to let them out."

This sobering concept sank into Caleb's swimming head. In a place this desolate—and it felt much more so than his own home, which had been full of animals, people, and life—a place where the ground sucked up an entire cornfield for no good reason—perhaps ghosts did wander the forests. Perhaps this was how other people lived, with specters among them, waiting for them to sleep. The food churned in his stomach. He sat in one of the cushioned chairs, trapped by its softness, its enveloping hold. The flowers stitched into its fabric danced woozily, as if in an undecided breeze.

"Are you all right?" Margaret asked.

"He's having a hard time hearing it, Margie, like those men."

"He's not like them."

William looked Caleb over, up and down, his filmy stare half hidden underneath his thick eyebrows.

"What men?" Caleb asked.

William unraveled one of his scarves, peeling the wool from a series of broad bruises in the shape of two very large hands. The fingers extended around the back of the old man's neck. "This is what they did to me," William said, "and they took a lot of our stores. Food, shoes, clothes. That's why I greeted you as I did."

The ringing of the shot sounded far away and long ago, and the echoes traveled all the way back to his barn. "Who were they?" Caleb asked.

"There were three of them," William said.

"Three," Caleb repeated, his insides convulsing.

"Never seen them before. They showed up in the same shape as you—dirty, half-starved, thirsty."

The three figures exited his house, their damage done. "Red scarves?"

William twitched. "You after those men, or are you with them?"

Caleb thought he might vomit; he tried to think of something else, but could only see the bright spray of blood beneath Emma. He tugged at his hair. He looked to Margaret for guidance, but she shivered uncontrollably, her mouth shut so tightly her loose skin became taut on her neck and around her cheeks and forehead. He thought of their bloody hands, touching the things he'd touched, their filthy bodies sitting in his chair. Their matted hair, with all those dangerous thoughts underneath, had lain on the very same pillow he'd placed his head upon. His heartbeat thickened and slowed down. He flexed his hands. "When did they leave?"

"Not quite four days ago," William said.

"Did you see which way they went?" Caleb asked, though he himself hadn't been brave enough to risk watching their departure.

William said that he hadn't, that he'd been unconscious and left for dead. Margaret, he said, had been in hiding in their closet, beneath a pile of blankets. Caleb wanted to tell her he knew how it felt to curl up in a closet like a hunted mouse. William stared out the window at the gathering drifts that were pushing against the glass, his face burning red. "I thought," he said, "that by the time I got to her, she would be gone." Tears formed in the old man's eyes, and he turned away.

"I saw," Margaret said, her voice so soft it was almost lost in the hum of the wind and the creaking of the house. "I saw which way they went." William's jaw stiffened under his patchy beard. "I didn't tell you because I knew you would go after them. I heard the doors open and I had to see if they had you with them. I'm sorry." To Caleb, she said, "They were going northeast. Toward Watersbridge."

"They could've seen you!" William said.

Caleb's bag had been placed near the cocoon, which had been rolled up next to a new ball of twine. She had washed the bandages and stacked them in piles. The straps of his bag had been repaired with even stitches and tight knots. He checked the chamber of his Ithaca and put a box of ammunition in his shirt pocket all the while trying to ignore the fact that an old woman had been braver than he. "Thank you," Caleb said, and shouldered his pack. He opened the front door and the comforting cold and familiar wind beckoned him. He tugged his gloves on with his teeth. The scarf smelled clean when he wrapped it around his mouth and nose.

"Don't go, son," William said.

"Caleb," Margaret said. "What about your mother?"

He leaned the Ithaca back against the wall, and replaced the box of shells in his pack, which he set on the floor. He thanked Margaret for her fine stitching. His gloves and his scarf he hung with some others on a rack of antlers that had been bolted to the wall.

"These men shot your mother," William said.

"They took my family," Caleb said.

"They didn't have anyone with them," Margaret said.

"No," Caleb said. "I meant something different."

William and Margaret both fixated on a gilded picture frame. It showed a young man, his hair flat to his scalp, his eyes dark like Margaret's, his face the same shape as William's. "You can ask the spirits," William said, "to bring them back."

Caleb's heart leapt, as if from the hayloft door and out across the fields. "Can that work?" he asked. "Does it?"

"Not yet," William said, "but we keep asking."

Caleb examined the bullets for imperfections. Even their smallest changes in grain, a slight wave in the metal, he knew by heart. He asked William so many questions about the appearance and whereabouts of the three men that William started asking Caleb questions as well, like what he was planning on doing when he found them. The inquiry stopped.

He dreamed of killers and scarves and untying his brother's boots and rising up to the dark sky, a ghost himself. He barely slept. In the moonlight leaking through the dusty windows, he crept from room to room, as he had at home, watching for intruders, filled with stories William told of souls unmoored from the stitching of a human body, wondering whether they would look like the white shirt his mother had let go over the rapids, translucent and moving with a spirit of its own. Late one night he heard the creaking bedsprings relieved of William's weight, and the old man came into the hallway, dressed in a thick sweater and many pairs of socks bundled and tied with bootlaces. The candle he clutched in his hand lit his face from below, turning his brows into evil shadows. He looked like the scarecrow the girls had made and stuck on the broken handle of a pitchfork in the middle of their vegetable garden. Caleb stood in front of him—dressed only in long underwear cleaned and washed by Margaret—the Ithaca loaded in his arms.

William nodded at Caleb sadly. "If you're going to do it, kill Margaret first," he said. "I don't want the shot to wake her, and for her to know what's coming. Better to sneak in now and do it quick. That's all I ask."

Caleb was so hurt he couldn't respond. He'd studied himself in the mirror—a vanity Jorah had eschewed—and—despite the haircut Margaret had insisted upon—concluded he didn't look like a killer at all. When he recovered enough to speak, he said, "I don't want to kill you. I'm watching out."

William's shoulders dropped with relief. "You can't shoot ghosts, son."

Caleb let the shotgun's barrel touch the ground. At the small clink of metal, William mussed Caleb's hair and went back into his room. Caleb's hands twitched at memories of patting Emma in the same way. The bedsprings confirmed William's return.

Caleb kept the gun in the bed next to him, rolled up in his pants so the oil didn't ruin Margaret's clean sheets. He thought it the kind of thing a killer wouldn't do.

WHEN SHE CAME to, Elspeth didn't know where she was or what had happened. At times, she'd imagined herself in one of the homes where she'd served as a midwife, and when the old woman woke her by pressing a cup to her lips or wetting her forehead with a moist towel, she'd try to get to her feet, to fetch the doctor's tools, to put the water on, to lay out the towels, but the old woman would push her head back to her pillow with a gentle hand. Others she'd remember herself back on the straw pallet at the foot of her parents' bed in the van Tessel home. In the mornings—a tick before first light—their father would rise to get the plants and flowers in order, to fill the vases and clear the lawn of any branches that had fallen in the night. Elspeth and her mother could sleep a bit more before they'd have to serve breakfast. She would nestle into her hand-me-down sheets and stained pillow and fall into her deepest slumber. The last few days had been her soundest sleep since, and when her eyes opened they weren't heavy or swollen. She felt right.

Caleb poked his head into her room and, upon seeing her awake, slipped in and eased the door shut behind him. She couldn't explain his sudden presence off the hillside. Most days she wouldn't see him until evening supper, and even then, he arrived after the prayer and didn't linger once the plates had been cleared. He looked strange, too, his skin pinker, his frame stooped slightly, as if the roof was about to cave in, and his hair appeared to have been cut with a dull knife. It came back to her, the white hot pain of the shot, the struggle down the hill away from their home—their home which had disappeared in the night.

Margaret entered without a knock and smiled at the two of them. "You have your mother's features," she said. Caleb shied away and played with the mended buttons on his shirt. Elspeth hadn't considered the shock of Caleb being in the world for the first time. She noted the sharp cheekbones that did not resemble Jorah's even planes, the dark brown eyes unlike her dusty gray, the peach skin that neither she nor Jorah possessed. The children had never known anyone but their siblings, and if they'd noticed anything strange about the fact they all looked so different from one another, they'd never spoken of it. Elspeth ached to unburden herself, to tell Caleb that he was not her child, that none of them were, but she prayed and realized that the weight lifted off of her shoulders would be dropped squarely on his and he looked too lean and worn for that.

The old woman ran her hands through the boy's hair. Caleb didn't flinch, but stood still as a frightened deer. Elspeth, her strength and mind returning, wanted to tell the woman to stop touching her son. She hadn't experienced such jealousy in a long time, not since the soft spots on the babies' skulls had grown over. On the wall hung a portrait of three children, clearly belonging to the old woman. Their looks were shared.

Two and a half years after she'd left the van Tessels and her parents behind, with snow falling hard and wet, plastering itself against the windows, gathering on the panes, Elspeth had cleaned metal birthing instruments in hot soapy water. Her red hand removed a shining set of forceps. She'd taken a job with a Dr. Forbes, and hardly considered Jorah, who spent his days with the animals and making furniture so that each time Elspeth came home, the house would be more full, more finished, more alien to her. Their house, as yet, contained only the two of them.

Dr. Forbes scribbled in one of his many black notebooks, a blue ribbon bookmarker dangling from the desk.

"Sir, if I may?" she said.

"Yes?" he said, not turning away from his note taking and, in fact, dipping his pen again.

She waited for him to finish. He removed his glasses and cracked his knuckles. Elspeth scrubbed at a small set of shears. "I wonder," she said, "if it's possible for a man and woman who are of different colors to have a child?"

Forbes laughed. "What kind of a question . . ." he began, then cleared his throat. "Of course, God would never approve . . ."

"Yes, sir." But she couldn't help herself. "I saw a couple walking—an Indian and a woman like me—and they seemed quite happy in each other's company, and I wondered. I'm sorry to ask."

He laughed again. "A woman like you? Hardly." His fingers toyed with his belt buckle. "It has been known to happen." He stood and thumbed across the spines of his notebooks, selected one from a high shelf, and flipped through the pages. His neat, cramped handwriting flew past. "Here it is. Yes, once, when I was quite young, I assisted Dr. Vashin as he delivered such a baby." He cleared his throat, the air dried by the woodstove, and read, "*The baby appears to be in normal health. The girl, fourteen years of age, also appears to be in fine condition. The birth did not give much difficulty or pose additional problems.*" He smiled at her. "My spelling certainly has improved."

"So it is possible?"

It took him a moment to recall what she was referring to. She could see the memory alight on his face and he flipped to another page in the notebook. He frowned. "It seems, and I had forgotten this altogether, that the girl's father made away with the infant in the night and dashed its head against a rock." He clapped the notebook shut, causing Elspeth to jump. She wasn't certain he'd been reading the last part and she worried she'd gone too far. "For the best," he said.

"But it is possible?"

He touched a hand to her waist. Elspeth allowed such advances without response, but he never moved past them.

"As possible as it would be for you and I to have a child," he said, his lips wet against her ear. But now she knew it would be futile, no matter the man.

She dropped the shears in the sink, and waved her hands to clear away the soap bubbles, and in the water she saw herself staring back and thought, as she often did then, of Gusta van Tessel, eyes wide and empty, staring up from the bottom of the bathtub.

THE FOLLOWING MORNING when Caleb saw his mother, she looked even healthier, more solid and more herself, though Margaret had taken the liberty of cutting her hair as well. It did her no favors—so short it made her face more severe, her features sharper. He heard Margaret on the stairs and shook his mother awake. "We need to go," he said, "they've been here. The men, the three men, they were here."

Few things in her life had provided Elspeth such evidence of God. She brought her hand to the cross at her neck, and then to her head. "Did that woman cut my hair?" Caleb nodded. She tried to smile. "Does mine look as awful as yours?"

"Worse," he said and laughed.

Elspeth noticed the boarded hearth. "What happened to the fireplace?"

"That's where the ghosts come in," Caleb said, and didn't have time to say anything further, because Margaret opened the door, and pretended to be surprised to find them both there.

"We're leaving," Elspeth said, and forced herself—through gritting teeth—to sit upright.

Margaret explained to both of them in great detail the dangers of moving Elspeth, saying she needed weeks, if not months, to fully recuperate from her injuries. Caleb began to panic. "So you may be able to leave before long," she began. He knew that soon wouldn't be good enough.

"I'll be fine," Elspeth said, with finality. She could not have this woman cutting their hair without provocation or invitation and filling Caleb's head with stories of ghosts and insanity. Then she noticed her clothes on the chair at her side. "Did you wash these?"

Margaret looked confused. "Well, yes, they were filthy." Elspeth yearned to be in Jorah's secure presence, if only in the scent of his old shirt. "They were covered in blood and muck, and—"

"We leave now."

"My dear . . ." Margaret began, but Elspeth closed her eyes.

"Leave me," she said. If God wished for her to follow these killers and was content to throw them in her path, she wouldn't wait for His next sign. A shadow passed over her. A hand went to her face, and she wasn't sure whose, but it was rough and chilled.

Once she heard the door shut, she rewrapped her chest. A quiet knocking at the door revealed the old woman. She didn't shy away from Elspeth's bare skin.

"William and I," she said, "are concerned about the boy." When Margaret understood that Elspeth wasn't going to speak before she'd finished, she shut the door. "We are of the opinion it would be best for him to stay here, with us, until you've done what you need to do."

Had the question been put forth a week earlier—as she lay in the dark shadows of the barn and the boy sloshed water into troughs, talking to the animals as he went—she would have said yes. After their journey, however, leaving him was inconceivable. "So Caleb told you what happened?" Margaret said he had. "And you think—after that—my family murdered—I would let my last child out of my sight?"

"No, dear, of course not," Margaret said and wrung her hands. "We have food and shelter and the boy seems so bent on . . . well, on killing."

Elspeth jammed items into her pack, not caring whose they were or where they'd come from. "We thank you for your help."

"I hope you'll reconsider."

Elspeth took some money from the toe of her boot, perhaps more than she'd intended, and threw it onto the bed. "For your troubles."

Margaret scurried away, and when Caleb knocked, Elspeth thought she'd come back to see if she had, indeed, reconsidered.

"I'm ready," he said. He traced the outline of the keyhole on the doorknob with his fingernail. "I have bad dreams in this house." Caleb hoped she would say something to let him know everything would be all right.

She yanked her bandage tighter. He heard the fabric strain. "Bad dreams," she said, "are nothing but."

ELSPETH LIMPED HER way into the kitchen, where William and Margaret had a full breakfast sizzling. Their backs stiffened at her injured shuffle.

"Surprised to see you up and about," William said and sipped a cup of coffee.

She didn't sit down, didn't eat. "I thank you both for what you've done, but Caleb and I are leaving today."

"Stay and rest up," William said.

"We must go," she said.

William's countenance darkened. "Margaret and I don't think you should follow after those men. No good can come of it." He tried to dissuade her with his tale of the killers, of the evil that came out of their pores, and the easy way with which one had held him by the throat while the others went through their drawers and stole anything of value. "And this place they're headed—this Waters-bridge—is no kind of place for a mother and her son."

The name shoved Elspeth back into the wall. Caleb, pink and new, had wriggled against her chest as she hurried through the dusty streets of that very town. The boy had cried, and she longed to duck into the church to calm him, but had pushed on. Circumstances—if they could be called that—made her return inevitable. And with the boy, a stolen son of Watersbridge. This, surely, had to be her reckoning. If so, she would go headlong.

Caleb—twelve and so different to her it made her shudder—entered the kitchen, sat down, and ate from the abundant plates of food. Elspeth had never seen him so at ease and it pained her. "Caleb, we have to be going."

He heard the tone of his mother's voice and shoveled eggs in faster. Margaret took a tin of muffins from the oven.

"Eat," Margaret said. "Stay. You need your strength, too, dear."

As if to prove she had plenty, Elspeth lifted Caleb's chair from the table—the boy's fork still clutched in his hand—a surprising show of power, even though it sent tendrils of pain to her toes and fingertips to do so. William raised his arms in acquiescence. Margaret retrieved a cotton bag from the pantry. On top of it she placed half a dozen of the steaming muffins.

"There's enough food in there to last you," she said.

CHAPTER 11

They could see Watersbridge down in the valley long before they reached it. The streets and clustered buildings were visible, and behind them the gray expanse of the lake. Caleb's stomach knotted in anticipation. The thought that they were close pushed them, and they tempted darkness when a snow squall rushed upon them, night lowering in an instant, the snow hard and fast as rain. It took both of them to lash their tarp to a maple tree, the wind toying with the material, the snow blinding.

The branches lent some cover and they each cleared a spot down to the earth to sleep on and they ate from the sack William and Margaret had provided—salted pork, pickled beets, bread with hunks of butter. After the comforts of the couple's house, the cold penetrated them deeper, sensing their weaknesses, until they became sore and tense. Elspeth tried not to think of the woman, how she asked to have her child, and slept a dreamless sleep, rising in the dim dawn to walk again, trailing behind Caleb, the town lost to trees and brush in the lower altitudes.

That afternoon, they came upon a burned-out building. It appeared to have once been larger than the Howell house, square but grand. Most of the frame held. Everything else had been prey to the flames. The scorched beams creaked and whistled in the wind. Caleb explored the remnants of the building, testing a step in a stairway that led to nothing. He shook a post. She saw how he changed in the midst of the charred remains—his face paled, his wide brown eyes avoided hers.

He climbed to the top of the staircase. His mother stood below, never setting foot inside the wrecked building. She coughed, a racking, terrible sound. "I burned the house down," he said. "I burned the bodies, and the house caught fire. All I had time for was you and the rifles and a little bit of food."

"You couldn't bury them," she said.

"No."

"I understand," she said, and she meant it, glad he'd set the fire: It gave them nothing to return to, nothing to compel them to turn back. The boy must miss it all, she thought. She wanted to give him something. "Caleb," she said, "Watersbridge is where you were born."

Caleb looked down at the buildings, a church steeple visible. He'd been born in a town that housed murderers. Margaret and William had difficulty discussing Watersbridge in front of him, choosing their words carefully, and he attempted to reconstruct and decipher all he could. "Mama," he said, "if I was born there, does that make me the same as those men?" It all seemed too much to grasp at once, and he wondered how other people understood it without difficulty. He kicked at a burned beam of the house. It twanged and shook, but held.

"No, Caleb," she said. "It doesn't." She wished she could reach out further than that, draw the boy from his trance, but she only had the energy to go forward and soon after he caught up and followed in her tracks.

CALEB FORGOT HIS soreness once they came in view of the trails of smoke rising from the chimneys of the town, and he raced ahead. Elspeth called for him to slow down, but he didn't listen. Above the tops of the pine trees, the steeple, topped by a golden cross, gleamed in the midday light.

When Caleb passed through a stand of oaks, a voice called out to him. The sound shocked him after such silence. By instinct, he crouched close to the snow, so close the chill stung the clean, bare skin where his hair had been cut. He put a hand to the butt of the Ithaca, tucked into the back of Jorah's bulky jacket.

A man clambered out of a ditch. He had long, stringy hair and one of his legs was made of wood. On the end was a boot, different than his other. "Hey, there, young master."

"Keep walking," Caleb's mother said.

Caleb couldn't help it—he wanted to see what the man had to say, and didn't wish to be rude to the very first person he met from the town of his birth, who hurried toward them, hopping out of the snowdrifts, one finger extended into the air, his white stubble shining in the reflection from the snow. "One moment, just one moment." From his shoulders hung a pair of coveralls, so beaten and worn that the straps now comprised more thread than denim. Under them, a stained red shirt was as vivid as a cardinal against the snowy backdrop. As the man moved closer, a small clinking sound, like that of tiny chains, accompanied his steps. Caleb saw that many of the dangling threads on his coveralls held needles— dozens of them. It was as if the man needed to repair his clothes so often that removing the needles meant nothing but lost time. They twinkled when he stepped into the path. "Could you spare some food?" he asked.

"We have none," Elspeth said, arresting Caleb's hand at the mouth of his pack.

The man scratched his chin; a welt bloomed beneath his fingers, as vibrant as his shirt. "Some coin, then? A tad of copper for the coffers?"

Elspeth moved in front of Caleb. "We have none," she repeated.

"Well, then, good day to you, sir," the man said, and stepped out of the path. In the darkness beneath the trees he ran his tongue over his teeth. Elspeth placed her body between the man and the boy, thinking that if they could put him behind them without incident, they were luckier than she imagined. "If you should happen to find some," the man said, "my brother, London, owns the finest inn in town, the Elm."

Elspeth took the boy's shoulder and kept him moving, not daring to look back and find the man upon them, a blade bright in his hand. With each step, however, her grip slackened.

Caleb's excitement for Watersbridge turned into something dark. His lack of knowledge already frightened him, like he'd only just come out of hibernation into a new world.

The smells of the town—bacon frying, horse excrement, fires burning—reached them before Elspeth let go of the boy. Once she did, Caleb asked, "Why did that man call you sir?"

"Some people don't know what they're saying," Elspeth answered. "Remember when your father had the fever?" The days then had been longer than ever for Elspeth, who dreaded nothing more than being stuck in that house for a whole winter as she watched out the window and in tumbled the first snow clouds. The children would ask her questions, and she would dream of their hands on her, their small, clamoring hands, all craving, needing, demanding something she could not provide. "For some people, the fever never breaks, and they wander through the world of

God with a piece of the Devil burning a hole through their brain, whispering into their ears."

"Father had the Devil in his brain?" Caleb asked, thinking this explained a great deal, that the small graveyard might have been the answer to that call.

"No, no, the Devil burrows down deep in some people, but not in your father, and not in you."

Caleb thought of the acrid smoke filling the pantry, the ticking of his mother's blood on the kitchen floor. He recalled his pride, the blossom of heat in his heart at having avenged his family. Elspeth relived the train trips, the babies, the families, and she again felt the grief of their loss. And as they neared the city, the wind erasing their journey, each of their heads rang with the belief that the Devil did indeed nestle in their skulls, and their foreheads burned with the sweat of his wicked imagination.

BOOK II

BOOK II

CHAPTER 1

C aleb trailed after his mother through the muddy streets, the snow compressed by boots, wheels, and hooves, and held his head down. He'd never seen so many men, or heard such thunderous noise. Every time he looked up, he worried that his chest would cave in and that the Devil picking at his brain would catch fire. Everything, it seemed, moved. "Are we going to the Elm Inn now?" he asked, twice, repeating himself to be heard above the din.

She grabbed hold of the boy's jacket and stopped him from colliding with a finely dressed man, who tipped his hat to Elspeth and hurried past. At her insistence, Caleb had jammed his shotgun into his pack, and had wrapped the protruding barrel with a blanket. She adjusted it roughly before they entered the main street, where carts passed freely down the center, and men clomped down the pine walkways and mucked through the foul streets shoulder to shoulder.

"But that man told us," he started.

"We can't believe him, Caleb," she said. "Some people tell you what you want to hear, others tell you what they want to say, and they can't all be the truth. Here, disbelief is as important as belief.

Maybe more." With that, she took his sleeve in hand, and the two of them entered the thoroughfare. He struggled to keep up. There could be no leisure in this town, she knew, and the boy would have to understand that. He could no longer be a child. But she couldn't bear watching it dawn on him.

The street opened into a small town green, the snow untouched and glassy. At the head stood an imposing church, whiter than the snow, its details lost in the glare of the sun. Behind it, a massive graveyard as big as the town itself stretched up a slow-rising hill. On either side of the green, as if lining up for communion, sat the various shops and stores, post office and barbershop, necessary to keep a small town alive. To the west, through the trees, the great Lake Erie, whose slate gray dormancy joined a sky that mirrored its color. Down the slope, two slivers of land jutted out into the water like a pair of hands straining for each other but never quite getting there, the almost-bridge that gave the town its name. In the embrace of those arms of land, men worked hauling ice from the lake to a boxy icehouse covered in workers like so many ants.

Elspeth forgot about the boy and released her grip on his coat. She almost expected the church bells to ring at her arrival, a sinner come to be burned. She had been in this church, prayed among these people, and buried her nose and mouth in her sleeve to block out the dust as she raced down these streets, Caleb nothing but a stolen babe swaddled in her arms.

The Brick & Feather Hotel offered rooms to let closest to the church—near enough that as they mounted the front steps, the bells intoning two o'clock rattled the panes of glass, shaking the posted notes. Elspeth remembered the hotel as a peaceable place. She gave Caleb the money to rent the room and quickly explained what to do, knowing that sooner or later her face would be recognized. It was a lesson, she said to the child, a test. She put her back to the wall and rested in a shadowed alcove next to a clock that ticked slowly and steadily. The rhythm of the pendulum echoed in her injuries as it reverberated through the wall.

The man at the counter introduced himself as Frank and met Caleb with a smile and Caleb responded in kind. Frank wore a crisp white shirt and a brown checked vest, upon which he wiped his glasses. His thick black hair had been combed away from his face and neatly parted on the left side. Caleb did as he was asked, and requested a room. He returned to his mother with the change cupped in his hands like eggs in a nest. They took the stairs, Elspeth obscured by the boy. In their arms they clutched their filthy and threadbare belongings.

"Sir," Frank said, and stepped out from behind his desk.

Elspeth didn't stop.

"Oh, sir."

Frank handed Caleb a tarnished bronze key.

"It'd be difficult to get into your room without this," he said. "Maybe you should give it to your father for safekeeping."

Elspeth's cheeks flushed hot. It was the second time she'd been mistaken for a man. She didn't dare turn around. She recognized the man's tone and stilted speech; he thought Caleb was daft. He'd gotten them both wrong.

"Thank you," Caleb said. "Sorry."

The words sounded up the stairwell.

The room was cramped, the two beds set in the shape of an L against the walls, an uneven-legged dresser against another. The wallpaper peeled from the wood, and it rustled in the wind that sought out the gaps in the beaten building. In the crook between the two beds sat a wooden stool, and atop that, a chamber pot.

Elspeth set her pack down at the foot of one of the beds. Caleb stayed in the doorway, his eyes squeezed with worry. "It's okay," she said.

His feet didn't respond. Several times he had to tell himself to walk before he could take even one step into the room and slide the pack from his shoulders. It slumped to the floorboards. Snow melted and dripped from their clothes.

"Do you prefer one of the beds to the other?" Elspeth tried to sound pleased.

He looked from the bed closest to the door, its heavy blanket faded to a dull pink, to the other, under the window, its honeycomb bedspread worn to holes in places. He heard a horse clop by in the street below and thought of his barn, the vast, open space, the clean air, his animals. "By the window." He shuffled over and sat on the bed. The springs shrieked. He flinched.

The enormity of the whole enterprise struck Elspeth with the child in front of her, the shotgun he pulled from his pack large in his hands, and she clasped the cross at her neck for something to hold on to. He cracked the breech, checked the shells, and snapped it back into place, and his face loosened and he relaxed against the wall. She joined him at the window and pushed the curtain aside. The streets teemed with people, each one a possible murderer, each one a possible threat to her. To him. She forced a grin and asked if he was hungry and he said yes. She was going to say they needed a bath first, a proper washing, but he looked so doleful and nervous that she changed her mind.

THEY ENTERED THE first restaurant they saw and sat down at the table closest to the door. Caleb scrutinized the men who occupied the other tables, and Elspeth—in turn—studied his expression for some recognition, a flicker of fear or a jolt of surprise. She wished she'd brought a gun with her, and told herself that their next stop would be the mercantile to purchase a pistol, something to tuck into her belt or the calf of her boot. Then she saw the familiar lump at Caleb's side—the barrel he covered with the scarf at his neck and the stock was hidden in the folds of Jorah's coat. The gun was long but not cumbersome, and one could dismiss it if they didn't know to look for it. She was unsure if its presence made her feel better or worse.

She read the menu posted on a slate above the counter to Caleb, and he sounded out the words and repeated them under his breath. "So we ask for it and someone brings it to us?" Elspeth continued without explaining—ham, sausage, steak, bacon and eggs. "So we use some of the money we have left from the hotel?" She said they did and thought the more she answered his questions the more dependent he would become and the less he would attempt to understand on his own.

Caleb went to the counter and ordered steak and eggs for himself and sausage and potatoes for his mother. Rather than carrying the remaining money in his cupped hands, he slid it into his front pocket like he'd seen the other customers do. It occurred to him that they wouldn't find the men they were searching for in such a place: bright light streaming through the white curtains, carefully painted walls and counters, tidy writing on the slate. He had imagined the killers so many times, and in none of his nightmares or daydreams did they occupy seats in sunshine, eating ham, their napkins tucked into their collars, reading the newspaper. These people were not quite wrong enough to have murdered his family.

Alone at the table, trying to sit as straight as possible with the pain in her side flaring at her every breath, Elspeth monitored Caleb at the counter, waiting for their food. She heard footsteps approach and a loud throat-clearing before she turned to see a man with curly, dazzlingly red hair and a moustache—both of which were patchy. He worried his fingers along the brim of the hat he carried in his hands.

"Sir, if I may," he said, and waved at the empty seat. Again she'd been confused for a man, and on this occasion, she realized how the mistake had been made—her hat slung low, her face dirty, her hair shorn, her shape covered by Jorah's old clothes, and her chest bandaged so tightly that it constricted not only her breathing, but her breasts. God had seen fit to hide her, but His purpose eluded her. The man placed himself at the very edge of the chair before she could answer. "My name is Charles Heather. I work for the Great Lakes Ice Company," he said, "and my partner broke his leg earlier this month. It was my fault." Charles Heather was on the verge of tears. "The company told me to find a stout man to replace him before the month was up, or I'd be let go. Are you, by chance, looking for work?"

Elspeth considered her options. They needed time to find the three men, and she'd never seen the killers. The descriptions that Caleb and William gave merely served to confuse her; they only spoke of the evil the killers exuded and the red scarves they wore. Elspeth had little money, as she'd left most of it with William and Margaret, a gesture she recognized as pointless. Most important, she understood her weakness, and the job would keep her from a birthing room. "I'm in need of something, yes." She lowered her voice an octave. "What's the work?"

Charles shifted back on his seat. He let out a hot breath. "Chopping ice from the lake and hauling it. You look like a strong enough fellow, but the work is hard, I won't lie."

Elspeth didn't doubt his honesty despite the nerves betrayed by his mannerisms. "But this accident—you caused it? What's to say you don't break my arm? Or kill me? Is the work so dangerous?"

Charles's fingers moved even more swiftly around the brim of his hat. He tapped his foot. "Yes, yes, I did cause the accident. I thought I had secured the pincers, but the ice fell onto my partner's shoulder. I need to make amends to him, to his wife and family."

Amends. Elspeth liked how it sounded. Charles asked her name.

"Jorah," she said, unable to conjure anything else. She had never used her real name in town, as she'd promised her husband she wouldn't from her very first trips away. "Jorah van Tessel."

Charles indicated Caleb with nod. "You're about a hundred and eleven short."

"I'm sorry?" Elspeth said. The question had already slipped out when she wished she could retrieve it; something about it had sounded too feminine, and she decided to limit herself to the fewest syllables possible.

"*The children of Jorah, an hundred and twelve*," Charles recited. "Your name. From the Bible. Ezra. Surely you knew that."

"You know your Book well." She glanced at the men seated around the room and—despite the pain it caused her—pushed her knees outward and hunched her shoulders, trying to copy their poses.

"My mother used to cover the windows in the summer to keep the heat out, and one summer—a particularly penniless summer—my mother had to use the pages of our Bible. She said no one reads Ezra. I guess she was wrong."

"I guess so." She wondered what Jorah meant by choosing his name—she had yet to come home with one child—much less all of them—when he took it. Maybe the appeal truly had been the way the word sounded, and its softness next to the harsh Lothute.

"So when I went to bed at night, and woke up in the morning, there it would be, Ezra, staring right at me." She expected Charles to start talking about Faith and Fate and she prepared herself. "I guess somehow I memorized it. Probably the only part of the Bible I could quote you, to be honest." He smiled.

Elspeth said, "All right."

Charles Heather stood and clapped his hands together. "You'll do it?"

She said she would.

Caleb, meanwhile, had been fascinated by the bustle of the kitchen through the open door. He could barely fathom food in such quantities—great bowls the size of washbasins laden with eggs, buckets dripping with batter for hotcakes and corn bread, links of sausage spooled like twine, piles of sugar as big as his head, row after row of glass jars of cider—it was like a fantasy. But the sound of Charles Heather clapping his hands startled him from his trance, and he turned with surprise to see the red-haired man standing over his mother, his bald spot shining in the afternoon light.

Caleb touched the Ithaca at his side, wondering how quickly he could untangle it from his scarf and yank it from the depths of the coat. He could not hear their conversation over the racket of the dining room. The man appeared gentle enough and his mother looked unconcerned. However, by the manner in which she cocked her neck upward, leaned out over the table, her arms crossed, her hands at her elbows, and adjusted herself every few seconds, he worried for her wounds.

Two heavy plates banged onto the counter behind him, and he took one in each hand, his elbow pressing his Ithaca into his side reassuringly. When he reached their table, the red-haired man readjusted the knife and fork where he'd unsettled them. "This must be your son—you can tell," he said and introduced himself to Caleb, who allowed the man to pump his hand up and down with vigor. "I won't interrupt your meal any further," Charles said, tugging his gloves onto his hands. "Mister—I'm sorry, did you tell me your last name?" His rusty brows knitted together.

"Van Tessel," she said. "Jorah van Tessel."

Caleb whimpered and Elspeth halted him with a glance. He knew better than to question the tone and tenor her voice had taken on.

"I shall remember it always," Charles said, with heavy import, and laughed. Elspeth didn't respond, and he pressed his hat onto his head. He elbowed Caleb and said, "Your father is a good man." Caleb picked up his fork and knife. "Right," Charles said, "I'll expect you at four o'clock to meet with Mr. Wallace at the Great Lakes Ice Company. Do you know where it is?"

"I'll manage to find it," Elspeth said.

"Well, it'd be tough to pick the wrong lake," Charles said and laughed again. He placed his hat atop his head, and Elspeth noted his scars and misshapen knuckles.

Caleb cut into his steak. He heard the wood creak as his mother sat back down, but could only watch the blood draining from the meat and gathering in the curve of his plate, unwilling to look at his mother until she glanced down at her food. Only then could he study this new person across from him.

A t three forty-five in the afternoon—according to the grand hotel clock—Elspeth left the Brick & Feather having told Caleb to stay in the room with the door locked, and headed west, downhill toward the lake. The Great Lakes Ice Company occupied the curve of land on the water, the unfamiliar machinery for the extraction of the ice—tall, dangerous-looking metal structures and beaten sleds with sharpened blades—close to the lakeside. Snow clouds gathered into a mighty wall over the water. The icehouse loomed to her left, in a direct line from the shore, and she heard the calls and replies of workers inside. As she went, she studied the postures and affects of the men she passed and reminded herself to widen her stance, to move her arms less, and to crouch down a bit with each stride. Every man's face possessed some kind of threat, some shade of darkness. Even Charles Heather, whom she found waiting for her outside the offices, an old train car, one of two set a bit apart from the bustle of the company. "Jorah," he cried in greeting. He shook Elspeth's hand warmly, then further enveloped it with his other hand. He rapped upon the door to the office three quick times.

He'd tried to comb his hair, and the effect sent his red curls spiraling off the side of his head like the petals of a flower.

Inside, a fire blazed in a stone hearth. The building contained one rectangular room, with evenly spaced windows. The only door was behind them. Three old men sat at a long desk, two bent over ledgers, the third clacking on the black and white keys of an adding machine but similarly stooped. A plaid flannel blanket hung on the wall, its reds and blues eaten away in places by moths. In the corner, a crib appeared to Elspeth like an apparition.

"I've brought a new man," Charles said. "A replacement." He cleared his throat. "A replacement for Mr. Acker. This is Jorah . . ."

Elspeth tried not to stare at the crib and waited for someone to acknowledge it. Surely it could not be real, in this of all places. Impossibly, the sun bored through the clouds to find its lacy adornments and made them glimmer. "Jorah van Tessel," she said, lost in the desire to peek over the edge of the crib.

One of the men—the eldest, judging by his lack of teeth and the white hairs coming from everywhere but his scalp—ceased his scribbling and put down his pencil. "Van Tessel, did you say?" Elspeth said yes, her mind fully enraptured by the illusion in front of her. The sure sound of fussing came from inside. The baby began to cry, tightening Elspeth's body like a string on a fiddle. Maybe, she thought, the Devil played a trick on her. No one seemed bothered by the child's plaintive call. "Are you of relation to Dedrick van Tessel?" he asked. The baby wailed.

Elspeth reeled. Torn from the crying, she saw the second oldest van Tessel boy, the smallest in size. Dedrick had been a scrappy child, always bruised or cut, whose clothes needed mending at least five times more often than the rest of the children. Dedrick spent hours in his room, serving punishment for hitting one of his brothers or sisters, but he also found ways to escape his confinement. Once he'd grabbed hold of his windowsill on the second floor, and from the kitchen below Elspeth watched his stubby legs kicking at the empty air before he let himself drop into the bushes. Her mother told her to keep silent unless Dedrick had hurt someone.

"No relation," Elspeth told the old man.

"Dead," the man at the adding machine said, and sniffed. "Fell off his horse, didn't he, Horace?"

"Cracked his neck in two," Horace replied, without pausing in his work.

"I'm sorry," she said. She couldn't imagine Dedrick grown. She tried to place a small beard on his jaw to make him appear older, but she ended up seeing him as he'd been. Elspeth thought of her father, too, tending the van Tessel gardens. But the years had gone so swiftly. Her mother and father had likely passed away. She envisioned two simple stones to mark their graves tucked in the corner of the van Tessel's property. "A cousin perhaps. Distant cousin."

"It's an uncommon name. Dedrick was an uncommon fellow," the eldest said. "Like Charlie here." The other men in the office chuckled. "But, alas." He snatched his pencil back up, picked some stray lint or hair from the point with his dirty fingernails, and resumed his work.

The baby's cries clawed at her.

"Horace, should I tend to the baby?" Charles asked. Elspeth grabbed hold of the table. Her relief at the baby's existence threatened to topple her. Her concern shifted to that of being discovered. Perhaps, she thought, something about her sympathy for the child colored her appearance: her skin flushed too brightly or her hands joined together the wrong way. Before she'd left the hotel, she'd inspected herself in the mirror and confirmed that without washing, and in Jorah's sagging clothes, she bore more of a resemblance to a man, and she'd been careful to maintain this appearance. She looked to Charles and affected his belly-forward posture and tucked one thumb into her belt loop, as she'd seen a fair number of men do.

"Things cannot possibly be so dire," Horace said, "that I would entrust a baby to you, Charlie." All three old men laughed, and Horace pushed his way upright, joints cracking loud enough to be heard over the adding machine and the crying of the infant. He put a hand to his back and pressed himself up straighter. "I'll see to her, I'll see to her."

"Should hope so—she ain't my granddaughter," the man at the adding machine said, and they laughed yet again.

Elspeth shifted so she could see into the crib, where the baby's face had gone crimson, her toothless mouth open wide, fists clenched in incommunicable fury. Horace picked her up and clasped her tight to his chest. Elspeth was surprised at the ease of his movements and the sureness of his grip. The baby saw Elspeth and the crying slowed and then stopped. She blinked her wide eyes. "She likes you," Horace said. "She doesn't usually take to strange men. Do you?" he asked the child.

The room lurched. Elspeth gripped the table more firmly, gave more of her weight to it, afraid she would pass out.

He brought the baby closer. Elspeth could smell it, the sweetness of its skin, and she reached out a quivering finger and ran the back of it along the child's cheek and a thrill spiraled through her. The rush of that soft skin. Everything inside of her moved faster, her heart larger, her bones stronger, her hearing clearer, her vision brighter. The memories she kept chained inside her broke free, including those she banished beyond all others.

She and Jorah had been on their own less than a year, and between the beatings Jorah took and the hard jobs that paid little, she'd convinced him to let her head out on her own to find work. She'd promised to use a fake name, for fear the van Tessels hunted their runaway workers, and to come home at the first twinge of trouble. He'd given her directions to the nearest town, where it took her less than a day of asking for work before someone pointed her to the doctor's office. Dr. Watt hired her before she understood the position. "Are you queasy around blood, Clara?" he asked. She shook her head no. "Do you have a steady hand?" She did. "A strong overall constitution?" She thought so.

The next day, she held a man's arm together while Dr. Watt sewed it up, whistling to himself, drawing the black string tight. Later than afternoon, after she'd washed the blood from her hands and Dr. Watt had commended her on her resolve, they'd gone to see an expectant mother. Throughout the examination the husband and wife argued over every aspect of their future child—whether it would be a boy or girl, what name they would give him or her, where he or she would sleep—and every disagreement circled back to a previous one and it started all over again. Elspeth had never before seen a woman yell at a man. Watt cleaned his pipe on his shirttail, untucked for this purpose. Once a week when the doctor checked to see how the baby lay in the uterus, the husband and wife would scream at each other until they were red-faced and sweating. Sometimes the doctor and Elspeth could hear them yell as they approached the boxy white farmhouse, the screams escaping through the open windows.

"Is this common?" Elspeth asked.

"On occasion," Dr. Watt said. "It's a difficult process for some. Most husbands aren't quite so tolerant."

Two months later, Elspeth was summoned from her hotel room in the middle of the night and ushered into the house by the husband, great concern on his face. The kitchen had been turned into a birthing room, a pot of boiled water perched on a Windsor chair, instruments laid out on a clean towel, the wife on the table with quilts and blankets piled under her, the room bright with light and warmed by the woodstove, and Dr. Watt smoking a pipe and massaging the wife's stomach like bread dough, his head cocked toward the ceiling as if maybe someone had called his name. The baby was breech, he explained, speaking calmly to both the mother and Elspeth about what he was going to do. He pressed hard on the lower part of the stomach and tried to shift the baby, but it would not budge. The process was too far along, he said, the baby had already begun its journey and sat too low in her pelvis to be moved. He plunged his hand into the woman, and she howled. Her husband called from the porch, where they could hear his heavy boots pacing. "What's happening?" he said

"Everything's fine," Dr. Watt said, but Elspeth could tell he was concerned. He bit hard on the stem of his pipe and then tossed it aside, the tobacco and ash scattering on the floorboards. "Not long now," he said, and sure enough, a small foot slipped from the woman and the doctor didn't hesitate to marvel at its size or vulnerability, and instead wrapped his fingers around the baby's ankle and began to pull. Elspeth could see the child beneath the woman's skin, the surreal lumps moving and squirming. She sensed the three of them—doctor, mother, baby—fighting each other, their wills pulling in opposite directions. Elspeth squeezed the woman's shoulder and gently probed her stomach and then her lower abdomen before she located the head and pressed down with the heels of both hands, and the tension between mother and child eased, and nature once again took hold. Another leg emerged, and then the girl's midsection, like a miracle. Dr. Watt yanked, impatient. Elspeth followed the head along its way with her fingers, applying pressure here and there when things stalled. The woman was small, but the doctor wasted no more time—sweat cascaded down his forehead, soaking a vee down his shirt—and with a great tearing he pulled, and the woman screamed and Elspeth wanted to hit him, balled her fist to strike. The head slid out and the doctor held the child—a girl—by the ankles he'd been yanking on for what felt like days and cleared her nostrils and her mouth and she wriggled in his hands. He gave her to Elspeth. She wiped the vernix and the blood from her body and face. She'd never seen something so pure, so untouched, and she marveled at the fragility and the stunning, electric life evident in every miniature movement.

Dr. Watt held out his hands to her and she pretended to find another speck of blood on the child's cheek and clung to it an extra precious minute. After she surrendered the baby, Dr. Watt swaddled her tightly and handed her to the new mother, whose groans of pain and rocking back and forth halted in the presence of her child. The father came in and the expressions on both of their faces made Elspeth understand that no mistake existed that this joy could not undo.

For weeks Elspeth possessed a new vitality; something vibrant had opened up to her. She longed to experience what she'd seen; she yearned to hold her own child. But the more she and Jorah tried to conceive and the more failure stacked up, the less she could recall the thrill and the harder it became for her to even move, her bones aching as everything ebbed away. Gusta van Tessel haunted her, and she once dunked herself under water, but broke the surface and clanged her fist against the side of the tub. She'd left Jorah the next morning to find another job as a midwife.

In the icehouse office, the man at the adding machine waved a piece of paper in the air. "Enough with the baby. I got two babies in here already," he said and slid the piece of paper across the desk to Elspeth. "Take this to Wallace. Charlie, show the man."

Elspeth wished to stay and let the baby stare at her for the remainder of the afternoon, but Charles grabbed the paper and gave her a light push. The other two men had resumed their scribbling, the scratching of their pens loud in the room like the gnawing of mice in the night.

THE INTERTWINED BONES of Caleb's brothers and sisters reached out to him, their mouths suspended in grimaces of pain. The terror when he'd sneaked out of the pantry at night haunted him. They would sometimes appear to move, or he would hear a breath or a sigh, but when he composed himself, nothing had changed. Emma's outline in the snow reassured him that she didn't shift in the night or twitch in the periphery of his vision. He'd sit in the yard next to her body, like he had in the long grass with Jesse, and he would will things to be as they had been, the deathly silence merely the comfort of family. This calm never settled upon him fully, and when he stood up, the nightmare continued as reality. He would get to his knees, remove his gloves, and brush the snow from his baby sister's face.

Not sure if he'd slept at all, he threw the covers aside and removed the scratchy nightshirt William and Margaret had given him, noting the bruises that ran up and down his legs and how his ribs protruded from his torso. He had a new hollow in his chest where he assumed his heart had been and he dressed as fast as possible. His Ithaca he once again fixed to his side before putting his jacket on, and he wound his scarf carefully around his neck to cover the section of the barrel that poked out from behind his shoulder.

In the lobby of the hotel, a fire crackled in the hearth. Men played cards at a table. Another sat in a chair, reading a book. Caleb tried to shake the ghosts that clung to him like spiderwebs. Frank stood behind the counter, the newspaper spread in front of

him, and Caleb asked him where he could find the Elm Inn. Frank
didn't look up and spoke to Caleb in a secret language of streets
and directions. When Caleb didn't move, Frank creased the paper
in the center and folded it over again, all with deliberation. "What's
your name?" Caleb told him. "Okay, Caleb." Frank repeated what
he'd said, only this time slower and using his hands. Caleb moved
only a few steps, and Frank sighed, opened the gate that led out
from behind the counter, and guided Caleb by his shoulders into the
street. From there, he pointed at the hitch outside the post office, the
light that illuminated the window of the barber's, the darkened doors
of the hardware, and explained to Caleb where he needed to turn
past the church in order to get to the inn. "It's on the side of the hill."

Caleb thanked him. The sky had already turned the color of
deep water, and Caleb was worried his mother might return to the
hotel and miss him. "Could you tell my—Jorah—where I went?"

Frank fixed him with an odd look. He lifted his chin. "What's
that under your coat?"

Caleb stopped. Frank motioned for Caleb to remove his scarf,
and Caleb slid the gun from its hiding place. Frank took a step
back. "It's my shotgun."

"Well, Lord, boy. You can't just go marching around town with
a gun under your coat. And you especially can't go marching into
the Elm Inn with a gun under your coat, as much as you'd probably
be smart for doing so." He held out his hand. Caleb folded his arms
around the weapon in a hug. "Come on, Caleb, for safekeeping."
He sighed. "You go in there with a loaded shotgun and you better
be ready to use it."

Caleb relinquished the Ithaca to Frank, who concealed it behind
his apron and looked up and down the street. "Careful now,"
Frank said and shut the door to the hotel, leaving Caleb alone in
the quickening darkness.

He followed Frank's directions, moving among the people. He tried to watch the faces for killers that would be emerging from their dark houses at this hour, but he had trouble keeping track of everything at once—his feet, the ground made uneven by the carriages and the horses, the crowds, and the bustling noise that shrank him. A trickle of water turned Caleb's attention to a shadowed figure lurking in the space between the barbershop and the dress shop. He'd just finished urinating. He held something shiny in the crook of his arm, and he slid it into his belt. Then he hitched his pants in a way that confirmed the presence of a gun, the addition of weight exaggerating the gesture. The gloom gathered around his face and Caleb saw nothing more than the barest silhouette. He coughed, a mean explosion of noise that made Caleb hunch and duck his head, and went on his way. Caleb stowed his fears, pushed aside the Elm Inn, took a deep breath, and followed the man as he passed the church. Caleb maintained a cautious distance, afraid the man would wheel on him any second, but he was too consumed with his own lurching, uneven steps to notice a boy behind him. As they walked along, twenty feet apart, the light gave out, and the black descended like a blanket. Caleb challenged himself to keep going, his dim awareness that they were mirroring Frank's directions growing into understanding.

The Elm Inn was indeed on the side of the hill, built on stilts. The whole structure had been made of rough pine, and—even in darkness, covered in snow—it appeared prickly, laden with waiting splinters. Light poured from the windows, as did loud laughter, shouting, and music. The man staggered up the steps, and brushed past someone vomiting onto the snow from behind the railing that surrounded the porch like an ill-conceived fortress. Both men were inside before Caleb could make himself mount the steep staircase leading to the front door. It didn't take him long to sound out the first two words scorched into the very wall of the building: ELM INN. The second part he didn't even attempt: VACANCY. A small shutter hung next to the word and Caleb flipped it to the side, exposing a NO.

The main room writhed with life. The inn had a large open foyer, where men played cards like at the hotel, but here women sat on their laps, wearing small outfits. Caleb noted the heat as well, barreling out of two enormous fireplaces—one to his left and one to his right. A bar ran the length of the building, obscured by smoke from the fire, lamps, cooking, cigars, pipes, and cigarettes. Staircases on either side led up to the second story, where a walkway led to rows of closed doors. A woman opened one, a disheveled man after her. He slapped her on her bottom and she rang a bell next to her door.

"Help you, boy?" In front of Caleb, a man sat squeezed into a chair. He was enormous, the size of a bull, his sides escaping over the arms of his seat. Caleb wondered how big a man could get. On his head he wore a hat that only served to accentuate the massiveness of his skull. At his feet were the ruins of a table. On his lap he held a metal box. "I say, help you?"

"No," Caleb said, and moved to walk past him.

The man sprang up with surprising quickness and put a firm finger to Caleb's chest. "Kid, you got to pay to even see what the Elm has to offer." He shook the metal box, and it rattled with coins.

"Aw, let the boy have a peek, Ethan," a voice said from behind the mountainous man whose hand—Caleb was certain—could have shoved him right through the pine wall and all the way back to the Brick & Feather Hotel. A disappointed Ethan gave Caleb a poke that knocked him back a yard, confirming his assessment of the man's power. "Don't worry me," he said, and spat toward a metal spittoon beside the door, the ground splattered with his many attempts.

The voice that had saved Caleb belonged to the same man who'd told him to come to the Elm in the first place. Caleb prepared to reintroduce himself but became confused when he saw the man owned not one but two sturdy legs. Caleb dismissed the notion that perhaps legs could be reattached in the larger world. This man had no stubble: His face was smooth and unwrinkled. Caleb wasn't able to see his scalp through his hair, and his clothes were certainly not held together by needles. They were, in fact, the nicest clothes Caleb had ever seen. They shimmered in the lamplight, which swayed with the movement of the room. This was an entirely different man. Who happened to look almost exactly like the man his mother had chased him from earlier that day. "Has the glamour of the Elm Inn left you speechless, young one?"

"What?" Caleb said.

"My child, you look as though there's something you'd like to say."

"I met someone who looked like you," Caleb managed.

"Ah, my lovely brother," he said. "And yet here you stand." The man smiled, and Caleb smiled back, realizing he'd made a joke. He liked the way the man talked. All of his words had a kind of magic to them, almost like they were music.

"He has a wooden leg," Caleb said, thinking it a very interesting thing to say until he remembered that, of course, the man's own brother would know this fact.

Yet the man laughed and the smile never left his face. "He does, indeed." He raised his pant legs, exposing dark socks supported by black bands and metal clips. Between the two, however, was pink flesh. "I, on the other hand, do not. My young friend, have you never visited us before?"

Caleb glanced around, surprised in the calm, enveloping presence of this man to find the two of them in a flurry of activity. "No. Never."

"Well, my dear boy, there is a lot to be learned here. Do you like to learn?" Caleb nodded, and the man reached out a clean hand tipped with perfect fingernails and patted him on the head three times. "Of course you do—knowledge is the key that unlocks all of life." He turned on his heel in a manner that Caleb had never seen, a manner that he hoped to practice in his hotel room as soon as he returned. Caleb followed in his scented footsteps.

EDWARD WALLACE WAS a giant of a man. His office was an old rail car, and he dwarfed the steps leading to it. He rested both hands on his cane as he spoke to Elspeth and Charles. He sat on the top step, his knees poking up like two mountain peaks. His back contained a permanent hunch from leaning down for people to hear him. Had he been standing, Elspeth imagined, she wouldn't have been able to make out a word over the saws and picks and the squeal of pulleys.

"Kind of scrawny," he said as if she wasn't there. He reached out and squeezed her biceps twice, testing. "Seems strong, though. Sure he can work the lake?"

"Of course he can," Charles said. Elspeth was concerned, though. For the most part her injuries had mended, thanks to Margaret's care, and though she'd done her fair share of removing stumps and rocks from the fields, she wasn't sure how she would tolerate the continuous exertion. She would avoid midwifery and in exchange, she would have to keep pace. Besides, Charles wasn't that much bigger than she was, excepting his belly. She studied him quickly and rounded her shoulders and pushed her hips forward to match his.

"We certainly need the manpower. That icehouse isn't going to fill itself." Wallace's face twisted. "Charles, give us some privacy, would you please?" he said. Charles's fingers played over his hat with frenetic energy. Elspeth was sweating, tensing, ready to flee, about to be found out, a woman among the men, an impostor and a fake. Charles thanked Wallace, placed his hat back atop his head, and walked several paces. Wallace shooed at him with his cane, and Charles shuffled up the hill, away from the lake.

Wallace leaned forward on his elbows, close enough she could smell something—pipe smoke, maybe—on his clothes. "He told you about the job, correct? The dangers inherent?"

"I'm well aware. Charles laid it all out for me," she said. Wallace was unconvinced. "And I need the money." He waited some more. "I trust Charles," she said.

This satisfied him in some way, and he rapped his knuckles on the railing of the stairs, and the cast iron rang like church bells. "Good, then. Best of luck to you both. Charles has his positives, but he can also be a bit"—he thrust himself up with the power of his cane and towered over her—"odd."

The odor of woodfire drifted across them, and Elspeth couldn't help but think of her own skin to the flames.

At the top of the hill, Charles leaned on the railing of the ice-house ramp. "What'd he say?"

"I begin tomorrow," she said.

He asked her to get a drink with him. The sounds of the other men had increased in her time with Wallace; they walked up from the lake, a steady mass of them, all chatting and laughing, happy to be done for the day, their collective heat bringing a wave of steam. She agreed, and regretted it as soon as the words had left her mouth.

As they merged with the crowd, Charles explained to Elspeth—Jorah—how they cut the ice from the lake with long saws and created a channel down which they floated the blocks. He pointed to all the stations on the steely ice. He and Elspeth would probably be on the banks of the water, he said, where they picked the blocks of ice up with a set of tongs and swung them by crane and pulley to a cart that would be taken to the icehouse by horses. The canal was a black stripe against the solid surface of the lake. She answered his questions about her family with a series of masculine grunts. He spoke of his own wife and their children.

They headed into a dingy tavern and Charles ordered two whiskeys. Elspeth didn't have the head or stomach for such things, but rather than give herself away, she threw the brown liquid back with a flick of her wrist and covered the blaze in her throat with her deepest cough.

"We had a boy die in birth," he said after he'd had another drink. "The cord had been wrapped around his neck and he lived for a few days, almost a week. The whole thing just about broke my wife clean open—me, too—and we set a place at the table for him before our other boys got old enough to object." Charles bit at his nails, mind stuck at his dinner table, and drank another shot of whiskey.

Elspeth feared the sound of her own voice as the alcohol invaded her, but a cloud had settled over the two of them, and if she had spoken, she doubted he would have heard her anyway. Her thoughts—those that she kept hidden even from herself—had broken loose and she couldn't hope to stop them.

She always pictured train tracks from above, lines and circles across the land like stitches on the earth. On that morning, she'd had to run to catch the train, and a porter had helped her aboard as the cars lurched into motion, the speed pushing her onto her heels. Snow glistened with melting water as they swept past. In the lowlands, the unending sheets of white gave way to patches of yellowed grass.

As usual, she hadn't planned on taking the child. Emma had

turned two and could speak in complete sentences and move around the yard on her own. Elspeth left at the beginning of winter, and tried to find a different type of work, but everywhere she turned she was deemed unfit, unprepared, or uneducated. To her, the cries of infants sang from every door and window, slowing her steps on the plywood walkways of town, calling for her to help. Unable to ignore them any longer, she went into the doctor's office she'd been circling for days and offered her services. The next morning, she crouched in her usual position, rags at the ready, pail of hot water at her feet, gleaming tools cleaned and laid out in neat and tidy rows. Everything waited in its correct place.

On the train home—the grass patches becoming more and more scarce as the train veered north—the baby didn't move. Elspeth tickled its feet, tried to get the baby to grab onto her thumb, her nipple, anything, but the baby refused. Elspeth wished for Jorah. The children had all fallen ill at one time or another, and he had nursed them back to health with herbs and medicines he stored in jars in a trunk at the foot of their bed. The baby turned blue, the splotches of color joining and deepening, the veins dark and threatening, and Elspeth debated running into the corridor for help, but she couldn't leave the child or risk the inquiry.

She waited too long. Before nightfall, the child stopped breathing, the blue fading, leaving the skin pale and rigid. Elspeth wrapped the body in a shawl, pressed it to her shoulder as if it were alive, and walked the corridor. The motionless child that she clutched in her arms had been taken by a God seeking revenge on one who spoke His word but would not follow His direction. He had given her no hints, no signs, direct or implied, that she should take this child. And now He'd shown her what He'd do to her for ignoring His wishes.

A man passed down the aisle as she did. She rocked back and forth on her hips, and placed a finger to her mouth, asking for quiet while the baby slept. The man gave a small bow of apology and stepped into an empty compartment to allow her to pass. She came to the end of the train. The icy wind tore at her clothes like claws. Elspeth couldn't look at the swaddled child. The stars maintained a fixed position above the train as it hurtled forward. She dangled the child over the tracks. She let go. The stars did not flinch.

In the bar, the tears came again. She dipped her head low so Charles couldn't see her. Surely this would give her away. Her cheeks burned as though she stood on her barstool and shouted her transgressions into the close air of men who'd toiled all day on the lake. Time would expose her. Though when she raised her head, she saw that Charles cried for his own loss.

"I don't know why we put them through that," he said, "seeing that plate every night. Maybe we were trying to let the other boys know how lucky we all are. It's difficult to be happy with what you have, isn't it?" Elspeth couldn't begin to answer that question. Charles didn't give her a chance, ordering another round of drinks and some chicken pies. Elspeth protested that she didn't have enough money. "It's my pleasure, Jorah," he said. Had she said she needed to get back to Caleb, she assumed Charles would have slid his stool back and excused her without a word. "Hard to feel lucky in this world," he said. "But today, I am." He punched her on the shoulder. "You saved me, Jorah."

CALEB SAT IN a soft chair in a luxuriant room that had a bath in one corner, surrounded on all sides by mirrors. A woman was in the bathtub, naked, but the man he'd followed inside paid her no attention. Caleb tried to do the same. When the man in the fine clothes saw the boy's discomfort, he chuckled. "Go ahead," he said. "You can look."

Some part of Caleb wanted to, but he shook his head no.

"A man of principle," the man said. "A dying breed."

The rest of the room shone with the reflections from the water, the polished wood walls and beams glittering. Even the bed seemed radiant; the bronze had been burnished and the very sheets appeared to exude warmth. The man sat on a lounge opposite Caleb. "My name," he said as he crossed one leg over the other, "is London White."

The unmistakable crack of a gunshot sounded from the other room, followed by shuffling on the hardwood floors. Caleb flinched. White made no move.

"My brother and I were born in this town. And where are you from—?"

"Caleb Howell," he said, embarrassed by his small voice. He knew there was a slight difference between *from* and *born* and he took pains not to lie. "From a farm."

White laughed. He laughed so hard tears rolled down his face. He wiped them with a handkerchief that he produced from his pocket. When his laughter slowed, he took one look at Caleb and began again. The scuffling in the other room escalated. Solid thuds knocked dust from the walls. Caleb wished he'd brought his Ithaca.

"I'm sorry. But, yes—a farm. And are you a hard worker, Caleb?" Caleb nodded. "Don't waste much time talking, I see. That's good. A great benefit to this establishment, silence."

A picture frame slid from one of the walls and shattered on the ground. In a flash, White crossed the room and threw open the door. He was gone only a moment. When he came back, he ran a silver comb through his hair and smiled.

A few seconds later another gunshot. The noise ceased.

"Yes, the benefit of silence." White took the time to seat himself, straighten his clothes all over again, and cross his legs with perfect leisure. He drew a watch from his vest by its chain and wound it, an affectation Caleb immediately admired. "So, what brought you from your farm to my doorstep?"

Caleb knew he had the right place—the Elm Inn was indeed a home for killers. He recalled Charles Heather talking to his mother. "I think you were going to offer me a job."

"I was, was I?"

"I think so." Caleb, not sure of himself, tried to affect confidence. "You were going to pay me to work for you."

"I wasn't," White said, and extended his hand for Caleb to shake, "but I will. We reward the bold here, as you shall find." White's grip was intensely strong. "Welcome, Caleb Howell, to the Elm Inn, and all her splendors."

CHAPTER 3

That night—their first in a real bed since leaving William and Margaret—Elspeth and Caleb were both racked by nightmares. Caleb's involved dark, furtive men sneaking into his house and stealing his gun. Sometimes he would reach for it, but he could never grasp it. Others, he'd aim, only to see nothing in his hand but one of his feathers. He woke and nodded off again, a twisting, sweating sleep stalked by an animal at the edge of his vision. When he finally managed to get off a shot, he tracked its blood through the woods and the trail ended with Jorah, dying on a mound of new earth on the other side of the hill.

"They wouldn't let me have my gun back," Caleb said as soon as his mother's eyes opened. Upon reaching their room, he'd searched their packs for a weapon. He'd found the hunting knife, which he'd unsheathed and placed under his pillow. "I left my gun at the counter and when I got back, it was someone different and he didn't know where it was."

"They probably put it someplace safe," Elspeth said. The boy had dark circles under his eyes. He played with the buttons on his shirt, his nerves frayed. For Elspeth, the dreams contained bundles dumped on railroad tracks, the sheets unfurling and leaving a naked baby on the iron rails. Gusta van Tessel floated above her, her hair and thin clothing waving in a starry sky as if underwater, her lips blue. The baby's feet and arms would stir, its large eyes searching for someone to pick it up, and its mouth would open wide and let out a piercing shriek.

She tried to shake the murkiness the dreams left behind and concentrated on Caleb, his boots tapping on the floor. His brown hair uneven from Margaret's haircut, he looked small in the space of the window, sitting low on the stool. When the children were infants, life had been simple. If they cried or fussed, she fed and rocked them. She became adept at slipping them out of her arms and into their cribs without their even stirring. There were times she woke in the middle of the night to silence, and made her way across the room to linger until the child moved—a sigh, a shift, a kick. Only then could she return to Jorah. In those days, there were simple problems with simple solutions. Caleb not being able to sleep without his gun was more complex. His foot shook in his dead brother's boots—boots she'd purchased on an abbreviated trip to Betherd that Elspeth had cut short before the child had been born, before indulging again—and the leather hammered out a rhythmless beat on the floorboards. She stood up from the bed, fully dressed, smelling as if she hadn't bathed in a week, knowing it added authenticity to her disguise, and went to retrieve the boy's gun.

Not having his Ithaca had banished all else from Caleb's mind. At his mother's receding footsteps, he took the hunting knife from beneath his pillow, replaced it in its sheath, and put it back in his mother's pack, careful to restore everything to its rightful order.

She wasn't gone for more than five minutes. She handed the Ithaca to him having judged its heft automatically, as she would an infant—eight pounds—and he cradled the weapon carefully. He checked the chamber and took the cloth from his back pocket and folded it several times to find a clean square of fabric.

"I have to go to work," Elspeth said. "How do I look? Dirty enough to be a man?" Caleb tore his eyes from the Ithaca and glanced at his mother. She'd turned into someone else. Caleb said she did. Elspeth hesitated, not sure if she'd made a joke, decided she hadn't, and left the boy wiping down the barrel of his gun, as if he couldn't bear to have someone else's hands sully the steel.

CHARLES MET HER outside the hotel, holding two steaming cups. He gave one to her and she took a careful sip of thick, black coffee.

"How's your boy?" he asked.

"Fine," she said, but she worried.

The morning was late in coming, under cover of dark, roiling clouds. The air smelled like snow, and Elspeth pulled her jacket close. "You'll get used to the cold, Jorah," he said, "but we need to get you some thicker gloves. Those won't last the day." He drew a pair from his denims and slapped them into her outstretched palm. "I always bring a spare. After work I'll show you to the mercantile."

Elspeth thanked him, the cold providing the rough edge to her voice so she didn't have to. The harshness of their breath and the snow packing under their feet constituted their conversation for the rest of their walk. There wasn't a soul on the streets except the occasional man headed in the same direction.

Lanterns drew a line from the icehouse to the canal upon which the frozen blocks would soon float up to the shore. The sight of the giant cubes of ice, almost as big as a man, made the nerves in Elspeth's stomach leap into her chest. She wasn't sure she could do the job. Maybe it would expose her for the fraud she was. Maybe the company would simply fire her. Or maybe Charles would fail to lock the pincers, and the ice would tumble onto her spine, and all she would know was a faint crack.

The lights reflected off the snow and hung a series of golden domes over the beginning of the workday. Horses whinnied and stamped their hooves into the frozen ground, their tack jingling. Elspeth and Charles joined a long line of men—none of whom spoke to Charles or greeted him as they did the others, with grunts or quick words. Elspeth retied her laces and pulled at her gloves. Somehow these small gestures took the edge off her apprehension. At the end of the line stood Edward Wallace, who leaned on a cane fatter than Elspeth's arm, and, despite his crooked posture, towered over them all. He held a ledger, which he glanced at when Elspeth and Charles stepped forward. He handed them each a pair of ice cleats, a series of metal teeth with adjustable straps at the toes and heels to fasten them to their boots. "Van Tessel and Heather—the cranes," he said.

Down the embankment to the edge of the water, they stood under a large post, jammed into the earth like a false tree trunk. Fifteen feet in the air, the post formed a T with another, this one parallel to the ground, the two held together by a swiveling metal bracket. On one end of the arm was a pair of metal pincers. On the other, nearly blending into the steely clouds, was an iron bar in the shape of a cross.

FRANK HADN'T EVEN finished shaking the cold from his arms when Caleb asked him, "How did you expect me to get my gun back?"

Frank hung his coat. "Morning, Caleb. How's the room?"

Caleb ignored him and repeated his question.

"Sorry, son, I must have forgotten to tell Wilkes whose weapon it was," he said as he moved behind the counter and rearranged the items that Wilkes had shifted over the course of the night.

"But—God's honest truth—I didn't figure you'd find much at the Elm Inn worth your time. I expected you back rather quickly."

Caleb accepted this explanation, and gave Frank his empty breakfast plate. "I enjoyed the eggs." Caleb searched his pockets for the rest of the money. He'd laid the coins on the bed and arranged them by size, then memorized the numbers on their faces. He'd wanted to know which was best, what he could buy for each one, and he clinked them together in his pockets as he stood in front of Frank. "Do you know where I can buy a pistol?"

Frank dripped some oil onto a rag and began to wipe down the counter. "A pistol? Caleb, I don't know you from Adam but I have to say, I'm a Christian man, and I don't know if I should associate myself—or this hotel—with someone who carries a pistol and finds himself at the Elm Inn at all hours of the night."

Caleb knew what one would buy a pistol for, but he'd studied himself in the mirror from the time his mother left for work until breakfast, and he didn't look like one of the three men in red scarves or the men at the Elm Inn—not like a killer. He looked like a boy. Even for a boy, he thought, he didn't look dangerous.

"The type of man I'm talking about is a man looking for trouble and trouble has an easy enough time finding folks on its own." Frank scrubbed at a spot on the counter, his forearms flexing where they emerged from his rolled sleeves. "So, Caleb, sorry to say, I think you and I might be done being friendly." With that, he balled up his rag, tossed it under the counter, and walked through the door to the kitchen.

ELSPETH AND CHARLES snapped the tongs onto a block of ice, the water sloshing under their cleated boots like liquid steel. Once they had secured the teeth, they walked over to the cross and each set their grip. Leather had been wound around the bar, but it had worn out in places and torn free in others. The apparatus groaned, the ice lifted, and the water dripping from its heights froze before it hit the hard-packed snow, pinging like shot.

"Jorah," Charles began as they pushed, swinging the ice to the sled, "is your wife home waiting on you?"

Elspeth strained at the weight. The bar required both a forward and a downward force to move. She pushed harder. Her wounds yanked at her skin; the bandages constrained movement. A groan escaped from deep within her.

"I'm sorry," he said. "I don't mean to pry. Maybe another time."

The thought of divulging anything made Elspeth queasy. Her secrets threatened to burst her at the seams every day. The constant pressure had become such an accustomed part of her that to live without it, she thought, would likely deflate her and she'd collapse to the ground like an empty burlap sack.

They dropped the ice onto the sled and the memory of the strain in her muscles tried to make her arms rise. She led the way back down the incline. The apparatus whined when they pulled it along with them, empty. "I had to ask," Charles said, "because I have a soul that needs some unburdening. My own wife—my own dear wife—has been trouble for me lately." He proceeded to list his complaints with his wife—her misunderstandings of him, her distaste for his work, her desire for a more comfortable life—in such detail that Elspeth gave up on listening and his voice became another sound in the rhythm of the work—the crisp squeal of the tongs as they snapped shut, the creak of the swivel as they pushed at the bar, the panting of their breath, and the small, measured steps of their feet on the packed snow, the teeth on their soles biting into the ice.

WITH HIS CONCENTRATION divided by every new man coming in the door, Caleb was not an attentive sweeper. Several times London White whisked past and pointed to a section of floor blemished by a small nest of hair or a clump of dirt. Eventually he took Caleb by the hips and moved him over to a splatter of cigar ashes. "How's your eyesight, Caleb?" he asked, and waved a hand in front of his face.

For much of the early morning, Caleb had debated whether or not to come to the Elm and begin work, but he always drew the same conclusion: There was nowhere else he would be able to observe the killing kind in such obscurity. Frank had said nothing from the counter as he'd slipped past, and London White had only pulled a pocket watch from his vest to comment on Caleb's tardiness.

Caleb toiled upstairs, supposedly sweeping the walkway that was lined with rooms identified by swirling, golden numbers affixed to the doors. The bells chimed irregularly in the morning, far from the symphonic clamor of ringing at night. From inside the rooms came muffled moans and rhythmic thumping that Caleb pretended not to hear. He had a notion of what happened between the ringing of the bells, but thinking about it made his eyes go blurry, so he pictured the killers. When the customers exited the rooms, some flushed and hurried, others languorous—as if they'd eaten a large and satisfying meal—Caleb would bend over his broom, pretending to inspect the floor, sneaking only a glance at their walk or their hair, trying to fit them with red scarves.

The panorama of the Elm Inn was best viewed from the walkway, and Caleb swept it again and again. There were half a dozen tables for cards, and the tinkling of coins being tossed on them could be heard under the constant roar of conversation and the

occasional disagreement. It was still early—the weak winter sun
trickled through the filmy windows—and White had told Caleb
not to worry about gunfire until the liquor had more time to
work. Caleb acted as if he knew what this meant. Women cir-
culated among the tables, and Caleb avoided looking at their ill-
fitting attire and the bodies they barely restrained. These women
were shaped differently than his mother or his sisters, rounder,
more fleshy. They brought drinks to the men, played with their
hair, sat on their laps, and whispered into their ears. Caleb's embarrassment made it easy to give his attention to the men, who
watched one another with wary glances. Many looked like the
raccoon Caleb had impaled in the horses' stall, their expressions
wild, their bodies plagued by nervous tics. Each carried the kind
of weight in his shoulders that bowed his back and hid his face
from the world. Caleb thought he would know one of the killers
if he saw them, that he would feel it as clearly as if he'd leapt into
icy water. No one in the Elm Inn gave him that shudder. Some,
however, struck a deep fear in his heart. One customer, frustrated
by something unknown that happened behind one of the closed
doors, caught sight of him on the upper walkway, the first time
someone besides White or Ethan had taken any notice of him, and
Caleb scurried in the other direction, lamely passing the broom
behind him. The man's longer strides caught up with him, and he
rammed his elbow into Caleb's back hard enough to knock the
broom from his hand and send it clattering over the railing and
onto a handful of patrons waiting at the bar. "Watch yourself,
boy," he said and tromped down the stairs.

Caleb heard a yell of annoyance and pressed his back to the
wall, out of sight from the floor below. London White came up the
stairs, broom in hand. He considered it, passing it from one palm

to the other. Caleb knelt and swept the last of the dirt into his hand. He didn't know what to do with it—he had been sweeping it up against the walls between the doors, rather than onto the card players and women below—so he dumped it into his pocket.

"When I was your age," London White began, making it clear he'd paid no attention to Caleb's work habits, "I was like my brother, living in the woods, making moonshine to sell to thirsty travelers, eating whatever we could catch—possums, rabbit, squirrel." He winced. "Then I sold a jar full of our best to a man in a nice suit. He rode the finest horse I'd ever seen. He wore the finest clothes. We feared men like that. Sometimes we'd give them our product for free." He wrung the broom handle with his fists. "Imagine that— the ones who could truly afford our wares and we'd give it to them for nothing because we were scared. I didn't like that feeling. Not at all." His knuckles went white. "I followed him home. He lived in a gorgeous house—windows and ceilings like a church, walls and floors as resplendent as the most magnificent of palaces. He had a beautiful wife—red hair to her shoulders, skin white as snow. Do you know what I did?"

Caleb shook his head. He could feel the dirt sifting through a hole in his pocket and trailing down his leg, tickling him. A smile began to creep across his face.

"I snuck into their bedroom at night and cut both their throats," White said.

Caleb repressed a burning urge to run. He had to stay. The knowledge that he was standing with and working for a murderer didn't shock him; it only confirmed his suspicion that he was in the right place. What did surprise him was his appearance. Caleb squinted at White, the outline of his jaw, the proud way he held his head, his upright bearing, and knew he'd never seen him flit across the frozen landscape from the hole in the barn. White was one of them, but a different breed.

"Was it the right thing to do?" He leaned on the railing. "Most would say no. But as I lived in their house and ate their food, my fear was gone. We do what we have to do so we can be unafraid." Caleb observed London White further: the precisely folded kerchief, the watch chain that dangled in an exacting crescent, the brightly, exhaustively polished shoes, the neatly combed hair. "And you, Caleb, I think you know that." He chuckled to himself. "One step ahead already. I knew it when you asked me—no, told me—that I was going to give you a job." He glanced at Caleb out of the corner of his eye and a glint of a smile flirted across his lips. "You're not afraid, are you?"

Caleb knew he needed to grow accustomed to lying. "No. I'm not." He saw an opportunity present itself. "I need to know something."

White patted Caleb on the shoulder. "Good boy."

"I need to buy a pistol."

White straightened Caleb's collar, buttoned an additional button on his shirt. "What you need is some new clothes. I shall bring you some." He licked his palm and smoothed Caleb's hair. "Shirt, pants, a new jacket."

"I don't need a new jacket," Caleb said forcefully.

White seemed to weigh his response. "Okay, Caleb." He picked a stray hair from his shirt and blew it from between his fingers. "A pistol? Whatever for?"

White turned to the front door, where there stood a stocky man with a wide smile and a nose that even from the upper floor could be seen as crooked, broken many times over. White licked his hand again, but this time patted down his own hair and adjusted his suit.

"Owen Trachte, in flesh and blood," White said, loud enough for the man to hear. "Polish the railings next," he said to Caleb, before descending the stairs. Owen looked to Caleb like a new kind of man—something he'd never seen before, different, even from London White. He didn't have White's smooth confidence, or the silent strength Caleb saw in his father, or the friendly openness of Frank at the Brick & Feather Hotel. Owen bore with him something different, a naked anger that Caleb thought, at unguarded moments, might be found on his own face.

Her hands raw and screaming with coin-size blisters, Elspeth sat next to Charles and sipped from a stein of beer. She didn't wish to go back to the hotel to that sad boy sitting on the stool with his rifle in his lap, waiting for a group of killers to pass beneath his window. So she occupied the same chair in the same bar from the previous evening, listening to Charles talk more about his life. He told her he'd come to this part of New York from the coast of Massachusetts, where his family had lived for generations, a long line of fishermen and whalers. He told her of the ocean, of going out in a ship as a boy until he could see nothing but the enormity of the world; how the calm seas exposed the curve of the earth, which dizzied him and made him afraid he could slide off at any moment. The Heather blood—his father had told him—did not run strong in his veins. Land, he said, was where Charles would need to make his way. And so he left Massachusetts to escape the constant lapping pull of the sea.

Like Elspeth, he'd traveled all over New York, seen much of the state—the mountains, the mighty river to the north, the vast stretches of green land between. But the shore of the lake, he said, had felt like home. The wind-powered waves were more than large enough for him. He'd been to Erie's center and jumped into the gray water and had been unafraid. The town's almost constant cloud cover suited him, as did the way the snows could move in without warning and alter the earth in minutes. "It struck me," he said, "as a good place to hide." He stroked his red beard. His moustache was frosted with ale. He smiled at Elspeth. "It's good to talk," he said.

"You didn't talk before?" Elspeth said. "To the man who was injured?"

Charles stared into his beer for a long time. Elspeth almost asked the question again before he said, "I guess Ben and I were never all that close." Elspeth thought maybe she'd spoken out of turn, that perhaps the accident had been worse than she'd imagined. The drink had worn them both down; their edges had softened and their usual care had eroded. "I have to apologize," he said. "I lied to you." He looked up at the ceiling. "About the Bible pages. My mother didn't put them on the windows of my bedroom." He traced his finger around the rim of his glass. "She put them in the outhouse. It got so stiflingly hot in there in the summer."

The admission made her laugh. It took effort for her to suppress her real laughter and move it down a register. Charles joined her. "Did you tell Ben that?" she said, thinking she continued the joke, but Charles stopped laughing abruptly. He drank for a long time, his Adam's apple rising and falling with each swig. "What about your wife? How did the two of you meet one another?"

It was Elspeth's turn to gulp down some more of her ale. "That's a long story," she said. The truth fluttered around inside her throat like a butterfly and she needed to leave before it flew out on its own. She gathered her coat. "For another time."

Charles begged for her to stay. "What about the gloves? We were going to buy you more gloves."

"The mercantile is open at this hour?" she said. The windows reflected the two of them, hunched over the bar. Beyond that, pitch-dark.

Charles's glance outside made him appear offended by the passage of time. "You're welcome to use mine long as you need them," he said. "After all, I owe you." Charles drained the rest of his drink, leaving nothing but froth dancing at the bottom of his mug. He signaled for the barkeep, who stepped out from the shadows and slid another beer in front of him, foam climbing over the sides and down his fingers as he grasped it. "Fatherhood," he said. "It's a wonderful thing, isn't it?" Charles's voice had taken on a new shape, something harder and sharper. "You have a nice boy. He's handsome and polite—much like you. A good boy." He spun a coin on the bar and snatched it up in his fist. "You've done well for yourself, van Tessel, you and your wife."

Elspeth thought of Jorah's countless hours reading to the children, schooling them, teaching them the ways of the world as best he could. He practiced long into the night in the living room— she could hear him parsing out the passages of the Bible, the thin pages crackling as he turned them. Caleb didn't figure into those memories; he'd been in the barn, where his small bed took up a tiny fraction of the huge building, alone in the loft, the hay heaped around him, thick and thin by season.

"You should get back to your wife and children, and I should get back to my son," Elspeth said, and rose unsteadily from her stool. As she left the tavern, she heard Charles slam down his mug and call for another drink.

CALEB HURRIED TOWARD the Brick & Feather—hoping to reach their room before his mother—but his head spun with lack of sleep.

Breathless, he sat on a windowsill to rest when he saw Frank on the other side of the thoroughfare. Caleb shook at the prospect of crossing the street, loaded as it was with horses and men and all their implements. He collected his courage and ran across the road, passing between two carriages, one holding a young couple, and the other loaded with firewood.

"Hello, Frank," Caleb said as he caught up to the man's long strides.

Frank, grim, tipped his hat but said nothing. He stopped in front of the barbershop. A horse whinnied from the post, and Caleb stroked its mane. The horse nuzzled against him in the crook between his neck and shoulder. He wondered how his animals had fared with the doors to the barn open, the weather invading, and the food scarce. "I'm sorry," Caleb said.

"You don't have anything to be sorry for."

The horse nipped playfully at Caleb's ear, and he ducked his head away. "I mean, I think you've got things wrong."

"Do I now?"

"I was raised on a farm, just me and my family. Some man in the woods told me to go to the Elm Inn, so I thought I should go." Frank glanced into the street in a manner that Caleb took for caution at being seen with him. "It's terrible," Caleb said, and he meant it. "Frightening." He next used a phrase his father had reserved for the worst the boys could do—like when Jesse broke the girls' dollhouse fighting with Amos, or when Amos had persuaded Caleb to jump from the loft door using only Elspeth and Jorah's pillows to cushion his fall. Caleb's deepest memory of the words, however, occurred when one night Jorah had told the story of the tower of Babel to the girls, who had said it reminded them of Caleb. Usually this sort of application pleased Jorah, who would praise the girls for finding the Bible in their lives. But this time he went quiet. They asked why they couldn't understand Caleb and he couldn't seem to understand them. Then their father said that if they didn't act, Caleb might be one of them. Outside the window, Caleb cringed at his words. "God help the heathens."

Frank slipped the hat from Caleb's head and laughed. "You cannot keep walking around looking like this." He steered Caleb inside.

A bell sounded as they entered. In the center of the barbershop, a thin man slept in a worn leather chair next to the woodstove, a book in his lap. His sleeves were rolled to his biceps, and he wore black suspenders and red striped pants. He snored lightly. Caleb didn't wonder why: The heat and the soothing smells in the room made his eyelids heavy as well.

Frank gave the man a small shake. "Teddy," he said. The barber opened his eyes. He licked his finger and placed the mark in his book. "Have time for two?" Frank asked, and Teddy noticed Caleb for the first time.

"Who've we got here?" Teddy asked and stretched. With a yawn, he brushed the chair clean as Frank introduced Caleb. Teddy took the blade to the strop, sliding it back and forth, and asked after Frank's wife.

"She's as big as a house," Frank replied. "But she's well. She sends her love."

"It's going to be a boy, Frankie, I know it," Teddy said, "and I've never been wrong. Have I?" He pointed a pair of scissors at Caleb, and Caleb shook his head no. "See, even the boy knows."

"My wife is expecting," Frank explained to Caleb, and answered his question before he could ask. "We're having a baby. Cut the boy's hair first, if you could."

"Of course. It's my policy to only nick the last shave of the day."

"I must always be last then." They laughed. Caleb liked how they talked and smiled at their jokes. Frank looked at ease as he held his palms out to warm at the fire.

Caleb hopped up into the chair. The barber put a sheet around him, and—as he got a closer look—asked, "Who did this to your head?"

"A nice old woman," Caleb said, "that my father and I met on our way here."

"She may have been nice," Teddy said, "but she didn't see too well."

He splashed a liberal amount of oil onto Caleb's scalp, passed his comb through it twice, very slowly, then began cutting. The hair fell in clumps onto Caleb's lap. He used to stand in line with his brothers and sisters when his father—always on a rainy day—cut their hair. Sometimes he told them the story of Samson, others he would recite Psalms, "*For innumerable evils have compassed me about: mine iniquities have taken hold upon me, so that I am not able to look up; they are more than the hairs of mine head: therefore my heart faileth me,*" or "*They that hate me without a cause are more than the hairs of mine head: they that would destroy me, being mine enemies wrongfully, are mighty: then I restored that which I took not away,*" and tell the children with a smile that by cutting their hair he was ridding them of enemies and iniquities at the same time. It was one of the only jokes his father ever told.

The night his father had killed a man, he'd paused in the tall grass when he'd heard Caleb's footsteps, and Caleb could see the clouds of his father's breath slow and then stop as he listened, everything made silver by the moonlight. The rain washed the blood from the grass, but it didn't erase what Caleb had witnessed. Two days later, the man dead and hidden away, Caleb walked about in a fever, and when he went into the house for lunch, his father was there, sharpening a knife. Caleb froze. He assumed his father knew he'd been the one in the woods with him.

"Shall I cut your hair today, Caleb?" his father asked, drawing the blade down the whetstone. Jorah did not ask questions in a manner that required an answer, but when Caleb said no, afraid of sitting under his father's eye, beneath the knife he wielded so effortlessly, Jorah went back to sharpening the blade. That evening, frightened of his reaction when his father performed his nightly sermon, he pretended to be late and waited for the prayer to end before he entered the kitchen. His father had glared at him with fire. A moment later, however, his look changed, softened, as if Jorah understood him in some small way, yet Caleb's fear never left.

"You okay, son?" Teddy asked. "You're shaking." Their voices faded. "Has he eaten today?"

He hadn't since breakfast—Elspeth's money had not lasted long—and being in the warmth of the barbershop with its pleasing scents and the rhythm of the scissors in his ears and the reassuring pressure on his scalp had made him groggy. The memories of his father were the last thing he thought of before he slid off the seat, dropping into a soft mat of hair.

ELSPETH CARRIED A small bag of licorice as an offering to the boy. The beds were made, and the room was cold; he hadn't been there in hours. The man at the front desk, Wilkes—the very same who'd held Caleb's shotgun—said he hadn't seen Caleb all day. Then he said, almost under his breath, "Suppose he could be at the Elm Inn."

"What did you say?"

"Nothing," he said, and smirked, but when he saw Elspeth's face, he no longer found it funny. "Frank told me your son asked for directions to the Elm Inn. That's when Frank took his gun. I figured you knew." Wilkes coughed. "The Elm Inn, sir, is a house . . . A place where men meet women."

He offered directions without her having to ask.

Obviously Caleb had listened to the man in the woods, with his rank breath and wooden leg. She ran despite the soreness from working the crane, the pain in her side growing and throbbing like a living thing. Though it slowed her, she didn't stop. She took the steep steps two at a time, rushed past the scorched wood confirming she had the right place, and opened the door.

The doorman—his mass dwarfing the chair upon which he sat—merely tapped the money box on his lap. The dim room and smoky haze took a minute to get used to and the first thing she saw when her eyes adjusted was Owen Trachte. She knew him instantly; he possessed the stubbed features and square shoulders of his father. The thought of Phillip Trachte, Watersbridge's only doctor twelve years prior, took Elspeth's breath away as swiftly as the kick of a mule. Elspeth hadn't had time to worry herself with being recognized, but her past had stepped out of the murk to remind her of her sins. The room grew hot and blurred, the details melting away.

"Help you, fella?" Ethan said, perhaps seeing the pallor on Elspeth's face.

"No." She collapsed into one of the upholstered chairs around the entryway. She loosened the scarf at her neck and tore the hat from her head.

The doorman looked at her sideways. "Ain't no resting place."

Elspeth's breath raced away from her, faster and faster until her lungs squeezed shut and her eyes searched the room for relief.

"Hey, hey, hey," the doorman said. He disappeared out of the clear center of Elspeth's vision and into the smudged periphery. He came back with two glasses, one filled with whiskey, the other cloudy water. She drank them between gasps, the liquid escaping out the corners of her mouth. He told her how much she owed him for the whiskey and then asked, "You seen a ghost or something?"

Elspeth didn't admit to him he might as well be right. Though she relived her sins daily, the memories had a gauzy quality to them, like a story she'd read a long time ago. Phillip Trachte had placed Caleb in her hands, but she'd lost many of the particulars to time. Owen hadn't been there, though he'd been a constant presence at Phillip's side. Owen's mother had died when he was small, but his faint memories of her and their false promise gave the boy an unsettling edge. His rigid posture always carried threat. On the seldom occasions when he was not allowed into the room with his father, he would lash out, breaking a glass or plate or stealing something from the jacket of an expectant parent. Elspeth couldn't recall how she knew this; she certainly had not witnessed it herself, but she figured that Phillip had told her of it. This adult Owen laughed, and she saw the gap in his smile where one of his friends had knocked his front tooth out with a fire poker. They'd been dueling—something picked up from a story Phillip had read to them. Elspeth had been in the office putting away an armful of supplies when she heard the roar of Owen's temper, the clash of weapons, and then his small, surprised yelp.

She understood why Caleb had gone to the Elm Inn. For Owen Trachte could only have grown into the type of man that associated with thieves and killers, exactly the type of man Caleb hoped to find. Somewhere in the sound of the bells chiming, chips falling, cards shuffling, matches striking, men yelling, and glasses breaking, she could hear his laugh. It had not changed. It, too, carried a tinge of violence. She fled from the building, dropping whatever money she had into the giant man's hands on the way out.

CHAPTER 5

The week passed quickly. More often than not, Elspeth vomited in the morning from the intensity of her soreness. But she grew used to the constant dull pain in her arms and the searing heat in her chest, and became unaware of their comings and goings. She and Charles developed a comfortable rhythm, despite his frequent tardiness to work and strange silences. Owen Trachte had not reappeared, and she convinced herself that he wouldn't be able to see past time and her disguise to recognize her. Yet the expectation of punishment stayed with her always.

On Saturday, Elspeth bought a dusty used suit from the tailor in town. She couldn't let him take her measurements—she said she was in a hurry—and so the suit did not fit well: It drooped from her shoulders like a wilted flower, but fit snugly on her hips when the jacket was buttoned. She hadn't realized how much she'd enjoyed the freedom of a dress prior to the last few days. Pants were constricting to her, and she had altered her way of walking, keeping her steps short and choppy, as if she always trod on the ice beneath the crane.

Sunday morning, she took a well-needed bath. The tub was ringed with dirt and she filled it again with clean water and washed a second time. Her hair refused to believe she was a man and she cut it with a straight razor and a pair of scissors she borrowed from Frank.

The process of bandaging her wounds had become less arduous and less gruesome. Scabs had knitted their way over the punctures. She applied a foul-smelling salve purchased—along with her own pair of gloves—at the mercantile and wrapped herself in bandages, tight enough that her breasts were no longer visible. A small dab of shoe polish wiped along her chin and jaw and washed away gave the faint impression of a possible beard. The tie took most of her time. She'd asked the tailor if he knew of a good way to teach a young boy the various knots, and the tailor had kindly given her a small pamphlet with drawings showing each step with looping arrows that represented the movements. Even so, it took her half an hour before the tie looked presentable. At last, she pulled on the suit jacket, leaving it unbuttoned.

She didn't ask Caleb to accompany her to church. She had always assumed Jorah knew the reason for Caleb's lack of God, but she'd never asked. Perhaps next week, when she could describe the service to him, she would ask why he'd waited outside—even in rain or snow—until they'd finished their prayers and why he would stare at his plate or his shoes when Jorah recited scripture.

Her clean skin tingled in the cold air. She tromped along the walkway, the boards echoing under her boots—shoes being too expensive but the boots cleaned and shined until the leather looked presentable—alongside others dressed in their best approximation of finery, something always amiss: a dirty cheek, a torn jacket, pants too large, shirt too small. In the other direction came the sodden; one drunk weaved close enough to Elspeth that she held out her arms to fend him off, the loose sleeves of her suit flailing, but he veered away at the last second. She wondered how many had spent their night and their money at the Elm Inn.

At the end of the green, the church glowed in the early morning sun, white and radiant. The golden cross shined with a godly luster, and the townspeople marched toward it like columns of ants. Elspeth followed the man in front of her into the church, down the aisle, and into a pew. The bench whined under their weight. Inside the church was bigger than it appeared outside, forty feet from ceiling to floor. On either side of the pews, stained-glass windows depicted the stories of the Bible: Noah and the flood, Moses and the burning bush, the beheading of John the Baptist, and the transformation of water into wine. She found comfort in their presence, recollecting Jorah's voice reciting the tales. The air heated with the congregants, who huddled in the front pews while the rear of the church remained empty. A balcony provided more unneeded seating. The organ began to play the processional and this calmed her enough that she shut her eyes. She sensed the choir, the deacons, and the minister shuffle past on the aisle.

A hand clasped her shoulder. Charles had made his way down the pew. People squeezed and shifted, and Charles sat pressed against her. "Morning, Jorah" was all he could say before the minister, an older man with intense green eyes, took the pulpit. Elspeth could smell the alcohol on Charles's breath, but he watched the minister with great concentration.

Throughout the service, she stole glances at Charles—his skin peeling from the wind and cold, his beard tangled—but if he noticed, he avoided her gaze and maintained his focus on the pulpit. During a sermon that detailed the travels of the three kings, and the hardships one must endure to reach a destination, it was as though God talked to her in particular. When the minister stabbed the air with a finger to emphasize a point, she felt put upon, attacked. Charles grasped her hand. His quick pulse thudded against her fingers.

His mother left Caleb a sheet of paper with a crude drawing of a church on it. His family used to sit in the main room while Jorah read from the Bible, his demeanor changing from peaceful to hostile as the day progressed. When Caleb had stopped attending, Jorah had said nothing, though he saved chores one could do alone and Caleb spent the day working.

Frank was not at the front desk of the Brick & Feather and Wilkes always eyed him with suspicion, so Caleb ate breakfast alone. The eggs were tough and cold, and the bacon had been overcooked as well, crumbling in his fingers. When he finished, he slipped his hat on low, and stepped out into the busy world.

Frank had told Caleb that the only things open on Sunday—Caleb knew he would avoid mention of the Elm Inn—were the Brick & Feather, the church, and the mercantile, which was run by Jews. Caleb didn't think he'd ever seen a Jewish person before and peered through the windows. A boy his age swept the floors. He looked normal, if a bit adult, dressed in an apron and neat clothing. A bell rang over Caleb's head when he passed through the door. He slipped down one of the aisles so he could watch the boy at his work. The owner of the store, who sometimes ate breakfast at the hotel, a thickly moustached man with bulging arms and stout shoulders—in direct contrast to the long and elegant building that housed his home and his livelihood—stood behind the counter, writing notes in a catalogue. He wiped his moustache with a napkin. Caleb knew at first glance that this was the boy's father—the boy was a moustacheless, smaller version of him. All the children, all of Caleb's brothers and sisters, had looked different. When Caleb saw Elspeth, he saw some of himself. Jorah, on the other hand, bore no resemblance to Caleb whatsoever. Nor to his siblings.

He walked purposefully to the display of pistols and ammunition. He studied the guns. The man noticed Caleb, cleared his throat, put the catalogue under the counter, and walked slowly toward him.

"In the market for a pistol, son?"

The word caused Caleb a slight pang. He looked from the man to his son and knew beyond a doubt that whatever Jorah Howell had been, he had never been his father. "I need a gun."

"How about the Colt?" the man said. "A fine pistol. Very fine." He removed one of the revolvers from the case and flipped open the cylinder. He handed Caleb the gun grip first. "I have to warn you, even a used Colt pocket thirty-two, which is what you have in your hands, is going to cost you almost ten dollars. Right now we're running short on the Army model—it's our most popular pistol—but that's twelve dollars, new. No one ever sells us back a used Army model. Do they, Seth?"

Caleb couldn't look at them, father and son, to see how the boy answered. The pistol was heavy, substantial, and as clean as if it had never been touched by human hands. Caleb saw how filthy his fingers were and blushed. He clicked the cylinder into place and aimed down the barrel of the gun at a bag of oats at the other end of the store. He placed the Colt back onto the glass case and rattled the money in his pocket. He had just over two dollars.

"May I ask how old you are? Maybe you'd like to come back with your father."

Caleb caressed the gun, but didn't pick it up again. "I hoped to buy it as a Christmas present. For my father." It surprised him how easily the lie came; it had jumped up from his throat like a hiccup. Before Caleb had slept in the barn, before he'd become the caretaker of the animals, during the bleary, sleepless nightmare days, Amos had taken one of the feathers Caleb kept in his pocket and scampered from the loft and toward the house, saying he was going to tell their father that Caleb was playing with girl's things. Caleb had slid down the ladder after him, but by the time he reached the barn door, Amos had almost made it inside the house, so Caleb, without thinking, picked up a rock and threw it. It sailed willfully toward the kitchen window, made a neat hole in one of the panes and landed, apparently, next to Emma, who'd been seated on the floor, painting a face on a corn-husk doll. Caleb had sprinted back into the barn, and disappeared into the darkness of a cow stall, where he hid between two of the giant beasts that regarded him with sidelong glances and absentminded chewing.

He heard his father's footsteps, moving with the same inevitable will as the rock, coming closer and closer. The cows—who didn't yet know Caleb as they soon would—betrayed him and moved to the edge of the stall, thinking they were about to be fed, leaving him standing alone. He fumbled with the latch.

"Caleb," Jorah said. Only a few weeks prior, Caleb had hiked to that square plot of land cloaked by gnarled moosewood, the newly turned earth smelling of spring, the murder fresh in his mind, and he didn't know which version of his father would appear to him: The one that regarded him with sadness or the one that set upon him with anger. Caleb shuffled to his punishment.

"Caleb, why did you throw a rock at your brother?"

Caleb tried to lie. He searched his mind for a good reason, a better reason than the one he had. Instead, he told his father most of the truth. He only omitted that without sleep, he'd been making strange decisions for days, forgetting to give water to the cows, dumping the slop bucket in with the horses. He expected fire and brimstone but his father only quoted, *"He shall cover thee with his feathers, and under his wings shalt thou trust: his truth shall be thy shield and buckler."* Jorah waited. "Do you know what that means, Caleb?"

This time he'd lied. He couldn't face his father any longer and he'd said that he understood and he was sorry. Jorah's mouth had flapped open and shut a few times, but then he'd breathed out of his nose and simply strode away.

In front of the gun counter, Caleb fumed at how all of his lies seemed to originate from Jorah, a web spinning ever outward. "My father has always wanted a Colt," he said. "My mother died"—here the shopkeeper covered his mouth with his hand—"and I thought I could do something special for Christmas." Caleb sweated with wickedness, but he didn't think he could be good again without these wicked ways and the purpose they were to serve. Moreover, it seemed to him that no one told the truth, and the more time he spent in this large world, the less he felt beholden to do so himself.

"That's surely understandable," the man said, and glanced at his son. "We do have a credit policy here. It's usually only reserved for our long-standing customers." Beneath his moustache, he smiled. "But you have a trustworthy face."

A small piece of Caleb, a sliver, wanted to warn the man, wanted his plans to be discovered, to receive his punishment, even as the shopkeeper leaned on the counter and went through the merits of each and every Colt pistol. He told Caleb what kind of game could be taken down with each one. Caleb saw the men again. The gangly one he would shoot like a deer, the bearded one a moose, the smooth, long-haired one a mountain lion. He listened to the descriptions of the guns, and he imagined each in his fist, making up for the failure of a man he'd mistakenly called father.

AT THE END of the service, Elspeth and Charles stepped out into the bright light of day. They squinted. New snow made the world ache. "Where's your wife?" Elspeth said. "Your family?"

Charles scuffed his feet in the snow. Other churchgoers milled about them, tying their scarves around their necks and buttoning their coats. Men draped shawls over women's shoulders. Charles itched at his beard. "If there was ever a time and place to tell the truth," he said, then trailed off. "They've gone away."

"Away? When will I get to meet them?"

"They're visiting her parents. It's nice, I think, for children to understand their family, where they come from."

Elspeth agreed. The minister shook hands along his way out of the church, and Charles removed his hat once more. Elspeth reached out to comfort Charles and squeezed his forearm. She had forgotten herself and squeezed harder, in what she hoped was a manly way.

"How about I buy you those gloves now? I'd be happy to. The store's open."

Elspeth held up hands covered in new gloves. The leather smelled fresh. She said she'd bring him his old gloves and he told her not to bother. They ran out of conversation. Wind channeled through the graveyard. The snow was stripped from the tops of the graves, leaving them bald and dark against the white backdrop.

"Do you think God can really forgive us our sins?" Charles asked.

"I hope so," Elspeth said. They faced the rows and rows of headstones, each lost in their own thoughts, Elspeth desperate to be overwhelmed by faith as elusive as the light through the trees.

IN THE LOBBY of the hotel, Caleb idly flipped through the pages of a newspaper, unable to read much of it. The Colt pistol he had tucked into his pants at the small of his back. Six bullets occupied the cylinder. He kept another dozen in his pocket. The shopkeeper had been kind enough to sell him a new Colt Army pistol for the price of a used one, and then had insisted on wrapping the gift. As Caleb had ripped the paper and hidden the empty box and the rest of the ammunition underneath his bed, his hands had felt like those of someone else, and the only thing that had returned them to his body was reloading the pistol again and again.

Elspeth surprised him by pulling a chair up next to his. They each sat in their own preoccupations. Elspeth felt like she was cooking a huge meal and every pot and pan, every kettle and dish, boiled over and she couldn't get to any of them in time. She didn't have enough arms, and couldn't make anything quiet down long enough to gather her thoughts. She saw the paper in front of him and pulled it toward her. She found an article about the gold rush in Klondike Creek and read it aloud. Neither listened much to the descriptions of the hordes of men driven by the promise of an easier life to the dangerous wilds of Canada, but the steady flow of words made them each retreat farther into the cushions.

Caleb examined his mother. Their hair was similar—hers a bit darker, but it fell in the same waves, contained similar cowlicks. His nose could be hers, but they were common, sloping and unobtrusive features. His eyes were brown and farther apart; hers were gray as the winter sky. She had his high, pronounced cheekbones, though her face was less angular. Still, he thought, he belonged to her.

CHAPTER 6

That night Elspeth dreamt of Charles. She sat in her rocking chair, watching out the window of the farmhouse. The day had just started and she could see the brightness expand on the landscape in front of her. Charles materialized at the trailhead, his back bent by a heavy, black bag. As he approached, his steps burdened, he passed a depression that burst with red ribbons unfurling across the snow, rolling endlessly, and the whole hill became covered in crimson silk. She met him at the door. They kissed.

When she woke, she still felt his lips on hers. She wiped her mouth with the back of her hand and washed her face, but it could not rid her of the echo.

Caleb slouched against the wall, checking the street, his pillow propped up behind him. In the darkness, his eyes were gaunt and sunken, as if the effort of watching had hollowed them out. "Where did you get those clothes?" she asked, noting the new shirt and pants, neither of which had been patched and repatched.

"The man at the Elm Inn gave them to me for work."

"Work?" she said. Despite the outfit, he looked poor and frayed at the edges.

"I'm only sweeping and cleaning up," he said. He couldn't believe how much his mother resembled a man, with her hair cut short, Jorah's old clothes, and the rinsed shoe polish shadowing her jaw. Something about her, however, a leftover twinge of pain or some unfound piece of shotgun pellet, worried him. He longed to tell her he'd been the one to shoot her, but in their rushed bursts of time together he couldn't work up the courage. "It's the best place to find them."

Her head fuzzy from sleep, she didn't know at first what he meant.

"The killers," he said.

Elspeth straightened the sheets and then the faded pink quilt on her thin mattress. The clock downstairs rang the hour. "I'm late," she said, and bound her breasts and dressed in a hurry, her back to the boy.

OUTSIDE, CHARLES WAITED with a cup of coffee. They stood for a minute, both facing the empty street, covered over once again with a thick coating of snow. The images of the dream roiled in her head.

"I can't wait for my family to return," Charles said before the door had even shut behind her. "My boys. I miss my boys. Graham's laugh—have I told you about Graham's laugh?" He had, but Elspeth had come to like hearing his stories, the way his whole body became involved, swaying, hands gesturing, feet stomping. "When they were small, his brother Stephen pulled his arm from the socket—it hung there loose as an empty sleeve—and I had a hard time popping it back in, because every time I did, he would scream and I would try to lessen the pain and end up not going quite far enough. My wife got the idea of distracting him, and she tickled under his chin, and soon we were all laughing—Graham's like a bird tweeting, high and fast—and I popped the arm back in." His smile vanished. "Graham got upset. 'You tricked me,' he said. And we had. But he only blamed me. It was always my fault." He coughed, expelling a thick cloud. "I'd forgotten that."

"You're a good father," Elspeth said. "Blame is difficult to maneuver."

He walked the rest of the way sullen and detached.

Jorah had never blamed Elspeth. Not fully. Perhaps he thought it their cross to bear together, but Elspeth knew they could not have children because of her. Dr. Forbes had told her so. He hadn't seen her in nearly a year, though his manner betrayed no surprise at her sudden visit. "I expected you might ask," he said. "I remember our conversations well." All of her hinting around had not gone unnoticed, apparently, and yet that was not the worst of his news: He had no remedies, no prescriptions, and no cures.

The men swung poles at the ice, undoing the night's slow, steady stitching over the wound they'd carved in the lake. The cracks echoed up the hill. The lamps hissed, hanging in a line from the icehouse down to the shore. The men on the lake worked in darkness, and with each passing day, Elspeth thanked God that she and Charles worked on the crane, near a bright light. They waited, drinking their coffee, hoping to time their last hot sip with the call to work. Until the men had cleared the canal and began sawing the blocks of ice out from the expanding hole in the lake, they had little to do. When the first block had been cut, they'd go to the water's edge, where the temperature plunged, to free the crane's joints and hinges from the coat of ice that had sealed them fast. They would strap on their cleats and jump up and down to get their blood circulating. In the same way, a man named Daniel patted the horses, shifted the blankets on their flanks, rolled and rubbed their leg muscles between his palms, trying to keep them warm until the first sled had been filled. The Friday before, one of the horses had pulled up lame on the first haul, and Daniel had screamed at Charles and Elspeth for overloading the sled. Daniel whispered close to one of the horse's ears, and Elspeth thought of how Caleb would excel at such a job. Much more fitting, certainly, than the Elm Inn.

"Jorah van Tessel," a voice said behind them. It was Edward Wallace. "I didn't realize you were paid to stand and do nothing. Charles Heather, on the other hand"—he rapped Charles's knuckles with his cane—"has earned a great deal of money for doing nothing."

"They're not finished clearing the canal," Charles said.

Wallace glared toward the shore. "Go help out in the icehouse until the flow starts. Be useful, Heather." He walked to his office, covering the ground in a few strides, cane knocking on the ice, bowing to squeeze through the door.

The icehouse was lined with stone and coal. Small gaps in the wood allowed air to circulate, keeping the room from retaining any heat. From the doorway, a sloping path descended into the body of the building. Blocks of ice rose into the air as tall as the tallest buildings Elspeth had seen, taller even than the roof of the church, though the steeple brought it closer to God. Pulleys and ropes hung everywhere from the great beams of the ceiling to hook and raise ice to the gaps at the top of the giant rectangular stacks. Men atop these stacks guided the blocks into place.

Charles hopped up onto a barrel.

"Aren't we supposed to work?" Elspeth asked him. No sooner had the words come from her mouth than she saw Owen Trachte standing in a small circle of men, talking and gesticulating. She flinched.

"Owen Trachte," Charles said. Owen was stuffed into the fabric of his three-piece suit, his massive neck and arms threatening to burst the seams, like an overstuffed sausage.

"He looks familiar," Elspeth said. The sight of Owen didn't concern her as much in the icehouse—she was well-concealed in her hat and scarf—but his presence rattled her.

"He's around sometimes. I think he sells parts for a machine company. Or hardware. Or ropes, maybe." When she didn't react, he continued. "His father was a doctor who drank himself to death."

"Maybe I knew his father," she said. She'd known of Phillip's habit, surely, and saw him sometimes at night in his office drinking and rereading letters from his wife, and she would find him in the morning, rumpled and reeking. He would leave the letters on his desk, and sometimes as he readied himself for work, she would pretend to search for something so she could read a few lines in his absence. "Do they look alike, Owen and his father?"

"A bit," Charles said. He drummed his hands on the barrel. "I don't know, actually. I didn't know his father well." Her discomfort twisted and turned within her. "I'm sure Wallace is safely in his office now," he said mercifully, "and we can sit down by the shore."

Elspeth's head spun with images of Owen after thrashing his friend—cheeks flushed, hole in his smile dark as pitch—and she wondered what he would do if he were to recognize her.

EVERY COUPLE OF days, London White asked Caleb to wash the sheets and towels, washcloths and underclothes. He wore an apron borrowed from one of the bartenders to protect his new shirt. When Caleb placed the dirty items into the old bathtub they used, he avoided colors and stains that he didn't want explained. White squeezed every penny out of the Elm Inn, and a cot had been set up in the corner of the laundry for days when it was not in use. After the first hour, the windows clouded with condensation, and the drying lines Caleb hooked from a sconce at one end of the room to the other would be heavy with sheets. Water puddled on the floor.

Caleb stirred the linens in the bathtub with the broken end of a broom. He liked to pretend he was steering down a river, as he'd seen in a book his mother had brought home. The book had only lasted a day. When Jorah had read a page and deemed it unacceptable, he'd burned it in the woodstove. The etching of a boy standing, the legs of his overalls rolled high on his calves, steering a raft down seething rapids had stayed with Caleb. He became quite involved in this daydream, waving and talking to people along the river, before the current took hold of the ship and he needed to bravely pilot his craft.

A girl, his age perhaps, with curled brown hair walked into the room. "What are you doing?" she asked. Caleb had never seen her before. She wore a small dress, the kind a girl half her age and half her size would wear, and it struggled to cover where her legs met her hips. If Mary had worn one of Emma's dresses, this was how she would appear. The look in her eyes, however, one of pain and weariness, made Caleb speak to her as if she were much older than he. "I'm sorry, ma'am," he said. "I was stirring the wash."

"Who were you talking to?"

Caleb shrugged and looked around the room, to insinuate he clearly hadn't been talking at all.

"Who were you waving to, then?"

He repeated his act of examining the empty room.

"I'm Ellabelle. You're Caleb. This is my room."

He ignored the cot in the corner.

"Do you talk? To real people, I mean."

"Of course." His voice made a strange leap and he turned back to his wash.

"Where did you come from?"

Caleb recalled London White's laughing at his answer to that very question. "My mother and I live down at the hotel." Something about Ellabelle made lying more difficult. He couldn't concentrate on what he meant to say—words tumbled out of his mouth without his guidance. Lying, he'd come to understand, took two things: fore-thought and memory. Both had been disabled in Ellabelle's presence. "I meant my father." He needed to figure out a way to end her questions before they began. "My mother's dead." He thought of Jorah's body, riddled with bullets. There was no way Caleb could have moved it to be with the rest of them, but his skeleton off alone in the dark corner of what had once been the house seemed especially cruel now. He tried to steel himself, rid himself of his guilt and anger toward a man he no longer knew as his father. They were strange feelings to have, with Ellabelle tiptoeing nearer on the wet floor. The room smelled of the laundry soap, a jarring cleansing odor, and Caleb took long breaths to combat a dizziness that swirled inside him.

"I said, I'm sorry to hear that," Ellabelle said.

"Oh, sorry. Thank you." Caleb leaned back and removed a pil-lowcase from the water. It steamed in the cold air. It dripped onto the floor between them. He'd opened the window a crack to help the clothes dry faster, and the wind that squeezed through whistled at the two of them. Caleb tried not to think of the horrific holes in the house and his days spent in the pantry.

"What happened?"

Caleb sloshed the water back and forth.

"What happened to your mother? How did she die?"

"I shot her," he said quietly.

Ellabelle came even closer. She sat on the edge of the tub. Her pale thighs, exposed when she sat down in her dress, pressed together. Every moment they didn't speak was filled with the sounds of the laundry, echoes upon echoes. Caleb thought she hadn't heard him. There were a million follow-up questions she could ask, and he prepared himself to lie his way out of it, to pretend it was all a joke. He forced a grin. She frowned. The only question that came from her was "Why?"

"It was an accident." It felt better than he could have hoped to have the truth loose in the air. The sheets sighed and shifted in the draft. Ellabelle touched her soft hand to his forearm. He refused to look at her, watching the whirlpools he created in the tub. "I'm sorry," she said, and Caleb couldn't be in that room with the overwhelming odor of the cleanser and the oppressive humidity any longer. He set the broomstick down on the side of the tub.

"Ellabelle?" someone called. She rolled her eyes, and White strode into the room. "Here you are. Hello, children." He lifted a pillowcase appreciatively. "Well done, Caleb. Fine job. This one," he said and pointed to Caleb, "takes true pride in his work. He'll be something someday soon, so you be nice to him, Ellabelle."

"She was just talking to me," Caleb said.

"I know," White said. "Time to earn your keep, dear." He extended a hand for Ellabelle.

"What is he now?" Ellabelle said, ignoring his request.

"I'm sorry?" White said.

"You said he would be something soon, and I'd like to know what he is now."

White's demeanor changed. "Let's not get ahead of ourselves." Ellabelle relinquished her tiny fingers. A bell rang close by, and Caleb wondered if it called for her. Before she left his side, she gave his arm one last squeeze.

ELSPETH STOOD IN front of a display containing a few dozen pistols. A young boy about Caleb's age knelt on the floor near the door, sorting nails into two buckets. Outside, a lake snow poured down heavy flakes, five or six inches on the street already, and the residents of Watersbridge were by and large staying indoors. The shop was empty except for Elspeth, the boy, and the shopkeeper, who spread his moustache with his thumb and index finger. "A pistol, eh?" he said. He introduced himself as Jakob. Elspeth shook his hand but held on to her own name. She'd found that not saying much reduced her risks. Besides, most of the men she'd encountered didn't waste words. "I apologize," Jakob said, "but do you by chance have a son?"

Elspeth pondered the shopkeeper's purpose: Maybe he aimed to sell two pistols, father and son, and double his profits. "Yes?"

"A thin boy with brown hair, brown eyes? Perhaps thirteen, fourteen?"

"Twelve," she said, and thought of her list of the children's names and their crossed-out ages, lost to the fire. It was strange for her—after all these years—to have one of the children out in the world, meeting people, drawing connections back to her. "How do you know him?"

"He's come through here," Jakob said. He invested the statement with a thick sense of meaning, but exactly what he meant by it Elspeth couldn't guess. "Are you sure you need one?" Elspeth figured the man was accusing her of being a poor parent, and Margaret asking her to abandon her son charged through her heart. "After all," he said, "Christmas is coming near."

Elspeth held up a hand to save the man from giving a long sales proposal, trying to contain her impatience. "Sir, if it's not too much bother, the pistol. Please."

Jakob—taking her attitude seriously—explained the advantages of the weapons one by one, taking the time to tell her what type of game she could take down with each. She knew that Watersbridge in the middle of winter didn't sport the best game, and yet he went on about deer, moose, and bears. Elspeth guessed that he needed his own peace of mind—and maybe that of his son, who pitched each nail into its bucket with a satisfying clink. Everyone, she decided, had to convince themselves that they were safer than they were.

The kiss Elspeth and Charles had shared in her dreams made her flush when she recalled it, and she would distance herself from him by refusing to talk for an afternoon. Charles's behavior, too, grew more erratic, whether because of her occasionally silent days she didn't know. Some mornings he would wait for her outside, the coffee steaming. Others he would arrive at work out of breath—long after Elspeth had loosened and oiled the chains and the crane—without apology. Or he wouldn't show up at all, and Elspeth would find herself next to a man who didn't rest or forgive her weaknesses the same way Charles did, who didn't take pause to stare out at the lake for minutes at a time, and drove at the iron bar in front of them without ceasing. His absences went unexplained. At times, she wondered if she smelled alcohol on him, and whether it was from the night before or more recent than that. *This*, she thought, *is how accidents happen.*

On her days alone, she missed him and the comfortable rhythm they'd developed. The job moved faster when he spoke of his family, and she shared small details with him as well, scenes from her childhood or the early parts of her life with Jorah, when happiness seemed possible. For all of the unpredictability, she appreciated his company.

Exhausted from fighting her dreams at night, by day she had no energy left to ward off her imagination. Sometimes she wondered if one of the men she worked beside could have killed Jorah and the children. Maybe Caleb would recognize him in an instant. Once, a shaft of sunlight struck the men pushing a block down the canal and it rested on one man, a slight figure who attacked the ice with particular vigor. The beam created a flutter in her chest and she wondered if God pointed the man out to her for a reason, but as she formulated the theory the light moved on to another man and another, shimmering against the frozen sweat and condensation slick on their coats. Perhaps they all were guilty. If the wind came from the east and didn't roar across the lake, she sometimes heard the cries of the baby in the office. To turn her ears from the temptation she would count her footsteps or concentrate on the creaking of the crane until her racing mind went blank again. She tried not to think of her family, or what people would do if she was recognized. Owen Trachte had not reappeared. After work, she would have two drinks to slow her mind, eat dinner—usually a small steak or stew, some days with Charles, others alone—and skate home on the icy streets, woozy with alcohol, her muscles too spent to control.

If the store was open even after she cleaned and turned in her cleats, she brought home dinner for Caleb: a pail with a sandwich wrapped in a cloth napkin, some cured meat, salted potatoes, dried fruit. Though the boy never thanked her or acknowledged the food, the pail would be empty the next morning. He returned from the inn while she slept and she left before he woke. She admired his closed eyes while he slept, how they fluttered behind his eyelids. She studied herself in the mirror and then looked to him, trying to pick out the similarities Jakob, Margaret, and Charles had seen.

Once she angled the mirror so they appeared side by side—as if in a portrait—and closed one eye and then the other, trying to gauge the distance between them. She would comb her hair with her fingers down across her eyes, and she'd tuck it back beside her ears, and she'd see it, too. *He could be mine*, she sometimes thought.

CALEB SWEPT THE Elm Inn inside, and cleared snow from the porch and the stairs outside. He and Ellabelle would sneak in a conversation here and there, before White told her to get back to work with a slap to her rump and a clanging bell. They avoided the subject of Caleb's family and his mother's murder and focused instead on the events at the Elm Inn. Ellabelle had a natural talent for mimicry, much like Mary, and she imitated the postures and faces of the frequent customers and would act out entire conversations she'd overheard. She said every word—even those that made Caleb blush—without blinking, then collapsed into laughter. Their laughter was often what alerted White, being such an unusual noise for the Elm, and the two of them became adept at hearing his elegant shoes coming up the stairs, and Caleb would run onto the walkway and start sweeping while Ellabelle would sit at her dressing table and prepare herself for her next client. Caleb hated to see Ellabelle's door closed, but he hated even more to see it open and a man thrust his hat on top of his mussed hair and amble back into the parlor, a grin on his lips. She'd reach up a thin arm and pull the string attached to the tarnished bell next to her door and if no one came, White would slide through the crowd and tap a man on his shoulder and whisper into his ear. Caleb hated to watch but found himself staring anyway, committing the men to memory so he could see the change in them when they exited her room.

White could hear the bells through the din of the bar—amid the jokes and arguments, the exclamations of dismay and exhortations of luck he could discern a single bell and its source. Caleb memorized London White's movements—his walk and his nervous habit of plucking his watch from his pocket and winding it—and he tried them out in the empty rooms where he stripped the soiled sheets. He was careful to keep these mannerisms from Ellabelle, though he didn't know why, and from Frank, who sometimes kept Caleb company during breakfast at the Brick & Feather. Most mornings the hotel was quiet, and Frank sat across from him, telling stories about his boyhood on Nova Scotia. Frank also encouraged Caleb to improve his reading with the newspaper, helping him through articles about President McKinley and the troubles with Spain. Often the size of the world made Caleb dizzy. It all seemed so far off, as distant to him as his barn. Caleb avoided thoughts of home, his family, and his animals. And yet every morning when he put on Jesse's boots he pictured his brother. A smile seen through the crowd at the inn or the sound of someone's laugh would remind him of Jesse, too, and he would move closer with his broom, trying to find the perfect instant where he could see or hear his own memory, but not well enough to break the spell. He wished he could pray. On these days, he allowed himself some precious seconds with the horses hitched outside and with one of the regular's dogs, Misty, who often escaped the house and stayed dutifully outside the front door all day, occasionally lowering her head onto her paws for a nap. Caleb would bury his face in her fur and listen to her belly rumble.

He scrutinized the men at the Elm Inn, and placed himself in the barn, his face flush against the rough wood. The biggest excitement among the patrons had been for Owen Trachte, but he had been the one man Caleb had noticed who did not come back, as many of the customers came to be familiar once he understood that the same men sat at the same tables and visited the same girls. Violence created little stir—even when someone got shot over bad cards, White simply ordered the wounded to be taken to the doctor, and the injured man would be carted off to laughter and things would return to normal. And though Caleb knew there were most likely men in the inn at all times who had probably killed someone—including its owner—he didn't see any of the men with red scarves. Caleb wondered if—before coming to have their laps caressed by women in small clothing and spend their day's wages on drink and cards—the customers sat down to a meal the same way his family had. He wondered if all fathers betrayed their prayers.

He reassured himself of his pistol's presence by shifting his hips and having its heft on his belt so he didn't pat the small of his back every few minutes. The sight of blood ceased to bother him; after what he'd seen, there wasn't much that could shake him. The sense of fear he expected to clutch his heart remained at large, nothing but a wild thought that drifted farther and farther away, as far away as the strange-sounding places in the newspaper, France or Spain or Mexico.

Until Martin Shane returned. It was a Friday, often the Elm's busiest day—but not the bloodiest, which, almost without fail, was Sunday—and Martin Shane slipped through the door, spoke to Ethan for longer than most, paid his entry, and skulked along the edge of the room to the bar.

Caleb swept the stairs, ignoring the rhythmic banging of a bed frame. The previous Sunday, Martin—all crimson with fury, his fair skin burning beneath his shaggy blond hair—had broken three chairs over the back of a man who had one of Martin's friends by the neck. When Ethan pinned Martin's arms behind his back, Martin saw Caleb, who stood in front of him, broom in hand. The sight of Caleb stopped Martin's screaming and struggling. Blood trickled from the corner of his mouth. Ethan's knee dug into his neck, but Martin paid no mind to the twenty stones bearing down on him, and his bloodshot stare didn't leave Caleb, who had been on his way to sweep snow from the porch so it didn't snap clean off the inn, but the strangling and chair-crashing had been in the path to the door.

"Go help wash the glasses, Caleb," London White had said as he approached the broken chairs and bleeding men. "The porch can wait for us to sort this out."

Caleb had not seen Martin since, and he'd looked for him to avoid him. The mere thought of the man's gaze made him squirm. No one paid much attention to the boy who swept, shoveled, and cleared glasses. Less than a week later, though, Martin waited at the end of the bar, thick-necked and wind-peeled. The Elm had yet to fill up, but men finished with work streamed through the doors and dropped their admission into Ethan's lockbox.

Caleb stole past doors doing their best to contain the grunts coming from inside until he stood on the balcony directly over Martin. He could see the freckles on Martin's scalp and the way half of his collar had tucked under his shirt. Martin spoke with the bartender, lifting his hands into the air, then pressing them together as if asking forgiveness. He reached into his pocket and produced some money, which he slid across the bar. White had told Caleb that chairs cost the Elm thirty-four cents apiece, but he charged customers fifty. A fine, he'd told Caleb, kept people honest. "Mistakes are meant to be learned from," he said, "not repeated."

The bartender took the money and stepped away, and Martin stood on the footrest under the bar and scouted the room. Caleb knew Martin Shane looked for him. He drew back against the wall and a bell rang close to his head and he jumped and turned, smashing into the soft chest of a woman. "That's going to cost you," she said, and adjusted her brassiere. She rang her bell and Caleb gasped. The customer on his way out of her room chuckled. "Jesus, kid," the woman said, "this ain't the place for someone who startles easy."

ON FRIDAY MORNING, Charles hadn't been waiting for Elspeth. As she walked alone past the dress shop and the barber's and paused outside the doctor's office—everything dark and hushed, the day seeming to gather itself, the sky over the lake fat with snow clouds, but nothing falling—she heard a whistle from the church. Framed by the columns and holding two mugs, Charles waved to her. Unsure of his purpose, she hurried across the street. Charles opened the door to the church, and they stepped inside the narrow hall meant to keep the cold from the congregation. He produced a key and unlocked the inner doors. Charles sat in a pew, Elspeth next to him. The church looked all the bigger in shadow.

"You have a key to the church?" Elspeth asked. Somewhere in the vast space water dripped.

"I used to be a deacon," Charles said. Elspeth was going to ask what had happened, but he plunged ahead. "Jorah, I have some things to confess."

"You've chosen a fine location," Elspeth said, trying to ease the tension that contorted Charles's face.

"All my talk of the boys—it's all been true, in my heart," he said. "And I don't know how I did this and I'm so sorry I lied, but—they're gone."

"Dead?" Elspeth said. Her own truth pushed up her throat.

"No," he said. "Their mother took them."

Everything slowed. Elspeth could count a minute between each drop of water, and if she'd seen one, she would have sworn it drifted slowly as a feather. She waited for him to continue, but he simply shattered. He dropped his head to his hands, which rested on the pew in front of them. His sobs echoed through the sanctuary. One, two, three times he lifted his head and thumped it against his knuckles. The whole pew rocked with the motion. Tears washed down Elspeth's cheeks, too, and she let them, unconcerned about what damage they would do to her falsely shadowed jaw. She composed herself, exhaling deep breaths and drying her eyes.

Charles, embarrassed, wiped his tears away as well. He took her hand in his and held it to his chest. "I simply thought you could understand."

"I do," she said, but resisted the urge to add anything more.

C ALEB HAD TAKEN refuge upstairs. The sheets were still moist; the smell of bodies clung to the air. Each room had one piece of decoration on the walls—a tintype, a painting. In this case, a mounted deer's head gazed at them with its glassy eyes. London White straightened the collar of his jacket. "There's a man down there looking for you," he said.

"I know," Caleb answered.

"I can tell him you've left; I can tell him to leave." He evened one sleeve with the other, and adjusted his cuff links. "But I must know what I'm harboring you from." Caleb told White about the fight, the chairs crashing and Shane's attention settling on him. White pulled his golden pocket watch from his vest and wound it several times. "Could be he desires you," White said, and it was clear to Caleb from his far-off tone that White was thinking aloud. Once he finished winding, he held the watch to his ear. "But I've never known Martin Shane to be a buggerer. That's not something we cater to." White regained his usual confident speech as he continued; he'd made up his mind about something. "Of course, exceptions can be made, but not for my best boy." White ruffled Caleb's hair, something he did often—in passing as he showed a customer up the stairs or glided through the crowd to a disturbance at the other end of the parlor. "I'll tell Shane he'll have to find some-one else," White said, and left.

Caleb sat on the edge of the naked mattress.

Sometime later, Ellabelle tiptoed in, her stocking feet soundless on the wood. She sat so close their legs touched and asked what was happening. "That doesn't sound right," she said after he'd repeated what White had told him. "Shane's not the type. Trust me." She elbowed Caleb in the ribs playfully. "I can always tell."

Under the vacant stare of the deer, Caleb suddenly longed to understand what transpired behind the closed doors. His mouth opened and he knew Ellabelle would answer, but he couldn't figure out how to ask.

"Do you think," she said, "that this has something to do with your mother?"

His mouth clapped shut on his question. "No," he said. He thought of the earthen mounds and the men they contained. He couldn't figure out how the murderers could have stumbled upon their farm by accident. They were looking for them, and they'd found them. Perhaps they'd found him as well. The thought didn't frighten him, but filled him with stillness.

ELSPETH RETREATED TO the edge of the water, where the first block of ice made its way to them, pushed along by the polemen, all in shadow. Charles readied the crane and the pincers and rubbed an oil-covered rag at the hinges. His cheeks had swollen from rubbing away the traces of his tears. They worked in silence.

With two blocks on the sled, the horses pawing at the ground, shuffling, ready to work, a crack like a gunshot echoed across the lake. Elspeth stopped. Charles looked stricken. For an instant she thought he'd been shot.

"The icehouse," he said.

A low rumble followed by a tremendous crashing shook the ground beneath them. Elspeth almost toppled over. The noise continued, never ending. The horses reared and one took off running, forcing the other with it. The blocks of ice had not been secured, and one slipped from the sled and the whole apparatus lurched onto its side, the other block toppling over and charging across the packed snow. Elspeth heard the tightening of the leather as the animals strained against the upended sled. Another unearthly crack sounded out from the icehouse. The horses galloped hard, the sled tearing the earth behind them and knocking over one of the light posts, then another, and the lanterns spilled their kerosene onto the snow, creating tiny suns, perfect orbs of flame.

Charles had already made it halfway up the hill before the rumbling stopped and the screams started, his cleats kicking up snow behind him, stumbling in the great gashes left by the horses. Elspeth followed far behind, passed by some of the men who worked on the lake, their jackets covered in a silvery glaze like sleet. The icehouse loomed above her, three stories of rough-hewn wood, looking weather-beaten but permanent. From the open door, cries of pain and alarm exploded and carried out over their abandoned posts.

Once inside, all was chaos. Blocks of ice the size of sheep had crashed to the ground and lay in pieces in the loose array of a herd, and between and among them lay the dozens of men who had been unfortunate enough to work in their shadow. The giant towers that had pitched forward left a gaping hole in the middle of the icehouse like a missing tooth, and an unholy light shone through the gap onto the floor, setting the horror in sharp relief. Arms and legs sprouted between shards of ice, as if mountains had sprung up without warning and trapped men in their rocky surface. Some worked to lash the remaining pillars to the railings of the upstairs catwalk, which Elspeth immediately understood to be not only pointless, but also potentially lethal to everyone in the building: If those blocks should fall, they could bring the entire building down with them. Others milled about, gathering in groups to pull, to lift, trying to free those who'd been ensnared by the avalanche. The agonized shrieks were unbearable.

Elspeth got caught up in the stream of men, whose current carried her down the wide ramp—scarred from the constant sliding of the sleds—to the floor, stepping over and across smaller pieces of ice that had slid the twenty feet or so to the door. There, a ruddy-faced man with blood spilling from a thin cut on his forehead yelled for her to take a side of a block of ice, through which she could make out the distorted image of a body. Elspeth took hold. She'd left her gloves at the crane and the cold burned her fingers. Her cleats, too, were at the edge of the water and the worn treads of her boots struggled to gain traction. The man counted to three and groaned loudly. Elspeth pushed as long as she could, until her arms caught fire and the breath burst from her mouth, and she fell to the ground as if all that had been holding her together was the air she kept in her lungs. They rested. They counted to three and tried again. It didn't move. Charles elbowed Elspeth to the side to get his hands on the block as well, and the bloodied man counted. This time the ice slid away, and exposed a man driven into the dirt floor. They didn't wait long—he was dead.

Charles put a hand to her shoulder and propelled her on to the next group, who were trying to move four nearly whole blocks from two men. They seemed to be on top of one another, three arms intertwining and jutting out from the ice. Elspeth looked around at the faces of the men gathered, grim and covered in muck and blood. She knew, as they all did, that their efforts were futile. But they needed to do something, to loose their fear on some task. They moved one chunk, and then another. The men had been crushed together, their cheeks touching, almost embracing. Blood mingled in the dirt floor.

Loud pops issued forth from the ice as it settled. Men shouted for help. A few others with broken limbs or superficial wounds screamed in pain, while others squeezed their heads with their hands, uninjured but stricken by the dreadful sight of a relative or friend taken from the world by nothing more than water.

Charles took a fistful of her coat and urged her along again. One foot, covered in a hole-filled sock, darned many times over, extended out from beneath a jagged hunk of ice. A boot lay untied a few inches away. The two of them managed to push the ice aside and beneath it was a boy. He couldn't have been more than thirteen or fourteen. The ice had dashed in the right side of his skull, and his face there had been flattened and split at the line of his scalp, revealing stark white bone and wet blood, purple from the cold. His mouth gaped open in surprise. In his hand he held a sheet of paper. Before she could tell him to leave it, Charles wrenched the message from the boy's grip. He held it out to her and when she didn't take it right away he dropped it to the bloody earth.

Her numb fingers searched it out in the muck. The note read: "*Stephen—Lunch at Noon? Meet me in Front of the Church.—Lucy.*" Elspeth placed it upon the boy's chest and draped one of his arms across it to hold it in place. With shaking fingers, she pressed his eyelids shut.

A look crossed Charles's face, one he tried to erase immediately but an impression remained like a faded scar. He stepped nimbly across the ice-strewn terrain and out the open door, where the sun had risen and turned the sky a dull gray. He darted off in the direction of town as if yanked on a string and Elspeth followed. She tripped in the ditch left by the horses when they'd stampeded away and regained her balance without so much as a glance backward from him. He disappeared down a path made by the workers in the mornings; the trail through the evergreens took them out of the wind and to and from the apartment buildings on the edge of town. It sloped downward, but the men had kicked footholds wide and even like glass steps.

At first she thought the same impulse that had driven Charles to the accident repelled him with equal speed, but she caught sight—between the slender trunks of the pines—of a man in a waistcoat and a corduroy cap twenty paces ahead of him. She heard Charles cry out but the man didn't break stride. Charles ran, even his cleated boots skidding, each time righting himself with a hand to the icy path, and when he got close enough, he lunged and threw both arms around the harried man. A hundred yards away, Elspeth rushed down the slick steps, thinking she would break up the fight before Charles killed him. Instead, Charles wheeled the man around and kissed him.

Like she'd heard a bullet whistling past, Elspeth ducked. The man didn't fight Charles at first, but after a long embrace he clutched Charles's shoulders and shoved him down a small embankment. Torn, the man hesitated and then hurried away. Elspeth stayed hidden and took stock of the quiet forest: No one else had seen.

Charles dragged himself onto the path and sat with his feet tucked under his thighs, his chin sunk to his chest, and his arms wrapped about himself. As she approached, he stood and she half expected him to kiss her, too, especially as his hand came to her neck tenderly. Then he started to squeeze. "Charles," she said, before his thumb closed off her windpipe. She didn't fight him; her final penance had come.

He gripped her throat tighter, and pointed a finger at her, a voiceless threat, and spots of light filled her vision and her legs began to go limp. She wondered what he saw in her eyes as she died. His attention shifted to something on the ground and he released her, and she collapsed, forgotten. She let her body relax and gathered air into her lungs. Charles pounced at a dark leather glove, finer than the unevenly stitched pairs they wore out day by day. He placed the opening over his mouth and breathed in hard enough to wilt the fingers. He eased the glove onto his hand and flexed it. Lost in himself, he left her on her back, gasping and retching. The lights in her eyes flashed across the gray sky like shooting stars, and then faded away.

A SOFT KNOCK sounded at the door. Caleb tapped the Colt at the small of his back. Ellabelle took his other hand in hers.

Martin Shane entered. The light from the lamp cast shadows onto his face. Caleb inched the pistol from his waist and cocked the hammer. Martin removed his hat and placed it on the dresser. His hands shook, Caleb guessed from drink, but as Martin moved closer and leaned down, Caleb saw that he was crying. He'd never seen such a large man cry before. Martin's unsteady fist wiped his nose and he dropped onto his knees, shuffling forward on them, his wet eyes fixed on Caleb. A dreamlike peace had come over him and he reached out to touch Caleb, though he was a yard away. Caleb started to sweat and his fingers went numb where he clutched the pistol.

Ellabelle hugged Caleb tight. "What are you doing?" she asked Martin.

Thunderous footsteps sounded on the walkway before London White stormed into the room, followed closely by Ethan. "Martin Shane," White said. Ethan pulled a sawed-off shotgun from somewhere in his massive bulk and aimed it at Shane's head, but Shane didn't flinch, didn't stop his movement toward Caleb. When he got close enough, Shane lifted Caleb's chin with one finger. The light flooded his face. He was terrified.

"Hell, maybe I was wrong," Ellabelle said. "Maybe he does want to fuck you."

Caleb didn't think he could move to raise the pistol.

"Martin Shane," White said again. "Step back from that boy or Ethan will take your head clean off."

The small click of Ethan's gun being cocked froze everyone in the room and seemed to bring some sense back to Martin. The big man stepped forward and pressed the gun into the base of Martin's skull. He pushed hard enough to bend Martin's head forward, but his eyes never left Caleb.

"It's okay," Shane said. "I'm this boy's uncle."

CHAPTER 8

The smell of urine made Caleb wince. Ethan had dragged Martin away, and White had said to Caleb, "We're going to settle all this out," then followed Ethan out of the room. A gunshot rang out downstairs, and Caleb flinched. Ellabelle put her hand on his shoulder to steady him. Caleb worried that they'd shot Martin rather than hear his story, and that in letting it happen, he'd killed a man the same as his father or London White.

"Wasn't him," Ellabelle said, as if hearing his thoughts. "That came from a card table." She got him to his feet and giggled. "You work here long enough, you know where the bullets are headed." The exchange with Martin had left Caleb with nothing. His body could do little but tremble. He didn't blanch when Ellabelle peeled his wet pants from his body, the fabric producing a sucking sound when it pulled away from his flesh, the pistol falling from his waist and onto the floor. This time they both jumped. If Ellabelle had been offended by the presence of the weapon, nothing she said or did betrayed it; she simply put the pistol on the side table.

"I've never had an uncle," Caleb said.

"Don't worry," she said. "It's not true. This happens every so often." She eased him back to the bed. Caleb's body went slack and he rested his head on the stained pillow.

Ellabelle went over him with a warm washcloth, wiping clean every crease of his body. He didn't possess the energy to refuse. After she finished bathing him, she patted him dry with a soft cloth, and soon the scent of rose powder reached his nose. Its scent lingered in the hallways, and at times he would see one of the women slap a handful into each of her armpits before she rang her bell for another client.

Ellabelle helped him crawl under the sheets. She pulled the curtains on the glaring winter day and snuffed out a candle that burned on the table beside his pistol. "Sweet dreams," she said.

ELSPETH QUIVERED WITH draining adrenaline. She tried to piece things together, but they wouldn't fit. She walked back to the icehouse and looped her scarf around her neck twice, afraid that Charles's hands had left a bruise, not that anyone would notice with all of the broken and wounded walking dazed through the snow. She heard the cry of a child, the baby in the train car, and her heart leapt, and she turned her head this way and that, trying to pick out where it came from, before an unattended sheep wandered by her, its bleating something her mind had twisted into something it wasn't. One man—whom she didn't recognize—dropped to his knees not far from her, a mangled mess at the end of his arm. He gripped his wrist with one hand and watched as the blood drained from the tips of his fingers, drawing dots and then lines in the tamped snow between his legs. Elspeth knelt beside him. He looked at her with glazed eyes. She reached for his wrist and lifted his arm higher, above his head. The bleeding slowed. He leaned against her. The blood dripped warm onto her shoulder and then her cheek. She drew his belt from his pants, which elicited a grunt of irritation or query from him, circled it around his arm and pulled tight. With the knife from his sheath she dug out a new notch in the leather and cinched the belt. A frantic man with a black bag in his blood-soaked hands knocked Elspeth out of the way and took over. He helped the injured man up and ushered him elsewhere without a word. Once he'd left, Elspeth realized it had been Owen, the bag in his hands very much like his father's.

The horses were gone, the screaming had for the most part stopped, and the milling workers had either taken up in small groups or disappeared—to where she had no idea. No one had made an announcement of any kind. No one had taken charge. She sat down on the edge of a trough, the water iced over, the horses' saliva dried in swirls and eddies. Fresh-looking men wandered from person to person, asking what could be done—their questions joining her own in a vast babble—and Elspeth knew they'd come running from town, alerted by the shaking of the ground and the screams that carried across the ice. Others created their own tasks: Some pulled the bodies from the icehouse and covered them in canvas; some had gone to work repairing the gouges in the earth from the horses' wayward journey; and four men worked to move the blocks of ice that had fallen from the sled, but they didn't seem to have any destination in mind but toward their origin, toward the lake.

LONDON WHITE ROUSED Caleb none too gently. He saw a pile of new clothes on the chair in the corner and White holding the Colt. He yearned to be back in his bed at the Brick & Feather, with its raucous springs and thin blankets, but the distance to the hotel had grown by miles since Martin Shane had arrived. As Caleb opened his mouth to ask why White had woken him, White pointed the pistol at him, and took aim. He made a light popping sound with his mouth—the sound of a tiny gunshot—then let the weapon dangle from his finger. He twirled the Colt, caught it in his fist, and replaced it on the table. His unoccupied hands pulled his watch from his pocket and he began to wind. "Is it true?" he asked.

Long ago on the unfinished road, his mother had told him she had no brothers or sisters. Jorah was not his father, but even if he was, he and Martin shared no visible similarities. He couldn't be his uncle, but somehow he felt familiar, as if they'd spoken before in a dream.

"Because if it *is* true, well, then, we have a whole set of problems." The winding of the watch became ferocious. White sighed in irritation at what his hands had been up to while he had been distracted, and he threw the watch next to Caleb's pistol.

"Then it's not true," Caleb said.

"That's no kind of an answer," White said. "What trouble are you in?"

"I'm not," Caleb said.

"We don't have many twelve-year-olds wander in here, Caleb. Much less twelve-year-olds with pistols tucked into their waistbands." Caleb wondered whether White had a gift for spotting sin. He witnessed enough of it; perhaps it revealed itself to him. Caleb fidgeted in the bed, even more aware of his nakedness beneath the sheets. "If you're in trouble and you're honest with me about it, I will take care of it."

Caleb pondered this opportunity for long enough that White took it as an answer, and patted Caleb's cheek with reassurance. He checked himself in the mirror, washed his hands, and slapped his face with water. As he watched his own reflection he said to himself or to Caleb, "Of course not. Martin has been prone to outbursts

like this. If you were indeed the Shane boy, you would be much . . ."
White inspected Caleb in the glass, his head tilting this way and
that, squinting. In answer, White pulled the sheets up tight around
Caleb's neck. "No," he said finally, after much study. "No."

"Mr. White," Caleb said, "what's happening?"

White pressed his hair into place, removed his jacket, slapped
it with an open palm—the dust glittering silver in the light from
between the curtains—and then slid it back across his shoulders,
where it fit like a second skin. "The proper question is," he said,
"how do we keep this from happening again?" He fetched his
watch from the bedside table, held it up to his ear, secured the
chain, and situated it in his vest pocket. He buttoned his jacket. His
hand moved over Caleb's Colt. "Turns out you might need this."
White rotated the gun on the table so that the grip faced Caleb. The
unsteady sensation Martin had set upon him flooded back stronger,
because there were so many things he didn't know. He wondered if
he was the Shane boy. The image of Shane's neck bulging beneath
Ethan's arm came back to him and he said, "Mr. White, please
don't kill him. Don't kill Mr. Shane."

White laughed. "Son," he said, "what good would that do me?"

A MAN STOOD over a cart full of the dead with the Bible in a
tremulous hand. His legs swayed on the cart bench, and he periodically bent down to steady himself. He wore denim overalls
and a hole-filled shirt: not the uniform of a holy man. He com-
menced a passage, then stammered and wiped something from the
pages with his forearm, flipped through them, the wind rustling
the fine paper, the sound like wings flapping. He struggled to keep
his place. "Damn it," he said as he lost his balance, regained it
momentarily, then slipped from the cart, the Bible falling from his

hands. He scurried after the book, and when he picked it up again he thumped it against his thigh to rid it of snow. Perhaps realizing what he'd done, he cradled the Bible in his outstretched palms, as if to ask His forgiveness for the rough treatment.

Elspeth watched this from the edge of the trough where she'd sat—covered in gore—for almost two hours. On occasion, a doctor—or someone acting as one—would lean down and ask if she'd been hurt and she would shake her head without speaking. One of them had handed her a cigarette before he ran off, in the direction of what she didn't know. She rolled the cigarette between her fingertips, crushing it, only dimly observing the tobacco drift to the ground, and the paper being taken by the wind when it had emptied.

The children came in an endless loop: stealing them, watching them grow older, listening as their sounds crystallized into words, Dr. Watt taking the baby from her outstretched arms and the elation ebbing from her body, the child she'd dropped on the train tracks crying out to her. Once, after a long absence, she'd sat down to a dinner that Mary had cooked, something that had apparently become customary with her gone, and the children all looked to Elspeth, expectant. How their shrill voices had angered her, how she'd wished they would stare at something else. They seemed hardly to blink. The angrier she became, the less they watched, and this stoked her fury. Caleb had been one of the last to look away, eating the center of his bread, pressing it against his mouth, licking off the butter.

The would-be preacher read aloud, *"But the rest fled to Aphek, into the city; and there a wall fell upon twenty and seven thousand of the men that were left."* He frowned and glanced around the bustling scene, but when no one took any notice of him—he did not spy Elspeth watching him—he pressed on. *"And Benhadad fled, and came into the city, into an inner chamber."*

Elspeth missed Jorah. It came to her like waking from a night-mare. Jorah would be able to find the perfect passage for this man, to give him the strength he needed to deal with the crushed bodies gathered in a heap at his feet. On her voyages into the city, she rarely thought of her husband—even when a man took a shine to her she declined out of her own disinterest, not out of loyalty to the husband who'd stayed on as her protector through all of her sins. Another man, after all, served her no purpose. But in the dimming sun, with all the horrors of the day receding, she wanted to see her husband, to touch the bony bumps on his shoulders, chalked with dry sweat, and have him kiss the top of her head where her hair parted.

The preacher's brow furrowed and the corners of his mouth tipped again, and he rifled through the pages. Apparently dissat-isfied, he returned to where his finger had marked the page he'd begun and he continued, *"And his servants said unto him, Behold now, we have heard that the kings of the house of Israel are merci-ful kings: let us, I pray thee, put sackcloth on our loins, and ropes upon our heads, and go out to the king of Israel: peradventure he will save thy life."* Even the casual listener could tell that the man hadn't picked a suitable passage, but Elspeth forgave him—as he apparently did himself—for he left the cart and walked away in the middle of another verse.

"That did not go well," a voice from behind Elspeth said. Edward Wallace blotted out the sky. He leaned on his cane and smoked from a pipe. In general, he appeared unbothered by the events that surrounded him.

"I suppose not," Elspeth said. Two men dragged a dead horse up from the lake.

"I hear you acquitted yourself well today, Jorah van Tessel," Wallace said. Bile rose in her throat. "Perhaps in pairing you with Charles we've underestimated you."

The mention of Charles made her blush. All of the jokes the men in the office told and the strange, oblique allusions coalesced in her head. "I don't believe so, sir."

"So are we in agreement?"

"No—I meant, sir, that I don't think that's the case. I enjoy the work."

Wallace grunted, and with a crackling of bones and joints, sat down next to her. He coughed a few times and they waited until his wheezing subsided. "In truth, Jorah, most of these men are meant for nothing more than this." He gestured with his cane to the panorama around them. The sun had escaped the tree line and drifted out over the lake and turned gold in its descent, Erie with it. In this new glow, the men moving the dead from the icehouse and the rest making repairs and consoling one another turned to shining statues.

"Come with me," Wallace said, and rose with the help of his cane.

ELLABELLE HAD WARNED Caleb not to spend time in the stables. "Not one good thing happens there," she said. Between the stalls, however, the heat from the animals chased the chill from his bones and a long-lost security welcomed him. A man named Gerry logged the comings and goings of horses, carts, and carriages. Caleb didn't like his leer when the night wore on and he'd snuck too many drinks from the bar, or how he lingered in the Elm as often as he could, loitering by the women's rooms, wearing an evil grin and pinching their rear ends, which always made them squeal and slap his shoulder. If Gerry had even slightly resembled one of the killers with his wiry strands of hair and yellowed teeth, Caleb would've shot him on the spot. Or so he told himself.

Night had fallen. The noise from the Elm reached into the stables, and so Caleb walked farther into its darkness, to the end of the stalls. The quiet eased the tension between his eyes. One stall held no horses; the latch had been broken from the wood. Caleb hooked his leg up and over the rails with a practiced agility and soon he'd fallen asleep in the hay.

He hadn't been there long when he heard loud voices. Caleb knew Gerry's slur, but the other voice didn't conjure a face as easily. "Aw, hell. White don't know what he's doing from one day to the next," Gerry said. "From one minute to the next, even."

The light from a lantern drifted down the aisle, and Caleb retreated to the rear of the stall. From his new vantage point, he could see the back of the man who'd started the fight Martin had waded into, swinging chairs. Martin's friend took off his hat and rubbed at his scalp. "He's taken a shine to the boy?"

"Don't you worry, Dax," Gerry said. "Marty proves that's the boy and White'll have to let him have him."

Caleb wondered if he'd underestimated Gerry; it sounded like he was trying to calm Dax down.

"Proof?" Dax said. "Where in hell's he going to find proof? The kid's been gone for fifteen goddamn years."

Gerry scoffed. "That boy ain't no more than thirteen. Probably hasn't got a hair on his prick yet."

"You know what I mean." He lowered his voice. "Martin said he'd pay me to take him. We could split it."

"Dax, don't be an idiot. I don't like White any more than you, but if you make off with that boy, there's only one place for him to come looking, and he's going to come looking with Ethan and a whole armory of guns."

A latch lifted, and Caleb heard the rattling of reins. "He likes the boy that much?"

"Does it matter how much?" A horse whinnied, and Gerry nickered at it. "London White," Gerry said, "don't like being thieved."

The hooves moved off, and so did the men.

Caleb exhaled. A noise rustled close, and he didn't have time to react before an arm reached through from the next stall and grabbed his neck. He smelled liquor and tobacco. The arm clenched tight enough that he couldn't scream.

"Looks like I caught myself a barn rat," Gerry said, his breath hot on Caleb's ear. "You been into the feed, rat?"

Caleb's feet kicked at the hay. The horses whinnied nervously. He reached into his waistband and wrapped his fingers around the Colt. Gerry yanked Caleb back hard, smacking his head into the wooden rail. The force of it must have surprised Gerry, and Caleb shrugged his arm off, scurried deeper into the pen, lifted the gun and cocked the hammer. Shadows cast by the lantern, which Gerry had hung down the aisle, prevented Caleb from seeing into the next stall. "Don't touch me," he said, his throat raw.

Gerry spit onto the dirt. "You heard us, didn't you, boy? You heard me tell that idiot Dax Hanson not to kidnap you? You heard me warn him about Mr. White?"

"Step out into the light," Caleb said.

"So you can line me up? I don't think so, son. Why don't you put that weapon down and we'll finish this chat?" Caleb caught a glint of thin hair and he pointed the pistol right below it. "Okay, now," Gerry said.

"Stay still." Caleb listened for the man's feet shifting in the hay. For the first time, he'd done what he'd hoped he would have the strength and courage to do and he had the advantage on someone. This didn't give him the elation he'd expected, instead he clutched his stomach to hold everything inside. "Who is the Shane boy?" he asked. Wind shifted something in the beams and the whole barn squealed at them.

"Martin Shane's nephew disappeared a while back—he'd have been about your age now, and so he gets it in him that every boy that comes around is his old lost nephew." His feet moved.

"Stay still," Caleb commanded. From this distance, he figured he could get maybe two shots off before Gerry could hop into the pen.

"I have to admit, though, Caleb Howell, you're the first one that's ever given me pause. Or," he said, "Mr. White."

"Mr. White thinks it's me?"

"Hell if I know what goes on inside that head of his. But this is the first time he's let Shane walk out without a scratch after pulling something like that."

Caleb squeezed his legs together. His stomach was warm. "Where does Martin live?"

Gerry laughed. "Martin Shane's been a friend of mine since you were nothing more than a star in the sky, son." He stepped out into the light and turned his back to Caleb to lift the lantern from the nail where he'd left it. He'd lost the fear that Caleb was going to shoot him, and Caleb didn't have any need or desire to kill the stable attendant, although he'd told himself he would if it had come down to it. He let his arm drop. Gerry whirled and punched Caleb in the jaw. Then the temple. Caleb crumpled, the gun in his hand, a full complement of bullets in the cylinder.

"You're lucky you got angels watching over you," Gerry said and kicked some hay on Caleb. "You ever put a gun on me again, boy, better make sure you shoot me dead." On his way out of the stables, he slammed a fist on one of the enclosures. The horses whinnied and reared at the outburst. The swelling didn't wait. If angels watched over him, Caleb thought, they didn't mind seeing him suffer.

ELSPETH HAD TO work to keep up with Edward Wallace's strides. Even with the cane and on unsteady footing, his long legs swallowed up a yard at a pace. He stopped to shake the hand of the would-be preacher, who beamed as if he'd been touched by God Himself. Inside, Wallace's office had been decorated like a well-appointed sitting room, with a rack full of periodicals between two overstuffed chairs. A fire popped and sang, the room dry and pleasant. Thick rugs deadened her footfalls, and Wallace shut the door to the cold and hung his cane on the coatrack. In the corner lay a crib, a yellow blanket folded over its rail. Elspeth clenched her fists. "Terrible tragedy," she said, her throat frail from the choking, her voice somewhere on a train with the baby.

"Yes, of course," Wallace answered. He wedged himself into one of the chairs and motioned for Elspeth to take the other. Though aware of the crib behind her, crouched in wait, she tried to ignore its call. She removed her hat and pushed her hair behind her ears, reminding herself to cut it even shorter when she was within the safety of the hotel. Through the windows, she could see the icehouse and the land falling off toward the water where workers had already begun to rebuild the line of lights in the ruts made by the horses and the sled. The small, round fires still burned.

"Charles tells me you can work numbers," Wallace said. He set his pipe onto a dish and took a ledger from under his chair with a groan and flipped it open to a page marked with a ribbon.

Elspeth had initially learned mathematics from helping her mother with the cooking, and the books the van Tessel girls had left behind, and had further improved her skills as a midwife—mixing tinctures, tracking changes in weights of mothers and children— though she didn't recall telling Charles. The attention, however, had already grown too much for her. She reminded herself of the cost of discovery. "No, sir."

"The bookmen need help," Wallace said, ignoring her. "Especially now, with new men coming on and families needing their final pay." He took two fountain pens from his breast pocket, uncapped them, and laid them side by side. "Jorah, let me be frank." He consulted his ledger. "You're not cut out for the line. The crew you and Charlie work on has been the slowest, day in and day out, since you arrived."

She thought of Charles's absences and of their many breaks, where she bent over and waited to catch her breath. Beads of sweat began to form at her hairline and at the small of her back. She'd been too confident about her ability to fool them. Wallace began making lines on the ledger, loud, final lines that must have signaled the deaths of the icehouse workers. Charles's feral expression came to her and the veins in her neck pulsed.

"But Charlie spoke highly of your intellect, and so . . . The position comes with a raise." Another mark struck out another life.

"I'm not that concerned with the money, sir."

"You have a son, don't you, Jorah?" His pen hovered over the paper. She wondered if anyone knew about the errand boy yet—whether his parents had been informed or not. "Wouldn't your son enjoy one day moving out of the Brick & Feather and into a home? Wouldn't he like to have a room of his own, perhaps? A growing boy needs a room of his own."

Elspeth ignored the surprising knowledge Wallace had of her and instead indulged in the daydream of her and Caleb living in a small house on the edge of Watersbridge. It was summer. Elspeth crossed the yard after work, and when Caleb threw his arms around her, she didn't care that her hands had been stained with ink and ran them through his hair anyway. Then, from the gaping maw of the open door, a baby cried. Wailed. And Elspeth longed to run to the child but Caleb clung to her tightly, as she had Amos, as Jorah had when he'd asked her about the children. She gasped.

"Horace, one of our accountants, has been forced to pay rent here while he takes care of his grandchild."

Elspeth needed to touch the blanket, to clasp it to her face and smell it, breathe in the scent of the child. The familiar itch came to her, a scratching at her core. "So the infant sleeps here at night?"

"Often, yes," Wallace said. He tapped his pen on the edge of his ledger. "It's no way to raise a child—in someone else's home." He slashed out another life.

Tears began to form and she heard the baby crying again. She wondered where they could go, how much money it would take to set her and the child up in a new town. She blinked the tears away. "I'm sorry—It must be the smoke from the fire."

Wallace seemed to consider this, then joined her in the lie. "I'll have the chimney checked," he said. "So—a promotion?" Wallace rolled something across the desk with the cap of his pen, and when it stopped in front of her, Elspeth saw it was a tight roll of bills tied with a piece of string.

The infant kept calling to her, needing her, and she knew she had to remove herself from that very small, very hot office if she were to breathe. She took the money. "Thank you," she said.

CHAPTER 9

In the alley next to the barbershop, Elspeth checked to be
sure she was alone and pulled her boot from her foot. She
banged the heel against the ice and a small, dark clump slid
from the leather. With the back of her hand, she pressed the money
flat, counted it, unrolled the bills from Wallace, added those to the
stack, folded it in half, and placed it in her pocket. She'd played this
game many times, the promises to herself not to purchase a train
ticket, not to gather supplies for the journey, not to think of the
child asleep and waiting for her, needing her. Yet with the money
in hand she could think of nothing else. Wallace had given her the
funds and told her where to find the baby, she told herself. He'd
made a point to mention how little Horace could provide for it, how
much it needed its own space, and she could already feel the child's
weight in her arms, how it grounded her.

When she passed the dress shop, the woman inside paused in
her work, her tight lips holding a series of pins between them, and
gave a hesitant wave. A boy stood outside the mercantile, shoveling
snow from the walkway. "Are you all right?" he asked her. She
mumbled something about being fine, but she caught her reflection

in the shop window and understood why the dressmaker had re-
acted as she had: She was coated with blood. "Would you like to
come in and wash up?" he said. "You could have some water."

Once inside the store, the heavy air, laden with food and
coffee, stifled her. She hunched and dropped her head between
her knees. "Are you sure you're okay?" the boy asked. "My father's there now, helping out, I guess." He took her by the elbow,
and she allowed him. "At the icehouse," he added. The image of
the boy with the broken skull and the smell of the icehouse—the
crisp, fresh odor of the ice; the sweat of the men; the sharp stench
of the dying—would not leave her, and she fingered the money
in her pocket for encouragement. They pushed through a set of
saloon doors at the rear of the store, and he placed her in a dark
room the size of a closet. The boy lit a lamp, illuminating shelves
full of family portraits, most of them small, no larger than a tea
saucer. She picked the boy out in many of them. Father, mother,
two sons. A family without greed, she thought. They stood erect
and proud, though in one image they dissolved in laughter. The
boy fetched a washbasin, a cloth, and a mirror. Her face and neck
had been painted with gore and it had dried and fractured on her
skin. She thanked him, her voice cracking into her own, not the
deeper version she'd been forcing from her belly.

"Father likes cameras," he said, as if apologizing for the photos.
"We carry them in the store. I don't know if we've ever sold one." Elspeth draped the cloth over her face and let the moisture loosen the
blood. "We're not even allowed to touch them, me and my brother.
Last week, my brother," he started, then must have thought better
of it when she rung out the bloody rag. "Father says rules are made
to keep us safe."

Elspeth turned this over in her head.

The boy erased a smudge from one of the picture frames with

his shirtsleeve. "No one needs reminders of Watersbridge, my mother says."

"I suppose not," Elspeth said from behind the cloth. She pulled it down her cheeks, the material rough. She scrubbed at her neck and imagined she peeled away parts of her she had no use of anymore. She saw Caleb lying in the gruesome muck with his head staved in, the ice that killed him inert around his lifeless form, melting from the heat left in his blood. "I have a son," she said, "about your age."

"I know," the boy said. "I've seen him. There aren't many children here."

The money made a slight bulge in her pocket. "I came for a gift for him."

The boy scratched his chin thoughtfully, probably something he'd seen his father do. "How old is he?"

"Twelve." She no longer needed her sheet of paper with all of their names and ages. All she had left to remember was Caleb.

"What kind of things does he like?" She shrugged. She couldn't conceive of Caleb running around, playing games with this small, dark boy. Caleb had grown up in the span of one morning. She knew she'd failed him. The boy wiped his nose with the back of his hand, staring at her. "Well, what does he like to do for fun?"

The question made Elspeth bury her head in the cloth once more, and she thought of him, so small and scared, cleaning her wounds, waiting to see if she would survive, the entire rest of his world erased.

CALEB HURRIED TO the Brick & Feather. The streets had emptied. He noted this, but he didn't consider why. He had wrapped his scarf around his face so that his bruises didn't show. Inside the hotel, he gave Frank a brief wave and bolted up the stairs. He burst into the room, thinking only of asking his mother about Jorah and the Shanes. He found her, however, bathed and dressed in her church clothes, a tie knotted tightly under the darkened jaw she'd worn since their arrival. In her hands she held a small package. He unraveled his scarf, and her look changed to one of horror. "What's happened?"

"It's not important."

"Of course it is." As the shopkeeper's son had for her, she took Caleb by the elbow and led him into the washroom. She filled the bath with hot water and began to take his clothes off.

"Mama," he said in reproach when she started to unbuckle his pants, even more nervous around her with the possibility of being the Shane boy clogging his thoughts. He turned from her to undress, and stepped into the water, covering himself. He had never seen this side of his mother, and he buried his questions and fought his embarrassment so that she would continue. He forced a smile and his face ached. She used a cloth to carefully dab at his cuts and bruises. He hadn't known her to be so gentle. Her touch, certainly, seemed that of a mother.

After she'd washed him, Elspeth rested her cheek on the edge of the tub. "I used to bathe you, all of you, as babies." She splashed some water onto his back with a cupped hand. The light played on her eyelashes. "I loved you so. Your skin was the softest thing I'd ever touched, and afterward, I would wrap us both in a towel to keep you close."

Caleb recalled Emma being bathed in the kitchen sink, her body red. The girls would be allowed to help, and Caleb peered at them from beneath the kitchen table, the same table upon which his mother had lain, close to death. "Mother," he said, aware he risked ruining this moment, "I was the one who shot you."

Elspeth went rigid. Her hand clutched the porcelain. "Why?"

Caleb made trails with his hands through the water, and tried to bring himself back to his raft, floating downstream. "The men had come. They'd shot everyone. I'd been in the barn, but I couldn't . . ." Every tear in his body had been wrung out of him. The emptiness moved down his limbs. "When you came in, I thought you were them, and I had to do something."

Elspeth combed the boy's hair from his forehead. "It's okay," she said. "It is." She sang to him in a soft, shy voice, "*O thou hearest when sinners cry, Though all my sins before Thee lie, Behold them not with angry look, but blot their memory from Thy book.*" Her voice echoed in the small room, and because she held her cheek on the tub, it vibrated through the water. "Do you understand what it means?" she asked. He nodded. "I have many apologies to give you, Caleb," Elspeth said, "and I hope you can be as forgiving."

The beating and the admission, coupled with the bath made him spent and sleepy, and he leaned his head against the porcelain. *For a moment*, he told himself, and shut his eyes.

Elspeth heard his breath even out, and his hand slipped from his lap and she saw that he was no more than a boy and replaced the washcloth. After a few minutes, she shook him gently, dried him off, and helped him into bed. While he slept, she went downstairs and ordered them dinner: steak, fried potatoes, and beets.

CLEAN, DRIED, AND rested, Caleb sat up in bed. His mother lifted the lid from his dinner. She'd waited for him, and she used the stool for a small table. They ate in happy silence, afraid to make a loud noise or a false move, unused to this fragile new contentment.

Sated and with empty plates, they both relaxed. Elspeth presented the boy with a gift. He undid the twine, pulling it so quickly it sent a smoke of fibers into the air. The butcher paper held a toy horse, its mane and tail lustrous and soft. It was brown with a white mark in the shape of an arrow on its forehead. Its teeth were exposed, painted brilliant white, and it raised its front left hoof, as if in greeting. "Thank you, Mama, it's nice."

"I know you must miss the animals of the barn."

He stroked the hair with his thumb. Of course he did, but he missed his brothers and sisters more. The quarrelsome noise of the Inn was much different from the noise of the Howell household, and Ellabelle couldn't measure up to Jesse.

While Elspeth cleared their plates and placed a hand on the door to bring them back to the kitchen, she said, "I don't want you going to the Elm Inn anymore. It's too dangerous. Don't get crossed up in something in which you have no business." Caleb opened his mouth to reply. "I'm your mother, Caleb. Rules are made to keep you safe." At that, she shut the door behind her.

The affection that had spread through Caleb over the course of the last few hours evaporated, and when he threw the sheets aside, his skin rippled with goose bumps. He already was crossed up in something, and he appeared to be the only one capable of remembering what they'd lost. No gift or toy pony could undo that. He could not be changed into a boy again for the convenience of his mother. He threw his hat and gloves on, not caring about the dried blood that mottled each, and left the Brick & Feather before his mother could return.

CHAPTER 10

Caleb crept along a ridge, the forest, black and endless, on his left and the town of Watersbridge behind him. The snow had melted and then frozen over in an icy sheen. The wind tightened his skin, made his cuts sing and his bruises throb. Ahead, the ridge curled toward the Shane household like the tail of a sleeping dog.

He'd asked Ethan about Martin—ignoring the twinge of betrayal at disobeying his mother—and Ethan had said the Shanes didn't venture off their land much, a trait Caleb appreciated. Ethan's gaze wandered over Caleb's beaten face, but Ethan didn't like to ask questions any more than he liked to answer them. Caleb said that he thought he'd walked past their house once, and—as he'd hoped—Ethan replied, "I doubt it; they live all the way on the edge of town." Ethan had given him directions with little prodding, and he'd finished by saying with great disdain, for he thought the Shanes too isolated, "They named the trail leading to their property 'Shane Road,' because no one else uses it." While he walked on it, Caleb wondered if the road didn't bear his name as well.

When he finally got a full view of the house, rather than the slivered glimpses he'd seen through the trees, he saw the eaves decorated with elaborate carvings, the doors similarly marked, and the yard littered with stone statues of animals, buried to their torsos in frozen snow. He waited for the barking of a dog, the bellowing of a calf to herald his presence, but no alarm sounded.

Someone crossed a window and Caleb lost his breath. Once, he'd fallen from the top of the hayloft ladder, carrying a bucket and rushing to finish his chores before Jesse. He'd thought he was going to die, that his lungs had broken. Yet that injury had a source. This had been nothing but a shadow flitting across the yellow light emanating from the glass, a movement as rapid and fleeting as a bat, and his windpipe constricted as surely as if Gerry had his arm around his neck once more. He pushed his hat up off his brow, chilling the gash at his hairline, the tingling sparks bringing him back to the world, to the dry smell of pine and the flapping of an owl's wings. High above, the tallest trees creaked in a breeze only they could reach. To Caleb it seemed as though the very air trembled with nerves.

He inched closer. On his hands and knees, he moved like a spider, and he imagined what they would think when they woke in the morning to such strange tracks. At the far side of the house, the brightest lights reached farther out into the darkness. He searched for a better view, pushing his way through the tips of small bushes poking through the snow. He scraped between the trees, under and over the boughs, the sap frozen but adhering to his coat, hat, and gloves, attempting to strip them from his body. In a small thicket of pitch pine, he found both cover and a gap in the branches, a hollow with only a dusting of snow, the needles and cones gathered into a soft rug, close enough to smell the woodfire. From his knees he could see three people. At first, they all had their backs to him, but then a large figure moved and exposed Martin sitting at the table. He slammed his fist on the seat of his chair and threw something with disgust—what Caleb could not guess. Another man took the seat next to him. Unlike Martin, he had dark, curly hair and reedy limbs. Caleb eased back on his haunches, cold attacking his body as soon as he did. The third figure was seated across from Martin, but he could see it was a woman from the bun in her hair and the shining implements that held it in place. The woman and the dark-haired man held hands and bowed their heads. They prayed. Martin, however, picked up his utensils. The similarity that Martin, too, avoided the family prayers compelled Caleb to say it out loud, testing its nature: "Caleb Shane." He clapped his hand over his mouth. The three of them ate, and he tried to calculate the hour, but time had warped when Martin had walked into the Elm, and Caleb could hardly figure if night was coming or going.

Soft, thick snow tumbled down. Unlike most in Watersbridge, which came from the lake and fell fast as rain, these flakes took their time in meandering down out of the sky, gliding back and forth. Between the languid flakes, he saw nothing else that made him want to believe Martin Shane's story anymore. No one had batted an eye when he'd hurled something across the kitchen, and Caleb could tell that the other people maintained a safe distance from him. Over the course of the meal, Caleb guessed the only noise came from the screeching of knives on plates and the clanging of spoons in bowls. The room contained no more congeniality or familiarity than the restaurant. He felt Elspeth's touch again, the care with which she daubed the blood from his wounds. A lifetime of memories told him he had been a fool to entertain the ramblings of this insane man. The city had spun him around and loosed him, dizzy and disoriented, on its wonders. Of course Elspeth was his mother. By telling him not to go to the Elm, he understood, she'd only begun to act as one. It had never been required of her before.

The meal finished, the woman inside turned to the basin beneath the window: She had his hair, his eyes, his lips; part of him had been taken and layered onto her like a veil. He passed his gloved fingers across his own features like he needed to be certain they hadn't been stolen entirely. He gripped the branches in front of him and pulled, as if the bushes were a quilt he could swaddle himself in. The woman leaned closer to the window and pressed a hand to the glass to shade the light. Caleb let go of the branches and slid backward, not able to turn from the house but desperate to get away. The woman spoke to the men and Martin joined her at the glass. The window clouded with the fog from their breath. Caleb thought perhaps he'd screamed. The branches snatched at his face, his hands. He finally emerged from the thicket. Snow whisked past as he scrambled up the hill.

The front door to the Shane house banged open to reveal Martin and the other man. Caleb stopped. In the crook of his elbow Martin had a shotgun broken open, and he cupped a hand near his mouth to light a cigarette. The other man reached back inside the door and produced a rifle. Caleb drew his Colt. The glow from the house only made it so far, and then the night might help to obscure the trail that would lead straight to him. Or so he hoped. The snow, for once, didn't fall fast enough to cover his tracks. The moon that had remained hidden behind the snow clouds broke free, and weakly illuminated the path at the top of the ridge. He tried to will himself up, to crest the hill and sprint back to town. But his muscles refused. He stayed crouched in a ball. He shivered. Sweat dripped from his scalp, off his earlobes and the tip of his nose. It stung his cuts. When he was very young—before the boys and girls separated into their own chores and their own groups—they'd played hide-and-seek and he'd always hidden in the same places, and he would

watch the shoes of Amos, Jesse, and Mary between the boards of
the sheep pen or from the corner of the woodpile, and they would
approach without hesitation, knowing he was there. As soon as
they came close, he could stand it no longer and simply ran, and
Amos, especially, would be angry with him for ruining their game.

Martin kicked at the snow. The two men talked, occasional
laughter poking its way through their conversation and piercing
Caleb's hiding spot. Martin locked the shotgun into place while
the other loaded his rifle. They cocked the weapons, but their pace
was leisurely as they walked toward the thicket. They approached
the tracks he'd left. He'd broken clear through the icy surface of
the snow and into the powder beneath, and he understood that
once the men's footsteps went from the cacophonous shattering of
the icy crust to the soft shuffle of powder, their demeanor would
change, and they'd put their guns to their shoulders and not stop
until they'd killed him. His knees locked, and he again felt like the
small and helpless creature that had watched through the knot in
the wall while his sister bled into the snow and his family followed
her, one after the other, into darkness.

The pair was less than a yard from his tracks, and Caleb could
smell the tobacco on the air, knew it would soon mix with the
metallic stench of gunpowder. Martin shifted his shotgun to his
hands. The other man stepped into the middle of Caleb's tracks
and Caleb popped onto his feet and raced for the top of the hill.
Without looking, he fired his gun once. The trigger yielded with no
resistance. Blinded by the darkness and the terror, he grasped the
base of a small oak and pulled himself up the steep incline, digging
his boots into the snow, trying to reach the solid earth beneath. His
foot struck a rock and he shot forward. Whatever stood in front
of him he grabbed, scrabbling toward the ridge. A glance back revealed his scarf hanging from a tree like an empty noose, exposed

in lantern light. He clawed at the ice itself. He found purchase on the broken stump of an elm and leapt for the clearing as a bullet pierced the wood. The splinters scratched at him.

The sudden freedom of the trail fed his legs and his lungs. He heard shouting and the report of the rifle. But with the thickness of the trees and the uphill angle, the pair had slim chance of a clean shot. It was their luck against his own. He slipped and fell and shoved himself upright again. The trail sloped downward, and as he rounded a bend he heard the sizzle of a bullet and then heard the solid thunk of it nestling into a birch tree. Thin as paper, the bark slid to the ground and rustled as he sprinted past. Their voices suddenly got louder; they must've known of a shortcut up the hill. He hugged the tree line, stayed tight to it when the path curved. Friendly with the close air of the Elm Inn, he'd gotten used to the indoors, and the sting of the bitter cold rattled like shards of glass in his lungs. He didn't know how close the men were behind him, but he didn't dare lose his concentration and his footing to check. Besides, he'd heard Amos and his father discuss taking aim and killing deer and squirrels by nothing more than the wetness of their eyes and the shine they took from the moonlight.

His feet settled into a steadier rhythm as the path leveled. He hadn't heard the whistling or dull thud of a bullet in a long time. The snow continued to fall, and he hoped that if the men had gone back to fetch a horse that his tracks would be obscured.

He neared town—the lamps shone over the trees and the noise of the inn echoed through the forest—and he pictured becoming a man like London White's twin, living in the woods, alone. He would get a dog and a horse and on cold nights he'd sleep beside them. He didn't think he'd miss people much at all. His breath raspy and ragged, he stopped running. In the sky, the rising moon excused itself behind the snow clouds again. Flakes continued their lazy descent. The path widened. He walked in the ruts of wagon wheels, where uneven rocks had long since been kicked away or ground into the dirt and he thought his trail would be harder to see. The noise intensified, sharpening into laughs and screams, the inn at its peak. He listened. Something else traveled on the air. He stopped. A low thunder rumbled beneath the sounds emanating from the inn. He jumped as far as he could, to the edge of the woods, then hopped again, and slid beneath a broken pine. His lungs burned and he suppressed an urge to cough as the hooves beat louder. The thin, dark-haired man from the Shane house stood in the stirrups—the horse steady enough in the snow and that he could trust its movements and scan the ground for prints. Caleb scooted farther beneath the branch, the cold there deep and invasive. The hoofbeats receded and then approached, slower. Caleb raised the Colt, his hands moving slowly, but they were numb from the cold and sweaty from the terrified run and the gun slipped from his grasp. The unmistakable sound of a man dropping from his mount turned Caleb's search more frantic. His fingers sifted through the snow. The man struck a match and Caleb saw the brief explosion followed by a dull illumination. It lasted a few long seconds before he heard the hiss of the spent match being thrown away. The man lit another. Caleb held his breath and knew the man did, too.

Somehow he found the gun. The barrel, however, had caught on a section of needles, and a thick icicle cracked and struck a branch on the way down, the din incredible to Caleb's fearful ears. "Come on out," the man said.

Caleb tried to see through the underbrush to line up a shot. Before he could, the man fired and snow dropped from the branches with a thump. Caleb could try to blast his way out, but from the trees he'd have to hope beyond hope to get lucky enough to hit something critical before the man could pinpoint his hiding spot and pepper it with bullets.

"I'm coming out," Caleb said. "Please don't shoot. I'm just a boy." It was a fact he'd forgotten over the last few weeks and it came as a relief. He wished he'd carried his mother's gift with him as evidence. He wanted to say it again, *I'm just a boy. Let's stop now.*

"Toss your gun out first."

Caleb slid the gun on the snow, and the man kicked it away. He pulled his hat down low; he couldn't let the man see his face, see the woman in it. The man trained a pistol on him as Caleb crawled out. He had a scar between his nose and his lip that interrupted his stubble. "Why are you spying on us?"

Caleb picked at some sap affixed to his coat.

"I don't care if you are a boy, I'll put a bullet between your eyes. Now, tell me, why were you spying on us?" Caleb said nothing and the man struck him with the back of his hand, knocking Caleb to the ground and his hat from his head. When he looked up, though, the man's expression changed. He sank down, his legs crossed, and he sat in the snow in front of Caleb, who pushed himself up onto his elbows. "You're him."

The horse, spooked by the shots, worried at the ground with a hoof and tugged at his bridle, which the man had in one hand. He dropped the reins, but rather than flee, the horse backed up a few steps, struck the ground anxiously a few more times, shook his mane, and calmed.

"I don't know what you're talking about." He didn't want to be the Shane boy. He hadn't had time to understand what that meant, or how he'd come to have two mothers.

The man's eyebrows furrowed and rose up in worry, the dark hair undulating in a dance. "But why would you shoot at us?"

"I don't know." He didn't want to admit to being scared.

"I'm Paul." He helped Caleb to his feet, then hung on to his wrist, and pulled Caleb closer and Caleb could smell the stew lingering on his breath. "I thought you might miss this," Paul said, and draped Caleb's scarf around his neck, cautious of his wounds. "What happened to your face?"

"I'm not who you think I am."

Paul located the Colt in the snow, wiped it off, turned it around, and handed it to Caleb, grip first. With it, Caleb regained his confidence and his mind cleared. "I'm going home to my father."

Paul wrapped the leather of the horse's bridle around his wrist twice and then let it fall loose again. "You can go if you do me one favor," he said. Caleb waited for him to continue for almost a full minute. He could feel his heart beating in his fingers where he gripped the gun. "Come to our house and have dinner. Sit and eat with us."

"How about I leave this town with my father and we never come back?" With that, Caleb put the gun in its familiar place at the small of his back and set off down the path.

The horse's bridle jangled and the saddle creaked as Paul relaxed back into it. He called after him, "That's not your father."

Caleb strode faster. His thoughts spun completely out of control and he couldn't catch any of them, and he stopped trying.

CHAPTER 11

Behind the church and next to the graveyard, a series of pale gray tarps covered the bodies crushed in the icehouse. Elspeth measured the size and height of the outlines, trying to find the darned socks, the bootless foot of the child who'd carried the message. She had to keep reminding herself that Caleb, too, was a boy, nothing more. His hairless body had been so pale in the bathtub, his arms and legs so thin, ribs showing. He'd burned the bodies of the only family he knew after living in and among their corpses for days, surprised expressions forever locked on their faces. He'd acted bravely in their honor and opened the door of the pantry to find he'd shot her. She couldn't imagine. What bothered her as she pulled the canvas over a pair of legs was that she hadn't tried to. Only a few hours prior she'd counted her money, bent on escaping and replacing him. Her anger at his leaving the hotel against her wishes evaporated and settled back upon her own conscience.

Every few feet a rock held the tarp in place, but the wind teased the material, creating a rumble like thunder. Some of the men quaked at the noise, shaken by the accident, their glances gone shifty, unable to quite meet one another's eyes. "Quite a mess," one of them said. Elspeth agreed. "All these sons and fathers," he said. "Tragic."

Elspeth bent down to move a rock into a firmer position.

"Where are you headed on this bitterly cold night, friend?" The man took a watch from the folds of his expensive-looking furs and wound it.

"I'm not sure," Elspeth said. "And you?"

The watch disappeared along with the man's arms into the bulk of the coat. Elspeth could see the shining eyes of some limp animal staring at her, and the bright gleam of its teeth. "I came to find you, actually."

Elspeth reached for her pistol.

"No need for that," he said. "Your boy has been working for me for some time now, which I assume you know." She said she did, dropping her voice even lower. He grinned, and between the flash of his teeth, the luminous fur, and the glass eyes it stared at her with, he glimmered like quicksilver. "You have different last names, I hear. He's a Howell, you're a van Tessel."

Elspeth considered shooting him and laying his body to rest with the muddy men of the icehouse, their day's sweat more, she guessed, than this man's lifetime. But she didn't know what lay within the confines of his coat, and that worried her. She couldn't leave Caleb alone. Not after all she'd done. "His mother," she said, "used to work for some van Tessels down this way, and I thought the name might help. Might open doors."

The man considered this. He tilted his head back and forth like he could shake loose the truth, but his gaze never left her. "Well," he said, "we all do what we can to get ahead." Again he seemed as though he found something amusing. "Caleb is a good boy. And totally unafraid, isn't he?"

"Yes," Elspeth said. "He's all that I have now."

With a stunning quickness, he reached out from his coat and pushed her hat back. Elspeth didn't have time to react before the hand had returned to the fur. It all happened so fast she questioned whether it had happened at all. The smile vanished from the man's face. Elspeth could smell him, a warm, exotic scent. "I wished to see you," he said. "That's all." He spoke with disquieting calm. "If ever you're in need of a game, the Elm's doors are open to you always, Jorah Howell." He turned on his heel.

She waited until she could no longer hear any trace of his footsteps, and then she began to run. Everything in her screamed to steal the infant and leave town. The urge was familiar and comfortable—she exalted in it, and it fed her, gave her stamina. The boots and shoes of every man, woman, and child of Watersbridge, drawn to the accident and then home to dinner and bed, had cleared the roads completely of snow. She passed the graveyard and climbed the hill, resting—out of breath, her injuries throbbing—at its apex to look down at the frozen body of the lake, a gray nothing that soaked up the light and gave little back. Twisters of snow blew on its surface. She took several frigid, deep breaths and forced Caleb's name and then his image into her head. She kicked off her boot, took the money from her pocket, and jammed it into the toes. Once she'd retied the laces she stomped on the ice several times to tamp down the money and the sound echoed over the water.

On the other side of the graveyard, walking north, she turned onto a small street, both sides lined by a knee-high rock wall, one side buried by frozen drifts of snow, but exposed on the other where the wind had stripped it clean. The small lane gave way to an even smaller path that skirted the lake. The chill crept up her legs. Only one house stood on the street Charles had described as his own. A large window was set in the middle of the building, and on either side of that were eighteen others, three on each side, for three stories. Between all the windows and staircases, landings and porches ran back and forth, up and down, in a seemingly non-sensical fashion; the house was surrounded by a skeleton of wood. Someone emerged from the broad front door—head down, collar pulled high, hands jammed deep in his pockets against the wind.

"Can I help you?" he asked. Elspeth recognized him without a second's hesitation: Owen Trachte. She stood closer than she'd been to him in twelve years, and despite his hat and scarf, she could see how time had hardened his baby fat into something severe and poked through with whiskers.

"Does Charles Heather live here?"

"You a friend of his?"

"I worked with him."

"Another." Owen whistled between his teeth. He told her he hadn't seen Charles all day. He asked if Elspeth had witnessed the accident.

"I saw what happened after."

"Tragic," Owen said. "Do I know you from down there?"

Elspeth pulled her scarf higher on her face. "I don't think so."

He extended his hand and introduced himself. Elspeth shook, happy that she wore her gloves, for some part of her believed that if Owen could grasp hold of her bare hand, he would recognize something in her touch. "I'm off to the tavern," Owen said. "You might find Heather there, Jorah."

"Are you sure he's not home?"

Owen pointed to a dark window in the upper corner of the building. "If he is, he's asleep." He scuffed his feet in the snow and lifted his shoulders, as if to bury himself deeper in his coat. "You coming this way?"

"I think I'll wait a bit. See if he comes back."

"Suit yourself," he said. "Don't wait too long, or I'll be chipping you out of the ice."

Elspeth laughed, high at first, then roughing it up as she remembered herself. They both realized the inappropriateness of the joke at the same time. She bid him good night and Owen moved on toward the dim glow of town.

A sign in the window read ROOM FOR LET. A tin box nailed to the wall on the porch contained twelve slots, each labeled by name in tiny, meticulous script. Elspeth stood back and attempted to dissect which staircase led to which room, which landing was available to which resident. After some tracing, she took the stairs up to one landing and then another, before she stood outside what she hoped to be Charles Heather's darkened window. She lifted chapped knuckles to knock on the glass, and when she saw her hand there, a sense of calm breezed through her. Charles would help. With all of his troubles—his kiss, his moods, his lies—he would be sympathetic to whatever pieces of her story she decided to present him with. He would tell her what to do with Caleb's boss, who seemed to know everything about her and even more about the child she'd raised as her own. They shared too many secrets for him to turn her away.

The slightest reflection came back at her and she saw how she'd changed her posture, how she stood there with her shoulders lowered, arms bowed, feet apart. How complete her lies had become. She didn't know whether to be proud or afraid. No response met her insistent knocking.

Back down the stairs, the wood groaning in the cold, she followed in Owen's wake onto the increasingly well-traveled roads. She needed the assurance of people—thinking how not all that long ago she'd walk into the fields in the evenings to escape the voices of the children—and she arrived at the restaurant, where the heat from the ovens and stoves clouded the windows so that they cried tears of condensation. As she was about to open the door, it flung back at her, and a crowd barreled into the street, their boots rapping on the planks.

She heard Charles's voice, slurred but careful, emanate from somewhere in the middle of the group. "I meant no harm," he said. "It's been a rough day for everyone."

She lurked on the edge of the mass of bodies as they shuffled out of the restaurant. A flurry of movement and Charles was tossed to the ground for the second time in a matter of hours. He lay curled in the snow. Elspeth circled around the half dozen or so men, trying to get closer to him. While she glanced from one diner to the other, napkins still stuck in their collars, Charles rose to his feet. His left cheek bloomed into a hundred small cuts from the granules of ice. A knot had already formed on his head. "I merely needed to find a partner."

"We told you about this," the cook said, and removed his apron.

"I meant no harm," Charles repeated. His hat had come off, and his shock of orange hair had been decorated with snow.

"Don't care—don't let me see you in this place again."

Charles put a finger to his nose and emptied one nostril and then the other of blood. He smiled, his teeth stained red. "Maybe you'd like to come and work with me?"

The cook launched himself at Charles, and the other men closed in, too. The speed of it surprised Elspeth, and it took her a second to get her weight off her heels. She reached through and around, her nails tearing at their clothes to get to Charles, grabbing whatever she could hold on to and yanking.

She caught a glimpse of him when he kicked away from the crowd, stuck his chin in the air, and grabbed a napkin from a man's flannel collar. He took both ends in his hands—each wearing a different glove—looped it around the man's neck and tightened. Charles leaned back and the man—a fellow of considerable size all the way around—toppled backward, Charles beneath him. The man's feet pawed at the snow. His face, ruddy before, turned purple. His neck bulged.

One of the men clawed at the napkin. Another lifted his boot over Charles's face. Before it came down, Charles's cold stare locked onto Elspeth. A shiver washed down her spine. The heavy sole fell. His mouth went sideways with a sickening crunch and the boot ground into his face. The man who had been strangled rolled away, coughing and gagging. The others grouped around Charles, and everything moved at once—arms, legs, fists, and feet.

Elspeth surged forward and tried again to pull the men from Charles, but they were too far gone, and she couldn't get within a foot of him without being knocked back by an arm or a hip. "You're killing him," she shouted. The men wouldn't let up. She tried to push through again and an elbow caught her square on the nose. The crack reverberated in her skull and she tumbled back onto the ice. Tears came. The stars in her vision became fireworks. Elspeth could feel the thrum in her skin—her nose, the swelling of her eye, the blood sliding around her mouth and down her neck.

A gunshot sounded out. It had no effect. The second stopped them, and they released their grips, straightened their shirts, wiped the blood from their fists onto their pants. Their breath sent fast-dissolving clouds into the air, and they came and disappeared like the blinking of fireflies. Owen Trachte held a pistol loosely at the end of his thick fingers, the barrel smoking. He jerked his head at the men, and they grumbled to each other before tromping back into the restaurant, their skin red with exertion and cold.

"Guess you found him," Owen said when the door had shut.

Elspeth mopped the blood from her face and spit more onto the snow. It pooled in her throat. The two of them appraised Charles. She could smell the alcohol on Owen's breath, and she saw his father, years ago, drinking in his office, reclining in his chair, his feet upon the windowsill. Charles's face had lumped and distended. When he breathed his nose whistled. The cold had either numbed Elspeth to the point where she could no longer feel it or the night had already started to leave them. She looked to the sky between the trees, but could not find any sign of light in the east.

Owen checked Charles's body, first one arm, then the other, then his shoulders and his collarbone, his torso, and his legs. "He's got a broken jaw, maybe some ribs," Owen said. He turned his attention to Elspeth. "They got you both pretty good." Owen squinted at her, and then placed his thumbs on either side of her nose. He pressed down. A burst of electric pain coursed through her and settled into relief from the pressure. Owen patted her on the shoulder and pointed to his own lumpy nose. "I've had my share." Elspeth heard the thunderous stampeding of Owen and his friends, the wails and squeals they'd emitted as they'd chased and attacked each other, the closet full of rolled white bandages that would need to be restocked every few months in winter, every few weeks in summer.

"Thanks," she said. He bent down and gathered up a ball of snow, which he packed in a handkerchief and gave to her. She pressed it to her nose.

"The bleeding should stop soon enough," he said. "You'll probably have a headache for a few days." He picked Charles up and tossed him over his wide shoulder. Charles grunted at being bent in half.

"Should you be carrying him if he has broken ribs?"

"Nobody else is going to," Owen said and set off in the direction of their home. Though she wasn't sure he intended her to, Elspeth matched Owen's short and heavy steps. She couldn't help herself. The guilt she felt for Caleb seeped into her thoughts, and she wondered if perhaps Phillip Trachte had drunk himself to death on account of her stealing one of his charges. "You learned to set a nose on your own?"

"Nah," Owen said. He fished a cigarette from his pocket and lit it before Elspeth could offer to help, the whole action taking less effort than she would need to tie her shoes. "My father was a doctor." Somehow he held the cigarette in his lips and managed to drag on it with one corner of his mouth and exhale with the other.

"He's gone?"

"Yeah. He taught me more than I wanted to know. He was my only friend growing up," he said, and Elspeth almost asked about the boy who'd knocked out his tooth but thought better of it. "I must have been six—seven—and I was too afraid to ride a horse. So he would get down on all fours and we would practice, the two of us. He'd rear up and everything. Prepare me. He was like that with a lot of things." Charles moaned on his shoulder. "So what did you boys do to get those men so upset?"

"I'm not sure."

"Looks like Heather got the worst of it." He readjusted Charles, who whimpered. "But he usually does."

Elspeth let the comment fade on the wind.

"I'll wake the doctor," Owen said as their house came into view.

"Can't you do it?" she said. "I'm sorry, that sounded rude. I just meant—you set my nose and I saw you at the icehouse today."

"I don't think I was much help there. I can do some stitching in a pinch, but that's about all." Owen spit some stray tobacco from his tongue. "A doctor lives downstairs. He usually works on animals, but he was my father's apprentice." He flicked his cigarette into the night. "I trust him."

"I guess I'll head back then," she said. Owen waved her away with a meaty hand. As she peeled off and walked in the direction of the Brick & Feather, she tripped again and again over clumps of ice and the hardened footprints of others. The cold returned, but Elspeth was certain it had never left.

Elspeth's hand stung, and she pulled it from her pocket like it was a rock, or a gun: cold, heavy, and inhuman. Her skin had torn along the knuckles and swollen on either side, so the gash looked like a series of mountain ranges cut by a river of blood. Somewhere in the fight she'd lost her hat, and she paused outside the butcher shop, and in-between the silhouettes of hanging pigs and geese she searched the ground like it had only fallen once she'd noticed it was gone. While her lungs and muscles coursed with the fight, her broken nose ached in the wind, and her ears rang from Owen's gun, she continued on, and in front of the hotel she almost crashed headfirst into Caleb, coming from the opposite direction. No sound but their footsteps interrupted the night. No one else ventured out in hours that were tipping from late to early. It was as if they were the last live souls on earth. Elspeth enveloped the boy in a hug and squeezed him until her arms ached.

After he'd ignored the one rule his mother had ever given him, he couldn't understand why she'd chosen this moment to show such affection. It was as though she knew where he'd been and what he'd seen. The courage he'd built up to ask her all of his questions drained away once again as she held him.

The boy refused to look at her. "Did you find something out?" she asked. She glanced over his shoulder as if the trio of murderers were right behind him. She noted the pistol in his hand, and tapped his wrist, as if encouraging him to put it away. He did not.

"What happened to your nose?" he asked, making out the swelling through the shadows. She looked old. Their time together had worn on her, and he saw the wrinkles that stress had dug into her skin. Her forehead bore three deep lines that colored her stern and worried. He held the door open for her.

"Nothing," she said. "Nothing to worry about."

Only once the door shut out the wind did they hear their hearts thudding vainly in their ears to combat the cold. The grand clock tocked in the empty space. They stared at each other for a while, waiting. Neither spoke, and to each it was apparent how much had changed for the small boy who went to live in the barn and the woman who tromped up the hill every few months, stayed a few restless months more, and then was gone.

AT TEN O'CLOCK in the morning, something heavy crashed in the hallway, and they jumped awake and winced in unison. Caleb pushed back the filmy curtains above his bed. The morning appeared thick with skies like smoke, the snow not yet falling. Wind buffeted the building. They studied each other. Elspeth had slept sitting up, and her limbs crackled with inactivity. She stretched one leg and then the other and loosened the laces on her boots. Her lips were caked with gore. Both her eyes had gone black. But it was her nose, and the thick vee of blood it had left on her shirt, that held his gaze. It had grown purple in the night, and though it looked relatively straight, a small lump protruded from its center. Caleb, for his part, looked much worse. His jaw carried a nasty bruise, the deep color of blackberries. On his temple, a thick knot pulled his eyebrow into a surprised arc and half closed his eye. Combined, they gave his face the appearance of leaning to one side, like a snowman that had begun to melt.

"Aren't we a pair?" Elspeth said.

Caleb's voice came out garbled from his swollen mouth. He repeated something he'd heard often at the Elm Inn. "The cards aren't falling for us."

"I got a raise at work," Elspeth said. "So it's not all bad." She attempted a laugh. From the edge of the bed, she leaned over to retie her boots and every heartbeat brought agony pulsating into her nose.

"We can't go yet," Caleb said. He picked up the toy horse his mother had gotten him only the day before; it looked ridiculous in the morning light. Leaving had only occurred to Caleb in rare stretches of quiet—coming home from the inn in the early morning, the hardiest birds trying out their songs, or among the drying sheets, the air pregnant with steam and the smell of soap—but he had always thought of Watersbridge as a transitional point: Either the murderers were there and they would kill them, or they weren't and Caleb and Elspeth would try another town and another until they ran out of world. As the days had passed, however, and the piles of their clothes had begun to accumulate, and their scents and belongings had filled the room, Watersbridge had become something like a home without either of them realizing it. Caleb returned the horse to its shelf. He took the pistol from the stool and tucked it back into his belt. Like he hadn't seen it in a very long time, he set the Ithaca on his lap and went to work cleaning it, the kind of chore his father had shown them but hadn't allowed them to perform on their own before they'd watched him enough times to walk his hands through it first, telling him what to do, step by step. The first time Caleb had cleaned Jorah's rifle he'd placed the gun upon a bright white towel so as not to mar his work, and when his father had seen the towel smudged with oil, he'd made Caleb wash it and sit on the creek bank to watch it dry. *"There they cry, but none giveth answer, because of the pride of evil men,"* his father had said when Caleb finally came in, the towel folded as neatly as he could manage and dry as a bone. The memory made him think of the Shanes' house, and though the Ithaca had been buffed to a bright sheen, he shook out his cloth and started all over from the end of the muzzle.

Elspeth wiped the dust from the mirror and adjusted her hair. Her black eyes and the thick bruise of her nose lent a certain manliness to her face. The throbbing worsened as she stood. "What are you going to do today?"

Caleb tilted his head as he answered. "Ask some questions."

She buttoned her coat and tied a scarf around her neck. "You be careful, Caleb. If you need me, I'll be down at the icehouse, in the offices there."

Caleb stared at himself in the shine on the shotgun barrel, where his lumps and bruises distorted his face beyond recognition.

THE ICE COMPANY had come to a standstill. At the shore, where the breath of horse and man usually created a constant cloud of exertion, only two men worked in silence, shrouded in scarves, repairing the bent and battered sled. Closer to the icehouse, a solitary figure reset a lamppost. The hulking doors were closed, yet Elspeth could hear the men chipping away at the ice inside. Next to the building, an oilcloth tarp wasn't wide enough to obscure the bodies beneath it—those that hadn't been moved to the church, or couldn't be identified, the worn soles of boots and the muddied tangles of hair protruding on either side. She didn't see the darned socks, or the small feet they held.

In the office, only Horace sat behind the long desk. The hearth was cold. He wore fingerless gloves and thick glasses, and his hair stuck up in a white horn, as if he'd been yanking on it all night. He had wrapped himself in the plaid blanket that had been hanging on the wall, and where it had once been, a large scorch mark marred the wood. The baby slept in the crib, her arms crossed and her tiny fists snug under her chin. Elspeth wished her sleep was as sound. Her desire to run flashed only briefly, like the tip of a memory.

"I see you, I see you," Horace said, "I must finish this one . . ." He went silent and scratched some numbers into a ledger. The figures piled up on the page. After an uncomfortable length of time, he set his pencil on his desk and pushed his chair back with a loud scrape. "What is it?"

Elspeth explained the promotion.

"You're smaller than the rest. I'm surprised you lasted as long as you did."

"Rest of who?"

"You worked with Heather?" he asked. She hadn't mentioned Charles's name. "Did he do that to you?" She reached a hand up to her damaged face. Horace laughed, exposing his pink gums. He slapped the desk. "Today's shot, but tomorrow, who knows? Who knows after something like this. You'll have to work in here, with us. Not much room to speak of." The old man pulled the blanket tighter across his shoulders. "He's a funny man, Charlie Heather," the old man said. "Always has been. He was a funny boy."

"You've known him since he was a boy?"

"Of course. He's Wallace's son. He practically grew up in this room—that's his crib." Charles's stories of the sea, of growing up in Massachusetts, had all been lies. Horace read her look and continued. "They don't share a name, I know. He's Edward's sister's boy." He lowered his voice to a conspiratorial whisper. "She abandoned him." Elspeth stared at the scar burned on the wall. It was roughly the shape of a bird. "She came into town one night, child in tow, and knocked on Edward's door like a stranger. The next morning he woke up and she was gone. She only stayed long enough to say that the father's name was Heather." The old man blew his nose into a handkerchief that appeared out of the blanket. "Maybe it was all that time growing up without a mother that turned the boy so . . . peculiar." She saw Charles in the snow, clutching the dropped glove, inhaling its perfume. "But you know all about that, don't you?" The man flipped open a different ledger, sending dust spinning in all directions. "If you didn't, we wouldn't have to find another promotion."

Elspeth ignored the slight, and turned her attention to the child. "I bet this little one knows nothing of what's happened," she said, and held out a finger to the infant, who clasped it in her tiny hand on instinct, but didn't stir.

"Oh, no, no," the man said, "she's been up all night—she just went down in fact. No, the kids know. They know better than we do. It's like when you see the forest creatures fleeing, you better run, because something's coming—flood, fire, pestilence." Elspeth moved her finger back and forth and the baby held on even in sleep. The man finally located whatever he'd been looking for and licked his lips twice in quick succession. "They understand it all a lot better than we think."

CALEB, TUCKED BENEATH his hat and collar, hurried down the stairs and toward the door.

Frank called out to him. "Breakfast?" Then, glancing at the clock. "Lunch?" He excused himself from a man fixing the door to the kitchen. Frank carried a newspaper under his arm, and plopped it on the table.

"What happened?" he said, lifting Caleb's hat, and then folding back his collar. Caleb let him: A part of him had hoped that he would. "My lord, Caleb." Frank pulled him into the kitchen and sat him on a stool. He said he'd only be a minute, yelled Caleb's customary order to the cook, and snatched his coat from the rack, which wobbled back and forth in his haste.

In the hours between breakfast and lunch the kitchen calmed down, and the staff sat in the corner, playing cards on a butcher's block. One dozed in a chair next to the door leading outside, his head propped against the hutch containing stacks of plates and rows of glasses. A cook, a kind, round fellow who winked at Caleb every time he'd bring his dishes in and place them in the sink, dropped off a plate of hash and eggs with two pieces of toast with extra pats of butter. It hurt to eat. His teeth were loose. The eggs and hash were easy enough to soften with his tongue and then swallow, but the toast he left untouched.

Frank, flushed and exuding cold, came into the kitchen with a brown bag in his hand. He withdrew a small tub, dipped his fingers into it, and said, "It's petroleum jelly. It doesn't hurt, but it'll guard your face against the cold. You're not going out today, are you?"

Caleb dreamed of a day spent in bed or at Frank's side, reading the news and watching the people come into the hotel, but he said, "I have to."

"I expected you'd say that." Frank slathered the jelly onto Caleb's face, heavy and soothing. He tapped the newspaper. "Care to read some before you go?"

Caleb wished it to be so easy, but he needed the kind of information only the Elm Inn could provide. He thanked Frank for his help and dropped his plate at the sink. Frank put Caleb's hat on with care to avoid the cuts and bruises and refastened the collar of Jorah's old coat, and helped Caleb roll the sleeves. Frank's hands smelled of the paper—of ink and pulp. Caleb ignored this last plea to stay in the safety of the hotel, and left out the back, where he gingerly opened the door and the cold gust that blew in woke the napping man, his sudden spasm rattling the glasses and the plates, ringing them like chimes.

ELSPETH SAW THE would-be preacher standing in the upper doors of the icehouse, his hands folded across his belly, hair falling out of place and into his eyes in the face of the wind. He radiated such peace that Elspeth changed course. Inside, a handful of men stacked broken chunks of ice onto sleds, struggling in dirt thick with blood. She climbed the stairs, and as she reached the catwalk, the preacher darted in the other direction. Elspeth picked up her pace, and the men below stopped their work to see who would dare raise such a ruckus while the ghosts lingered. She hoped she apologized with her eyes. "Sir," Elspeth whispered, but the preacher did not stop. "Preacher." He sped up and crawled under the thick ropes that lashed the remaining stacks of ice to giant eyebolts they'd fastened to the walls. "Wait," she said.

The men below leaned against the sleds, watching the preacher race toward the opposite staircase. One of the men said something to the others in a whisper harsh enough to ascend to the walkway, and the preacher, in the echoes of this unheard comment, stopped. He faced her and forced a smile. "Hello."

She'd been wrong. Rather than the ease of peace on his face, it had been the emptiness of utter despair. He looked down at the men. "Would you mind if we went someplace more private, my—my son?" They both knew this term had no place between them; Elspeth must have been at least five years older than he.

He led her to a storage room where chains hung from the ceiling and bolts the size of her thigh were stacked against the walls. Buckets of harness oil and axle grease filled the room with dizzying odors. Yet the preacher insisted on shutting the door. The lamp had been turned low. "Now," he said, "what is it that you need help with?" His voice threatened to crack with each syllable.

Elspeth longed to explain to someone, to receive some sober advice and perhaps leave turning over a Bible quote in her head as she would if she'd been speaking to Jorah, though she'd witnessed how poorly equipped the preacher was to handle such chores. Seeing him, however, she recognized she'd break him if she asked for much. "Would you be so kind as to say a prayer with me?"

Relief poured over the preacher's face, and he looked even younger with the lines of concern lightened. They bowed their heads, and he sank to his knees and Elspeth followed. They said the Lord's Prayer together. By the time they finished, his cheeks were wet and he blinked away tears.

"What is it?" Elspeth—who felt no better—asked.

"I'm sorry, I should be providing you with counsel, not the other way around." He got up and brushed the dirt from his knees. He offered Elspeth his hand and helped her to her feet.

"It's fine," she said.

"Well," he began. "This whole thing"—he waved his arm around him, to encompass the icehouse—"has been too much for me." His voice split into multiple registers, alternating high and low. "I know it's silly to complain when men have lost their lives and children their fathers and wives their husbands, but I don't know how to bring these people peace."

People rarely asked Elspeth for advice. A doctor she'd worked for—the doctor who had left her with Emma—once had asked her, "What is that head so full of that I feel like I can never ask you a question, for fear of it spilling over?"

"All you can supply is an ear," Elspeth said to the preacher. "If you can't give solace with the Bible, don't try to."

"I don't know my way around the Book as I should." He fingered the thick links of a chain. "You're going to tell someone, aren't you?" She swore she wouldn't. "I craved something of my own," he said. She knew this impulse well. "I used to walk past this perfect house next to the church on my way to work in the furniture factory, and some days on the way home I'd stop and sit in the grass and just look at it. I thought about it all the time, everything behind those windows being mine. When the factory moved to Rochester, I was fired, but the man who lived in the house had been promoted. The preacher—the real preacher—convinced me these were signs from God. It wasn't difficult. The Lord had made me stay and now I could get what I wanted. I'd been put so very close."

"Can we be blamed for wanting?" she asked him.

"We can," he said.

A small breeze rocked the chains, and they clunked together.

"'*Do you hear the call, my son?*' he asked me."

Elspeth didn't have to ask, didn't have to look at him to know his answer and that he hadn't meant it at all.

ONLY A FEW scattered men lounged around the Elm Inn. As with most mornings, the sun coming in through the windows without the curtains pulled or without curtains at all cooked the previous nights' sins: the smell of alcohol more pungent and insidious, the odors of moving bodies more bracing, urine and stale smoke and cooked meat all congealed into one mass. Caleb grabbed a broom someone had rested on the doorframe—probably Ethan sweeping up broken glass or someone's teeth—and brandished it like a weapon, unable to conceive of working. A door banged open upstairs, and Ethan's hulking frame backed out of it. At first it looked like he carried a pair of boots under his arms, but after a few more steps, Caleb saw a thin stripe of skin and then trousers. Ethan maneuvered himself around the bend toward the staircase, his back scraping along the railing, the balusters sounding off-key notes. It was plain from the way the man's head swept along the wooden floors that he was dead.

"Boy," Ethan called, spotting Caleb, "come and help me with this one."

One insinuated many to Caleb, but he wouldn't dare ignore Ethan's request. He scampered up the other staircase and hurried along the walkway. Ethan lifted the man's torso with a hand in each armpit, and Caleb took up his ankles. His socks had fallen down into his boots, and the skin felt hot. But Caleb soon realized it wasn't heat that shocked his hands, but the intensity of the cold; the man was like ice. Ethan smiled, one eyebrow cocked under the bowler White always asked him to remove indoors. "Whose fist you hit with your face?"

Caleb grunted and found a new grip on the rolled cuffs of the man's pants. "No one," he said. The man's eyes had lolled deep into his skull, the color there like the set of pearls White lent from girl to girl, whoever happened to be his favorite at the time, whoever— he'd told Caleb—could fetch the best price. Caleb had seen eyes like those before and he'd covered them with a set of buttons from a pair of overalls. The scent of early morning on the hillside came to him, something fresh and earthen, and it turned to rot.

"Ethan," Caleb said, once they'd gotten to the bottom of the stairs and the big man had dropped his load with no ceremony whatsoever, the dead man's skull bouncing on the floor. Caleb set the feet down with all the care he could muster. "What are you going to do with the body?"

"What we do with the rest," Ethan said. When gunshots rang out in the inn, the first thing Caleb did was to find and identify the gunman, see if he struck a chord in his guts, and once every-thing calmed, someone would call out, "Somebody go and fetch the doctor." The next morning there would be a deep pocket in the snow on the side of the building, smeared with the dingy brown of old blood. He'd come to learn the joke, to understand their cruel humor. Ethan wiped his hands on his pants. "Don't you worry about stuff like that. You stick to sweeping and doing the laundry for now. Someday maybe you'll be able to quit the ladies' chores and move on to the men's."

"How would I find someone," Caleb said, edging the dead man's legs parallel to one another with his toe, "who would be willing to kill a man?"

"Now that, kid, is a man's chore." Ethan stretched his back until it cracked mightily. "You mean to kill the one who done that to you?" Ethan hoisted the corpse again and motioned with a nod for Caleb to follow suit. "I suppose I could do it. Depends on the job." They shuffled across the gaming floor, Ethan kicking chairs and tables out of the way as they went. "Killing's like anything else—there's a right man for it."

Caleb couldn't believe he hadn't asked Ethan these questions sooner; everyone else took such great pains to protect him that he'd stopped asking lest he hear the same careful, uninformative answers. "What if I needed someone to go kill someone someplace else?"

Ethan paused while he fiddled with the latch on the door, holding the man's entire upper body with one large paw. "Ol' Jackson Ramus, that's who you'd call." Jackson Ramus. The name didn't seem real to Caleb. He checked it against his images of the men. "Of course Ramus died three, four years ago." Ethan pitched the door open and the cold wind knocked Caleb backward. Ethan didn't notice. "He was supposed to be tracking a woman whose husband said she'd been kidnapped. And he found her all right, found her in the lying-down game with another man." Ethan didn't slow moving across the icy landing to the railing. "Ramus was a smart man—maybe too smart, maybe not smart enough—and he figured if he came all the way back to ask the husband what to do, he was sure the husband would send him right back the way he came to kill this new man and the cheating wife."

Ethan stopped when they got to the edge of the deck. Caleb spun around, thinking they were going down the stairs when the legs were yanked out of his hands and the body flew through the air. Ethan slapped his palms together. "Of course, Ramus was also what you might call a lazy man. Lazy man with a gun is not the kind of man you want to find yourself next to." The body landed facedown, the snow leaping into the air with a massive, rushing noise, and settling over the man's clothes. "So he shot them, both of them. And came back home."

Caleb looked at the body splayed out in the snow, everything at unliving angles. He could barely listen to the words that followed.

"But Ol' Ramus got it wrong. When he came back, the husband was so upset, he shot Ramus between the eyes, stuffed his killing fee inside his mouth, and then shot himself right in his goddamned broken heart."

THE PREACHER'S STORY hummed in Elspeth. She stepped over the repaired tear in the earth. Wallace stood outside the icehouse, looking up at the great doors. She hurried toward him, but Wallace appeared to be in no rush himself. He turned and saw her expression. "So you've heard." He sighed, and the sudden condensation gathered around his head with the heaviness of the thought. "Charles has always . . . Charles has been a good boy. He's always been a good boy."

"I don't understand. Are you trying to keep me away from him?"

He patted her reassuringly. "Quite the opposite." His hand angled her face into better light. She feared he'd wipe the shoe polish from her jaw and crack his cane over her skull. "Did he do that?"

"How can you keep standing up for him? Cleaning up his messes?" She heard her voice climbing into the feminine territory she'd been so careful to keep hidden.

If Wallace noticed, he didn't betray it. "Oh, what we do for our sons." He knocked on the door like he wished it luck, and headed toward his office. "You're welcome to the job, all the same," Wallace said, not bothering to turn around.

CHAPTER 13

T hat night, Elspeth fought off sleep for Caleb. When he arrived home, she ate with him, despite the intense weight in her eyes and the soreness in her body. Her hands hurt when she moved them, and every time she blinked, her vision bloomed into oranges and reds. She asked Caleb about the inn, and his responsibilities there. As his mother, she thought, she should inquire more about how he spent his days and nights. His responses were minimal: grunts and nods. Words, it appeared, had left him.

Caleb was wary but happy that Elspeth took an interest in his search in some tangential way, that she hadn't forgotten the scattered bodies in their home. Over and over he watched Ethan ejecting the corpse from the deck of the inn, and its horrible flight, and the empty whush as it landed. When he took out his pistol to clean it, all she did was ask him to wait until they'd finished eating, and so for the time being he tucked it back into its familiar spot behind his belt. He cut his food without scraping his plate and chewed quietly, because the meal seemed to be a solemn occasion, a preparation for something that he didn't understand.

Past the barn down a small worn runnel that had dried up long ago, a stump had overhung the edge of the hill, half of its roots dangling, hanging on to the air itself, and Caleb would stand on the dead wood and sense everything in front of him, and nothing below. One spring morning he'd followed the dried channel and at the end found nothing but a drop-off. He'd thought he'd never be able to recapture that feeling, but since the murders, he experienced it all the time.

"Do you remember how Amos would sit on that old crate by the pigpen for hours?" he asked, the memories, as always, grounding him. "Watching his shadow move across the grass? At first he'd been punished with it, but then he liked it?"

Elspeth didn't remember, and couldn't know if she'd been gone, had forgotten, or had simply not paid attention. "He was punished a lot, wasn't he?" she finally said, and Caleb rolled a piece of apple with his fork. The church bells rattled the glass in the windows, shook the water in their cups. On more than one occasion, Elspeth glimpsed the toy horse she'd purchased for him and she cringed, knowing how badly she'd misread the situation. The gun waited on the bed with the boy's cleaning supplies. She couldn't turn the clock back on him, no more than she could cut a child's hair and call it a baby again.

THE NEXT DAY, Caleb arrived at the inn to a pile of dirty bedding. He separated the items by order of their drying times, washing the few blankets first, followed by the sheets and the pillowcases. In the white mass immersed in the tub, he saw the dead man, watched him sail through the air and break upon the snow, felt the sharp chill of his ankles in the water. His empty eyes stared out from the bubbles. Caleb wondered if he had a family, if they missed him, and if they thought of him. Some days Caleb forgot to think of Mary, and he tried to picture her as he pushed the broom handle back and forth, the sheets gurgling in its wake, and finally saw her laughing and kicking the chickens aside as she rushed to the kitchen, her apron full of eggs. A violent thump from the other room dislodged his memory the way the sun moving behind a cloud will evaporate a shadow. When he tried to conjure her up again, she was gone. He hoped his mother remembered her sometimes. He missed his brothers and sisters with a soreness in his arms and his chest that had nothing to do with the work in front of him. Despite the steam in the air, he felt parched, dried out.

After he'd hung the last sheet, he walked upstairs, his mind made up. He had to look. He wondered where the souls went, and saw the translucent suits described by William and smelled the dry fire of home, the choking stench of the bodies. He heard the roar of flames and the frantic hooting of owls. At first, he stood far from the window, afraid to see the dead man again. He sat on the bed. The one piece of artwork on the wall commemorated the duel between Aaron Burr and Alexander Hamilton. Caleb admired the peaceful look on Hamilton's face, and the angelic radiance that emanated in a golden halo around his head. Burr's pistol exploded in a cloud of gunpowder, and Hamilton's chest bore a mortal wound, all at the same time. Caleb thought the painting captured the speed with which things happened. On the dresser, someone had left a newspaper, exclaiming that a grave full of nine hundred bodies had been uncovered in a place called Boston, where workmen had dug holes to stick a train underground. He struggled over the words, and wasn't pleased that he'd taken the time to do so. Frank had steered him away from such stories, preferring the heroism of the president or the tales of everyday people who did brave things like rescue a child from drowning or save a dog from a burning building. Caleb wondered if other people found things as confusing as he did.

Assured that the world outside contained as much dread and violence as the world he'd encountered, Caleb went to the window and peered over the sill. A body, indeed, lay in the snow. Something moved as well, and he pushed open the sash. Snow cascaded down from the eaves at the disturbance and once it had cleared, he leaned his head outside. The wind fluttered his hair. The ground appeared to be littered with bodies, dark shapes that he strained to see more clearly. One of these inert forms possessed the brown curls of Ellabelle. Caleb's heart dropped. A second passed, though, and her arms began to move, then her legs. He exhaled and rested his head against the side of the window frame. Ellabelle shifted her limbs again, producing a swooshing sound. She'd made snow angels, a whole host of them. She peered up at him. "Caleb?"

There was another body, though, one that didn't move. This man had fallen face up. His legs did not twist at unnatural angles. It wasn't the same man Ethan had thrown from the porch. This body belonged to Gerry. His eyes were open, and his stable boots muddied the snow at his feet.

Ellabelle called Caleb's name again. The gash in his head pressurized, as though it would tear open and spew blood until he, too, lay in the snow, an expanding puddle beneath him. London White had killed Gerry. Or had Ethan do so. Maybe Ethan had misunderstood their conversation. Caleb assumed it had been on his behalf—he may as well have pulled the trigger himself. He heard Ellabelle calling from outside, the voice seeming to come from another land altogether. He backed away from the window, his head pulsing, thinking he might vomit, retching and crumpling to one knee. The Colt fell from its station and slid across the floor. In the inn a bell rang, an early customer finished, another welcomed.

THE AIR WAS warmer for the first time in weeks, the clouds not charging in with violent purpose, but lolling across the sky. The ice gave way rather than snapped under Elspeth's feet on her way to Charles's apartment. A few squirrels emerged from their homes and scampered around the thoroughfares. Owen Trachte held the door open for Elspeth and they'd passed each other before he recognized her. She wondered how deep the recognition went. "Nose looks okay," he said. She thanked him for his help.

She'd been waiting in the hotel, drinking coffee and drumming her fingers on her knees, not sure what to do next. A piece of her said to leave Charles alone, to go to work at her new job, where she could collect some more money before she and Caleb moved on to another town. But every time she thought of their departure she saw the golden steeple of the church, the cross that emanated light, and deep inside was reminded of the weight of her sins. She no longer had the strength to carry them around, nor would busyness or movement sate her. She prayed on the tattered couch in the lobby of the Brick & Feather. Her thoughts were unfamiliar as they sprinted past, a jumble of dead bodies and Jorah's voice intoning Bible verses, cut up and stitched together until they made no sense. At the thought of Caleb, however, they slowed, and in her head she prayed for him, for Charles, and her own soul, though she knew it was beyond saving.

"He's up there," Owen said. He flicked his thumb toward Charles's room. Elspeth thanked him again and hurried up the narrow staircase. Charles yelled for her to go away when she knocked, but she ignored him. The door was unlocked. Everywhere there were papers: books, ledgers, newspapers, letters, envelopes— some torn open, others untouched. Stamps littered the floor like pebbles in a stream. A dining table and two chairs would have taken days to unearth they were so covered in materials: maps, tintypes, drawings, plans, notes, photographs, reference books opened and stacked on top of one another. Bookshelves of all sizes gave little order to the clutter, their shelves so overladen they bent into nervous smiles. The grimy windows on either side of the room failed to illuminate much, the papers making everything dusty, the air itself almost smoky, and Elspeth coughed and licked her desiccated lips. On a folding cot lay Charles, braced by several pillows, his face encased in bandages, his arms and one leg likewise.

"What is all of this?" Elspeth asked, picking up a newspaper dated three years prior.

"I'm in pain enough without you wasting time getting to the point," he said through a small slit in the bandages, his jaw barely moving. He shifted in the cot, the material groaning beneath him.

"Why did you have them move me off your shift?"

"I'm sure you know. You've seen enough."

"Did you even have a wife?" she asked. He said he did. "Why should I believe you? You lied about your whole life."

"I didn't."

"What about Massachusetts? What about growing up a fisherman's son?"

"I thought they made me more interesting to you. You, who'd come out of nowhere like an angel." He snickered. "But what do I gain by lying now?"

"And this wife left and took your boys?"

A small fleck of blood appeared at the corner of his mouth and it spread on the bandage, soaking the stark white. "My wife suspected me, the way I am."

"But you had children." In all the mess, she glanced around for a photo.

"The mind is powerful," he said. "And for a while, I could make it do what I wished." He tugged at his bandages. "But this was lying in wait." With each of his breaths, the stitching on the cot sighed and the joints clicked. "And now, we do what we can."

"You loved your sons."

"Of course I did," he said. "I do."

"I know you're a good man." She thought again of Caleb tending to her and the horror he must have experienced at opening the door to find the results of his bravery. "Mistakes," she said, "are correctable."

"These aren't mistakes," he said. "These are facts. But I am sorry I lied to you, Jorah."

"I'm sorry, too." His pointed look as the boot had lifted over his face sent a chill through her. "My name isn't Jorah," she said. She was more surprised to say it than Charles appeared to hear it.

"Whoever the hell you are," he said, his back going rigid and lifting off the cot. He writhed in agony. "You're here to kill me? Say yes. It's okay. I want you to. Let's all keep our secrets."

Elspeth drew herself up and picked her way across the dusty library to his side. She touched him lightly and he jumped. Despite her broken and bruised nails, she couldn't guess how her hands hadn't given her away. With her small, battered fingers, she flipped the lock on the door.

"No one's here," Charles said at the sound. "Go ahead and shoot. Send me out of this world." He sobbed. The bandages on his face contorted. "Please. I can't take any more."

The purple fingers protruding from his cast were within a hair's breadth of her hip. The pistol tugged at the back of her trousers. Holding up one hand in defense of her action, she took the gun from its hiding place and dropped it on the cot next to Charles's leg, within easy reach of his hand.

"You don't think I've tried?" he said. "I can't. I'm a coward."

"I'm not going to kill you. You're the only one who knows me." First she removed her hat and scarf. Then she unlaced her boots, struggling with the mud-caked knots. She pulled off her socks, and her bare feet stuck to a rainbow of stamps. She unbuckled her belt and let her trousers fall to the floor. Charles shook on the cot, the canvas screeching. Her sweater required some force to pull over her head. It sizzled with static. Her hair stood on end. She unbuttoned each button of Jorah's flannel shirt and shrugged out of it.

"Jorah, stop," Charles said. She glanced at the gun but it hadn't moved. "Whatever your name is, just stop."

Her Jorah had waited in their bed. It was early summer. He hadn't yet built the closet or the dresser. Their room had no walls, but the beams that would soon support them reflected the lamplight, clean and white, and everything beyond in their new house was darkness. The air smelled of fresh pine and cedar. She undressed in front of him, but as she reached her undergarments he looked away, and she sat at the foot of the bed and removed them alone. He lifted the chimney and blew out the lamp, and let the darkness settle onto the sounds of their breathing and the small clink of the glass sliding back into place. When she slipped under the covers, his hand pressed onto her belly, his skin warm and rough. Her body changed, grew more capable, tightened into something stronger. Her belly, however, remained the same, and no amount of effort could fill it. "My name is actually Elspeth."

"You don't have to do this," Charles said.

Elspeth stood in her undershirt and a sagging pair of wool drawers. She shifted her weight and paper crunched underfoot. Even in her state of undress, sweat rolled down her legs. The shirt caught on the pins she'd used to fasten her bandages, and she pulled each from its housing, lining them up on a stack of newspapers that covered the bedside table. As she did so, she pressed her right arm across her so the bandage did not fall. Once she'd removed the pins, a ritual she'd repeated enough to perform without looking, she unwrapped the bandage, the layers peeling away with a soft sighing. Her breasts fell loose. The shot continued to heal, some mere white pocks, others scabbed over in a dull crimson. Her cross remained around her neck. She tucked her thumbs into the waistline of her drawers and worked them over her hips until the fabric whisked down her legs. She stepped out of them.

"Okay," he said. "What now, Elspeth?" The bandages around his lips grew slowly darker. Her hands felt empty, her arms yearned to cover her nakedness, but she forced herself to stand there. "Do you want me to say I'm surprised?" he said. "Do you want me to say I didn't know?"

"What?" An unknown draft crept up her shins and her thighs and shrouded her. The sweat prickled on her skin.

"I didn't know at first, not right away." He coughed and sank deeper into the mattress. "But soon enough. Why do you think I took so many breaks if not to cover for you? Why do you think I said all of that to you in the church about our understanding one another?"

"When then?"

"I spoke to you once at the tavern, maybe the second night of our working together, and I talked about my boys, and I saw it—something, I don't know, motherly, feminine. I confirmed it over time."

Elspeth wrapped her arms around herself and sat down in the pile of clothing. She let her head rest against the side of the cot. "Who else knows?"

"I don't know," he said. "It took me a while to figure out how many knew my secret. They found out, though." A bottle of salve rolled across the floor where she upset it. "They will find out, Elspeth."

She crossed her feet, revealing the bright stamps stuck to her soles. One in particular stood out to her, a violet eight-cent, the man staring off into the distance, a sad, bewildered expression mapped out in the lines of ink. Elspeth plucked the stamp from her skin, licked the back, and affixed it to the foot of Charles's cot, where he readjusted and began snoring softly above her.

ELLABELLE'S CLUMSY FOOTSTEPS entered the room. Caleb lay on the floor. He couldn't control his breathing: It came out rapid and shallow but drew in with enormous gasps, his whole mouth opening wide. In his pain he hoped he would die, felt sure he would, that something inside of him had rotted.

Ellabelle knelt close and brought his head upon her knees. Her skin—cold and wet from the snow—soothed his feverish forehead. She smoothed his hair, calming him and said he'd be okay, he only needed to breathe. Before he could pacify his lungs, he forced out the words. "He killed him."

"Who?" Her curls tumbled from behind her ears as she looked at him. Something sweet hung on her breath. Her cheeks weren't red from the snow; they stayed pale. She looked frozen.

"Mr. White. He killed Gerry."

"Of course he did," she said. "It's okay. He's coming."

"What do you mean?" Caleb asked.

"I thought something was wrong—I told him to come."

"He killed him," Caleb repeated.

The crisp, measured steps they'd learned to listen for when joking or telling stories rang in the hallway and then in the room. Ellabelle didn't move. White first readjusted the blankets where Caleb had mussed them and then sat in the same spot, looking down on the two of them.

"Caleb, does Mr. Wilcox's end not meet your approval?" he asked. He dragged his watch by its chain from his pocket and turned the wheel. Caleb's head swam and his lungs had not fully recovered. He panted like a dog. "Gerry Wilcox, the stableman?"

"No," Caleb said. "I didn't want him to die."

"So those injuries on your face, those did *not* come at the hand of Mr. Wilcox?"

"That doesn't mean he has to die," Caleb said.

"I see." White rubbed his temples with his thumb and middle finger. "Not that I need to elucidate my reasons for you, Caleb, but I simply cannot have my employees beating upon one another. Mr. Wilcox had been warned against this type of behavior. Ms. Ella-belle, has Mr. Wilcox ever wronged you?"

Ellabelle pursed her lips, hard in thought. "Probably," she said. "I've gotten good at forgetting the nasty ones. It's the kind ones that stick."

"Of course, my dear. Very poetic," White said. "So, Caleb, you may rise with a clean conscience. Mr. Wilcox's fate did not rest with you." He crouched down and put his hand over Ellabelle's, the pressure increasing gently on Caleb's forehead. White smelled of talc and soap. "You don't have to worry."

He got up and appraised himself in the mirror. "Now, Caleb, have you any ideas as to the whereabouts of his compatriot Dax Hanson? That would also be appreciated."

"Why? So he can end up at the doctor?"

"That's up to Mr. Hanson. These men, Caleb, do not have our best interests in mind. I may tell you that much." White checked his watch and snapped it shut. "Ellabelle, customers."

Ellabelle kissed Caleb on the forehead. "You relax now, Caleb. It's good that Mr. White is here to take care of you."

"Thank you, Ellabelle," Caleb said, and he meant it, though relaxing was clearly not possible. He understood she didn't possess some part of her that other people did. White didn't have it, either. Caleb didn't know what to call it, or even how to describe it, because it wasn't simple right and wrong. Sometimes, he wondered if his mother was missing it as well.

Ellabelle left the room, but before she did, she placed a pillow under his head, and he lay there on the floor, staring at the holy Alexander Hamilton, his chest blooming with blood, listening to the growing bustle of the inn, wondering which bell meant Ellabelle had seen another client, not certain if he cared as much as he once had, until his breathing returned to normal.

ELSPETH STIRRED a pot of soup for Charles, the ladle scraping along the edges of the tin. The air smelled of wet newspapers, a sour, musty odor. She'd dressed herself in Jorah's flannel shirt, forgoing the underclothes and the bandages. Without them, the constant vise around her lungs had loosened. "I'm sorry I lied to you," Elspeth said. Her real voice sounded unnatural and she was aware of it traveling up her throat and onto her tongue. "I came home, less than a month ago, and my family had been murdered. Caleb was in the barn, hiding."

"Everyone?" Charles shifted on the cot. "They killed your children, and—your husband?"

"We think they might be here," she said. "The murderers." She suddenly worried about Caleb asking questions at the inn, her frail child among killers. She flushed with embarrassment.

"This is the place to hide, I suppose," Charles said, and pressed no further. "I'm sorry, too."

The soup hissed on the stove, as she had ignored it for too long, and she pulled the pot from the heat. "What would you do if I wasn't here?" Elspeth asked.

"My father would come, after some time."

"But he's not your real father?"

"He's been my father as long as I can remember." She poured the soup into the cleanest bowl she could find, wiped a spoon on her sleeve, and cleared one of the chairs by the kitchen table. Charles groaned when the stack of papers she'd moved from the chair to the floor toppled over but she ignored him and held out a spoonful of broth. "Owen checks on me from time to time," he said. The slight gap in the bandages parted as he opened his mouth.

"He's a—friend?"

Charles scoffed. "Not in the way that you mean, but yes, he is a friend."

They heard a whisper of music coming from somewhere, so nonsensical to each of them that they didn't move, drinking in the subtle sound. Neither mentioned it once it had passed.

"Who was the man I saw you with after the accident?"

"Someone important to me," he said. "As you witnessed, the feeling doesn't seem to be shared."

"Did he work the lake before me?" she asked. "As your partner?"

Charles shut his eyes. He talked to himself, saying something over and over and she wanted to lean in to hear, but what she could see of his expression told her it was private and not to be shared.

"What is all this?" Elspeth asked, letting him know the inquiry had ended, motioning to the reading materials stacked on every surface.

"Again, some things that are important to me aren't to others."

She ladled the soup into his open mouth. She'd been fed like this, not long ago. She couldn't recall if she'd ever thanked Caleb or made him understand how brave he'd been or that she'd be dead without him. She supposed he knew. Once the cup had been emptied and she'd wiped off Charles's mouth, he asked her to leave, not angrily, but with a simple request. She obliged, and as she did so, his body slackened and he deflated on the cot, his body making hardly a ripple beneath the thin blanket she pressed over him. She dressed in her old clothes. The bandages she left behind, the pins still in a neat row.

CHAPTER 14

aleb waited for Elspeth in one of the plush chairs in the
lobby of the Brick & Feather. Despite his nervous excitement or perhaps because of it, he periodically had to
shake himself awake, not sure if he'd fallen asleep, and if he had,
for how long. Outside, it continued to warm, and some of the snow
melted, the drops from the rooftops making discordant music with
the ticking of the clock. He allowed himself to daydream of his visit
to the Shanes', how the woman who looked so much like him would
embrace him, lifting him off his feet and spinning him around before
they both collapsed, dazed and laughing. As the daydream wore on,
however, they tired of him, like the girls' favorite dresses, made from
ribbons and lace his mother brought, which would fray and dull until
they grew to hate wearing them. He worried the woman would hold
him and feel within him the lies and the failures that stacked up on
his chest at night and made it hard for him to breathe, as if maybe
he'd be heavier to her, and she'd hold him at arm's length and wonder
how he'd gotten so full of rot and poison, not knowing what he'd
seen or what he'd had to do. And maybe she wouldn't ask. Or maybe
he wouldn't be able to say. When he saw Elspeth he would ask her

the questions that had been burning holes in him. Engrossed in his thoughts, he didn't notice Frank standing above him, holding a plate of cookies. "Where's your father?"

"He got a new job."

"Caleb, this morning someone told me they'd seen you leave the Elm Inn," Frank said. "Are you still working there?"

Caleb mumbled that he was. His lips tight, Frank asked Caleb how things fared there, and Caleb said they were fine—he didn't fancy a lecture. "I know it's not your fault," Frank said. He took a deep breath. "When I was a boy," Frank said, "and we lived in Nova Scotia—do you remember where that is?" Caleb said he did, and recalled the map Frank had shown him of a peninsula shaped kind of like a duck's foot. "I worked with my father. He was a blacksmith and a farrier and everyone assumed I would follow in his footsteps—especially my father. But I never liked the heat, and I hated the noise." He laughed. "That fire scared me, Caleb. It sure did." A trio of men talking by the hearth all began singing. "One day, after I'd made a horseshoe, a perfectly nice horseshoe, one of dozens, I told my father that I didn't care to be a blacksmith any-more. Do you know what he said to me?"

Caleb didn't. In all of Frank's stories Nova Scotia and his child-hood had sounded so wonderful: the skies full of the calls of loons and the songs of flycatchers and kingbirds, the days spent jumping into piles of hay and fishing from the rocky coast. Caleb had seen it all so clearly and this unhappiness made no sense.

"He told me we each make our own way in this world, and if the forge wasn't mine, then so be it." Frank rolled up the newspaper in his fist. "Do you understand what I'm saying to you?"

Caleb watched the people on the walkways, everything busier with the sun out and the cursed cold lifting. "I don't think my father minds what I'm doing."

"I wasn't speaking about your father."

"London White certainly doesn't mind what I'm doing."

"Mr. White is a difficult man to walk away from," Frank said. "But you can, you know." Caleb had seen too much to believe him. "You're a boy. He wouldn't dare do anything." Caleb couldn't help himself. He laughed. It sounded awful, even to him, a bilious, nasty thing. He covered his mouth and a cold shame settled over him. While Caleb knew he meant well, Frank couldn't possibly guess at even a fraction of what went on at the Elm Inn. He was aware he might end up empty-eyed and broken in the snow, Ellabelle's angels all around him. As he turned to walk away, Frank bit into a cookie and offered the plate to Caleb, and when he declined, Frank handed him the newspaper, smudged and crumpled from being twisted in his sweating hands.

THE DRESS SHOP in Watersbridge didn't open often. A sign in the window proclaimed in flowery script, FOR BOUTIQUE APPOINTMENTS, PLEASE SEE MR. JAKOB ROTH, MERCANTILE. When Elspeth peered in, however, a woman bent close to a dress on an armless torso, pins in her mouth. This woman, the same woman who had waved to her—one of the only small kindnesses she'd met in Watersbridge—was also captured in dozens of photographs in the back of the store. A tiny light appeared in the dark, almost forgotten place Elspeth had reserved for God. Bells signaled her arrival.

"Do you have an appointment?" the woman asked. Elspeth said no, and the dressmaker remained focused on her work. "That's okay. How can I help you?"

"Something simple," Elspeth answered. "For my wife." The store wasn't much bigger than the room she'd shared with Jorah, one side lined with bolts of fabric on long spindles, another contained shelves loaded with folded dresses, some labeled with a name in the same fluid script as the sign. The occasional glinting pin and a few small scraps of fabric, too small even for a pocket, dotted the floor.

"Would you like to come back with her?" the woman asked. She fixed the hem of the dress an inch higher, stepped back, tilted her head this way and that, and undid the pins to let the hem fall back to its original length.

"She's not here," Elspeth said. "But she's about my size."

The woman glanced back at her—the first time she'd done so—removed a piece of lace from an embroidered box, and spun it around the neck of the dress. "Have many people noticed?"

Elspeth stopped protesting before she could even start. Her broken nose pulsed. Her vision went black, then white, then a hazy confusion of both. "Not many, I hope."

"People don't pay attention to anything but themselves these days." She emitted a grunt of exasperation at the dress and wrapped the lace around her hand to tidy it. "You stopped binding your bosom."

Elspeth noticed her shirt dipped in the center, a subtle shadow, nothing more.

The dressmaker chewed on the end of the tape measure she had around her neck. She removed a dress from one of the shelves. The fabric was heavy but beautiful, a deep blue, shiny but not ostentatious, with careful buttons and clasps. It looked expensive, but between the flood of emotion and fears that overpowered her, Elspeth couldn't object. The woman tapped the nameplate affixed to the now-empty shelf. ROBERTSON, it said. "Dead," the dressmaker said. "Don't worry about the cost—I'll be glad it can go to someone." She got out a sheet of paper and wrote a note in her long, looping scrawl and once finished, she folded it twice and handed it to Elspeth. "Take this to my husband at the mercantile. Only him. Only Jakob."

Luck had proved so hard to come by that she didn't dare spoil the miracle by asking questions. Instead, she offered her thanks and started to lift the dress by its shoulders to let it fall to the floor, but the woman pressed Elspeth's hands together. Hers were small and chilled. "It will fit."

CALEB HAD EXPECTED Elspeth hours ago. He couldn't stand Frank's pained expression any longer and he'd moved to their room. For close to an hour he soaked himself in the bath, his fingernails never ready to give up their thin crescents of dirt. He used them to comb his hair, flattening it down, though pieces shot up in places, like weeds poking through a stone walkway. From the shelf above his bed he selected the nicest shirt White had given him and his cleanest trousers. With some spit and a sock he tried to clean his shoes. After he tucked his shirt in, he figured out how to button his suspenders to his pants and drew them up over his shoulders, where they fell slack. Once he finished, he sat on the stool, afraid he would muss his pants and wrinkle his shirt. So he paced, following the paths of the warped floorboards.

A low boom echoed through the hotel. A crack extended down one of the windowpanes as the explosion reverberated through the building. It felt like the detonation had come from within himself—as if his heart or his stomach had finally given way to the constant pressure. He passed a hand up and down his torso to see if he was still whole. Out the window, he could see down the thoroughfare to the church at the tip of the green, and next to it, a crowd.

"WELCOME BACK," JAKOB said when he saw Elspeth. "I trust the Colt pistol is to your liking?"

Rather than responding, Elspeth handed Jakob his wife's folded note. His smile faded. She worried that she'd been turned in by the dressmaker, and that any one of the pistols in the case between them could be turned on her.

"Okay," he said. He ran his thumb and his index finger along his moustache, and then wiped his hand on his shirt. "Let's find what you need."

The thunderous boom shook the store, and Jakob caught a glass that fell from a shelf behind him, but elsewhere came the sound of items crashing to the ground. Elspeth's knees buckled and she latched onto the counter. She saw her own wild expression reflected in the glass.

"They're dynamiting graves," Jakob said, "for the icehouse workers." He stepped out from behind the counter, and called, "Seth, take inventory of what's been broken. Isaac, listen for the bell."

From the depths of the store came matching shouts, "Yes, Papa."

The note had been left on the counter, Jakob's moustache wax marking his fingerprints. All she could make out before following after him down the overcrowded, labyrinthine aisles was the word *husband*.

CALEB LEFT THE Brick & Feather, his patience gone, and marveled at the great number of people outside; more, it seemed, than ever before. In the graveyard behind the church, the crowd would back up as one and the dynamite would sound. When the mass of onlookers moved, Caleb prepared himself for the shaking of the earth.

A large man unhitched his nervous horse outside the barbershop, and Caleb stopped to run his hand along the beast's muzzle. The horse's muscles relaxed, the tension dissolving into leftover anxious quivers. "You like horses?" the man said and dabbed sweat from his forehead with a handkerchief, his hair pasted to his scalp by the moisture. "You have a way with them." Caleb thanked him and the man said, "This is Art. I don't think I'll be able to calm him 'til they're done making those graves. Best to bring him home and let him worry there."

Caleb watched the crowd back up again and he laid his hand along the horse's brow, standing on his tiptoes even though the horse had lowered its head to him. The explosion came and went and the horse snorted, nothing more. The man patted it along its flank. He fished something out of his pocket and handed it to Caleb. HANK WALSH, BREEDER OF FINE STALLIONS, it read. "If you ever need a job, son."

Caleb played at the edge of the card with his thumb, holding it between two fingers, and a frost settled over him—he couldn't imagine going to work for someone like Hank Walsh or even owning a fine horse. Caleb couldn't picture anything at all outside of the feverish crack and flash of gunfire. He knew as he wandered down the crowded road that he would never pass a day without seeing killers exiting his house, Emma's limp body, or Jesse's dull eyes. He threw the card into the muck so he didn't waste any more time on it, and watched the water seep into the paper and the letters run.

The bells on the door to the mercantile rang. The boy his age came sprinting from the aisles, and another who looked like an even smaller version of their father trailed behind him, then caught up. They wrestled and jostled to be first behind the counter, the larger one winning out and shoving the other to the floor.

"Can I help you?" the boy asked, out of breath.

Caleb took the Colt from his pocket. The boy stuck up his hands and he and his brother laughed. Caleb didn't understand what struck them as funny. "You know," the boy said, "I'm making like you're robbing the store." The brothers laughed some more. Caleb tried a chuckle, but it came out like a cough.

"I'd like to trade in this pistol."

The boy whistled. "No one's ever turned in a Colt Army model before, have they, Isaac?"

"No, sir, Seth," Isaac answered.

"Are you thinking about money or trade?"

Caleb said that he wanted the money to spend in their store, and the boy explained to him how much he could give him, considering Caleb had payments left, and they shook hands on it. Seth, the older of the two boys, brought Caleb to an aisle not far from the counter with Isaac following close behind. The first vase Caleb saw he loved. A yellow daisy had been painted on a blue jug, and Caleb thought it to be the exact type of thing the Shanes were sure to have in their home. He also picked out some cloth napkins—"A big seller," Seth assured him, with Isaac nodding for emphasis—some salt and pepper shakers in the shape of horses, and a needlepoint that said MOTHER in scripted letters that he would hold in reserve, just in case.

He clutched the final item in his arms, even as Seth wrote them up, and presented Caleb with a sheet to sign. Caleb scribbled something on the page—too excited to re-create the fine circles and lines Frank had taught him—and grabbed his packages. A note drifted to the floor from the counter, and Caleb bent to pick it up. He couldn't help but read it. *"This man is in danger of losing his wife. My dear husband, we are to reconnect them. Love."* He almost told the boys how sad the note sounded when he handed it to them, but decided against it, figuring he'd rather they didn't know.

JAKOB AND ELSPETH shared the load of parcels they'd settled on—an overcoat, two hats—one for winter and one for spring—gloves, perfumes and powders, undergarments, boots, and a couple of dresses, not as beautiful as the one she carried under her arm, but fine enough for everyday wear. They unburdened themselves on the front counter, and Elspeth sorted through everything, unable to believe this sudden rush of good fortune. The older of the two boys stood next to his father, a smile on his face.

"What's happened, Seth?" Jakob asked. "You look awfully pleased."

"That boy was here and he traded in his Colt pistol," Seth said. "No one trades in a Colt. Isn't that right, Father?" Jakob inspected the gun and the paperwork. "Did I do something wrong?"

"No, Seth, no," Jakob said and placed the paperwork in a file behind the desk. "Sir, I think your son just came in here and sold a pistol."

Jakob tore several sheets of butcher paper from a roll on the counter, pulled a knife from his belt, and sliced a dozen even lengths of twine. Elspeth's nerves jumped and twanged, and she wished for the men to hurry up.

"He bought a vase and some other things for his mother," Seth said.

Elspeth busied herself wrapping the dresses to hide the tears that threatened to form, folding the paper over with firm creases. "Wonderful," she said. A foreign joy spread through her. She thought of her trips back to the house, tromping up the hill, a portion of her bag and its weight devoted to her children, to the gifts she'd present them. "His mother will be thrilled."

"Seth," Jakob said, "go find your brother and make sure he doesn't need any help." The boy didn't protest but lingered a bit, tidying the top of the counter before Jakob gave him a light pat on the rump that sent him on his way. Once he'd gone, Jakob continued wrapping Elspeth's packages, his tongue stuck out in concentration. "Pardon my saying so," Jakob said. "But your son, he could use some more time with his mother."

Elspeth inhaled, surprised, her nose flaring with pain. "I suppose you might be right."

The shopkeeper tied the last package tightly, and slid the neat stack across the counter. "You see," he said, "he told me she was dead."

"I'm sorry he lied," she said and picked up her items. "Things are not always easy."

CALEB'S EARS TINGLED without his hat; he'd been afraid to muss his hair. The road that had been endless with guns at his back only took him a third of an hour to walk, and before he could prepare himself he'd arrived at the Shanes' home.

Out of the reach of the dynamite, Caleb could only hear the slightest pop and the earth withstood the intrusion; the house appeared as sturdy and solid as ever. Yellow light poured from the windows even though a fraction of sun still topped the slate roof. The statues he'd seen half frozen in the dark appeared to be poking their heads out of the snow with curiosity, wondering about the small boy with combed hair bearing gifts.

He stood there for a good while—until the sun extinguished itself beyond the horizon and the cold crept out of the shadows—before he could force himself to the door. The first rap of his knuckles wasn't loud enough to hear. He cleared his throat, which squeezed itself shut every time he thought of meeting his real mother. His second knock brought a scuffling of boots and the low sound of voices from somewhere in the house.

Paul answered the door, his coat on and his dark hair pressed beneath a hat. When he saw Caleb, he stepped back and placed a firm hand on Caleb's arm and took him into the house. He removed his hat and coat and let them fall to the stone floor of the hallway in which they now found themselves.

"Kelly," he called, "Martin." He laughed and put his head on Caleb's shoulder while he hugged him, his hair soft on Caleb's neck. He led Caleb into a large kitchen, the ceiling high and striped with huge beams. A weak fire smoked at the far side of the room, which contained the table Caleb had seen through the window and a series of shelves full of dishes, bowls, and cups. The middle of the room held a countertop crowded with the beginnings of a meal, jars and eggs and white paper, unfolded and holding a thick steak, the blood bright red in the creases. They stood by the stove, which exuded heat. A door to their right opened, giving way to Martin Shane pulling his suspenders up onto his shoulders, which made Caleb suddenly self-conscious of his own sagging low. He shrugged in his coat, trying to situate them better. A wide smile split Martin's face.

"Sam," Martin said. He clapped his hands.

Paul put a quieting finger up to Martin. "Tell me your name again," Paul said.

"Caleb."

Martin's expression darkened and he looked askance at Paul. "Caleb," he said, his mouth drawing out the syllables. "Of course. So good to see you here." His smile returned. He pushed Caleb's hair back, and Caleb wished he'd combed it back to begin with, if that's what they wanted. Martin ran his fingers across Caleb's bruises and Caleb tried not to wince. "Kelly!" Martin yelled. Paul never let Caleb leave his grip, almost as if he thought Martin would break him if he let him go. Martin, for his part, continued to paw at him. "You'll stay for stew?" he asked. He pulled Caleb's coat from his arm, and it was all Caleb could do to keep hold on to his presents, switching them from hand to hand while Martin yanked the other side of his coat off.

A door creaked and the men turned as a group. There in the doorway, wearing a black dress, her hair knitted up in an intricate bun atop her head, stood the woman that had stopped Caleb's breath. Her presence stunned them all, and Paul lost his hold on Caleb, who stumbled forward. Kelly opened her arms, and he, uncertain at first, went to her and settled into her embrace. She got down on one knee, and he perched himself on the other, though he was nearly as big as she. Her cheek was cool and smooth against his. She smelled like cooking, like baking bread.

"I'm Kelly," she said into his ear.

Paul said, "Welcome Caleb."

Kelly rocked him in her arms. He'd never been so engulfed by another person and he wished he could sleep there, and that all his travels and all his worries would disappear into the night like a quick exhalation.

CHAPTER 15

People had waited on her for most of her life, Elspeth
thought while she bathed. After leaving the relative
comfort of the van Tessel estate, someone had always
awaited her arrival: Jorah had waited in the woods and in their in-
complete house; Mary and then the rest of the children—growing
like grass in her absence—had waited for their mother to appear
over the lip of the hill; Caleb had waited for her amid the gruesome bodies of his family; and he'd waited for her to find the men
responsible. This last task she had spent little time on, wary of her
own tenuous place in Watersbridge and distracted by her work on
the lake, by Charles, and by the idea of another baby. And now, she
waited on—and prepared for—Caleb.

She leaned back and dipped her hair in the water, letting it
rush in around her ears, shutting out the world. She rolled over
and scrubbed her face hard with her hands, the pain immense, the
calluses on her palms scratching her cheeks, and emerged without
the smudged complexion that had given her the shadowed look of
a man. To her hair she applied some of the oils and powders she'd
received from Jakob and brushed out the knots and gnarls. It was as

short as Caleb's and she swept it to the side and pinned it in place. The room filled with the scents of crushed mint and rose hips. Soft and loose, the dress felt strange on her body, much different from the stiff constraints of the pants she'd worn to the lakeside—sweat- and mud-caked as they were. In the room's lone chair, she had the odd sensation of her feet growing heavier and she stood to avoid the Devil's tug. She speculated on the gifts Caleb had purchased for her, and these imaginings made her buoyant. Besides overused and broken items from the van Tessel children, the only gift she'd ever received had come from Jorah on one of his few voyages into civilization. He'd come home with a torn ear and a dark bruise on his neck, and presented her with a velvet box of hairpins. On the end of each, a small animal had been cast and painted with a careful brush. She, in turn, had passed them along to the girls, who didn't like to waste them in their hair, where they could not see them, preferring to use them to fasten flowers to their chests. The memory soothed her. Perhaps an hour later, she patted down a pocket of air in her dress. One hand clasped a shard of the broken mirror that hung in the hallway while the other dusted powder onto her cheeks, lessening the severity of her black eyes.

The room had fallen into darkness before she raised herself to light the lamps. One lonely match shook in its box. She said a small prayer, asking for the match to last long enough for them both. It struck on the first try, and once it fizzled down to a manageable flame, she lit one lamp, then the other. She held the match in her fingers, the flame burning slowly, dancing in tremors and waves. She didn't dare breathe and put it out. When the heat crept close to her fingers, she shook once. As she watched a small ribbon of smoke make its way up toward the ceiling, she imagined the cool surface of the vase, the weight of the clay.

"LET THE BOY breathe," Paul said.

Kelly relented, and Caleb made a show of readjusting his clothing from her latest embrace, but really, he'd enjoyed this one as much as the first. Martin served stew, thick with potatoes and earthen carrots, strung with beef. Paul tore him a chunk of bread.

"So, Caleb," Martin said. Paul shot him a warning glance that Caleb followed, but Martin plowed ahead. "How old are you?"

"Twelve."

"Twelve," Martin said with great purpose. "That's getting close to manhood."

Kelly and Paul exchanged a look. "What brought you here to Watersbridge, Caleb?" Kelly asked.

"My mo— My father," Caleb said. Then, changing his mind about lying to all the expectant faces, "My mother."

"Did your mother or your father ever talk to you about where you came from?" Paul asked. He propped his elbows on the table and dropped his bread into his stew.

"She told me that I was born here."

Martin shook his fists with joy, Kelly brought a hand to her chest, and Paul pushed the bread around his bowl with his finger.

"So then," Caleb said, his fist tightening on the bag of gifts he'd placed by his seat, "you're my real mother?"

Kelly brought her bowl to the stewpot, even though she had yet to touch her spoon. Paul tapped Martin with the mouthpiece of his pipe, which he loaded with tobacco and tamped down with his pinkie. Martin touched his brow like he'd been struck with a sudden headache. To try to please them, Caleb took a bite of his stew and smiled. He wanted to return to the happy dinner, but his other hand clenched the bag harder, rolling the top under his fingers. Kelly's chair screeched across the floor as she set it near him. "Caleb," she said, and pushed his hair away from his forehead again, "your mother was my sister, Kaitlyn. And your father was her husband, Samuel. You were—" She sobbed, a big, gasping sound. "I'm sorry. You were named for him. Samuel."

Caleb dropped the bag of treasures to the floor. In spite of himself he asked, "Where is she?"

"Someone stole you," Martin said. "Kidnapped you, right out from under us." Paul shushed him and lit his pipe. His bread had soaked up the color of the broth and turned soft and dull. Their utensils all remained clean and unused.

"Where is she?"

"Your mother—my sister—" Kelly said. "She passed on."

"Passed on?" Caleb said, sure he knew what she meant but not wanting to.

The stew gurgled. The tobacco in Paul's pipe made a small crackling noise and the scent reached Caleb, sweet as the forest in summer.

"She died," Martin said. Paul and Kelly each said his name at the same time, but he continued. "She died when she gave birth to you."

The words struck Caleb with a quickness. "To me?"

"It's not your fault, sweetheart," Kelly said. "It wasn't anything you did."

Caleb couldn't begin to process that another life had been lost because of him. Instead, he focused on Elspeth. Maybe, Caleb thought, his mind shouting, speaking too quickly for him to hear, Elspeth had taken him away because she didn't wish for him to live without a mother. Or to live without a father. Why, then, would she leave so often, and when she came back, keep herself from him—from all of them—even when she sat in the same room? The pipe smoke that had begun so sweetly now tasted like dizziness, like his mouth when he woke up sick. The world slid away from him and he looked up at it as though from the bottom of a well.

"This is a lot—an awful lot, Caleb," Kelly said, and he put his head on the table, the soft napkin on his cheek, the heat from his bowl close to his forehead. Before he knew it Kelly helped him from his chair and up a set of dark, narrow stairs. He worried, for a moment, that he'd been poisoned, but Kelly's arm around him told him different. She carried the bag that contained the gifts he'd purchased for her, the shards of the broken vase scraping against one another. In his hand he still held his spoon.

She pulled back clean-smelling sheets, and Caleb slid in, fully clothed.

"You need rest," she said. She pried the spoon from his hand. She kissed his cheek, then his nose, then his other cheek. "Poor child."

A FAINT NOISE roused Elspeth. A mouse scurried across the panes of moonlight cast on the floor, and it disappeared behind Caleb's empty bed. She turned down a corner of his blankets and ran a hand along his pillow to feel the small indent where his head had rested. She felt ridiculous in her perfumes and fancy clothes. She undid her hair. She slid off her shoes and shed her dress, which she hung from the only available hanger, run through an eyehook in the ceiling that awaited some long-missing decoration. The dress swayed back and forth.

Her dreams came quickly: icy, sharp nightmares in which she walked a set of creaking planks in front of a crowd of people: the

children she'd taken—Emma, Jesse, Mary, Amos, and Caleb; their
mothers and fathers, who screamed for her blood; the small skeleton next to the train tracks, with its delicate finger bones, its incom-
plete skull; and Jorah. A firm hand pushed her from behind and she
plummeted for minutes, hours, before a set of pincers hanging from
a crane closed in on her, piercing her below her rib cage, jerking her
to a stop. The blood flowed down her legs and dripped from her
feet. The crane moved, out over the gray enormity of Lake Erie,
until it reached deep water that had not yet frozen, and the pincers
released her into the raging waves from such a great height that
she sank so deep she could not hope to swim to the surface. As she
approached the flat light of day, she crashed into a solid layer of ice.
She pounded. But the ice would not break.

She kicked herself awake, out of breath. One man's gaze stood
out from the crowd that had already begun to fade from her
memory. He'd placed a hat over his heart, and he didn't yell like the
others. Once the pincers tore into her flesh, he'd slipped his hat back
on and turned to go without a word. The name Shane—ignored for
so long—rang through her, and she wondered about all the nights
Caleb had spent away from her. The dress moved in some unseen
wind, the hanger scratching back and forth, producing an awful
squealing that sounded nearly like laughter.

"YOU'RE AWAKE," THE voice said.

"Yes," Caleb said, and he felt the same cold stone in his bowels
he'd felt in the barn, his face against the wood, the stench of his
own urine flooding his nostrils.

"It's Paul," he said. "Don't be alarmed. I know it's been too
much for you to take in all at once."

Caleb sat up. Paul's shoulders hunched, and his hands cupped around something Caleb couldn't make out in the dark. Kelly hadn't drawn the curtains, and Caleb could see the fat moon, heavy in the sky.

"I know that whoever raised you did well," he said. "Maybe they weren't the ones who took you. I can't be sure. But I'm here to warn you." A creak came from the hallway. Paul and Caleb froze. They waited. Something—an owl, maybe—passed by the window, and Caleb jumped. Paul put his finger to his lips.

"Martin Shane is an unforgiving man," Paul said once enough time had elapsed that their suspicions quieted. "One who's unlikely to wait to see whether someone is guilty or not. Do you understand what I'm saying to you?" Caleb nodded. "When you disappeared, Martin and your father—they looked for you, far and wide, all over the state. Weeks, months at a time, they were gone." Caleb envisioned a man who looked like him galloping across the wide-open places he and Elspeth had crossed. "They found a woman who thought she may have seen you at the train station," Paul said, and though Caleb thought he'd remember such a thing—riding on a train—he didn't interrupt. "She said she saw the doctor and a woman holding a newborn infant. They questioned that doctor, and he never wavered, not even a little." Paul pulled at a loose string: a tear beginning in the knee of his pants. "Martin and your father went up and down the tracks, stopped at every station, town, and in-between. They exhausted themselves. I don't know that they slept. Horses gave out by the handful. When they returned, they stayed up all night in the living room, pouring over maps and newspaper reports, each and every word of the woman who thought she might have seen you. And they'd leave again, midnight, noon, it didn't matter. Whenever a new thought struck them, they'd be off again.

"It was less than a year before it all got to your father. Every time he came back he'd be more and more like a skeleton. Less and less of him. And it was like he couldn't see anything in this world anymore. He didn't say much to me, or to Martin, either. And then, one night, they were riding into Watersbridge and your father meant to cross the ice as a shortcut home. Martin said it was too warm, the ice too thin. Your father didn't listen. Martin had turned his horse around and had only gone a few paces when he heard the ice cracking."

"My father's dead," Caleb said, needing to say it out loud.

"They looked for him that night, dragged some lamps down to the water, tied a rope around the waist of a man named Edwin, who'd been a friend of your father's, and let him shuffle out onto the ice. I was there. On the way back, Edwin shook his head before the light even touched him, like he'd been shaking his head the whole time. If it hadn't been your father, and if people didn't know of his heartbreak already, they wouldn't have even bothered."

Caleb tried once more to picture a bigger him riding across the plains, following train tracks that melted into the distance, but all he saw was a gaping hole in the ice that turned clear and still and then froze over completely.

"All this riding and all this hunting turned Martin into a different man. Hell, he was a boy then. Not much older than you." Caleb saw Martin's wild eyes as Ethan pinned him down in the Elm. "Every penny he earned he used to hire trackers, hunters: whoever he could find. Trouble was, around here, people had already helped as much as they could, and they'd seen what had happened to your father, and they'd seen what had happened to Martin, and the whole thing scared them to pieces. And it had been two years by that time. You were gone, vanished. But Martin, he kept looking. Every cent he had, he'd find someone who wouldn't feel guilty taking his money. Sometimes Martin would go along with them, and he'd pull out the maps, the plans, and the words of that woman, and it'd start all over again."

Paul toyed with whatever he held in his hands. "I could tell soon as I saw you on the trail that you'd been through things. You have some of the same look about you that your father had, that Martin has." Caleb wanted to tell him about Emma, Jesse, Mary, Jorah, and Amos, and how he'd burned their bodies and he'd burned their home. He wanted someone to stand up and scream for him, to acknowledge all that he'd lost. "Your mother, your father, your family, whoever it is," Paul said, "are not safe from Martin. Some of the men he hired would come round here, and they were killers. Empty-souled killers."

Caleb imagined the glint of Jorah's hair, the small explosion of powder that preceded the man falling in the fields. He walked around the mounds on the other side of the hill. He smelled the earth the following morning. A killer looked at the barn. A red scarf fluttered, and then another and another. He saw the long hair, the stooped walk, and he knew what had happened. "Where did they come from?"

"Who?" Paul said, only half present.

"The men Martin hired. Where did they come from?"

Paul gave the object in his hand to Caleb. Wrapped in dark fabric was a roll of money. "Kelly and I have been saving that," he said, "all our lives. Whatever we could keep from Martin we did. Sometimes he'd find it and he'd go off and buy another drunk tracker, another man itching to let loose his bullets."

"Where did they come from?"

"We want you to know that you can stay here, and we'll put this money to making you a life. Kelly and I, we'd take care of you," Paul said. "But if whoever brought you here is important to you,

you take that money and you run. You get far enough gone that you're not on those maps Martin spreads out."

Caleb didn't care about the money. To him, it was nothing but paper. "Where are the killers?"

A sudden demonic glow flared out the window like a sunrise, followed by a holler. "He's burning it all—the maps, the papers, the accounts, the newspapers—now that you're here." Paul's eyes squeezed into a frightened squint. "This release"—he tipped his chin toward the window—"will be followed by the thirst for another." He closed Caleb's hand around the wad of money. "Go."

Caleb gathered up his few belongings. The broken gifts he ignored. He looked around for the Colt before remembering he'd traded it in for a bag of junk. He longed for his Ithaca and felt too light without it.

In the kitchen, Kelly stood at the window, watching as Martin threw sheaves of paper into the blaze and then poured a bottle onto them that made the flames leap. From the way she stiffened, he knew she sensed him there, the same way the animals would only partially acknowledge his presence. He lingered, not sure what he hoped for, before walking down the front hallway and into a night filled with Martin's rhapsodic screams.

ELSPETH PICKED HER way down the stairs in new shoes that necessitated that she gather up her skirts to see where she stepped. The hotel had begun to wake, some rumpled men stumbling in from the night out and others straightening well-pressed outfits and drinking coffee. A few women were scattered among them, dressed in elaborate fashion. The room smelled of cleanliness: soaps and subtle perfumes. Out of habit, Elspeth expected Charles, carrying their mugs of coffee.

Frank recognized her, but it took a while, even with her standing right in front of him.

"Elspeth," she said.

"Elspeth," he repeated.

"My son," she said. He brought his cup to his mouth but failed to drink from it. "Have you seen him?" Frank shook his head. "Do you know where he might be? It seems as though," she said and struggled to keep her composure, "he has taken some of his belongings with him."

"Did he take his shotgun?" Frank asked. The gun, cleaner than the day she'd bought it, occupied the shelf above Caleb's bed. "That boy isn't going anywhere without his gun," he said. "Why don't you come talk in the back?"

He grabbed her elbow roughly and pulled her through the kitchen and into a back pantry filled with jars of jams and jellies of all colors, shelves of cookbooks, and sacks of flour and grocery bags labeled with crooked letters. Frank shut the door and left them in the dark. Another explosion of dynamite in the graveyard shook the tiny room.

"Look, ma'am, sir, whatever the hell you are today," he said, "this is none of my business, but since I've spent some time with Caleb: Have you given any thought to what you're doing to that boy?"

"Not enough," Elspeth said. "But more lately. Thank you."

His hand touched her stomach, then slid quickly down and into her groin. His fingers pressed against her. "Why?"

"To avoid being recognized," she said. "To stay out of trouble. To keep myself from the same sins."

"That boy doesn't have a chance," he said. "Not a damn chance."

She was glad for the darkness. "I know."

His hand raised to her. She could sense it looming and waited for the blow, tilted her head back to receive it. Finally, the punishment she'd deserved for so long. "My wife is pregnant," he said. "I'm sad for the world that will meet our child." The hand lowered and he tossed the door open. The new air hit Elspeth's face and her tears turned cold. Another explosion sounded, this time unsettling jars and a bag of flour. The cooks busy making breakfast halted, ready to catch falling objects, then resumed their work, the whisking of eggs sounding to Elspeth like the claws of an animal hunting. She wished it would hurry up and find her.

A gain Caleb heard the beat of a horse's hooves chasing him back to the center of Watersbridge. The graveyard was quiet. The bodies lay beneath lamps strung up for the occasion, and in their golden domes the empty graves yawned at their prey. When he reached them, he braved a glance back and saw nothing there. No horse followed him. Martin Shane did not appear out of the gloom, smoke hanging about him, emanating from the folds of his coat.

Dawn approached and things were beginning to brighten, objects emerging from the black to reveal themselves as everyday bushes and trees, not men with scarves sighting him down the barrels of their rifles. He slowed. By the time he reached the Brick & Feather, his hysteria had subsided, and his mind had focused on one objective: leaving.

The wad of money sat heavy in his pocket. In the quiet of the hotel, the carpets softened his steps. From the counter, Frank gave him a sad smile. Caleb opened the door to their room to reveal Elspeth awake and already bundled, her bags under her arms, and dressed, once again, like a woman. His frazzled mind could barely process this transformation.

Elspeth had waited all night for the boy who appeared before her, and she had forgotten in her image of him the lump on his skull and the bruised cheeks. After Frank had spoken to her, she'd stood in the pantry for long enough that her clothes had become saturated with the scent of coffee. In that time, she'd thought of all she'd put this small boy through, everything that he'd suffered and fought, the images and the ghosts that she knew would hound him the rest of his life. Her only conclusion—made all the stronger by forgetting entirely about his beating—was that she needed to leave him.

"I couldn't bring myself to ask," Caleb said. "I tried." He unraveled the scarf from his neck. "I'm not your son."

"No," Elspeth said. The animal that had come after her had found her, had already begun to devour her, and with the fear and guilt radiating from her body, it was like liberation. "I took you."

Time passed. Caleb shrank to his haunches, and Elspeth could hold on to her bags no longer and set them on the floor. She kept her coat and hat on, her sweat profuse and sour. They could hear the church bells calling the mourners to the funeral, and the scratchy shuffling of their steps. Elspeth watched the long streams of people dressed in black, their heads down. After a while, she turned to him. Caleb's mother and father had been kind people, she began, and she'd decided they would make it easy not to sin again. "You understand, I assume, that I took your brothers and sisters also?" She made the statement coldly, because if she'd soaked it with the breadth of her emotion, she would not have been able to continue. She didn't have to protect the boy from her fear because she no longer possessed any. She would lay herself bare.

She explained that because his mother and father were such sweet, loving people, she thought she would be able to return to

Jorah and the small family they already had and she would be satisfied. Those children, with their curling hair, their burbling sounds,
their reckless steps, would be enough. Caleb's mother—"Kaitlyn,"
he said, "her name was Kaitlyn"—was sturdy and prepared, almost
calm, when Elspeth arrived. She kissed her husband at the time
when most women screamed, and she bore down on the pain. "She
was brave," she said. Elspeth knew she could not steal this baby.
This would be a good child and a good family.

"I fear, Caleb, that if I tell you the rest . . ." she said and trailed off.

"Tell me everything," he said. "I know she died because of me."

"Not because of you," she said, and began to cry for him. She
continued. The blood began to seep out, first a small rivulet that
neither Elspeth nor the doctor noticed, as they were so busy and
the mother—"Kaitlyn," she added—was so calm. When the drops
began to splash Elspeth's ankles, she pointed the small pool out
to the doctor, who told Kaitlyn, "You're doing fine." But Elspeth
recognized that he needed the baby out because the mother didn't
have much time. "I wanted to warn her, even as the color drained
from her face and her eyes began to roll," she told him. "I should
have, even though it would have done no good." The baby came. A
small boy, bald as a potato and just as full of lumps. "You." Once
he'd left her body, the mother released, and her body seemed to collapse in on itself, her face gaunt and her legs mere spindles. Elspeth
took an ankle in her hand, the heat escaping. The doctor yelled for
Elspeth to clean the baby, and she did. He cried right away, and she
swaddled him, alert and strong already. She held him close.

Caleb's father—"Samuel," he said—came in, and he screamed
and prostrated himself onto the floor, his knees sliding in the blood
and excrement. "Take him away," Samuel said of Caleb, "take the
baby away."

Caleb blanched at this. She continued.

"I did as I was told." She waited for Samuel in the nursery, but he never came, not even as the hands on the clock hit eight, nine, ten, eleven. Not that night, not the next morning. The doctor went home. In that time, she convinced herself—because she was a sinner and easily convinced—that God had told her to take Caleb, using Samuel as a mouthpiece. "I stole you," she told Caleb, "and it was a wicked thing to do."

The admission didn't satisfy Caleb as he thought it would. He assumed Elspeth finally voicing her mistakes would relieve the pain like the removal of a splinter. It didn't. "And now," Caleb said, standing, "they're all dead, everyone, and my uncle's going to come and kill you."

Elspeth adjusted herself on the bed. "Then that will be the end."

He pressed something into her hand and she touched his, warm and soft, and dragged the tips of her fingers across his palm when he pulled away. She opened her fist to reveal the wad of money. "We're leaving," he said. Caleb tucked his Ithaca under his arm and yanked at her sleeve.

"You're coming with me?"

"We can find the killers," he said. He began to throw their belongings into the old pack—Margaret's stitches still taut.

"Caleb," she said, "I'll wait. It's enough now."

"No!" He couldn't calm himself, nor could he force her to care. Everything appeared in swirls of color and movement and every beat of his heart told him to sleep, that the world moved at all the wrong speeds, but he banished these thoughts and continued to stuff their pack with whatever remained on their shelf. He filled his pockets with shotgun shells. "He sent them."

Elspeth thought he meant God. He stuffed items into their flimsy bag. "Wait, child," she said and took hold of his wrist to stop his packing. "Who? Who sent them?"

"My uncle," he said. "Trying to find me." The words spilled out, and it was as if he saw them crack on the floor like eggs, and he recognized that without him, his brothers and sisters would still be alive. It was his uncle, his fake mother, his town—everything about Caleb had become death. He didn't wonder at Kelly being unable to face him. The poison coursed through his veins.

Elspeth didn't have much experience trying to soothe Caleb and so she did all she could: She wrapped him in her arms. When she let him go, the shoulders of her dress were wet, and Caleb blushed and wiped his nose on his sleeve. "I'll talk to him," she said and hushed him before he could argue. "We'll find out where those men live. I'll try to explain to Mr. Shane."

"No," said Caleb. "He'll kill you." He refused to see anyone else murdered. "We have to go. Now."

With each tantrum, he looked smaller to her and her responsibility grew. "He'll be at the funeral. I'll talk to him at the church." She gripped the boy's hand. "He won't shoot me in a house of God."

Caleb couldn't guess what she planned on saying, how she figured she might excuse herself, but he didn't have the strength to argue. He understood his father's end: how he'd steered his horse onto the ice, the animal trusting him, skittish at first, but then he'd encouraged it with some whispered words and a strong tug on the reins. Caleb knew his exhaustion.

They joined the procession of mourners. Along the way, the stream of people gained tributaries, more coming from the side streets and out of the restaurant and mercantile, until they filled the road from gutter to gutter.

Elspeth tried to unlearn in two hundred yards what she'd spent a month affecting. The dress hung—floppy and insubstantial—off her frame, and her face stung from the harsh soap and scented oils, tender without the shoe polish on her jaw and neck. The steeple hovered above them, and as they approached, the bells rang—even the straining of the ropes on the pulleys audible in the silent shuffling mass. Elspeth no longer considered the bells an alarm signaling her failures; she heard them as encouragement for her newfound freedom. She held no secrets from this world.

Caleb looked for Martin, but he stood no more than shoulder high and could see only backs and torsos. The church had been filled to capacity, everywhere one looked the pews and aisles crawled with black clothes and faces contorted in grief. They climbed the steps to the balcony and found a pocket of space. More mourners pressed them to the back wall, against a mural depicting a series of angels lifting souls up to heaven, their arms outstretched in serene acceptance. The usually majestic stained-glass windows were deadened by the slate gray sky. Caleb stood on his tiptoes, and could make out the pulpit and the lectern, each dressed in black, and the candles of Advent burning on the altar. People sat on the floor and stood in the aisles. In the center of the sanctuary lay a block of ice. The organ began to play, low and insistent, the notes stretching long and resounding through the building. The choir came through a door at the side of the church—briefly stymied by the crowd clogging the aisle—but the congregants cleared a narrow footpath, and the choir members tried to affect some semblance of formation and decorum on their way to the chancel. Next came the minister, and he waited for those seated in his path to stand and pack themselves together, flattening into one another so that he could pass. As he fought through the horde, his patience clearly tried, his smile tight, another commotion erupted at the rear of the lower level, and Caleb located an alley in the crook of a man's arm to see London White, with Ethan clearing the way, taking no note of the crowd, strolling to a seat in the first pew. Elspeth watched mourners scatter like insects for her son's boss, who wielded his black suit like a weapon. White ended up in the front left pew, Ethan next to him on the aisle. The minister's face grew red at his presence, but White ignored this and serenely opened a hymnal.

In the balcony Caleb and Elspeth were jostled as well, and she put a protective arm around the boy. Her hat was knocked from her head. Harsh whispers erupted, and Elspeth could see the disturbance coming toward them as a fishing line disrupts the water. Martin Shane broke through the pack, his elbows high to clear room. He gnashed his teeth. In his belt, he carried a pistol. Elspeth maneuvered herself in front of the boy. Now that she'd received what she'd asked for, she had no clue as to where to begin. To Elspeth, Martin Shane didn't look anything like he did as a young man, twelve—almost thirteen—years prior. She'd only seen him once or twice, hanging back in a quiet corner while she met with his sister. Then he'd been a rosy-cheeked boy with hair the color of wheat, his eyebrows bleached almost white by the sun, his nose freckled. The years had been unkind. From his manner, she put no faith in the church to protect her child. However, when the minister requested those who could to take their seats, Shane merely exhaled liquor-stained breath onto them and gave his attention to the pulpit. The minister—the real preacher, back from Rochester—spoke loud enough to carry over the coughing and shifting of hundreds of bodies.

Shane moved decisively and Elspeth wished she'd brought her gun, but she'd told Caleb they'd go unarmed into God's house. As the big man clasped the boy's arms, however, she prayed for a chance to lodge a bullet in his heart. She scratched at him, their movements met with exclamations elsewhere in the balcony, their struggle rippling outward.

The choir began to sing. "*In heavenly love abiding, No change my heart shall fear, And safe is such confiding.*"

Caleb had no room to fight. His feet left the floor and he didn't know what Shane intended and he clenched his fists and pounded at him. No one noticed, least of all Shane, who lifted Caleb onto his shoulders and leaned against the wall. Elspeth ceased her clawing. Caleb found himself in the hot air at the ceiling. Shane smelled of smoke. Elspeth and Caleb exchanged a look that neither could decipher, something of confusion and weariness.

The voices of the singers below—"*Wherever He may guide me, No want shall turn me back*"—comforted Caleb, slowed his heartbeat, though he could sense it in his tongue and his wrists. He stared at Shane's towhead, where the gaps between the thin strands of hair were covered in splotches and dark spots. It had been five or six years since he'd ridden on Amos's shoulders for the last time; his hair had been brown and full. From his new perch, he could see the entirety of the room: the huddled choir, the block of ice on a black tarp, the stained-glass windows that reminded him of the candy his mother had given him long ago.

The church heated with all the bodies, even as outside the snow came down, the storm gaining energy, the mild reprieve of the last few days only that. It piled on the sills and attacked the panes of the windows. Between words of the sermon, one could hear the drumming of the fat flakes trying to work their way inside. In this hushed reverence, the minister left the pulpit. He was shorter than Caleb expected, with a full head of white hair, green eyes, and a neat beard. He placed one unsteady foot, and then the other, on the block of ice. A member of the chorus, a bald man, half stood when the minister's feet slid, but the old man steadied himself with his arms outstretched, the Bible in one hand. "On this, God's Earth," he said, "there are no accidents. The word *accident* doesn't appear in His Book." He shook the Bible in his hand and almost slipped again.

Elspeth watched Shane and Caleb interact, gauging whether the boy would change his mind and stay with his uncle. Caleb bent his head low, entirely too large to sit on someone's shoulders. They didn't look alike, not exactly, but a certain similarity about their bearing and their mannerisms struck her. The closeness with which they observed the ceremony made her believe the boy would indeed remain in the place of his birth, and continue the life she'd disrupted.

"We can only be masters of God's world for moments at a time," the minister said, "before He decides, in His infinite wisdom, to remind us of His power and of our tenuous station on His Earth." Elspeth sank. "Eden only lasted so long."

The service continued on and on, and the mourners began to forget about their loved ones, more concerned with their uncomfortable seats, tired legs, and the rising temperature in the building. Several times Shane fell asleep, his head lolling to the side and resting on Caleb's thigh before snapping back to attention. As the three of them remained forced together, their tensions melted as surely as the ice at the center of the sanctuary, the red carpets turning dark.

The ceremony concluded with Edward Wallace reading a list of the dead, the bell tolling for each man. Elspeth wondered who the young errand boy had been, whether the note he'd carried had been his own. Caleb couldn't help but offer up his own names, those of his brothers and sisters, and Jorah, and his father, Samuel, and—especially—his mother, Kaitlyn. Each chime ran through him. Once the last echo of the last ring faded away, the choir started to sing, but the people ignored them, pushing toward the exits, forgetting about the snow-clogged streets and sharp wind. The choir could not process down the center aisle, and they gathered in a clump behind the crowd fighting to leave, their song dissipating and then going silent altogether. Elspeth made no effort to move. Martin stayed in place until there was room enough to lower Caleb from his shoulders. The balcony emptied slowly. Martin put his hands on his hips and watched the last of the grieving exit the building, an elderly couple arm in arm, each supporting the other. He spoke. "What do I say to you?"

After all that time, Elspeth thought, words were so small. "I took him," Elspeth said. Martin rested his hand on the butt of his pistol. Elspeth started to tell him the circumstances of his sister's death, but then decided against it because it was an excuse. She cleared her throat. "I have raised this boy—not well—but I have raised him as my own."

"He's not your own." A group of three men attempted to carry the black tarp that had once contained the block of ice from the church. They accidentally formed a spigot and the water drained out and they fumbled to raise the edges, only succeeding in making things worse. "He's mine."

"I'm not yours," Caleb said, his whisper growing harsh, his voice cracking. Neither of the adults listened. They watched the water slosh out of the tarp as if it held their problems, and ignored him.

"I'm sorry about your sister," Elspeth said.

"And my brother," Martin said. "I spent my life—we spent our lives, ruined our lives, lost our lives, trying to find him."

"I was never where I should have been," she said. It was then that she noticed the fury on the boy's face, straight and vicious anger that shoved out the fear that had dominated it since she'd woken in the barn.

"The men you hired murdered my family," Caleb said to Martin. He stomped on the wooden floor, and it traveled through the church like the ringing of the bells. They were turning him into a child, and it infuriated him. "All of them. Jorah. Amos. Emma.

Mary. And Jesse." He lifted up his foot. "These are Jesse's boots. My brother."

"He couldn't have been your brother," Martin said, but from far away. Dazed, he reached a hand behind him, searching for support. He balanced himself on the arm of a pew. His eyes moved across the mural.

"He wasn't," Elspeth said. She turned to Caleb. "None of them were. I took them. All. And I'm sorry for their mothers and fathers, and their brothers and sisters, and their aunts and their uncles, too. I'm sorry." The wind blew, and the bell whispered somewhere above them, pinged by specks of ice. The relief straightened her back and made her breathe easier as sure as removing the bandages from her chest. "I would ask for forgiveness, but I know I'm beyond it."

"They were my brothers and sisters," Caleb said and pressed a finger into Shane's chest, his head tilted toward the man's face. "My family is dead. Murdered. By people you hired." The syllables echoed in the now-empty church.

"A family, too, those men," Martin said. "The Millard brothers." He drew his pistol from its holster. He weighed it on his fingers, and Elspeth thought he meant to turn it on himself. Caleb prepared to jump in front of his mother. Martin placed the gun in the collection box at the end of the pew, where the barrel jutted out from under the lid. Much to their surprise, Martin began to sing in a small warble, a hymn from the service, *"The busy tribes of flesh and blood, With all their lives and cares, Are carried downwards by the flood, And lost in the following years."*

CHAPTER 17

The trail to the new graves had already been worn to dirt. The clumps of charred earth and rock displaced by the dynamite littered the snow. Elspeth trailed a few feet behind Caleb and Martin, nervous about upsetting whatever unspoken agreement they'd reached. All Martin had said was "I'll show you," and he'd motioned for them to follow him. The driving snow made her blink involuntarily. From deep in the cemetery, farther down the dirty path, someone began to wail, the cries rending the air.

The heat of the church left Caleb's body, and he imagined it peeling away, like a snake shedding its skin, layer after layer. "Are my mother and father buried here?" he asked.

Though Martin's face had gone slack, his expression destroyed, Caleb's question deepened the injury. "We buried them on the highest point on the property," he said. He chewed on his lip. "You probably passed right by them."

Caleb considered why he couldn't sense their presence or know that his flesh and blood had been so close to him. The concept was familiar but as he tried to lash it down to understand why, to remember it clearly, it, too, drifted off into the relentless snow.

Martin kicked at the ground and sent pebbles and packed ice into the grave. "Come here," he said to Elspeth. With a blackened stick, he drew a map in the snow to the home of the Millard brothers. He spoke slowly and clearly, and Caleb was reminded of how practiced Martin was at giving directions through the passes and forests. He only paused to blow his nose. Elspeth clutched each word, and pictured the map in her mind. The lines didn't last long in the blizzard.

"O ho," a voice came from the gray depths. "The whole family." London White, Ethan, and Owen Trachte walked out of the murk. "For such pious people to run so quickly from church, we were worried something was amiss." White wore a black overcoat accented with mink's fur and a matching hat, while Ethan had rolled his shirtsleeves to his elbows, his skin raw in the cold. Owen's hands remained in his pockets, and he refused to look at any of them. "Isn't this happy," White said. Elspeth watched his glance sink to the quickly disappearing map, and before she could take one last look, Martin scuffed it out with his toe. "And what are we planning on this day of mourning?"

Ethan unbuckled his vest, revealing two large pistols at his waist.

"Mr. Trachte here has spun me some fascinating tales," White said. "Children gone missing, men changing into women, murder, betrayal, greed . . . quite a yarn, indeed."

Martin and Elspeth both edged in front of Caleb.

"Protecting the boy?" White said. The snow collected on the brim of his hat. He clucked his tongue. "It's not him I'd worry about."

"Just take the kid," Owen said, and White whirled around and stared at him until he mumbled an apology. It was strange, Elspeth thought, to see someone so powerful so cowed.

Somewhere close by, a small group sang a dirge. Elspeth thought she heard—through the snow, wind, and distant cries of the stricken—the harsh racket of gravel and ice hitting a coffin. She wondered if she could get to one of Ethan's pistols in time. He slid his hand from the grips, as if daring her to try.

"Allow me to explain your futures to you," White said. "My town—my lovely home—has no need for kidnappers. It's up to Mr. Trachte's discretion what punishment best fits that crime. Caleb"—he bent down—"son, we have room for you in the stables. That position has been recently vacated." He smiled. "Doesn't that sound delightful?"

Caleb was going to tell him he'd never take Gerry's job, that he'd only stayed at the inn long enough to find the killers and that he would never, ever return. Before he could speak, however, White signaled to Ethan, and the big man surged forward to grab Caleb. Shane got between them and the two men tussled before Ethan grew weary of it and flung Shane aside. Elspeth, too, tried to stop Ethan, but Owen pressed a hand to her midsection. Ethan grabbed hold of Caleb's wrists, turned, and heaved the boy across his shoulder as one would a string of fish. Elspeth elbowed her way around Owen and reached out for her son, but Owen tackled her and put his knee to her back.

Caleb screamed, but in the snow, thick as wool, the sound didn't extend far, and if it had it wouldn't have been thought of as anything but the empty sorrow of one of the bereft. He could feel his mother being ripped from him, each step Ethan took like a stitch of his soul breaking. "Mama," he yelled. His hand strained for hers, but Ethan's powerful strides carried him away and Elspeth could not get out from under Owen's weight. Soon, in the mist and the falling snow, he lost her. It was as if he'd been torn in half.

Over all of it, he heard a gunshot. He cried out again. He

screamed until he went hoarse. He tried to wriggle out of Ethan's grasp, but the giant arm clamped down tighter with his every movement. Ethan shifted Caleb and said to White, "My pistol. Shane must have grabbed it when he came at me."

White rewrapped his fur around his neck. "Seems as though Mr. Shane has taken himself to the doctor. A fine thing, him being so close."

ELSPETH STOPPED FIGHTING against Owen. She'd caused Caleb such anguish. Maybe the best thing for the boy was for her to be gone. It wouldn't be long, she thought, before she grew indistinct and fuzzy in his memories, her features forgotten. Owen let her up and held his arms out, palms toward her, as one would a wild animal, until she reassured him she wasn't going to run after the boy. "They're not going to kill him," she said. Owen said he didn't think so. "London White doesn't have much need to lie," he said. He led her down the row of graves. Martin Shane's leg stuck out of one like a dead stalk, the snow on the far side—where a marker would stand—decorated with his blood. Owen covered her eyes, an outrageous nicety, and she slapped his hand away. Shane stared at her, jaw askew, one arm under his body, the other along the wall of dirt, like he could claw his way to his feet and out of the grave at any time. She said a prayer for him, and for who he used to be, the polite, straw-haired boy who had been too shy to speak in her presence.

Ethan's pistol lay nearby and Owen blew the snow from it and checked the cartridge. "I knew I knew you," he said. "Some kind of far-off dream, a nightmare from childhood. Somehow, I knew your face, but it took a long time to figure. Twelve years passed since I knew you. Then I saw you in the church, dressed like yourself, and it came to me like a lightning bolt—shocked me all the way to my toes." He pulled her away from Shane's dead body. "I'd almost forgotten you. Another year, two, who knows? I'd have no idea, a small spark of a memory I could never locate."

"What do you want from me?"

He let go of her, but tapped her upper arm with the pistol as a reminder. "You taking that baby ruined my father."

"He'd been crumbling long before I got there," Elspeth said. Most mornings the sharp clink of empty bottles had sounded as he'd lifted his medical bag to show her to her duties for the day.

"He was never the same," he said. "Business wasn't the same. People didn't blame him, but all the things that they'd been unwilling to say behind his back before they said to his face after." They had climbed almost to the top of the hill and Owen pushed her not in the direction of his room but toward the small forest that edged the town. "We had to find other means to stay afloat. My father, after all, needed his drink. And I needed my father." They entered the woods, the thin maples without leaves, the sap frozen on their trunks like tears. He walked with concrete purpose. They pushed through some scrubby pines and in a modest field stood a lonely cabin. "Do you know what I do here?"

"No." She dragged each breath up and out of her lungs. Her feet had gone numb. Finally she would pay her debt to God.

"This is where my father and I took the victims of Mr. White, and the men who preceded him and those who will come after— Watersbridge has and will always have someone in need of our particular services." She saw the thick, black soot at the mouth of the chimney, and thought she could smell the metal tang of blood. His grip eased. "The first were difficult. My father showed me what to do, and thereafter he would sit on a stool in the corner, too drunk to do much, but knowing that he had to stay, that he couldn't hand it all over to me. Not yet."

"I'm sorry," she said. "But why don't you stop?"

"We had a dog when I was a child. It was nothing more than a starving mutt that my mother found sleeping under our clothesline one day. But I loved it," he said. "His first year there was a vicious winter—you couldn't see out the windows or use the door the snow was so high. The dog couldn't go outside, not with all the snow, and so my father and I dug tracks and tunnels so it could at least walk around and relieve itself." Both of his hands bore scars and burn marks. "When spring came, that old dog just couldn't leave those tunnels and paths. It stalked that yellowed grass to dirt and wouldn't stray for anything. And one day, it walked a few small circles and lay down, dead." He worked a finger down his collar and pulled at it. "Why come to Watersbridge after all these years?"

She could tell the roof of the small shack had been replaced many times, tar paper rolled on top of tar paper, the layers visible and nails shining under the eaves. "It was my punishment," she said. "For my sins."

He reached over and examined the cross at her neck, and while his index finger played over the dent the pellet had made, he pursed his lips and gathered air to speak, then let it escape. He nudged her closer to the house, and she noted the dip in the earth that drew a straight line from the woods to the door. "People like White, they don't let go of employees easily."

"And now my son works for him."

"He's not your son," Owen replied. He brushed the snow from what turned out to be a bench in the shadow of the shack. "I've spent so many hours—years of my life—on this bench. When I first came here, I could curl up and sleep on it." He lay down and his legs dangled off the edge, and the bench became lost under his bulk. He sat up and tugged Elspeth onto the seat next to him, though the bench could hardly accommodate them both. "Have you ever smelled a man burn?"

"My son did. He had to burn his brothers and sisters after the men Shane sent killed them all." Elspeth shuddered at the image of Caleb lighting a match to the bodies of his siblings, his hairless face glowing yellow. "That's what I came here for. For him. And for them." She tucked her cross into her shirt. "Or it should have been."

She could see the pieces click into place in Owen's brain as the understanding dawned on his face. "White assumes I'll kill you." Owen turned the gun this way and that in his hands. He held it out to Elspeth, who waited to be sure he meant it. With a flick of his wrist, he spun the gun toward her, and gestured again. She grasped the cold bone grip.

"Seems like it's happening all over again," Owen said. "The Trachte men, doomed to repeat ourselves." He dug his heels into the snow, back and forth, creating two parallel canyons. "You take care of that boy."

"That's all I want now."

She left him in the clearing, sitting on the frozen bench, digging with his boots, certainly knowing that if she managed to take Caleb, White would find a replacement soon enough, someone who would be more than willing to add Owen to the ashes.

THEY LOCKED CALEB in the room where he'd observed Ellabelle and her snow angels. The serene, holy expression on Alexander Hamilton's face did little to ease the roiling of his blood. He imagined the death of his uncle over and over, his body tumbling to the snow, the shot appearing as quick as Hamilton's, the gun flaring like Burr's. After some time pacing and seething, the lack of rest and the removal of immediate threat dropped him on the floor and he fell asleep on the rug.

When he came to, London White sat on the bed. His legs were crossed. He held a large knife in his hand. The blade had been chipped and bent slightly, but the edge shone from constant sharpening. He held it to the light. "One night, not long after I bought this place, I crept upon my brother's camp. I held this knife to his neck." He flipped it on his fingers, grabbed the hilt in his fist, and slammed the blade deep into the footboard. "Do you know why I did this?"

Caleb pushed himself onto his knees. The knife's vibrations produced a twanging. "I needed to know I could, if I had to," he said. "I felt nothing, no fear or hesitation." White drew the knife from the wood, licked his thumb to wipe the dust from the weapon, and slid it into a sheath beneath his coat and vest. He rebuttoned his clothes and adjusted his sleeves so the proper amount of crisp white shirt extended from beneath his jacket. "You have been given a wonderful gift: the gift of no responsibilities, no ties, no attachments."

"What have you done with my mother?" Caleb asked. He'd been severed from his last attachment, but he needed to know for sure that she was dead.

White's face hardened. "That *thing* is not your mother."

"What's happened to her?"

White sighed. "Owen Trachte is not the kind of man to take injury kindly. It has been put out of its misery." He opened the door wide enough for Caleb to see Ethan standing there, and closed it behind him. The clicking of a key sounded through the room. This angered him further. He didn't care if White saw him out of control; he didn't care what White thought at all. He screamed for them to let him out until his eyes filled with colorful dots and he got too shaky to continue. He kicked the door once and after the second, Ethan unlocked it and pointed a stubby finger at him, "Kick that door again and you'll wish you were your uncle."

WHILE ELSPETH SPED toward Caleb, she tried to repeat the directions, starting with heading north on the line Shane had described. He'd drawn pictures of all the landmarks and the first would be a trio of hills, a rock outcropping. But her mind kept being overrun by Caleb's hand reaching for her. His fingers were small, his nails purple in the cold. She didn't know where his gloves had gone; she couldn't recall if she'd seen them in the graveyard. His screams were so loud to her that she grunted to herself to try to mask the noise, the snow thinning out toward the top of the hill that stood between her and the Elm Inn. A hawk swooped low over the lake, dipped one wing, and circled in increasingly tight patterns, before diving into the trees, where she could track it no longer.

Before Caleb had returned from work at night, she'd hovered in an anxious state of half-sleep. Only once she heard the knob turn, the creak of the bedsprings, the sound of his boots hitting the floor, and his clearing breath as his head met the pillow could she truly rest. She didn't know if she'd ever sleep again. Ethan's pistol held five bullets and one empty chamber. She reset the cylinder.

CALEB'S FEET DANGLED into nothingness. If he shut his eyes, he could bring himself to the loft door, watching the house, his family readying for bed, the smell of the fire drifting over and connecting them. When his eyes opened, though, he saw the dent in the snow where a corpse had lain that night or even that morning. The blizzard had slowed to the point it could no longer be referred to as such, downgraded to a common lazy lake squall, but the wind had been in his favor, and drifts piled against the inn. The drop would be thirty-five feet to the ground, but the snow made up a good eight of that, and he thought the knotted sheets would lower him ten more. He couldn't figure the numbers, but he knew in all likelihood he would break a leg if not his neck, and he'd be another body waiting to be collected.

He gripped the sheets. He tested them, and the bed he'd tied them to held firm against the wall. Carefully, he turned around so that he faced inside the room. He leaned back, the sheet in his hand, and flexed his legs outward. The feeling of freedom threatened to choke him. He didn't dare look down. With one step back, and then another, he walked on the side of the inn. The wind picked up. The bed shifted, and the sheets jerked, and his hands burned briefly with a stinging fire, and he fell. He leapt from the hayloft door. He aimed for the shovel. The lands he'd claimed rushed to meet him.

SHE SAW SOMETHING moving at the window. She took cover, obscured by a tree. By the time she saw her son, it was too late. She watched Caleb slip and stifled her scream by biting down on her scarf, terrified to alert the giant man or his boss. She plowed through the snow. When she reached him, his hair had been plastered back with sweat and his hands bled from the blanket, the skin sloughing off in papery sheets. She leaned her ear close to his mouth. Nothing happened. She willed her heart to stop so she could have complete silence. He breathed. She hugged him to her breast. She brought him closer and closer until her arms hurt.

"Mama?" he said.

She silenced him with a finger to his lips, pointed at the inn to remind him of the danger, and carried him off, her steps short and heavy. Once they could no longer see the inn through the trees, she put him down.

"I'll be okay," he said. "You came for me." They didn't have much time, so she pulled him to his feet and they raced side by side, away from the Elm Inn, whose raucous noise could be heard over the cracking of branches and the wheezing of Caleb trying to catch his breath.

BOOK III

CHAPTER 1

At the edge of the forest, they watched the rear of the Brick & Feather, where nothing moved except the odd curtain and one of the cooks dumping dishwater into the snow. They'd traced a wide path through the woods behind the hotel to retrieve their supplies, her pistol, and the boy's shotgun. Elspeth—fearing White and Ethan might be waiting for her inside—told Caleb to keep to the trees, and to run if anything at all seemed amiss. "Don't wait," she said. "If I'm not back in ten minutes, you go." She didn't linger long enough for either of them to consider where he would run to, and she stomped through the unbroken snow, her knees high. He watched her carve a straight line across the perfect surface, wind-blown ripples frozen like tiny waves.

Without her, he thought, he would have nothing. He imagined getting up in the Brick & Feather, the sheets on the bed across from his pulled tight, the pillow untouched. After a while, his worries overtook him and he crept out of the forest and followed in her footsteps. He hadn't gone far when she came around the corner, her church dress exchanged for her old work clothes, his Ithaca protruding from the bottom of her new coat. She waved him back into the woods. She'd brought the linens from their beds and tore them into strips to wrap around his hands. When she finished, she held on to his wrists and pulled him to her, and they leaned against each other, his head almost to the bottom of her chin.

THEY WALKED, AND muscles they'd forgotten stretched and tugged at their bones. Neither had much to say. After an hour of following Martin's precise directions the cold, the trees, the snow, and the rhythm of their steps hardened time into one familiar mass. Every couple of hours Elspeth would make them stop and drink and sit for long enough to catch their breath. During these breaks, she would recite Martin's directions as if predicting their future, and Caleb would fill in a detail here and there that she'd forgotten.

Late in the afternoon, Elspeth listed two more landmarks and then an old cabin. Martin had told them the family that lived inside had been friends with the Shanes for years and would happily welcome them. "It'll be nice to get a hot meal and spend the night in a bed," Elspeth said, despite the concerns she tried to mask for the boy's sake, thrusting her hands into her pockets so they didn't stray to the pistols—Ethan's and her own—that she wore at her waist. "Don't tell them where we're headed, though. We can't be too careful."

The closer they got to the house, however, the path twisting around a small hill and over a frozen creek, the deeper her worries. It struck her that they shouldn't have to blaze this trail through the drifts, that the family should have come this way to hunt or to resupply their stores for winter.

"How are you feeling?" she asked.

"Fine," he said. "Do you want me to take the lead?"

She said no and labored on, the ground tilting up, and what bothered her—as it had not long ago—was the lack of life: no noise, no smell of smoke on the air. Her heart beat faster. The cross at her neck bounced against her chest with each plodding step.

"You're walking too fast," Caleb said. She stopped and found him twenty yards behind, his bandaged hands holding his shotgun, the tips of his fingers bright red.

"I'm sorry," she said. "I want to get there before dark so we don't surprise them."

Caleb glanced at the sky. The sun would not leave them for another hour, maybe an hour and a half, and the house must be close. He rechecked that the Ithaca's safety was off.

The trail opened into a clearing at the crest of the hillside, and there stood two log walls and the stone chimney of a house. Caleb blinked back tears. His mother's pace didn't waver, and she walked right into what remained of the cabin, stumbling over beams and debris beneath the snow.

"We'll have a nice fire," she said.

Caleb joined her at the hearth, which she wiped clean with her gloved hands.

THEY'D BUILT A hearty fire, and spread the tarp beneath them. The cabin's two walls gave them protection from a biting wind that had kicked up once the sun had gone down. They didn't worry about the smoke—they knew the Millards were a half-day's walk, and even if the brothers came upon them, the ending would be the same.

"It's not much, is it?" Caleb said of their meager rations.

"I thought Martin's friends would welcome us," she said, though she hadn't packed for more than the two days' journey to the Millards'. One of the logs tumbled from atop the others, startling the boy. His collar hung from his neck, and his eyes had taken on the hollowed-out darkness of his uncle's. Elspeth wondered at the toll her actions had taken. The whole time they'd walked, she'd gone over permutations and possibilities, searching for a way in which her son would survive the next day. She considered leaving once he fell asleep and continuing on by herself, but he would keep going, too, and even if she was killed, he would try to avenge them.

"It was an accident," he said. "The fire. And shooting you."

"I know," she said.

He worried about sleeping, and of the nightmares that awaited him. For the first time, he told his mother of the dreams that had plagued him in the house, and how he'd moved to the barn to avoid them. He talked about his time in the pantry, and how he couldn't remember much but he could remember everything. "Some nights," he said, "I would wake up lying next to Jesse, and I wouldn't know how I'd gotten there. I would think he'd blinked, and I couldn't remember if it had been a dream or not." He told her he'd heard Emma giggle from the snow, and watched Mary try to pull herself from the stove. One night Amos had urged him to come out from the pantry, and he'd complied and waited in the stark moonlight, kneeling at his brother's side, urging him to speak again until the day started to break and he had to crawl back to his hiding place.

Elspeth pulled her scarf up to wipe her tears and breathed into it, the closeness reassuring. She'd laid the two pistols at her sides. "Your father taught me to shoot," she said.

"He's not my father," Caleb said.

"He protected us," she said. "He made us a family." Caleb opened his mouth to speak, but instead poked the fire with a stick. She needed him to hear about the quiet, happy times. They didn't occur to her often. "He used to worry when he left me alone to work or get supplies. So he took me hunting with him to learn to shoot. We would bring a lunch with us, some hard-boiled eggs and bread, sometimes jam if we had it, or—on the best days—smoked ham. He and I would follow the stream down the hill, through the fields, and into the forest, and we'd lie down there and your father would roll his eggs on my stomach, cracking the shells." He'd kissed her, his hair draping her face.

"Did you kill anything?" Caleb asked.

"Of course. Deer, squirrels, beavers, raccoons, even a turkey." She inspected Ethan's pistol with the help of the firelight: the worn curve of the trigger, the smooth grips, and the stained barrel. It was so heavy, she wasn't sure she'd be able to aim it with one hand. Again she went over the next day, and this time the brothers were saddling their horses in front of the house and they opened fire the moment they saw Elspeth, who couldn't even lift her gun. Jorah had told her to fire with her exhalation, to remain within herself but without thought. This, like everything else, seemed impossible.

She couldn't stand to look at Caleb with what awaited them and she excused herself to find firewood. At the first tree, she bent her head to the trunk, prayed to God, and let the rough bark absorb her tears.

As she walked back, Caleb saw his mother as half of what she'd been long ago, that mysterious figure who left for months at a time and then resumed a central role as if nothing had happened and then left again, and half of what she'd become in Watersbridge, with the pants and boots of a man, and the hat, coat, and scarf of a woman. Her stride, weighed down by her armful of wood, contained some of each.

She added a log to the fire and sat close to Caleb. She'd become softer to him in a way that owed nothing to her clothes or her hair. He heard her lick her hand and then pat down one of his many cowlicks.

Around midnight, the sky cleared and the stars began to show themselves, singularly, and then in bunches, like Caleb's freckles in the summertime. She drew closer, and stroked the back of his cheek with her cold fingers. He held still, not wanting her to know that he was awake and risk her stopping. Neither slept and neither spoke as the wet wood hissed and the fire popped, the stars multiplied and deepened, Caleb kept awake with thoughts of murder and Elspeth of death.

The items on Shane's list dwindled down to a handful, and Caleb and Elspeth responded by walking closer and closer to each other. Still, Caleb couldn't help but think of his father and uncle, and the thunderous hooves of their horses as they rode in search of him, his father standing in his stirrups and Martin leaning close to his horse's neck, the speed enough to yank their hair back. They crisscrossed the land, riding through dust, rain, snow, and leaves; hills, valleys, fields, and forests.

Around midmorning Caleb and Elspeth reached a battered train trestle spanning a frozen river, the ice silver. The supports looked like a series of Xs, as Shane had described them, and the bridge itself consisted of horizontal ties a yard apart, sandwiched between two pairs of massive timber beams that ran the width of the river. No train tracks had been laid leading to or away from the trestle, though they could make out a path through the trees on either side—whatever plans had been laid for the tracks had been scuttled. Caleb rolled spare shotgun shells in his pocket to distract himself, but as his mother scanned the bank for a way

down, all he could envision was his father plunging through the
ice and into water so cold it burned.

The wind funneled straight down the canyon cut by the river,
and the snow whisked along the ice, creating a low whisper that
made Elspeth shiver. She mapped out a plausible way down the
banks, but then she saw the expression on Caleb's face. "It'll be
okay," she said. "The ice is thick. You can tell by its color."

"My father, he died looking for me," Caleb said. Elspeth bowed
her head. She didn't know what else she could learn that would
make her understand the trail of misery she'd created any more.
"He went through the ice."

She turned from the bank and climbed the incline to the bridge,
which, to her, looked deadly: Some of the supports were broken,
some dangled from one side, and the ties had been coated in a thick
hump of snow and ice honed by the wind. She hadn't thought to
steal two pairs of cleats from the Great Lakes Ice Company, which
would have made her realize the confidence she tried to project for
Caleb's sake. She kicked at the snow on the first board and made
a gap big enough for both feet, and stepped onto the bridge, her
boots sliding and then stabilizing. The air wrapped around her and
she understood how easily it could throw her off, twenty feet into
the snow at the ends of the bridge, but from the center sixty or sev-
enty feet to a sure death. If one plank gave in to age and wear, all of
their searching would be for naught. She put this out of her mind,
and once she moved onto the third tie, she beckoned for Caleb to
follow. He hesitated. She managed to turn around and was going to
go back to help him, but he ignored her and slid his shotgun down
the back of his coat and—both arms out for balance—hopped over
the gap and onto the trestle. When Elspeth faced forward again, the
bridge seemed to stretch on for miles, but she didn't want to show
fear in front of him and she dug new footholds and continued.

Nearly halfway across, she toed a plank and it let go of its mooring and tumbled to the river below. After a few seconds, they heard it hit the ice with a hollow rattle. The gap between the ties was too wide, and Elspeth edged over to the beam facing the wind and wiped the snow from the wood; if she should be knocked from her perch, she'd rather it pushed her onto the bridge. She crawled on all fours, trying to carve grips for Caleb as she went. The beam was wider than the ties, but the ice was thicker and harder, and she couldn't get down to the bare timber and prayed for God to let them both cross safely.

Only after his mother had gotten close to the other side of the gap did he inch toward the beam. A slip would kill him, smashing him onto ice the color and strength of steel. Out of the corners of his vision things shifted and moved, but when he turned his head all would be motionless. It dizzied him. He splayed himself out on the timber, his back foot twitching as it left the tie behind. The exposure to the wind was stronger than he'd expected, and he struggled to dig his toes into the thin veneer of ice left by his mother. A gust tore down the canyon—he could hear it coming and see the snow torn from the trees—and they braced themselves, Caleb pressing his cheek to the ice, Elspeth crouching onto a plank. The wind clawed at his clothes and tried to loosen his grip. His chest and arms cramped. One of his fingernails cracked from digging into the wood and the pain raced up his arm and he roared. When the wind died, his mother leaned out to him and held on to his collar the rest of the way. The worst had passed, and they sped up, still cautious but with the other end in sight.

Twenty feet from the bank, Elspeth risked a glance back at Caleb and her right foot slid out from under her, and then her left. She threw out her arms and her chest hit the tie, knocking the wind from her lungs. Caleb yelled. Her legs dangled in the air. Her hands had a tenuous grip. Caleb rushed his steps but could not get to her in time. She threw one boot over the edge of the board as both hands gave out and she somehow rolled her body onto it, ending up on her back. She heard Caleb vomiting. Her breath came in quick, scratchy gasps.

Caleb wiped his mouth with his glove. He scraped loose some snow and used it to rinse. His fear at seeing his mother fall had caught him by surprise and slammed him in the gut. He was ashamed. "Are you okay?" he asked.

Elspeth waved him off. She had not yet caught her wind enough to speak. When she did, she rose, keeping her hands on the tie until she was sure of her footing. She kicked the next board free of snow and ice. "I'm okay," she said.

As she stepped onto solid ground, the overwhelming stillness of it collapsed her. Her body quivered from the tension. Caleb joined her, his knee touching hers, and he drank from a jar of water. "I'm sorry about your father," she said. He passed her the jar and her hand shook with the hammering of her heart.

THE BRIDGE CROSSING had sapped much of their energy, and they pressed on as they had to Watersbridge, trudging through snow-drifts as if in a trance. The breaks ceased—if they'd stopped they might not be able to start again until morning. At midday, Caleb passed a sandwich to his mother and they ate as they walked and when they drank, the water sloshed from the jar onto their chins and chests.

Elspeth's mind had run out of ways to predict their fates, and she concentrated on how much she'd missed having her son at her side. When the snow turned to powder or they walked through a blanketed cluster of trees, she listened to his breathing, measured and soft. She moved in step with him, near enough that when the way narrowed and they had to part and pass one at a time, the cold invaded her deeper, and she wished that her wounds would return so she could rest her arm across his shoulders. The wind intensified and she lifted her scarf over her mouth and motioned for him to do the same, though she had long ago gone numb.

MIDAFTERNOON, WITH THE sun bright enough to warm their skin and peel their cheeks, they passed between two rocks that stood like the horns of some ancient beast. She stopped and hugged the boy. Caleb buried his face in her scarf. His mother rocked back and forth and he swayed with her. Over his shoulder, she looked back the way they'd come, and she followed the flight of a turkey vulture in the distance as it traced the horizon, and toward the end of its path a shock of orange flared in the distance, between a pair of trees. She thought of Charles, alone and broken in his apartment, his mementoes scattered around him.

They'd reached the end of Martin's list. Around the bend they would see the Millard home. Caleb hoped that the farm would be as broken and empty as everything else they'd encountered, the skeletons of the brothers visible in the middle of the house like those of his siblings. It only seemed fair.

The main house sliced through the snow like an ax blade, the roof heavily pitched and punched through twice on either side by windows. The barn was like any other, though in need of paint. A majestic oak towered over everything, its bare branches seeming to gather the whole homestead in an embrace. Pens for the cattle stood empty, the snow undisturbed. The barn doors remained closed. Smoke drifted from the chimney, and they noted its lazy ascent. Elspeth took one pistol and then the other from her waist, tested their weight, and raised them, craning her head in an effort to aim. Caleb sighted down the barrel of the Ithaca.

They'd both expected something more: vines like snakes wrapped around the fences, black clouds and barking dogs, rusted cages filled with bones. A horrible screeching filled the air, and Caleb swung the shotgun left and right, trying to find the source, his finger beginning to tighten on the trigger. Elspeth stayed him with a tap to his forearm, and pointed to the roof of the barn, where a series of weather vanes lined the peak, pointing in their direction, sounding their alarms on rusted bearings. The wind died. The screeching halted, and a horse, which seemed as unnerved as they did at the disturbance, stood up in the paddock closest to the house.

CHAPTER 3

They stood in a grouping of trees with a clear view of the house, the barn, and the paddock and waited. The horse occupied itself rubbing against the fence and protectively trotting around its perimeter. After an hour, nothing more had happened. Elspeth untied the bedroll and tarp from her pack, shrugged out of her coat, removed her gloves, and stuffed them all out of sight at the base of a tree. Caleb followed her example, tossing aside his blankets and extra clothes. She unwound her scarf from her neck, did the same for the boy, and rolled them up and dropped them into the pile. She didn't think the scarves would weigh them down or get in their way; she'd wanted an excuse to touch him once more.

The sound hit them both at the same time: the crunch of snow, the huff of breath. Instinctively, they looked to the house, but the noise came from somewhere on the path. She signaled for Caleb to position himself on one side of the trail behind a thick tree trunk. With her pistols raised, she inched forward until she reached the broken stump of an evergreen—jagged with splinters the size of her fingers—and took cover, aiming down the bend.

She dropped her pack. She couldn't tell which gun to aim first but decided on Ethan's, and tried to keep its bulk steady. All Caleb could think of was his earlier failure, and he gritted his teeth until they ached. The sounds got louder, and he blinked, his vision blurry. His heart beat in his fingertips and he could no longer feel the trigger. A man appeared between the rocks, his head down, his red hair bright in the sun.

"It's Charles," Elspeth said in a hissed whisper, and Caleb relaxed his posture. He knew, however, that he had not acted fast enough, that he had failed once again. He flexed his finger a few times to make certain he was capable of pulling a trigger.

Charles shuffled along, his jaw bound, strands of his beard flaring out between the strips of gauze. Thick bandages tied his hands to the grip and forestock of the rifle, winding their way around the weapon and his wrists. His thumb and trigger finger had been left uncovered.

"What are you doing here?" Elspeth asked.

"He might be one of them, Mama," Caleb said. He advanced, raising the Ithaca. It hurt him, somehow, to have this man intrude on them.

"I told Owen," he said. He forced the words out between his teeth, his jaw unmoving. "I made a mistake."

"But why are you here? Do you know the Millards?"

"Only by name," he said. "Three of them, two of you." He gestured with his gun, one arm dragging the other with it. He winced. "Are they home?"

Elspeth regarded the two of them as they squinted through the glare and Caleb relayed to him all that they'd observed. Her boy looked so small next to Charles. The sun exposed the pallor of his skin from all the late nights in the brothel and she reminded herself once again that he was only a child. She'd put him through so much.

Charles, too, had endured pain in her name, and had followed her into the promise of something far worse. "Caleb," she said, "why don't you get Charles some water?" She pointed up the hill.

The jar sat in the bottom of her pack, where Caleb had once found gum and candy, and he unscrewed the lid and poured some water into Charles's mouth. Most of it ended up on his bandages. "Sorry," Caleb said. He understood then, and his hands screwed the lid back on of their own volition, and he placed the jar on the stump and left Charles trying to suck the moisture from his gauze. His mother was gone. All of their footprints gathered around the trees, and then one set split off, down the hill, toward the Millards' farm.

He raced back, snatched his Ithaca from where he'd leaned it against a rock, and sprinted after her.

Elspeth ran crouched over, taking a path that put the few trees in the yard between herself and the windows. She made it to the wide, scarred trunk of the oak tree and slammed into it, hugged the chilled wood with her pistol-laden hands. The horse corral was to her left, the house to her right, not twenty steps away. She prayed for Caleb and Charles to stay where they were, for them both to be safe, and bolted for the building. An indentation in the ground surprised her, and her leg jammed into her knee, her ankle taking all of the weight, and she tripped, crashing into the stone foundation of the house.

Caleb saw his mother hit the rocks, and swallowed his scream. He got to the oak just as she picked herself up from the snow. He held his breath. She shook off the fall. No one came bursting from the front door; the brothers didn't storm out of the house firing their guns. He got to the wall as his mother reached the front step.

She shouldered open the front door. Wind swept in and around her, making the curtains on the opposite side of the large living room dance. The room held seven or eight chairs in a semicircle around an empty fireplace, a black stain from the smoke rising all the way to the ceiling. A threadbare rug occupied the floor, and an empty picture frame hung on the wall. A staircase in the back right corner and a door directly to her left were the only other ways in or out. Caleb was there, behind her, and she jumped, startled, and then tried to body him back outside without turning her attention from the room.

Silence except the door creaking back on its hinges.

"Mother," a voice called out, "the door blew open." No one answered. "Damn it," the voice said. They heard a chair scrape out in the next room. Elspeth readjusted her fingers on the triggers, and pressed harder against Caleb, trying to shove him to safety, but he fought against her. "Run," she said to him, "please. Please, Caleb, run."

He stopped pushing and stepped to the side. He brought his gun to his shoulder. He heard each crack of gunfire early one morning. The lifeless gazes of Emma, Jesse, Mary, Amos, and Jorah all flashed through his head, and looked to him, hopeful.

The door opened. They caught a quick glimpse of the kitchen. A young man came into the room, a hunk of bread in his hand. His mouth was full, his cheek distended. Caleb recognized him as the gangly man whose glance had urged him back into the sharp hay of the loft, the man who'd killed his family. Here his legs, knock-kneed and thin as cornstalks even in patched trousers, seemed they could barely hold his weight.

"It's him," Caleb said. "He did it."

"Oh," the young man said, crumbs tumbling from his mouth. He disappeared back the way he'd entered. Caleb squeezed the trigger of the Ithaca, but too late. The shot peppered the door and clanged into the kitchen beyond it. Elspeth emptied both pistols, praying that one of the bullets would luck its way through the plaster and into the man. She heard scrambling but no cries of pain. She cursed herself. She drifted apart from her body, as if instructing someone else's hands to empty the smoking shells from the cylinder. Ethan's pistol she let fall. Frantic, she pawed at her jacket pocket, unable to find the opening. At last, her hysterical fingers closed around three bullets and she jammed them into the chambers and slammed the cylinder shut with her palm. Every second that the other Millards didn't stampede down the stairs, firearms in each hand, Elspeth viewed as a blessing. She forced Caleb back into the far corner of the room, where she could see both the staircase and the door.

Caleb, too, expected the other Millard brothers to thunder out of the kitchen or in from the barn, and against three gunmen they had no hope. He wished his mother had waited for Charles. Something squeaked from the kitchen. His mother slapped an arm to his chest, impelling him to stay behind her. The door opened a sliver, and Caleb pushed his mother's arm aside and fired. The knob dropped from the wood, a large hole in its place.

A spindly leg kicked the door open and the man, cheeks still full of bread, cocked a repeating rifle. Caleb's shot went right, and the Millard flinched before firing at them, the room exploding with noise and shrapnel. Elspeth rushed her three shots. She put herself between Caleb and the Millard, drawing herself up to seem bigger, like a bear lifting onto its hind legs. The bullets ripped into her body. Each one announced itself with a blazing flare of pain. Shin. Meat of the thigh. Forearm. The gun slipped from her fingers. The bullets ceased to matter. She collapsed back against Caleb. She fought to stay on her feet, to keep him as long as possible, but she could not combat the sudden weight of her body. She tried to move her mouth but it was too far away from her thoughts.

The thump of the bullets made him gag. His mother draped over him and he yelled for her to get out of the way. The man slunk back into the kitchen. The door drooped from one hinge. Her head was between his arms, heavy on his chest. He succeeded in ejecting his spent rounds and loading two more with hands that looked very small, the shells very big. The Millard's rifle preceded him out of the kitchen, the muzzle flashing again and again. Caleb heard bullets hissing past. Splinters and shards struck him. He squeezed his eyes and the world went white. He opened them when he didn't die. His mother was upon him but she was not moving.

Elspeth struggled to reach the surface. Her son squirmed behind her, and she saw the gun in his hands. He sat by the side of a creek, fishing, and she dropped a ruined shirt into the water to make him happy. She wanted to apologize and couldn't recall if she had, and she tumbled through the floor, moving fast, light and darkness swirling.

The Millard headed for the freedom past the open front door. Caleb fumbled with his Ithaca and tried to untangle himself from his mother. He brushed her hair from his eyes and mouth. The man stopped short of the threshold and fired. A blast from outside vaporized a chunk of wall. The Millard covered his face with his forearm and fired blindly. He wheeled and cocked his rifle. The shell soared through the smoky room. He pointed the gun at Caleb, who pulled the trigger on his Ithaca. His elbow slammed into the wall. The Millard lifted off the ground—one of his boots left behind— and skidded across the floor, his other sole scraping a black streak on the marred wood. Blood burbled from his mouth. His shoeless foot kicked, still running. The exposed sock had a stain in the shape of his toes on the bottom. His knuckles rapped a dying code on the floorboards.

Charles limped into the house, pushing two fresh shells into his gun.

The smell of gunpowder and the dying rasps lingered. Wood settled, buckled, and broke. His mother sprawled across him, her eyes open, her mouth agape. Caleb hurled his Ithaca like he'd never hated anything so much in his life. He began to cry. He pressed his forehead against his mother's, gently at first and then harder. The bruises on his face sang with pain, and the nicks and scratches he'd gotten had left new cuts, and he bled against her. He banged his skull on her skull, bone on bone, and ground his skin against hers. When he pulled away, his blood had smeared her brow crimson. This made him cry harder, and Charles handed him a handkerchief. Caleb dabbed away the bright splotches of blood, and then tried to wet the bandage with his tongue or spit but couldn't manage any. He wiped her forehead, only making it worse. He expected her to react to every touch. Each time she didn't, he lost a beat of his own heart.

Charles used his rifle like a cane. His right shoulder and arm were wet with blood. He sank to the floor.

"Casey, are you there?" a woman's voice called from upstairs.

Charles pushed himself up with his gun, but couldn't straighten fully. The stain on his shirt expanded. One of his knees gave out and the leg bent underneath him awkwardly. He'd gone glassy and drained of color, making his orange hair and beard brighter, and Caleb thought he must look like one of William's ghosts. Whatever strength Charles had was gone, the reserves exhausted, and he dropped his head to the floor.

Caleb didn't know how to get out from under his mother with the kind of respect she deserved, so he settled for rolling her onto her side and inching his way out from beneath her. His feet had fallen asleep and they tingled with each step. He nudged the bare foot of the Millard brother. His face had been shredded and his neck torn open by the Ithaca. The gun had ended up next to the Millard's foot, and it looked foreign to Caleb, the trigger guard bent, the muzzle dinged, the wood cheap and overworked by polish.

Caleb climbed the stairs to a dim hallway with two doors, one on each side. The left stood open, and there an old woman lay in bed. The shades had been drawn on the low, squat windows, but sunlight crept in at the edges. Her thin gray hair sparkled, but her skin was dull and cracked. The walls had been papered with flowered prints, and Caleb thought he could smell them before he saw the dresser laden with rows of perfumes and powders. The old woman wheezed and searched for him, her eyes drifting back and forth, milky white and blind. Her long, thin fingers held covers that buried her up to her neck. "Could you fetch me some water?" she asked.

"Where are the rest?" Caleb asked. She didn't answer but coughed so violently he felt certain she didn't have long to wait.

The other door in the hallway opened almost by itself. The narrow space allowed for three beds against the far wall and a long squat dresser along the near. The cant of the roof forced the Millards to align the foot of the bed with the wall, the head in the center of the room. The bed closest to the window had been slept in, the sheets dirty and yanked from the lurid striped mattress, while the other two were covered in dusty blankets with large lumps beneath them. Mindful of the graves on the other side of the hill and the countless bodies beneath the tarps in Watersbridge, Caleb threw back one of the blankets to reveal nothing but a pillow and some neatly folded sheets. Dust filled the air. It tickled his throat and dried out his eyes. When it had cleared, and he'd wiped away the tears, he saw that the dresser, too, was covered in a thick film. He wondered what the drawers held; whether the man downstairs had a collection as he had. He emptied out his pack, and there, at the bottom, was his feather. Against the blood and dirt on his hands, the feather looked blacker than ever, a darkness he could sink into. With the back of his fist, he wiped a square of the dresser clean and placed the feather in its center.

On his way out of the bedroom, his jacket snagged on a series of notches etched into the doorframe. At first he understood it to be a list of victims, a roll call of the dead that he scanned for his brothers and sisters, but instead he found the same names repeated over and over again, leapfrogging one another: Leonard, Oscar, Edmund, and Warren. The uneven carvings recorded the heights of the boys, and he traced over the letters, digging his nails into the deepest wounds. He resisted the urge to measure himself and add his own name.

He granted the old woman's wish, happy for something purposeful and easy and not knowing what else to do. In the corner of the room, a toilet table held a pitcher, a crystal glass, a washbasin, and a silver comb. She patted the cup reassuringly when he gave it to her. Once she'd taken a small sip and replaced her head on the pillows, she said, "I forgot all of your stories."

He collapsed onto a plain chair in the corner next to the table. He stared at his hands and pressed his thumbs along his fingertips, searching for feeling.

"I can remember one, I think," she said. She brought the cup to her lips again, and it clicked against her teeth. "Could I trouble you to open the window, my son? Let some of that summer air in for an old woman." Caleb pushed the curtains aside and she winced. The window wouldn't budge at first, but then yelped and went up halfway and stuck. He did the same with the other. The winter air lashed at his face and hands, the curtains undulating like living things. There was blood on his sleeve and Caleb couldn't register what it was or where it had come from.

The old woman smiled. "When I was a girl," she said. The wind blew in, gentler, and the cold restored the flush to her cheeks. The sun smoothed her wrinkles. Caleb stared at the prisms made by the bottles and mirrors that crowded the room, casting all the colors he'd ever seen onto the ceiling. With his index finger he pushed one of the perfumes, and the rainbow traveled across the wall by the window and Caleb's gaze followed. Two new horses rested in the paddock, saddled and glistening with sweat. He saw below him the other two Millard brothers, laughing and exchanging punches. The bearded one slapped the other and then took off running toward the barn. His brother tackled him. The horses shifted out of the way, used to such roughhousing. Both Millards—and their brother—had a pronounced widow's peak that pointed down to their thick eyebrows, and a thin nose that ended in a small knob. Their eyes were almond-shaped and accentuated by the deep lines beneath them. They chased each other around the horses' enclosure, hooting.

He wondered what they would do with the bodies. Would they burn them as he had his siblings? Would they bury them in the yard when spring came? Or would they leave them in the snow like London White, awaiting some devil to take them away? There had been one time—after he'd discovered the graves, when he'd stopped listening to the prayers—when he'd tried to understand, and he'd asked his father a question that had been bothering him. "Why, if heaven is above us in the sky, do we stick the dead underground, closer to the Devil? Why not burn them and let them go into the air, nearer to God?"

His father had stared at him for a long while, and Caleb expected a Bible verse, but Jorah had bitten the inside of his lip. "Sometimes we just like to keep them near to us."

Once the Millards saw the tracks and the hole in the side of the house, Caleb would be trapped. When they saw their brother, the Ithaca by his feet, Caleb would be dead. He could run down the stairs and out the front door, but they would likely see him before he got very far. The windows were too small for him to fit out of if he tried to jump. He clutched the windowsill. His broken fingernail screamed with pain but from far away.

He tried to fit names to the men outside, and the one downstairs, but none of them looked like an Edmund or an Oscar or a Leonard or a Warren. The curtains brushed against his face with the breeze. The bearded brother leapt onto the back of the other and drove him into the snow. The long-haired one slid out from under him, his movements as smooth as they'd been entering Caleb's house. An emptiness in Caleb's stomach grew with each gesture. The bearded brother slapped the snow roughly from the other's jacket in apology. Caleb took a shotgun shell out of his pocket and stood it on the windowsill. He did the same with another. And another. His pockets emptied and he watched the brothers advance on the house. His heart fluttered. He heard footsteps. The shoes and boots of Jesse, Amos, Mary, and Emma joined in a raucous army calling his name, ready to play another round, annoyed he was still out there, and he could already feel himself giving in, knew he would scream out and run, daring them to catch him.

Acknowledgments

I have been extraordinarily fortunate to have the support, friendship, and love of a great many people. My heartfelt thanks go out to:

My family: Mom, Dad, Anne, Meredith, Zoey, Brian, and the extended Scott and Strayer families. You raised me, you read with me, and I'm happy to share this book with you.

The Springer and Rogers families: Melissa, Alan, Susan, Chancellor, Paul, Becky, Fred, Judy, and the aunts and uncles and cousins who have welcomed me as one of their own.

Margot Livesey, who fifteen years ago sat down with me and encouraged me to keep going, and every day since has taught me how I can be a better writer, a better literary citizen, and a better person.

Hannah Tinti, for showing me the way with remarkable generosity.

My friends and readers whose guidance, jokes, and sanity I clung to: Urban Waite, Laura van den Berg, Chip Cheek, Pauls Toutonghi, and Jaime Clarke.

My amazing friends Mike Morrell, Peter Sax, Michael Hunt, David Lukowski, Josh Elliott, Matt Salesses, Katharine Gingrich, Cam Terwilliger, Shannon Derby, Kevin Alexander, Dan Pribble,

Scott Votel, Shuchi Saraswat, Kirstin Chen, Megann Sept, Sean Lanigan, Pei-Ling Lue, Leslie Brack, the magical Yaddo group, Paul Beilstein, Amanda Goldblatt, Jett and Chris Brooks, Mary Cotton, Jane Dykema, Randall Lahann, Kevin Wilson, Josh Weil, Ryan Call, Mike Rosovsky, Jason Reitman, Wendy Wakeman, Jesse Donaldson and Becca Wadlinger, Celeste Ng, Tom Perrotta, Julianna Baggott, Christian Botting, and Jamil Zaki.

All of my teachers, but especially Daniel Wallace, Jim Shepard, Pamela Painter, Christine Schutt, Joy Williams, Mako Yoshikawa, Rick Reiken, Ben Brooks, Don Mitchell, David Bain, Jay Parini, John Casey, and Thomas Mallon.

Ladette Randolph, Stacey Swann, Chris Boucher, David Madden, and all of the literary magazine editors who were kind enough to work on my stories.

The Corporation of Yaddo, which provided me with inspiration, confidence, and friendship. This book would not exist without the time and space you've given me.

The Sewanee Writers' Conference, the New York State Summer Writers Institute, the Millay Colony, the St. Botolph Club, the Virginia Center for the Creative Arts, and the Bread Loaf Writers' Conference for providing me with support and a sense of community.

Laurel Phillips, and some wonderful libraries and librarians— Skidmore College, Wellesley College, Morse Institute, Saratoga Springs Public Library, Wellesley Free Library, among others—for research help.

Everyone at Grub Street, especially Chris Castellani and Sonya Larson, for the great work you do. My workshop students always motivate me and remind me how lucky I am to be able to discuss writing and literature.

Janklow and Nesbit, especially Stephanie Koven and Amanda

Schweitzer, for taking the book to new places, literally and figuratively.

Harper and HarperCanada, for all of your hard work and support: Jonathan Burnham, Iris Tupholme, Jane Beirn, Shannon Ceci, Maria Golikova, and everyone who has had a hand in bringing this book to life.

Sarah Rigby and the staff at Hutchinson, who cheered me at every turn.

Barry Harbaugh, editor extraordinaire, for calming my (almost constant) fears and going above and beyond at every turn.

P. J. Mark, the world's greatest agent, who took a chance on a very rough piece of a book and showed me a light at the end of a tunnel that at that time seemed very dark and on the verge of collapse.

Taylor, most of all, for your unwavering support, sacrifice, and love. No matter what was happening, no matter how busy or stressed life was, you always encouraged me to do whatever it took to get this book finished. Thank you for believing in me.

About the Author

JAMES SCOTT was born in Boston and grew up in upstate New York. He holds a BA from Middlebury College and an MFA from Emerson College. His fiction has appeared in *Ploughshares, One Story, American Short Fiction*, and other publications. He has received fellowships and awards from, among others, Yaddo, the Sewanee Writers' Conference, the New York State Summer Writers Institute, and the Tin House Summer Writer's Workshop. He lives in western Massachusetts with his wife and dog. *The Kept* is his first novel.